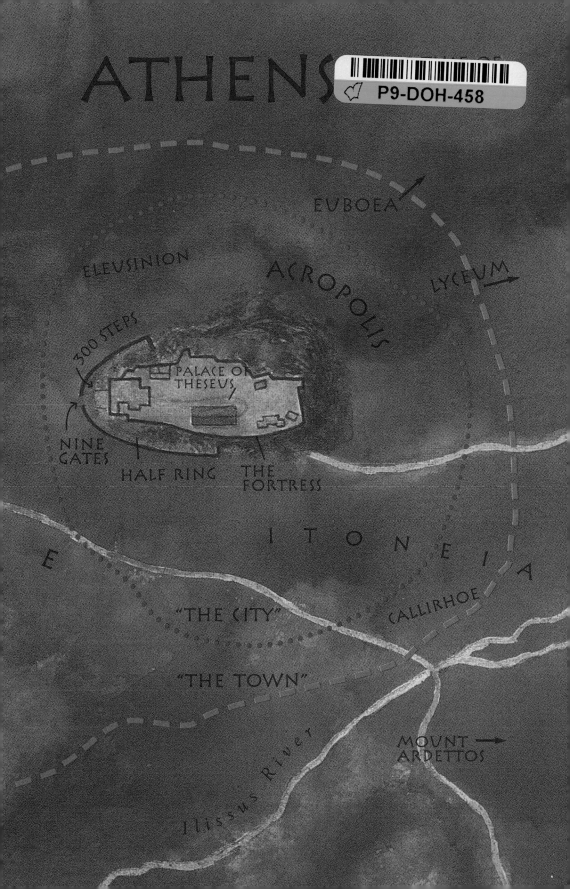

ATHENS

P9-DOH-458

EVBOEA

ELEVSINION

ACROPOLIS

LYCEUM

300 STEPS

PALACE OF THESEUS

NINE GATES

HALF RING

THE FORTRESS

I T O N E I A

E

"THE CITY"

CALLIRHOE

"THE TOWN"

MOUNT ARDETTOS

Ilissus River

LAST

OF

THE

AMAZONS

Also by Steven Pressfield

The War of Art
Tides of War
Gates of Fire
The Legend of Bagger Vance

STEVEN
PRESSFIELD

Last of the Amazons

DOUBLEDAY

NEW YORK
LONDON
TORONTO
SYDNEY
AUCKLAND

⚓

PUBLISHED BY DOUBLEDAY
a division of Random House, Inc.
1540 Broadway, New York, New York 10036

DOUBLEDAY and the portrayal of an anchor with a dolphin are
trademarks of Doubleday, a division of Random House, Inc.

All of the characters in this book are fictitious, and any resemblance to
actual persons, living or dead, is purely coincidental.

Library of Congress Cataloging-in-Publication Data
    Pressfield, Steven.
    Last of the Amazons: a novel / Steven Pressfield.— 1st ed.
        p. cm.
        1. Theseus (Greek mythology)—Fiction. 2. Athens (Greece)—
    Fiction. 3. Women soldiers—Fiction. 4. Amazons—Fiction.
    5. Sieges—Fiction. I. Title.
    PS3566.R3944 L37 2002
    813'.54—dc21   2001047672

ISBN 0-385-50098-x

Copyright © 2002 by Steven Pressfield.

All Rights Reserved

Printed in the United States of America

June 2002
First Edition

Book design by Terry Karydes
Maps by Richard Grider

10 9 8 7 6 5 4 3 2 1

For Lesley

PRIAM: Once before now I travelled to Phrygia where the vines grow, and there I saw a host of Phrygian men with their quick horses. . . . I too was numbered among them on the day when the Amazons came, women the equal of men.

—Homer, *The Iliad*

This was the origin of the Amazonian invasion of Athens, which would seem to have been no slight or womanish enterprise. For it is impossible that the Amazons should have placed their camp in the very city, and joined battle close by the Pnyx unless, having first conquered the country around about, they had thus with impunity advanced to the city. That they encamped there is certain, and may be confirmed by the names that the places thereabout yet retain, and the graves and monuments of those that fell in the battle. . . . For indeed we are also told that [a number] of the Amazons [who] died were buried there in the place that is to this time called Amazoneum.

—Plutarch, *Life of Theseus*

LAST

OF

THE

BOOK ONE

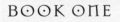

MOTHER BONES

A TAME AMAZON

≋≋≋≋≋

When I was a girl I had a nurse who was a tame Amazon. Of course such expression is a misnomer, as one of that race may be domesticated no more than an eagle or a she-wolf. Selene however (this was her name, "Moon") had been detached at age nine from her *skyle*— the words for "battalion" and "family" being the same in the Amazon tongue—and sent to dwell among civilized society, at Sinope on the Black Sea, and had thus become conversant with settlement ways. She could not endure such confinement however; at age twelve she stole a horse and weapons and fled home to the Wild Lands. As a grown warrior Selene fought at Thorn Hill against the Trojans and Dardanians, at Chalcedon against the Rhipaean Scyths, and at the Halys against the fifty sons of Admetus. She could speak Greek and served both as adjutant and envoy, as well as commanding in the *hippotoxotai*, the fabled Corps of Mounted Archers. She held the rank of wing captain in the Great Battle of Athens, in which Theseus and his allies of the Twelve States, after months of fighting, at last beat back the army of women.

Selene surrendered shield and bridle at the pass between Parnes and Cithaeron, where the graves of Amazons may still be seen, alongside her lover Eleuthera, "Freedom," who bore numerous wounds, and to secure whose ransom and release Selene yielded up her own liberty. Selene was never shackled or stockaded in my father's service, but held by her word alone, and so served honorably, governing my sister, Europa, and me until my sister's fourteenth (and my eleventh) year.

You eldest of my daughters reckon the bloodbath that transpired at that season. Each year I recount the tale on this eve of the festival of the Boedromia, beneath that horns-skyward crescent called by men an Amazon moon. None of male sex, father, brother, husband, or son, may learn this chronicle now or ever, nor any fraction, so have we all sworn, even you youngest, donating our blood in the Iron Rite of Ares. Repeat with me now: who abjures this vow shall perish at our hands, so pledge we all.

Arise now, children. You youngest, take the hands of your sisters and follow me, Mother Bones, into the outer court. None will disturb us here. Double your overcloaks and set them in a ring upon the earth. The night is warm. Nestle at one another's sides, resting your backs against the walls or trees. There. Let us form the Moon Crescent whose name is *labrys*, "double axe," while I at its apex recite our lore. Listen well, daughters. Each verse I narrate, sear into memory. You eldest, who have heard the tale each autumn as you grew, accept this charge: if I alter so much as one stanza, bring me to book upon it, for our incantation wants naught of legend but truth alone. And when you come to impart this history to your own daughters, recall this commission and transmit these wonders uncorrupted, as I to you.

Selene feared the race of men. They exuded self-dignity, what she named *anaedor*, "no breath" or "without soul." She called Greeks "stick people," by which she meant they creaked, stiff and wooden. Nor did she confine such reproach to men, but included Mother as well, and the women of our farm and of Attica entire, of whose behavior Selene could make no sense and in the presence of whose everyday acts, as the haggling with vendors or the chastising of servants, she often lowered her gaze, a gesture I have seen repeated by others among the Amazons, whose notation is of embarrassment for the actor observed and the courtly wish not to compound this by making her conscious of a witness.

Selene feared this quality in men, this obliviousness. It was what permitted them to tread on a beetle and not hear its cry, or rend the sheath of the earth with a plough and not feel her anguish. Yet Selene and her race, as all savage nations, were capable of appalling cruelty. God help the man, or woman, who fell into their clutches when they defended their honor or painted their faces for war.

Amazons believe in hate. Hatred is sacred to Ate, to Hecate and Black Persephone, and to Ares as well, whom they call with the nymph Harmonia their progenitor. Ephesian Artemis, whom they worship, was the greatest hater ever, they claim, surnamed Void of Mercy, and even Harmonia, whose name means concord to civilized folk, means rancor in their tongue. Amazons believe that mothers hate daughters and daughters mothers, that sea hates sky, and night day. The world is held together by hate, which is in their lexicon a bounty and divine dispensation. Lovers must hate one another before they may love, and to this end the bonding ritual which Amazon novices perform at eight and twelve, when they formalize their *trikonai*, the notorious "bonds of three," is constituted of a savage type of hand-to-hand brawling they call *anitome*, "anytime anywhere." Kicking, biting, eye gouging, all are sanctioned. The elders form a circle about the fighting girls, plying with horsewhips any combatant perceived as slack in her attack. Once over, the fight and its memory, the Amazons believe, form a bond which endures such that no warrior thus bound may ever desert another.

Selene cuffed Europa and me regularly. Nor were these love pats, but such blows as to fetch us off our feet. As frequently she caressed us, and many times must be scolded by Mother or Father for expressing affection at inappropriate moments, as in the presence of priests or elders. She slept in our beds, or we in hers, till we were six.

The shield and bridle that Selene had surrendered were objects of supreme fascination to my sister and me. Father did not display these as trophies, not wishing to dishonor Selene; in fact he sought more than once to return them. Selene would not take them. They came to be stored in a chest in the loft above Father and Mother's room. Europa and I soon learned to pick the lock; we would mount to the attic and linger all afternoon, absorbed in the scent and sensation of these artifacts. We marveled at the workmanship of the bridle, which was ox-hide rimmed with ivory and electrum, the right cheekpiece depicting a griffin taking down an elk, the left a crescent moon, and a snaffle bit of pure gold. Selene's shield was of bearskin, from the densest pack across the shoulders, crescent-shaped and three layers thick, laminated with a glue of elk sinew and faced with the skin of a black leopard. On one's arm it felt like a timbrel drum, taut in its ash frame, astonishingly strong for something so light.

Selene smelled. Mother would not permit her into the formal rooms of the house, as the odor she exhaled, so Mother claimed, clung to every garment, to her hair, and even to the walls themselves. "Can you not smell it, children? Good God, what a stink!" Mother chased our governess, often with a broom, to peals of our laughter. For Selene's part, she abhorred the house and entered it only under compulsion, as civilized folk will a tomb. She could not hear in a house. I recall Father, seeking to chastise her for some transgression, calling her before his big counting desk. "Why the devil won't you listen, Selene?" Her silence drove him wild. Finally he realized she could only hear him if he bespoke her out of doors. Soft worked better than hard. No blow or threat availed, nor gifts, however precious, to bend her counter to her will.

Selene permitted herself a solitary vanity: her hair, which was jet, of such luxuriance as to appear almost beyond human. She curried it as a horse's mane, of which it reminded me, and dressed it, apart from men's eyes, in the following manner. The top mass was first thrown forward from a part running ear to ear across the crown. The horsetail falling rearward was divided in four parts and cinched by four silver clasps, one for each cardinal direction. These were lifted off the neck and rolled together into a sort of broad horizontal bun, as gentlewomen of Cyrene do, which was then bound tight to the rear of the head by an ox-hide thong called *xaella,* "clothesline," which itself is wrapped four turns about the head. The xaella is a weapon, a garrote. Its ends are tipped in elk horn and etched with the battle-axe of Ares. Once the rear was set, the thrown-forward forepeak would be drawn back, half of its mass cinched at the crown, to form a horsetail with its excess, the remainder woven in among the four quarters. The effect of this, either loose or topped with the Phrygian cap of doeskin, was both glamorous and fear-evoking, as the mass of hair seemed at once to make its wearer half a head taller and, as well, provide a helmet of its own, to cushion a fall or blow. The worst thrashing Europa and I ever received from Mother came when she discovered us dressing our hair in this fashion.

It became Selene's wont, each autumn round the anniversary of the Great Battle of Athens, to "borrow" javelins and steed by night from Father's stable and make away into the hills, holding fugitive for as long as a fortnight. At the first of these decampments, Father outfitted posses and published bounties for her recapture. Yet it became clear that no rider could overhaul her, or face her wrath if he did, but that Selene, left to her devices, would return of her own, sated by whatever trials or wonders she had undergone and content to serve out her sentence, so to say, for another twelvemonth. Never would our governess recount her adventures, despite Europa's and my most piteous pleadings, save in the form of songs, whose verses appeared nonsense at first but later came to impart their cargo of wisdom.

These rideaways, as we called them on the farm, became if not condoned, then tolerated. My father came even to joke of them, inquiring of Selene when she planned to fly the coop this year, that he might draft his schedule around the date and hire on in advance a surrogate to supervise the children. Selene herself could not predict the hour of her absconding. She went when she went.

The bucks of the farm called Selene "Titless"—what they in ignorance took *A-mazos* to mean—though never to her face. In fact the term Amazon derives from the Cimmerian *Ooma Zyona,* "Daughters of the Horse." This was meant pejoratively. The Cimmerians (who only acquired horsemanship latterly) sought to offer insult to their rivals of the plains. The Amazons viewed this with contempt. They never use the word Amazon to describe themselves; Selene employed it only in converse with Greeks and then grudgingly, because it had gained currency. Likewise she transposed Amazon names into Greek, as Alcippe, "Powerful Mare," or Melanippe, "Black Mare."

They lusted after Selene, the swains of the farm, as they did all the maids, nor was Selene averse to grappling with him she favored, yet none could temper her or draw an uncoerced smile. Only beneath music's spell would she relent, the proper tune proffered by the proper suitor, and then only with such a sorrowful and distant measure as to render her yet more remote.

There had been others of Selene's kind in Attica then, taken like her of wounds after the Great Battle. Several had been made mistresses; others placed in service. All ran off. Chained or bound, they died. Only Selene, constrained by her pledge and her care for my sister and me, abided. She acquired notoriety. Town people would contrive occasion to visit the farm, nosing about to observe one of that race called in the Scythian tongue *oiorpata*, "man killers." "Has her right breast indeed been seared off, to better draw the bow?" "Do you permit her near weapons?" "What holds her from running?"

Once a dame of the district of Melite, the aunt of Prince Atticus, to whom my sister would become betrothed, upbraided my father for exposing his daughters to such unholy influence. "The children will grow to be savages! Who will teach them to card and spin? How will they learn to hold seemly silence?"

My father believed girls should ride and run, nor grow effeminate, squeamish to take game or trek alone in the dark. Who better to impart such arts than a wing captain of Amazonia? Father admired Selene. He wore his custody of her with a covert pride, as one might holding the leash on a she-bear or a lioness. He felt protective of her. For men hated Selene on sight, and women more so, which phenomenon never failed to both stir and alarm my sister and me, and in the presence of which both of us were struck with a rage we could neither name nor exonerate.

Theseus himself, lord of Athens, owned acquaintance of Selene and had dispatched communications to her on occasion, including gifts which she disdained and, to our awe, discarded. On a spring noon in my eleventh year the king traveled out specifically to speak with her. Never had there been such a day! Here down our lane advanced Theseus, monarch of Athens and Eleusis, master of Crete and the islands; he who had brought the dominion of law to Attica, binding within one polity the fractious barons and purging the land, in Myrinus' phrase, of the brigands of misrule.

Theseus was our father's kinsman, the king's mother Aethra and Father's mother Polycaste being cousins, and both Father and his brother Damon had accompanied Theseus a generation previous on his first voyage to the Amazon Sea; yet never in memory had he trod the stones of our estate. He arrived by carriage, not horse or foot, for he had broken a bone in his thigh some days prior and must gimp about by means of a forked staff. Ah, yet, when he came! Who had beheld a handsomer man! Taller by half a head than my father, himself tallest of the district, and carved as from oak. The pelt of his forearms, burnished gold from the sun, made me shiver, and his curls falling to his shoulders bore such a sheen as put one in mind of wild harts and martens. It took slender imagination to understand how Antiope, the Amazon queen, could have fallen so beneath his spell as to desert her own kind and even do battle against them, at this monarch's side.

My sister and I scrutinized great Theseus' apparel: a simple white tunic with a blue border and a rust-colored overcloak, clamped with a brooch of gold in the shape of a sponge. Here was the story:

Once during Theseus' early tenure as king, a commoner had approached the palace seeking a hearing. He was informed that our lord was at his bath; entry was permitted to no one. But the king heard the man at the gate and motioned his guardsmen to relent. He received the fellow while still in the tub and rendered his judgment, which happened to be favorable. When the nobles learned of this they were outraged by its want of dignity. But the gesture endeared Theseus to the commons, so that to this day to act "from the bathtub" means to bypass channels and move immediately with compassion. In gratitude the petitioner presented Theseus with a golden charm in the shape of a sponge, which the king prized beyond all other honors and set in place on his garment, men said, before even his brooches of royalty.

So too did he act on this visit to our home, saluting Father as "Elias, dear cousin and friend," and Uncle Damon as "my fellow black sheep." He disburdened himself of all signia of rank, surrendering these to my sister and mother as a mark of respect to them, and when he sat apart with Selene beneath the oak (which ever after came to be called the King's Oak) it was a sight of wonder to those of the farm, above all the hands who despised her, to behold with what deference the king bespoke the captive maid and with what grave attention he received her response.

We could not know of that which he informed Selene, namely, the critical wounding in battle of her lover Eleuthera, three months' trek east in her homeland on the Black Sea. The report, months old, had only the day before reached Athens by ship, and Theseus, honoring ancient oaths, had felt bound to impart it to Selene in person. Amazons may only take lovers in threes, the triple bond they call *trikona*. Hell, they say, will take any one of the three in place of any other. This is the stem of valor in battle, the Amazons believe, for each triple-mate may donate her life to preserve her comrade's. Selene and Eleuthera were such mates. Nor could one tell by studying Selene's face what grief or resolve she formulated on that account, by so little did her aspect alter. Only later that evening, tracking her like spies, did my sister and I discover the charm of flint and horn she had hung upon the camphor tree which stood alone upon the farm's east-facing slope. This the Amazons call an *aestival*, which term has no equivalent in Greek. It is like a ticket one leaves for a friend to attend a chorus or dance. An aestival is a pledge to set one's own life in place of her lover's and, failing that, signalizing the vow to reunite with her in hell.

Theseus well comprehended these savage tenets and tendered warning to my father, speaking apart in the aftercourse of his interview with Selene, that she, driven now by a mandate superseding that pledge which held her in indenture, might claim her release or even seize it by her own hand. Father understood this as well. Both men were aware of the imperative held by all warrior races to serve honor before survival. This too might impel Selene to run.

We children divined this as well and more, intimates of our governess. We knew the romance which bound our king to the Amazon Antiope, who had fought at his side in the Great Battle. Perhaps the king yet loved Antiope, long perished as she was, or feared the magic of Eleuthera, who bore the war name of the Scythians, *Molpadia*, "Death Song." Our girls' eyes never left the monarch, seeking in his demeanor some hint of heartsoreness, which we thought we detected, unaware of its actual source. Nor did the youths of the farm, restrained by their own diffidence from approaching, dare bespeak the king in such frank manner as the governess. We could see them mutter to one another as men will. "What's she got, that wild bitch, that sets her so high and mighty over us?"

They hated Selene before, and more now, so that this night, after the king's party had departed, the bucks came for Selene in her kennel, a bark lean-to alongside the room I shared with my sister, and dragged her forth to the dark. When Europa and I made to scream, Selene fixed us with a glare that commanded our silence, which she herself would maintain, we knew, and bear mute all the men would do, though we flew anyway to Father and Mother, but neither would come at once, though we implored them, knowing the ravagement of person being inflicted on Selene with each moment's delay. Father believed that on the farm, as on a ship, the hands sometimes may not be ruled but must work out their malice, and him or her judged most outcast must bear the toll. I hated my father in that hour. Perhaps he too feared Selene's flight yet knew not how to quell it, or felt his mastery of her failing or proving false. He departed to her rescue indeed, but absent haste.

Mother held Europa and me from following, and, tugging us to her breast, made to account. "Selene is not a person as you or I, children, but a wild creature who may bear that which to a human being would be intolerable."

"Do you mean she may be violated, as drakes in a gang assault a duck?" This my sister demanded and received a blow for her insolence.

Mother restrained us long enough for the men to work their evil: then, Father reappearing, with a look released us. We understood we might tend Selene now, and flew to her.

Men gave it out that what came later was payout for the way she was shamed, or grief at the news she had borne. It was neither. For one of her race, who had surrendered and served, no further shame was possible, nor was grief grounds for vengeance but only *altare*, union with the fallen, as the Amazons call it in their tongue.

Selene did not run away that night. Rather she called Europa and me apart, to that plane copse where she had schooled us in silence, and over three nights imparted to us her history. When an Amazon senses the hour of her death approaching—when wounded or ill, say, or on the eve of some battle before which she has received a vision or sign of her impending end—the law of her race commands her to "make her testament." She gathers her daughters and imparts her chronicle. Such account, Selene conveyed to us, rarely takes form as a narration of events, but may contain as much of visions and dreams as of waking adventure.

These annals Selene now delivered to us, as I this night pass them on to you. She told of her childhood upon the eastern steppe; of the arrival by sea of Theseus twenty years past; how the king had won the heart of Antiope, war queen of Amazonia, and fled with her to Athens. Selene told of the fury of the Amazons and of the marshaling, beneath Eleuthera, of their own clans, reinforced by the male tribes of the plains, Scyths and Maeotians, Thracians and Tower People, Massa Getai and Thyssa Getai, and fifty other nations, and of this army's three-month trek west and assault upon our city. These wonders Selene narrated with such unwonted urgency as to strike my sister and me with dread (for why would she offer her testament unless she was preparing to die?) yet we were bound to silence by our love for her and the awe in which we held her.

On the third night she led us apart to that toppled wall we children called the Viper's Pocket and there, inserting her arm to the shoulder within a cleft, felt about and withdrew a stone adder, the serpent yet torpid with the night chill, whose poison the Amazons employ to produce that state called in their tongue *adraneia*, "no turning back." Clamping the snake behind the neck, Selene set its nostrils adjacent her calf. She uttered no cry, nor moved, as the fangs entered her flesh and she struck off the head with her sickle. Her blade prized apart the snake's jaws and extracted the fangs, deep as the joint of a thumb. She sang:

> Kallos *beauty*, orge *wrath*,
> *Heart speaks but none listen*
> *Save we on this path.*

Now look you there, daughters and granddaughters, beneath the moon, to that drystone wall which yokes the shearing pens to the gate of the lane.

From there, on the noon succeeding that night, Selene came mounted on my father's stallion, which she had stolen from its stall moments before. Between the steed's jaws set the golden bit of Selene's bridle; on her forearm rode the war shield of bearskin and black leopard. She whipped the beast to the gallop, while the boys and men of the farm raced in a gang to cut her off.

Scyllus the goatherd Selene drove through with the flung javelin, there before the wall, striking him in the solar plexus with the full force of her throw, enlarged by the horse's rising moment so that the herdsman did not even stagger but was nailed, as a plank beneath the joiner's mawl, against the boards of the gate, slain before his mouth could gape or arm ascend to direct the alarm.

With the bow Selene slew Dracon the foreman, there beside the spring's hollow, and at a gallop leapt the wall, loosing a second shaft as she flew, which took the boy Memnon square in the throat, slicing voice box through and severing the column which supports the weight of the skull, so that he dropped like a sack of stones, life-fled before his carcass hit the dirt. And here Mentor, called Top

Hand, who had abused Selene most brutally and handled her most with contempt, seeing her vault wall and palisade and bear down hard upon him, wheeled to flee.

Now from the Amazon's throat, which had endured so long in mute forbearance, ascended that war cry which even to recall at the remove of years sends the gooseflesh coursing, and, snatching the woodsman's hatchet she bore in the stead of a battle-axe in the brace across her shoulders, she slung this weapon upon her fleeing prey at a dead run, its warhead whistling end over end to fix him between the shoulder blades and plunge a full hand's breadth deep into sinew and bone. The force of the blow drove the brute face-foremost into the dirt, where he struck and bounced, arms neither flung wide in agony nor extended before him to break the fall but hanging slack at his sides, and slid upon his chest as a stone skipped across a pond, to skid crown-first into the wattle underpan of the sows' trough, dead as a rat and as void of locomotion.

Selene's mount's hooves thundered past and, strewing straw as she heeled him hard over, slewed round the corner and raced away up the slope, trampling the grafted vines which had been staked out just that forenoon. She vanished beneath the olives of the rise, leaving naught but hoof-punched dust to drift and settle, punctuating her flight.

2

ELEUTHERA MEANS
FREEDOM

Two nights later I woke to find my sister flown. I knew at once she had fled to follow Selene. The transom beneath the eaves was our accustomed escape (as our little room had no window and no outer door); in moments I was up and over, barefoot, and away into the woods.

There must have been fifty hiding places employed by Europa and me, to any of which she could have flown, yet my feet bore me toward that plane grove, our academy of silence, where Selene sacrificed a dove to the moon at each solstice. Once in winter when I had stamped there with the cold, our governess had made Europa and me (for one may not be scourged apart from the other) stand nightlong in frost so hard we lost sensation to the waist. I crested the slope now, lungs heaving, only to have a blow unseen cut my feet from beneath me. I plunged, on my back in my nightshirt, to discover a form atop my chest and a blade at my throat.

"Who has followed you?"

It was Europa. She was naked. Dark as it was, I could see three slashes carved in echelon into the flesh of her breast. This was the *matrikon*, the ritual self-mutilation practiced by the Amazons on the eve of battle.

"What have you done to yourself?" I cried.

My sister's horse Redhead waited, laden with kit.

"You mean to track Selene!"

Europa hissed me silent. "Why did you follow, Bones?" (This is the name I was called as a child, for the dearth of meat on my frame.)

"Take me with you!" I begged.

Europa had mounted to the crown of the slope and held there, motionless, listening. At last satisfied that no one had tracked me, she skidded down and again seized me by the wrist. "There, feel it?"

She thrust my hand between her legs.

"I bleed woman's blood."

The hair stood erect over all my body. My sister's first moon flow. She was a woman now. I could see from the churned earth that she had been dancing. She turned from me in a state of exaltation and elevated both arms toward the moon, which was her namesake, Europa "Broad Face," as it was Selene's "Full Moon." Her breath steamed upon the air. I marveled to behold her in this transport, impaled in ecstasy upon that shaft which lanced silver between the trees.

"Take me with you, sister!"

"You must keep this secret. You heard the men today!"

Indeed at dawn this day Europa and I had trekked into the city to the site of the Assembly and there watched from the *peuke* copse at the brow of the Pnyx (along with other children, slaves, and women debarred by law from deliberations of policy) as the men debated Selene's fate and what action to take regarding her crime and flight.

Outrage had been fierce and immediate in the wake of the farm-yard massacre. Before the blood of the slain had dried, their male kin had been sent for, while the dames swarmed about their slaughtered sons and husbands, wailing in woe and horror. Bring horses and weapons! Muster a posse! Father was appointed captain. My sister and I could see him stall. As an hour slipped away, and another, in the marshaling and provisioning and assigning of arms, the zeal for pursuit abated. Common sense told the futility of launching after Selene. Who could overhaul the Amazon, who had the postnoon's start and gained more with each hour? Selene would run her mount till it dropped, then steal another and another, while the company on her trail must trade for or purchase fresh animals, through a country already made disgruntled by its prey's passage, nor could an armed party pass through alien states absent permission of their princes. Theseus himself did not wish to make a case of this, when his ministers informed him of it later that day, reckoning other affairs of state of far more pressing urgency, namely the increasing boldness of certain barons, agitating for independence from the crown, not to say their allies in the Assembly, who sensed, perhaps, a slackening in Theseus' support among the people and sought to exploit this for their own advantage.

The day passed, and another. Rage at Selene moderated, succeeded by grief for the slain and a darker sense, never absent among superstitious country folk, of a god's hand in the play. Perhaps heaven had willed this holocaust. Surely the dead could make no claim to blamelessness. And their kin, however passionately they may have wished for revenge, were poor men with few resources and less influence.

And so all sought to put from mind this unhappy episode, the running-amok of an obscure and doubtless half-mad governess. But one man, Lykos, the son of Pandion, who was brother to Theseus' father Aegeus and felt himself cheated of Athens's throne, hated Theseus and bore him malice for this and other ills long past. Lykos perceived in the event of Selene's crime and flight the chance to work evil to his enemy. So he set himself to inflame the people, declaring in assembly that such lawlessness unpunished would inspire further mischief—not the harmless outlawry of boys or men but that of women, most pernicious and foul. This struck a chord. For what husband or householder—Lykos incited the males of the Assembly—

may close both eyes in sleep, when tame governesses sling fatal darts and fly unscourged to alien lands?

The orator recalled to his hearers that epoch, so few generations past, when fathers could not even name their own sons with certainty, such was the promiscuity of women. Here at Athens our king Cecrops had founded the institution of marriage, by which the unchaste nature of the female was at last governed and the rights of property accession, father to son, established in accordance with heaven's will.

"How scandalous, men of Athens, if our city, where God first bound female to male in holy matrimony, should be the site of this ordinance's overthrow. Here too did divine Demeter first tutor man in bringing forth the bounties of the earth. To our fathers she taught cultivation of the soil and husbandry of animals, by which arts, shared by us freely with all humankind, has the race of men elevated itself from the slough. Here our fathers founded the twin pillars of civilization—agriculture and monogamy. Will we, their sons, permit both to perish? Let this wild woman get away with murder," Lykos railed, "and we might as well strike the city and return with her to cleft and mire!"

The Assembly met then as now outdoors on the hill of the Pnyx, presided over by Theseus, and from this vantage Lykos gestured to the quarters south, west, and north, recalling to his countrymen the siege of the state, only one generation past.

"Have you forgotten so soon, men of Athens? Let me remind you, then, of that hour when the hordes of Amazonia made their camp on the very stones upon which we convene today and kindled for their cookfires the timbers of our homes, which they and their savage allies had razed entire, driving us before their host in terror. Nor did the ranks of the foe stand slender or attenuated, but in depth twenty shields, with battalions of male auxiliaries, wild Scythians and Thracians and Issedonians, Black Cloaks and Tower People, Massa Getai and Thyssa Getai, painted Tralliai and screw-maned Strymonians, archers and slingers as well as armored infantry, and cavalry above thirty thousand. Nor could we repair to our estates, gentlemen, for the army of Amazons had captured all, laying waste the countryside from Eleusis to Acharnae, while we ourselves starved and rationed water, huddled on the Acropolis behind a palisade of timber and stone. Have you disremembered, men of Athens? Has this little scrape escaped your recall?"

Lykos called on Theseus to mount a pursuit of the Amazon Selene by a fleet and army. He so agitated the people that they stood upon the instant of approving a motion to pursue the fugitive all the way to the Black Sea if necessary, exacting vengeance not on her alone but whatever remained of her race, wiping them out at last and for all time.

Our king rose upon his hobbled leg. The herald set the speaker's *skeptron* in his hand.

"Men of Athens," Theseus began, "I stand in awe of this demonstration of spirit. Would that the commonwealth could call upon such zeal in all her perils. Yet you will acquit me, I hope, if I detect within our speaker's fervor a subtler and more duplicitous scheme. What do you care for this issue, Lykos? I daresay you would not part with a parsnip for the sake of this female Selene or the victims of her wrath, none of whom you could even name before yesterday." The king indicated his president's throne. "You'd like this seat, wouldn't you, Lykos? Or failing that, the satisfaction of ousting me from it? Lykos! Your name means Wolf and like a wolf you stalk me."

Murmurs greeted this, and cries from both parties.

"What I shall do about this wild woman," Theseus resumed, "I know not yet. But I know what I will not do. I will not pursue her across oceans. Not from fear of rivals, however skilled in their manipulation of their countrymen's passions, but because it is simply not worth it. I will not elevate the moment of this lamentable homicide by my participation in the pursuit of its instrument."

Theseus set forth an alternative. If Lykos craved so fervently the capture of this savage maid, let him lead the party in person. The state would foot the bill, declared Theseus, and he himself would donate twenty battle mounts, trained and tractable for sea transport. "Name your ships and men, Lykos, and I will fund them. If you return with your prize, may all glory redound to you."

It was with no slender amusement that Europa and I, not to say the Assembly entire, played witness to Lykos' recitation of alibis to duck this chore. He retreated beneath a storm of derision. The Assembly adjourned.

Now at midnight in the plane grove, my sister dressed and drew her riding cloak about her; she took Redhead's reins and moved to mount. "Do you remember Selene's testament?" she addressed me.

Of course I did. I could recite it by heart.

"And her story of Eleuthera's warrior oath?"

Of course.

"If Eleuthera lies now near death in the Amazon homeland," my sister spoke, "and Selene has flown to aid her, then I must go too. To preserve her if I can! I would gladly die beside her, or for her."

None but a younger sister knows the thralldom in which she stands to her elder. It rubbed even harder with Europa, for she was such a prodigy as rider and runner, fastest of our district, boys included, and possessed of the wildest heart and keenest wit. Now she was a woman, set to launch upon the most brilliant of adventures, while I, her mealy brat sister, must not only wither at home, bereft of her and Selene, but act out the pretense of ignorance to all who would quiz me later. I feared too for my dear sister. She was just a girl! I loved and hated and envied her all in the same breath.

Europa saw it. She drew me to her. "You must second me now, Bones, as Selene seconded Eleuthera. Do you remember the story?"

Indeed. Selene had told it a hundred times; we begged for it, my sister and I, never tiring of its recitation.

Selene's elder mate of the triple bond called trikona was that Eleuthera whose life she had preserved by the sacrifice of her own liberty in the aftermath of the Great Battle of Athens. At the time of this childhood chronicle however (the one my sister referred to), Eleuthera was fourteen, Selene eleven—the same ages Europa and I were now—in the homeland of the Lycasteian Amazons, on the Wild Lands north of the Black Sea. Amazons may not renounce their virginity until they have taken the lives of three foes in battle. At that time Eleuthera had claimed one and bore his scalp on a rawhide thong at her waist. This night of which Selene spoke, a raid had been made by two hundred, Eleuthera's clan and others, upon a party of Phrygian freebooters encroaching on their country. Eleuthera, emerging from the fray at a hard gallop to that defile where Selene and the other novices too young to fight waited holding the second string of horses, had skittered across the plain (it was winter, the earth iron-hard) calling to her younger mate to vault and ride; victory was theirs and no pursuit. Mount and follow me!

Selene had sprung to the back of Eleuthera's two-horse, whom she had just finished "running off" to get him his second wind, and heeling him with all her strength had barely held her elder in sight, with such joy did Eleuthera's primary mount, a big long-legged gelding called Soup Bones, bear her across the frost. At last reining-in, Eleuthera had permitted Selene to draw alongside and, stretching her lance moonward, held out upon its shaft two scalps of men, slick with blood and the still-steaming flesh of the crowns from which they had been torn. Eleuthera here howled such a cry of joy, Selene told my sister and me, as made the down of her arms stand up stiff as boar's bristles.

"Now by the laws I may take a man between my thighs," Eleuthera had cried, laughing. "But I shall not. Never! But make these my children"—she elevated the scalps—"and by them, and all that follow, preserve the free people!"

This was Eleuthera's warrior oath. My sister had imbibed the tale a hundred times, for she would beg to hear it, untiring, and Selene never denied her. I devoured it too, wondering at the manner by which our governess imparted it, ever the same, so that we came, Europa and I, to recite entire passages. My sister's soul drank the song as a horse hard-ridden sucks water from a forest pool, and Selene, perceiving and approving, enlisted her whole heart in consummating our conspiracy. She drew Europa to her, and me, inflecting the tale with her touch as well. As she told of Eleuthera's horse, we felt her knees press our flanks; her fingers played across our shoulders as hoof strikes on the steppe; she kissed us and flattened our breasts against hers so that the smell of her hair and the heat of her flesh reinforced the tale and became indivisible from it. She became Eleuthera to us, and as she, Selene, had surrendered in love to that warrior maid whose name means Freedom, so Europa and I fell in love with her.

I begged my sister to take me with her.

"Of course you cannot go, Bones. But you may aid me if you will."

I would! Just tell me how.

"Buy time for me. Conceal my flight. Play the warrior when they grill you. Offer nothing. Back me as Selene has backed Eleuthera."

I knew she was duping me. I could tell as she took my shoulders in her hands and bent her gaze to mine in savage confidentiality. She was ceding me a spy's errand and passing it off as a hero's. Yet she was my sister, my champion and mentor and ideal. What option did I own but to obey her, and make my peace with being left behind?

3

HANDSOME DAMON

Europa's flight set the city on its ear. Within hours ships had been secured and provisioned, men recruited and officers assigned. The running-amok of a captive governess was one thing; but that a respectable maiden of good house (and one who, when she reached fifteen, would be betrothed to Prince Atticus, son of the illustrious Lykos) could be so seduced from her wits as to make off in the train of such a savage, this set the public cauldron to the boil. Whose daughter was next? Whose sister, whose wife?

Censure for Europa's flight fell upon Father, who was denounced not only for not placing a sturdier watch upon the maid (he should have known she would fly!) but for appointing a wild wench over his daughters in the first place. As for me, I came under as fierce an assault as my sire, for our offense was viewed not as a clan or tribal matter but a crime against the state, to wit, inciting an insurrection of her women. Ministers of Lykos and others came to the farm and interrogated me under oath.

Where had Selene fled?

I did not know.

Where did I think she had flown?

I could not guess.

I was arrested. Armed men tore me from my mother's skirts and bore me in a waggon into the city, where I was placed under detention at the town home of the baron Peteos, a hero of the war with the Amazons and father of Menestheus, who would one day rule the state. Such sequestration, I was informed, was for my own protection. I scorned this, until the first stones began crashing against the shutter boards.

Mother had been permitted to bring my clothes and weaving. But she too had come under suspicion. Before darkness had fallen that night, a mob surrounded the house and was only dispersed by the king's guard hastening from the palace. Nor was this corps of vigilantes constituted of men and boys, as one might expect, but women, even respectable matrons known to Mother, not to say girls my own age, some of whom had been my playmates. How they howled for our blood!

Now it is a fact that in a crisis of lawlessness, one often discovers discharge not in the law but in the outlaw. Thus it ensued that Father's brother Damon, the rogue of the family, materialized as our deliverer.

Damon was our handsome uncle, seven years Father's junior, who doted upon my sister and me, as happens frequently with bachelor kinsmen possessing no issue of their own. Damon had farmed our estate with Father up until the Great Battle with the Amazons, in which he had fought against the army of women, at first with distinction, then later, apparently, with no small notoriety. He had taken their side, at least for an interval. Athens had set a price upon his head in that season; we children could never ascertain the particulars, for as soon as one of our elders commenced to speak of the occasion, a general clearing of throats would ensue and all sprats be banished from the room.

At any event, Damon had had to decamp out the bolt hole, as

the bailiffs say, making his living thereafter by piracy and the hunt. It was he, when my sister and I were small, who made us to understand Selene's shame at capture.

"You must remember, girls, that Selene in her own eyes has committed the supreme sacrilege of her race, that is, to deny to her lover Eleuthera, whose soul stood in her care due to the gravity of her wounds, the boon of a glorious death. No panel has convicted Selene; only the heart within her bosom, by which she stands self-indicted and self-condemned."

Uncle had always favored Selene. He brought her cheeses and rare fruits from his travels; she would accept from him what she would from no other. I never saw them speak. Rather, each would take station across the court from the other, at such time as other business was being transacted and other traffickers filled the lane, so that a glance might pass between them, unremarked by strangers, yet freighted with volumes comprehensible to themselves alone.

Had Uncle been Selene's lover? He was so dashing, and she so comely, that our lasses' hearts must conjure aye. Yet never, for all our snooping, could Europa and I catch them at so much as the exchange of a word.

"Among warrior races, pride is all," Uncle made us to understand. He told us of the flint daggers the wild tribes carry and of the rite of *autoktonia,* double suicide. "This is the act Selene was charged by the code of her race to perform when her mate Eleuthera's wounds, and her own, made capture inevitable. I was there when we took her surrender, on the mountain track between Parnes and Cithaeron. Both women's horses had been killed days past; Selene had borne her lover, near death, seeking to mount the pass at Oinoe. Each time the hill bandits of the district had spied them out, wounding Selene further, twice nearly capturing both. Some dozen of these villains had her birdlimed inside a shepherd's hut when our patrol chanced upon them.

"We drew up in wonder to behold this warrior, despite her injuries a specimen of peerless pride and beauty, arise from her covert and advance toward us, bearing her lover's unconscious form in her arms, with her own hands weaponless and extended. To take an Amazon alive was a prize unheard of, and promised such distinction that our captain, moved as well by motives of clemency, granted her appeal—to reprieve the one and enslave the other."

That had been seventeen years ago, six years before my birth and three before my sister's.

Now, in the event of Europa's flight, Damon had returned to Athens and been welcomed. He had volunteered for the posse and indeed been elected one of its sergeants of cavalry. The squadron would embark with the dawn. Father must sail and so must Damon. But how could they? To abandon Mother and me? To leave us to the mercy of the mob?

The hour was past midnight; Uncle, Father, and Mother conferred in the chamber of our detention, while I feigned slumber on a pallet against the wall.

"There is only one solution," Damon pronounced. "The girl must sail with us."

He meant me. I must accompany the posse.

One may imagine the protests put up by Mother and Father. Had Damon gone mad? To take a child upon the sea! And into such peril! "Where will she be safer?" Uncle countered. "Out that door?"

For minutes Father and Mother refused to hear him. They proffered brief after brief in opposition. Each failed on its face.

"Bones must go with the ships," Damon offered with finality. "And not under protest but with a will."

If Mother and I sought to return home now, he attested, we would be stoned. Not this day perhaps; Theseus' guards might beat our enemies back. But in time and without fail. "The city's derangement may be wicked, but it is real and it will not go away. Only by aligning ourselves with the mob's cause—all of us—can we slip this noose."

By now I had abandoned all pretense of slumber. So that Uncle might meet my glance and flash a hopeful spark.

"What do you say, Bones? You speak the Amazon tongue. You know your sister's ways and Selene's. In a crisis you may speak to them or for them."

My inclusion in the posse, Damon insisted, would be no small asset on such a delicate chore. But most crucially, he stressed, the act would demonstrate to the city that our family, women as well as men, stood on the side of civil order and in opposition to chaos.

It worked. The following dawn Father, Uncle, and I joined the squadron of four—*Euploia, Theano, Herse,* and *Protagonia*—where it waited on the strand at Phaleron Bay. The tally of men at arms had been trimmed to eighty, and cavalry stalls fitted amidships, as it had been decided that the company must ferry sufficient horses to mount at least half the whole. For in that vast wasteland into which the pursuers proposed to venture, a dismounted party could neither track nor overhaul its object. Without cavalry, if our men won a victory, they could not follow it up, and if they suffered a defeat, they would be ruined utterly.

Here was how the vessels were launched. First Theseus and the priests, officiating from an altar of shingle, sacrificed a black ram to Persephone and a bull to Poseidon. The prayers were chanted and the vessels blessed, the holy cargo of myrtle and rowan plaited into the prows. Wives cast garlands of agnus-castus, sacred to Aphrodite of Navigation, and put up that hymn to the Daughters of Night, whose verses I had always thought referred to shepherds

Across Night's field
fare you safely, beneath that canopy
woven not of stars
but of our love

but now, I realized, meant sailors on the sea.

The rollers were greased and the shoring timbers whacked clear by the boatswains' mallets. The men braced up the ships with their shoulders to keep them from careening. The craft were heavy, freighted with goods for trade—oil and wine, weapons and armor, everything except the horses, which were held by their wranglers in rope pens on the strand. Now the sailors took their launching stations outboard of the gunwales, and each, planting his soles on the shingle and seating the loom end of his twelve-foot oar inboard against the centerbeam, with the shaft braced against his thole pin so that the blade extended five or six hand's-breadths beyond the gunwale, set his chest to this and heaved in unison upon the beat. The vessels groaned, prow-first, toward the sea. The false keel tracked down its trench; the rollers screamed; smoke ascended, in wisps and then clouds. When the vessels' prows had nosed into the sea far enough to float, the first eight horses were loaded aboard each, hoodwinked, up a ramp which was then taken up as well and slotted in place to form the door of the undecked stalls amidships. The last four horses, yoked as a team, joined the men in warping the ships out again (as they had nosed back into the sand, thanks to the weight of the horses) till again they were elevated, lifted by the sea. Then these last four animals were loaded too, up the short ramp, and this was set in place barring their stalls. I had been recruited with the wranglers to gentle the beasts, who now balked and bellowed in fright as the ship yawed against its hawsers and the men sprang to their benches.

How gallant these lads! How caught up in their adventure! Flown from their hearts was all recall not only of my sister Europa, the object of their enterprise, but even of Selene, whom they hunted on orders of the Assembly and the state. Did any give thought to her? Not even Father or Damon in that hour. Who knew her? Who apprehended the gods she served, or those imperatives of love or honor that commanded her?

Only I.

As I sought my berth in the foreships, out of the oarsmen's way, Selene's voice arose unsummoned within my breast. Her apparition ascended before the inner eye; I heard again her testament, which she had imparted just three nights prior to my sister and me, mandated by the foreknowledge of her own end to come.

Who would speak for Selene?

Only I.

I felt the last scrape of sand beneath the keel. I heard the hawsers' slap and the chanty, "Cast off and pull." The ship slewed, seeking balance between her oar banks, and then her prow set toward open water. The motion caught me sick, as it did the horses, who now in alarm evacuated bowels and bladders, sending this broth in cascades onto their footing timbers and through these to the bilges.

Heaven preserve us, the ships had launched.

We were on the sea.

4

DAUGHTERS OF THE HORSE

Selene's testament:

⊗⊚⊚⊚⊚⊚⊚⊚⊚⊚⊚⊚⊚⊚

I was born not in Amazon country but ten days north, among the Black Scythians. These are not black-skinned, as Ethiopians, but black-maned; fierce fighters, women as well as men. My mother was Cymene, daughter of Prothoe, who had dueled Heracles hand-to-hand and been slain by him before the Typhon's Gate of Themiscyra, capital of Amazonia. Mother could speak Pelasgian and Aeolian Greek, and wished me to learn for the free people's sake, though among our race speech, and its handmaiden, reason, are considered stages of degeneration, inferior to action and example, which is the language of *Ehal*, Nature, and of God. Among my people speech is parsed; even infants babble little, rather are schooled to make themselves known as horses and hawks, without sound. It has been my disfigurement, for my race's weal, to have learned letters among civilized society. This art has severed me from God and from the free people.

Men say God made the sky. This is mistaken. God *is* the sky, for creation may not stand apart from Creator, but all that is, is, and is God. First from the sky issued the thunderbolt and the hailstorm; for a hundred times a hundred thousand winters these reigned, solitary. Then came eagle, and falcon, and all creatures of the air. These lived a thousand millennia, never touching earth, for she had not been made, but dwelt happily upon the air and within it, which itself was all their sustenance, of food and spirit. They were a part of God and were God.

Sky craved communion and brought into form Earth, our mother, charging her with his bolts of fire and cleaving her belly to bear ocean and mountains and inland sea. All these were great and holy and were a part of God and were God.

From Sky came Horse. In the beginning Horse flew, more swiftly than the eagle, and in fact was called by God "steppe eagle," as she is to this day by the free people. Horse was first to form societies. Before Horse's coming each creature dwelt apart and solitary, in communion only with God and Earth. Horse invented language. Her tongue was holy, God's own idiom, which speaks in silence, without even the cast of an eye or flick of a mane. This language yet endures, but may be heard by humankind only within the stern clash of battle.

Hear, O People, the peal
of God's sacred tongue, resounding alone
atop Ares' anvil, hammered into hearing
by the mawl of valor.

When humankind appeared, they were weak and puny. Horse nursed them on mare's milk and blood, and raised them as her own. Horse led the clans to water when thirst parched the plains and to vales of fruit and forage when famine bore them hard. When swift fire raced across the steppe, horse commanded the people, Leap upon my back; and bore them at the gallop to safety. Horse taught them to hunt the shy hart and the wild oryx, the mountain eland and the gazelle. And when grim famine stalked the land, Horse instructed the people: Eat of my flesh and live. Without these boons and others numerous as the lamps of heaven, the race of mortals would have perished a thousand times over. Always Horse preserved them. And when the free people in thanksgiving sought to make sacrifice to God, they offered up that which they revered and venerated beyond all, their savior and ally, Mother Horse.

Horse taught the free people her ways, to ride and raid; she schooled them to bear winter's hardship and summer's travail. Her flesh she donated in every part, from the casings of her organs, with which the free people bore water, to her sinew for bowstrings, her gut to stitch wounds. From her mane the free people wove rope and winter cloaks. They used her hide and hooves and even her teeth, grinding these for beads and dyeing them into belts for their maidens' loins. The people were happy. They ranged God's estate in freedom, wanting nothing which Horse and their own hands could not provide. They would have roamed so forever, had not the gods, by their own discord, intervened.

For that race of humankind which knew not the horse dwelt in misery and abjection, scratching its living, as swine do, of acorns and the roots and grubs of the slough. Prometheus the titan took pity on them. He stole fire from heaven, when Zeus of the Thunder expelled the generation of immortals elder to himself.

Prometheus gave fire to man.

Horse feared fire. The free people fled from it as well. But those bog-bound of humankind discovered the arts by which it could be made their patron. Meat they roasted, and grain; they tamed the wild rye and barley and made these to grow at their bidding, imprisoned within their walls, and by the close flame to bake these to bread.

With fire came pride, as Prometheus (whose name means Forethought) well knew, whose object was the overthrow of heaven. And in his pride man tore the flesh of his mother, the earth, rending her with the beaked plough, to sow the seed by which he would stoke his arrogance.

Man knew speech now, and collected into towns, stinking kennels abhorred by God, where not even His holy storm may penetrate, but walls and ramparts keep it out. Man lived in hovels, reeking with smoke and sooty with ash. These made his hair smell, and the dirty rags he wore to clothe his nakedness; his hands stank with it and his skin grew ashy and abraded. The free people drew scent of these creatures and fled, as horses do, from his foul and malodorous approach.

Men's language succeeded the language of birds and horses and the silent tongue of the free people. The stem of his speech was fear, fear of God and God's mysteries. Man sought by naming things to denature them and deplete them of the terror they held for him. His words were harsh and disharmonious, and as remote from true language as the screech of bats is from the music of the stars. Yet among our captains it was recognized that those encroaching tribes as Pelasgians and Dorians, Aeolians, Hittites, and such, who coveted our lands and the herds which ranged them with us, made speech with words and employed these as weapons. So some of our race must learn their tongue to resist and confute them. In each generation a number were chosen. I hated and feared this, for God had cursed me with facility for this art, and I hid myself each time the war queen's gaze scanned among the people.

I had a friend Eleuthera (such was her name in Greek) and her I loved beyond moon and stars and breath itself. Among my race, any who displays promise as a leader may not grow to womanhood among her own, lest her mates, out of their love for her and fear of seeing her elevated apart from them, work mischief to damp her gifts. So she is sent away to allied tribes, where she is tutored in the arts of war and politics, to return only after her moon's blood. When she was ten, and I seven, Eleuthera was called to this commission. All light left my heart at this hour and when they came to me, the ministers, calling me to learn the languages of men, I resisted no longer.

I was taken out, dressed in doeskin with my hair beaded and parafinned, to the trace which runs from the Gate of Storms to the sea and along which the traders' trains pass. A war-schooled mare carrying a foal was staked out with me. The traders took me across the sea to Sinope and placed me in a proper household, under whose law I became what they call a *sinnouse*, a sort of companion to the daughters of the house, who is above a slave but beneath a sister. I learned the Greek tongue, both Aeolian and Pelasgian, to speak and spell.

The family was not unkind to me. The father offered no insult and in fact shielded me as if I were a daughter. But he would not let me ride or run, and when I reached once to touch the crescent saber mounted above the hearthstone, he slapped my hand. "No, child, this is not for you."

I dwelt in the women's quarter, learning home craft and music, to spin and to weave. Days I studied; nights I lay apart and wept. My heart longed for home—for the sky, which was God, and the wild earth, our Mother. I missed the sweet voices of heaven which spoke in birdsong and the chirrup of the prairie marmot, the spirits of thunder and the flood and ebb of the sea of stars. When I caught scent of the stable, the horse-smell racked my soul. I ached for the Wild Lands, even their pains, for sharp stones beneath my heel, the sting in the nostrils of the frost-bound steppe, and her gifts, the warmth of my Eleuthera's arms about me in the night.

There is no word for "I" in the Amazon tongue. Nor does the term "Amazon" exist. This is a foreign invention. One says "the daughters" or, in our tongue, *tal Kyrte*, "the Free." Eleuthera, as I said, is a Greek word; my friend's true name is Kyrte.

Among tal Kyrte, one says not "I," but "she who speaks" or "she who answers." To express herself, one says in preface, "This is what my heart tells me," or "She who speaks is moved thus." One of our race does not perceive herself as an individual apart from others, mistress of a private world divisible from the internal worlds of others. When one of my people offers speech in counsel, she does not produce this as a Greek might, from his own isolated disseverment from God; rather she summons it from that which contains her; that is, allows it to arise from that ground which has no name in our tongue but is called by the Thracians *aedor* (in Greek, "chaos") which is the sky, which is God, that which animates all things and inhabits the spaces between things, understaying and undergirding all.

Before she speaks, one of the free people will pause, sometimes for no small interval. This the impatient Greek takes for slow-wittedness or stupidity. It is neither; rather a distinct and disparate manner of viewing the world.

In Sinope when I heard people use the word "I," I experienced it as a thing of evil, recognizing its wickedness at once. Even after I learned the hang of it, and came to use it myself, I hated it and felt it a bane which would consume me if I kept its usage too long.

The term of my indenture was defined in this manner. When the mare (whose worth was my tuition, so to say) foaled, and that foal grew to saddle age, I might school it and ride it home. I could not wait for this, however, but stole another horse and weapons. I fled home, believing I could put this "I" behind me. But it had sunk its malign roots into my heart and contaminated me, that I might never truly return to the Daughters, not as I had once been, at one with them.

When one of tal Kyrte misses steppe and sky, she longs not just for their beauty but also their cruelty. For among the free people the foreawareness of one's death, and heaven's indifference to it, is the keenest and most brilliant pleasure, rendering all precious. This is the supreme mystery, the fact of existence itself, before which mortals may only stand in silence.

The city people hated and feared this mystery. Against it they had founded their walls and battlements, not so much to repel invaders of flesh as to hold at bay this unknown, to blot it from their hearing and wipe it from their sight.

This is why they hate tal Kyrte, the free people. Our existence recalls to them that before which they have flown in terror. If we can live with it, in fact live *in* it, then they must be less than we, to have erected such edifices to its exclusion. That is why they hate us and why they came, Heracles first and then Theseus, to destroy us.

Once in Sinope I saw the great Heracles. He was old then, past forty, with his famous Labors behind him, but still brilliant. The whole city tramped out to see him.

The bards praise Heracles as the solitary hero who plundered our queen Hippolyta's virgin belt. This is a lie. He came to the Wild

Lands with twenty-two ships and a thousand men at arms—and not such clods as one sees with stone-point spears dull as billhooks, but iron-armed, in cuirasses of tin and silver, shields bronze-faced and heavy as waggon wheels, and helmets of electrum and gold.

They wished to see him wrestle, did the people of Sinope, and set the prize of a bronze cauldron for any standing past the count of ten, and a talent of silver for him who took the great man off his feet. You could see Heracles cared little for such sport, bored of it long since, but he still threw with such violence all who dared close with him that levity departed the tourney, and wives feared for their husbands, lest this son of Zeus snap their spines, not knowing, even so far past his prime, his own strength.

I trailed him afterward through the streets, compassed as he was by his corps of toadies and tufthunters. His strength, one perceived, was not of men but of gods; you could believe he had slain the Nemean lion bare-handed, whose skin he yet wore, so dense was the pack of muscle across his shoulders and so massive the columns of his thighs. Yet what struck my child's observation was not Heracles' might but his sorrow.

He was not free, nor had been ever, but a vessel formed (and deformed) of heaven. God had bequeathed him glory imperishable, a berth among the stars, and charged him to overturn the order of the world. This, Heracles had done. He had performed his labors.

I studied his eyes, in the glimpses one could catch between the press of idolaters. Once I thought his gaze met mine. Did he know me for the race to which I belonged? I believe he did, and at once.

He had defeated us, and others would follow, seeking to emulate his glory. Yet his aspect spoke now, I perceived, of grief and contrition. *I performed my Father's bidding,* Heracles' eyes seemed to tell mine, begging their remission. *I had no choice.*

Heracles, as the world knows, had come to the Amazon Sea twenty years earlier, first of the southern races to bear arms against the free people. He came with thirty companies of infantry and five of cavalry and encamped before the Typhon's Gate of Themiscyra. This was at the rising of Arcturus, when the clans of the daughters of

Ares gather from as far as Libya, and, declaring he had been sent by King Eurystheus of Mycenae to bring home our queen Hippolyta's virgin girdle, tantamount to demanding her submission to him as a concubine or whore, he called out to single combat any and all champions of the free people.

Hippolyta reckoned at once the evil borne by this man and the woe it foretold for the nation. But the young bloods could not see past the outrage he offered. They clamored, these daughters, to be first to face him. Hippolyta commanded forbearance. She would deflect Heracles' purpose. She would deny him the fight he had come for.

Hippolyta stripped her girdle and offered it in peace, appending tokens of respect, honoring the invader's enterprise and lineage as child of Zeus. Heracles accepted with gratitude, to his credit grasping the purpose of this device and wishing, since he had achieved his aim, to depart without bloodshed.

But Melanippe, "Black Mare," who held that year the post of war queen, and Alcippe, "Powerful Mare," her commander of cavalry, could not bear this affront. Pride spoke to them out of their strong hearts, inciting them to battle. What force had deranged their reason? Who but Zeus, devious-devising, to grant, by their vanquishment at his hand, honor to his son Heracles.

There is on the landward side of Themiscyra a dry course called the Raceway, where the traders' market stands in summer but which on this day had been cleared for the games in honor of Phrygian Cybele. Onto this field the pride of the free people rode. They sent an unbroken colt into the Greek camp, sign of challenge understood by all, and called Heracles out.

On that day he slew in single combat Aella, "Whirlwind"; Philippis; Prothoe, my mother's mother; Eriboia of the electrum helm; Celaeno; Eurybia, who had slain a leopard with her bare hands; Phoebe, called "Manslaughterer"; Deianera; Asteria; Marpe; Tecmessa; and at last Alcippe and Melanippe themselves, champions of the free people.

The harpers tell it thus: that Heracles' famous lion skin, which he wore draped about his shoulders, impenetrable to all save its own claws, had preserved him from the darts and axes of the daughters of Ares. This is nonsense. My mother was there and saw it. This she told: it was no beast's hide beneath which Heracles took the field, but iron armor of such weight and thickness as no other could bear and still move and fight. The flung javelin caromed off this black-smith's plate, even at point-blank range, and Heracles was so strong that though the impact might arrest his advance momentarily, it could not knock him off his feet. Sword and spear were as straws against him, and the mass of his great club, which an ordinary mortal could barely lift, staved our bronze shields and helms as tissues of flax.

In a duel of honor, single combat is law. Yet who, male or female, could stand up to such a prodigy one-on-one? My mother made his height at six and a half feet; I would declare him taller, even when I saw him at Sinope at over forty years old. He could kill an ox with a blow of his fist, men swore, yet I saw him as well outsprint in the races even the swiftest lads and all the men. Such physical primacy bred a fearlessness that made his precocity even more formidable. Nor were these the sum of Zeus' gifts to his son, but supernal vision and reflex as well. At Sinope he put on a demonstration. He stood at the neck of a stone runway, hemmed by barricades, while three war-riors, doughtiest in the city, slung javelins from inside a dozen paces. No one could hit him. He could snatch an arrow out of the air; side-step its rush and catch it by the shaft as it flew. Stones and sling bul-lets he caught in his fist or dashed aside with his club, as boys on the line-field bat away the bowled ball.

So they advanced to their doom at Themiscyra, the champions of our race, one succeeding another, like knights hurling themselves from a precipice. Heracles took his girdle prize, its luster now ampli-fied by blood, and sailed home.

A calamity of such scale had never befallen the daughters of Ares—the loss in their prime of the flower of the nation. My mother's generation grew to womanhood in the shadow of this shame, and my own imbibed as mare's milk both the trauma of that vanquishment and the foreterror of some more catastrophic over-throw, borne upon us by the next wave of invaders, successors to Heracles, who must ineluctably follow.

Champion of our generation was Antiope, granddaughter of Hippolyta and triple-mate to Stratonike and Eleuthera, the most brilliant archers and riders of the day. Antiope it was, even as a child, who resuscitated the nation. At that time the ancient rite of *mastokausis*, as the Greeks call it, the searing off in infancy of the right breast, had fallen from favor. Antiope revived it. At seven years she ordered her own mutilation, that all strength, as she grew, would accrue to the muscles of her shoulder and back, and no womanish flesh impede the draw of the bow and the cast of the javelin. Not one of our generation failed to emulate her. When at age ten the trikona of Antiope, Eleuthera, and Stratonike were called to study war with the northern tribes, they went with hearts singing with joy. They elevated to a peak unprecedented proficiency in the use of the *pelekus*, the double-bladed axe, and roused the generation of youth to mastery of the javelin and the Cimmerian bow. The practice of the steel-rimmed discus they learned and taught, to hurl from horseback, taking a man's head, helmet and all, at one howling swipe. Antiope's flesh she trained to be superior to heat and cold, hunger and fatigue, and schooled her string from colts, driving them again and again into the storm beneath Zeus' bolts, to fear neither riot nor havoc, but to love battle and drink with joy from the well of strife. About her she assembled a corps of champions—Eleuthera; Stratonike; Skyleia; the younger Alcippe; Glauke, "Grey Eyes"; Xanthe, "Blonde"; Euippe, "Beautiful Mare"; Rhodippe, "Red Mare"; Leucippe, "White Mare"; Anteia; Tecmessa, "Thistle"; Lyssa; Evandre; and Prothoe—a match and more for the paragons of old, and dedicated, all, to the reclamation of preeminence for the race. Their zeal fired not only our nation, the Lycasteia, but the Themiscyra, Chadisia, and Titaneia, and the clans and tribes as far as the Iron Mountains and the Belt of Storms. The elders looked on with pride as the plain rang with horses and young women training in the arts of war.

Antiope's gifts were not of valor alone, but statecraft and generalship. The combat of solitary champions, she persuaded the elders to debar, drafting in its place cohesion of cavalry and unity of assault. She called for return to the old ways. At her impetus the Corps of Mounted Archers was reorganized into companies, squadrons, and wings under commanders accountable not to those beneath but those above. She reinstituted the crescent charge and the assault called "chest-and-horns." For her hand Antiope fashioned a type of javelin unknown heretofore, weighted with iron in its core and warhead. Such a missile was too heavy to throw, even on the run, unaided. But catapulted by a sleeve extender, to amplify the leverage of the shoulder, and hurled not sidearm but overhand and from horseback, to add moment to its launch, it could be propelled to devastating effect. Antiope added a belly-band for her mount, with a step stitched in, so that she could plant her sole and rise at the gallop, driving the big muscles of her legs and back into the cast. At seventeen she could splinter a pine big around as a man's thigh. At twenty-four, when she acceded to the post of war queen, she had strung upon her lance the scalps of twenty-nine enemies slain hand-to-hand upon the steppe.

Let the next invading heroes come, be they Heracles' sons, or any army of champions seeking to emulate him. Not armor of adamant, nor the ramparts of hell itself, would preserve them.

Time passed and they did come, led by Theseus, prince of Athens.

I had not been born to daylight in Heracles' prime. This time, for Theseus a generation later, I was present and grown. Eleuthera was there too. She was twenty-two and a wing commander; I nineteen and her lover and friend.

BOOK TWO

THE RIVER OF HELL

5

PHALANXES OF IRON

Mother Bones:

⟨⟨⟨⟨⟨⟨⟨⟩

Within the forepeak of a ship, where the beam of the cutwater seats into the head timber of the keelson, is a cramped kennel used for the stowage of sails. It is called the wreath locker because into this space the priests, at embarkation, lade the holy boughs of myrtle and rowan, an offering to Poseidon and the daughters of Proteus.

> *In peril on the salt waste*
> *Turn ye home again to these,*
> *Lest you lose your way.*

It was to this closet that I repaired when the posse launched in pursuit of Selene.

No female is welcome aboard ship; her presence is considered unlucky. And though Father and Damon spared no exertion to moderate my disquiet, and no other offered overt insult, yet I could find no congenial berth. I hid. The locker was cozy; it smelled sweet from the scrubbed linen and wreaths of myrtle. I tucked into a ball within the folds of the sails and sought solace in slumber.

The ships as I said were four, *Theano*, *Euploia*, *Herse*, and *Protagonia*. They were undecked "fifties," reconfigured to hold six double horse stalls amidships. Oarsmen were thirty-four, with a captain of infantry, two wranglers and a cavalry sergeant, a ship's master and his steersman. All took their turn at oars, even Prince Atticus, who commanded the armada entire.

Passage to the Amazon homeland would take sixty days. The squadron would traverse waters no Greek save Jason, Heracles, and Theseus himself a generation prior had ever sailed, at such a remove from civilization, men feared, that Zeus Himself was unknown, but such savage races ruled as knew neither manners nor law nor deference to heaven.

Indeed I hid. The usages of the sea were alien to a child, and repellent. I was sick. I could keep nothing down. Ashore each night I yet felt the lurch and yaw of the main. I huddled in a fleece at Father's side, wretched as a trussed sow. How I missed home and Mother! How I longed for my snug little bunk and solid earth beneath my tread. The fourth day out I had this dream:

I was home, trapped by mischance in Mother's closet. She came swiftly, responding to my cries, and commenced beating at the door to free the latch. I was so relieved! I blinked awake, eager to rush into her arms. But it was no storeroom door against which my cheek was pressed, but the sodden timbers of the ship's keelson, and no mother's palm hammering but the tempest-driven sea. The ship pitched and slewed. I was sick again and cramping in my guts. A gale had got up. Through the deck I could see the sail drawing full. I sought to escape again to slumber. When I next came to, the sea's concussion had redoubled.

The ship was bucking now. Sky had gone the color of lead; squall-driven torrents lashed the deck. The sail was brailed up to quarters, then eighths. Clewed to a patch no bigger than a pot holder, it drove the ship like a courser. The heavens went black; cold rose off the deep. By God, the storm had struck fast! Only moments earlier the ship had raced on a high line; now she plummeted to trenches and canyons. Salt summits arose on all quarters. I gaped out upon mountains the color of iron.

I was puking again. I set both palms upon the futtock timbers and braced against the heave. How could this crate of spars stand such a pounding? A crewman reeled from topside into the locker. "Father Almighty"—I could see his breath shoot like steam—"spare me for my bride and babe!"

A dire keening cut my kennel. These were the forestays, singing in the gale. Suddenly they snapped, with the concussion of a bull-whip; the sail tore loose and, moments later, mast and yard vanished into the storm. At home Selene had schooled my sister and me to feel contempt for death, and this had seemed a fine idea on dry land. Now on the main my flesh revolted. Fear screamed from every sinew. My tongue was ash; my limbs quaked as if palsied. But the harder I struggled to be brave, the more terror-stricken I became. Father! I burned to burst from my hiding place and, crying his name, rush into his arms. Then I glimpsed him, on his feet amidships, as the ship dove into yet another trough. He had seized a man of the crew and driven him to his bench. I saw Father shout into the fellow's teeth, a cry of such rage as I had never imagined him capable. He shoved the man down and thrust an oar into his fists. The ship careered wildly now, not only fore and aft but up and down, and side to side. Two men grappled the steering oar, useless now in such steep seas. The poor horses! They had long since been driven from their feet. On knees and flanks they lowed like cattle.

The storm was on us now. The universe had contracted to a disk of iron-colored deep no broader than a bowshot. We had lost all sign of the other ships. On one side, seas ascended; on the other they crashed and withdrew. One sea mounted at a time, its mass obscuring sight and sound of its successors, and with it the ship must duel one-on-one, employing all her skill and courage, while she readied for the next and the next after that. Sea succeeded sea, each resounding with malevolence, each different from the sea before. One became a connoisseur of seas. Those which rose gradually, solid at the crest, were the easiest. Into their faces the ship pulls bows-on, aligning her keel with the axis of their advance. Those seas with shoulders may be slipped at the low point, but invariably at their backs arise greater seas and steeper, transversely driven, so that crest becomes shoulder and shoulder crest in such immediate alternation that the men at oars must often haul and back water in successive strokes, the oarsmen's task rendered diabolical by the press of the gale which twists and wrenches at their blades, seeking to wrest them from their grip.

Again and again seas rose. At last ascended the One. I could see it coming. It mounted and mounted and, when I thought it could mount no more, mounted again. I could not believe a sea could be so tall. Twice the height of a mast, if we had still had a mast, and broad as a castle, it loomed like a fortress and crashed like a battlement of stone. Thwarts snapped down the vessel's length; men were swept from their benches like dolls. Salt sea frothed to the gunwales; the weight drove the ship under. Men were crying, soundless, amid the thunder.

Over she heeled, so nigh vertical that a man could reach out with his finger and trace his name in the wall of water. Then she rose. Tons emptied over her rails; the vessel righted, yawing violently onto the opposite beam. I saw two horses, yoked head to tail, spill over the gunwale as casually as a comb of honey at the lip of a wine bowl. The beasts did not even bob, but plummeted like lumps of lead. Seamen beholding this gaped, waxen as ghosts.

The ship righted. Men clawed and swam to their places. So many thwarts had been staved as rendered half the oarsmen benchless. Worse, their wreck had ruptured the integrity of the hull. I heard a ghastly sound and realized it was the timbers warping. You could sight down the gunwale and watch it bow like a celery stalk. The hempen girdles, the *hypozomata* that bound the exterior of the hull, were now all which held the ship from disintegrating. I could not believe the sound as they warped and torqued. Strips of timber began shredding from the hull. Planks and carlings tore past, gale-driven. I saw one strike a fellow as he labored to set a beam; the blow sheared his ear and half his scalp clean as a cleaver. The man did not even notice until the blood, streaming horizontally in the gale, painted a swath before his eyes.

His need drew me from my covert. I waded to him, hip-deep in the seas which swamped the ship. But the prow behind me plunged in the afterpass of a sea; I spilled down the cataract, fetching up against the sail locker, upon which I remained impaled by the weight of water. The man saw me. Such a cast illumined his eye as wrought my terror to yet greater epitomes. For he seemed to descry my apparition not as one of this life perceiving another, but as one already dead to her first beheld upon the other side.

Uncle appeared beside me. He clutched me to him, shouting something I could not hear. Suddenly a hand seized his shoulder. It was Father. Before I could speak, he had wound a line about my waist and, binding this to his own, bawled to Damon that both must resume their benches. Father hauled himself—and me, yoked to him— to a shattered thwart and there, reseating his oar, set back to labor.

How excruciating that toil! Hour succeeded hour. Men's frames racked and broke. The horses' suffering surpassed description. The walls of their stalls had long since been splintered, yet the beasts themselves remained roped in place, not only hobbled fore and aft, but tethered to the footing timbers of their stalls. As each sea passed over, their heads and necks were driven under. Such horror: to see their hooves only, thrashing above the seas. Then the ship rights herself and the beasts, in whose goggling eyes terror finds no more eloquent depiction, heave up into God's air, manes and forelocks running rivers, to gasp the salvation that may endure only another breath.

I peered into the faces of the men at oars. Rivers of brine sluiced from their beards. Their long hair stood sideways with rime shooting from it. Into a trough the ship plummets; for a heartbeat the cosmos becomes pacific. Then that sound ascends and the ship, rising, shoots anew into that maelstrom which not all the howls of hell may replicate. My own hair, snapping like a pennant, became bound about the oar against which I too pulled, with palms riven to pulp, beside the bulwark of my father. How valiantly he labored! Nor did he toil alone, but all up and down the benches men strove with as much resolution and as little hope. I was seized with compassion for these gallant, luckless men. How brave they were! How nobly they persisted into the teeth of doom!

Last of terror's stages, Selene had tutored Europa and me, is busyness. This succeeded now. Men simply had no time to fear. Each instant arose freighted with so many exigencies that fear could no longer shoulder in. How insignificant one felt! I beheld Father and Uncle, the bastions of my universe, and knew both as but stalks within the maw of the Almighty. I spoke into Father's ear, as casually as if he and I sat at ease upon a bench at home.

"Selene has not fled to the Amazon homeland, Father, but to Hell's River in Magnesia. Europa will have followed her there, seeking to overhaul her."

How did I know this? Perhaps a god whispered. Yet I knew, certain as my own death.

Father's eyes never lit on me, bound as all to Atticus and our pilot. Yet he heard and believed.

The men rowed and rowed.

How long the trial endured I cannot say, save that at last, when I swooned into the lap of my father, the men yet maintained their resolve, until, the tempest's fury at last abating, the vessels sighted haven and rushed toward her to embrace their reprieve.

6

A TRANSIT TO THE
UNDERWORLD

∽∽∽∽∽∽

The companies trekked to Hell's River by tens, with me yoked to my father by a rein of rawhide, that I might not bolt at bogeys ascending from the mire, or, if I tumbled into one of the bogs of the approach, be roped to safety. It was raining. Chill sheets drenched the parties, turning the track to slough.

Sixteen days had elapsed since the squadron's deliverance. It had taken that term for the four ships to reacquire one another, each having fetched up on a different shore, and, once reunited, to refit the vessels, see to the wounded and lost, and to permit horses and men interval to recover. As early as the second night, Atticus and the officers had interrogated me.

What intelligence had I imparted to Father about Hell's River? Had Selene indeed fled there and not to the Amazon homeland? Why would she do this—and how did I know?

I recalled to the officers that the incitement for Selene's flight had been the report, conveyed to her by Theseus on the noon of his visit to our farm, that her lover Eleuthera stood now in peril of her life, somewhere in the Wild Lands above the Black Sea.

"Amazons bond in threes," I heard my voice address the captains, "and believe that hell will accept any one of this trikona in the stead of another."

"What does this mean, child?" Prince Atticus pressed gently.

"I cannot know for certain, sir, but common sense tells that Selene will make first for some portal of the Underworld and there offer sacrifice, perhaps of her own life, beseeching the gods to spare her mate Eleuthera's."

A second council was held that night, and a third when all four ships had at last reunited. A number of speakers confirmed the existence of such sites as I had suggested, where the tributaries of the River Styx—Acheron, Cocytus, Aornis, Lethe, and Phlegethon— twine in their circuit beneath the earth.

The nearest, at Raria on the Magnesian coast, was Fire River. This was the one I had been inspired to cite and the one for which plain sense argued the most compellingly. Its entrance lay within ten days' ride of Athens. It could be reached entirely by land, requiring no sea crossing (since Amazons fear and despise the salt element). And it was the only one on Selene's likely track, that is, to the ultimate destination of her homeland.

At the twelfth dawn, then, the patched flotilla put back to sea, retraversing the expanse across which the storm had driven it, to beach three days subsequent on that strand of shingle called the Hollows, in Magnesia, again on the mainland. A party of twenty was detailed to guard the ships, while the main body, fifty or more under arms, commenced the tramp inland seeking the portal to the Underworld.

This proved a desultory shuffle, as several among the crew who had personal acquaintance of the site had reported that "Fire River," so daunting in its appellation, was nothing more than a subterranean sump void of supernatural substance, a tarry trickle stinking of sulphur and bitumen. The stench was so foul, these fellows recounted, that neither bird nor beast inhabited the region but only lizards, serpents, and slugs.

The belt Father had cinched about my waist was of a type whose usage he had acquired in Amazonia twenty years previous, on the original voyage under Theseus. The Amazons call it an *astereia*, a "star belt," and the Greeks a riding wale. Selene wore such a wale always, for, as all horsewomen know, nothing comes in handier in the company of fractious mounts than a good length of rope, as lead, halter, hobble, or lasso.

So tethered, I advanced in Father's train. A stink ascended from the ooze, vile as eggs gone rotten. Men packed their nostrils with moss and bound muffles about their faces.

There was no village and the only locals, a runt race calling themselves Rarians, "Womb People," over whose greased topknots even I towered, spoke a form of shore Pelasgian so antique than not even our mates from Brauron or Marathon could savvy it. Heaven knows how these beggars made their living; perhaps they rustled lizards or swamp cats for the hides. Their fingers were no greater than my toes, and the stunted limbs from which these nubs protruded appeared more like the paws of some species of nocturnal rodent than the extremities of God-spawned humankind. Their mantles were of rat skin and opossum with the heads and tails still on, while both male and female ran naked from the waist down. Their loins they smeared with particolored mud, perhaps for its protective shell, or, as Prince Atticus reckoned, they were just plain dirty. Coin or gold meant nothing to them, but they would jig with glee over any artifact of fired clay. They coveted drinking cups, which our men carried strung to packs and belts, and would offer any tale for one. Yes, they had seen an Amazon. Make that ten, or a hundred! A young girl, indeed! Of roan hair, wasn't she, or did we say raven? Three times these denizens directed our companies to the Portals of Persephone, the debouchment from the Underworld (they claimed) of the River of Hell, each sortie revealing a less illustrious backwater than the one before.

At one point Damon achieved a parley with their headman.

"These wart bastards worship the Womb Goddess" was his report to Atticus and the captains. "We're trespassers. They won't steer us near the cleft, bet on it, and may strike a ruckus if we stumble too close. Here's more to chew on. Every swamp breed I've heard of are master poisoners. These may tip their arrows, or paint thorns, even set sharpened stakes for us to tread upon."

The posse slogged on all morning. The country was asphaltine swamp, into whose ooze the men's tread sank to the ankles. What elevations there were rose only inches above the mire; vegetation was canebrake and deerwood, whose stalks, dense as the shafts in a quiver, could not be prized apart but must be hacked through with the bronze axe, while a canopy enforced a stoop upon even the runt-iest. Beneath this vault the natives of the marsh glided with ease; they tracked us, so close you could hear their sparrowlike gibberish, while our party thrashed in mounting vexation. Men hung their footgear round their necks and slogged on, while leeches fastened to their crotches and armpits. The companies, at last breaking through to an eminence, rallied upon a shelf in the lee of a face, attempting to fire stalks of sodden pulp for warmth. Father wrapped a fleece about my shoulders and trundled to take counsel with the com-manders.

I leaned against the cliff, out of the rain. The morning's labor had drained what little hope I yet held for this site. Of all the self-advertised Rivers of Hell, if in fact such a site was Selene's object, who was to say this was the one to which she had made, or that Eu-ropa had believed so and followed—and what made us think that either of them was still here? Such were my ruminations, when a cry came from the men on the shelf.

They were jigging and hooting, pointing to the rock at their feet. A trickle of flame meandered within the cracks. This was *naphtha*. Dragon's blood, the men called it, though a child could see it was but some naturally occurring form of flammable liquid bitumen. The men called for Atticus and the officers. I scooted forward to hear.

At the brink of a bluff a flammable trickle spooled netherward, self-extinguishing into a natural well five feet across and twenty in depth. Steps had been carved in the funnel, looking ancient as Cronos. At the base could be distinguished crude glyphs. A cleft led into the earth, such as a man might squeeze through sideways, and whose terminus, if there was one, could not be made out.

Atticus, Father, and the captains worked forward through the press of men. The pilot Leon, whose spark had ignited the find, grinned up from halfway down the steps. He held a flint and horn charm, an *aestival* such as Selene had hung on our camphor tree the night before she made her break.

"This trash was looped at the brow of the bung, Cap'n. What d'you make of it?"

Father recounted the charm's significance. It was Damon, however, and four others chosen by lot (beans from a shaken helmet) who entered the crevice. The ingress was so close-fitting they could not scrape through in armor, but must shed all body plate save shields, rolled after them through the slot, and javelins to be used as spears, as the eight-footer was useless in such a strait, and the bow as well. Down they went. The remainder of the outfit clustered about the inlet, hallooing for reports as they descended. I begged Father and Atticus to let me accompany the party; my size would let me slither where grown men could not, and I could both speak the Amazon tongue and read its sign. Father would not hear of it. "Damon will reckon all you can and more. Find a seat and practice silence."

Here, then, is Damon's account of this descent to the Underworld, as I many times heard him retell it, both in that hour and in subsequent seasons.

Damon's tale:

I was picked because I had some of the Amazon lingo, and was well known to Selene, should we butt into her. Then too, if the lass Europa were indeed down this dungeon and repented her recklessness, it'd serve her to parley with me, her kin. I suffer the phobia of close spaces, but there was nothing for it. Wedge down we must.

The party was five: two brothers called Ironhead and Colt, both peerless horsemen—a lot of good that would do down this rat hole; Phormion, called Ant for his strength, who wanted no part but proved doughtiest of all; and my cousin Io's boy, Mandrocles, a lad of great courage but who couldn't swim. You'll see how this figures soon enough.

We wriggled down. The first twenty feet was close, but we could stand; daylight still filtered in. Ant took the lead and called back what was coming. It got tighter. We had to crab sidewise, then stoop; after that it was all fours, like miners; then belly-down like a snake. We spooled a rope marked in feet. At a hundred Ant balked. "This hole's going nowhere, Sar'nt." He was so close ahead I could touch the soles of his feet but fear made him shout. I poked him on. The shaft must lead somewhere or there wouldn't be steps at the entrance. "This ain't the mouth, Sar'nt, it's the asshole."

Ant crabbed on, nursing a lighted taper. "A cavern, mates!" We spilled like turds onto a sand flat before a lake of bitumen, a bowshot across. A gallery rose thirty feet above us. There was a tar beach, wide enough for two score to stand. I ordered all to hold, not to foul any spoor. The lake was tar, thick as broth. Little falls of naphtha cascaded into it. Glyphs painted the walls, not animals or men but spirals and rosettes, magic signs.

"Is this the Underworld, sir?"

"Yes, and I'm the Hound of Hell."

Sandal treads showed in the torch flare. A woman and a girl. You tell a print's freshness by edges fallen in. But in the tar the walls held sharp as if carved in stone.

"Could be ten days or ten minutes."

They had been here, Selene and Europa, that seemed certain. Who else would wriggle into this hellhole?

"Did they cross the lake, sir?" Ant asked.

"They didn't fly," answered Colt.

"Then do we have to cross too?"

I ordered all to scan the walls for sign.

"Amazon!"

Mandrocles cried this, making all jump from their skins. But he was only playing for the echo. His mates cursed him and laughed as men will with relief from fright. The oldest was twenty-two. They began spooking each other for fun, fancying beasts in the bowels of the lake.

"How deep, you reckon?"

"Step in and find out."

Then: a sound.

"What was that?"

From across the lake.

"Sounded like a horse."

"You're cracked!"

"Like hooves on stone."

All listened, breathless.

"If it is a horse," Colt offered, "it's a hell of a sprat, eking through that crack we just crabbed through!"

None dared voice the obvious: the cavern might have another entrance. Across the lake.

I called Selene's name.

No answer.

Again, identifying myself: "Selene, do you have Europa?"

Nothing. I ordered the men to hold their torches clear of the surface and follow across the lake. I probed in calf-deep, waist-deep; then the bottom dropped away. Ant followed, then Colt; the others were too scared to stay behind. We swam, shields propelled like skiffs before us, javelins and brands atop. Mandrocles clung to Ironhead, dog-paddling. The distance must have been a hundred feet. We came out soaked in tar to our beards. The smoke from our torches smudged the ceiling. Suddenly winged harpies thundered by the thousands. Bats. The men plunged in terror as the flock shrieked from the vault. It took eternities, it seemed, to recover breath. The banshees had fled deeper into the cave—or toward an egress we had yet to discover.

"Have a look ahead, Colt."

"What, alone?"

"Give it a squint."

"You're the sar'nt, Sar'nt. You go."

"I am the sergeant. And I'm telling you to go."

We groped on, along curtains of stalactite. A scream. Colt's brand had lit his oil-soaked beard. We pressed about him, beating out the bushy smudge. Ahead plunged a manhole.

"I ain't going down there, Sar'nt."

I led down a shaft steep as a stairwell, then along sandhills of some extinct river. I had expected bones or crypts, but there was nothing. Just walls and galleries, spooky with the drizzling of unseen cataracts.

"It's far enough, Sar'nt," pronounced Ant.

He wanted to call it a camp. Let our mates from above carry on.

"We're not here to bivouac, Ant."

Ironhead repeated that we'd pushed far enough; more must reinforce us. Colt seconded this. We had done our bit; let our comrades take it from here. Of a sudden Colt shuddered and lurched, as if shoved from behind. His speech choked off; he looked down, fingers reaching to his chest.

From his breast jutted the warhead of an arrow.

"I've been shot," he said casually, as if remarking the passage of a cloud. Blood burbled from his nose and over his lip. I heard Ironhead bawling in anguish behind me. I reached to haul Colt clear (for it was certain a second shaft would materialize instantly) but he dropped so fast my arms couldn't catch him. He fell as only the dead fall, unstrung at every limb.

With a cry his brother dived to his side. I confess I thought of neither; it was Ant who, maintaining sense, covered his grief-mad mate with his shield. At once a second shaft thundered into the oak-and-ox-hide chassis. I had recovered my own wits enough to reckon the direction of the attack; I seized Ironhead by the hair, as he still cared for naught but his brother, whom he sought to reanimate, as the horror-stricken often will, simply by the intensity of his grief. Ant and I hauled him behind a face of rock. All had dropped their brands, which lay on the oil ooze, setting it to blue flame.

"Goddess and ye Princes of Hell!" a female voice cried in Greek. "Take this, the first!"

From Selene's throat arose that war cry of Amazonia which turns men's spines to squash, echoing and reechoing about the cavern.

What of our valor, you ask? Not a jot remained. We began screaming, myself not least, as if our cries could carry back up to our companions still in daylight. *Help! Help!*

Selene was above us, somewhere in the dark. Boulders plummeted from the galleries. The very roof of the sepulchre seemed to sunder.

"Come forward, two!" Selene cried in Greek. "And two go free."

She meant she needed three heads to appease the Lords of the Underworld; she had one in Colt. Each of us wheeled to the others, ready to take the deal if we thought we'd be among the pair to skate free. Shame sobered us. Without speech, all knew what we must do: rise and run for it.

"I'm not leaving my brother," Ironhead swore.

His whisper carried like a shout.

"Rise and join him!" A third shaft ripped the ooze.

"Europa!" I cried into the black. "Are you there, child?"

No reply. This made me certain she was to hand, ordered mum by Selene. God help us if the lass drew down on us too. We snatched the brands; Ironhead and I grabbed the heels of our dead mate; we elevated shields and bolted. Along the dry river and up the staircase chimney, Ant took the lead. We tore down the tunnel leading to the lake. We could hear Selene's tread above us, sprinting along the gallery down which the bats had fled. Colt's corpse we dragged like a sack of onions, skull banging on the stone.

The lake shone black, dead ahead. Selene had gotten around us. From the shelf above, stone after stone plunged; from there one woman could pin us all day. We must break past, and hell take the hindmost.

Out we hurtled, flinging ourselves shields-first into the lagoon. I heard my cousin's boy, Mandrocles, that cry which follows being hit. Ironhead and I still hauled Colt's corpse. The lad Mandrocles had been struck by a boulder; half his face had been staved. He could not swim. Terror seized him; he wheeled for the inward shore, that ledge we had just stepped from. Stones the size of melons crashed around us. I seized the lad and shouted into his face: "You can't go back! She'll kill you!" He sunk his teeth into my hand. I let go with a howl. He clawed for the inboard shore.

At this instant Selene broke forth. I saw her vault from the gallery above, an axe in one hand, a brand in the other. She slung the torch. The lake erupted.

She had lit the soup.

The surface-slick of naphtha roared to flame. I plunged below. Fear wrung my breath; I dumped shield and lance and catapulted to the surface. The first sight was the hair of my arms incinerating. I heard, rather than felt, my beard catch fire. The lake was aflame. Instinct taught my arms to sweep before me; for an instant I could breathe, then the surface reignited. Something tore through my shoulder: an arrow shaft bound the joint. I felt no pain, only vexation. Selene was above on the shore.

She fired point-blank. I felt the flesh of my neck tear as the warhead ripped beneath my ear. I swam with the strength of terror. Ant dragged me onto the far shore. I turned back and saw Selene, on the hellward bank, dragging Mandrocles' spent form from the fire. She lifted him by the hair and hacked him off at the neck. The Amazon raised his dripping, flaming head impaled upon her axe and howled a cry of such savage joy as only could be loosed here, at the gates of perdition.

Into the asshole tunnel we wormed, Ant first, then me, then Ironhead. Cries came from above, our comrades at the cavern's mouth. One had snaked down, threading a rope. It was my brother Elias. Ant sought to pass the line to me. It jammed. "Grab my feet!" he commanded. I obeyed, calling the same to Ironhead behind. Now from the latter's throat arose such a cry as may never from memory's vault be eradicated.

"She's got me!" Ironhead bawled. His grip clamped my ankle like a fetter. He was being drawn back, out of the tunnel. Such shrieks rose from his gorge as to turn blood to water. Later, when the parties went down to collect the corpses, Ironhead's was found thus: Selene had caught his ankles at the bung-end of the burrow (she had apparently swum the lake of fire) and wrapped them with her star belt, the plaited rawhide band her horsewomen's race wear about their waists. She had set her heels against the stone and pulled Ironhead out, hacking him off first at the knees, then at the waist, then at the neck. The head she kept. We never found it.

7

EUROPA

Mother Bones:

❦❦❦❦❦❦❦

Thus Uncle's recital. It requires scant imagination to conjure the state of his comrades remaining aboveground throughout this ordeal, compelled to endure first the cries of those trapped beneath the earth, themselves powerless to bear them succor, then to scent the black asphaltine smoke, ascending first in wisps, then pouring in clouds from the upper stone, followed by yet more grievous dirges of anguish, resounding close within the cavern's mouth; while our own agents plunged to aid their fellows, and at last the ghastly aspects of the survivors, two only of five, as the earth spit them forth at our feet. Uncle could walk. He escaped with burns, a gash in the neck, and a shaft through the shoulder, while Ant, astonishingly, clambered clear with no wound at all. The graver toll was internal, that horror occasioned (as Damon told us later) by any duel with warriors of Amazonia, so unnatural and even monstrous does it strike the senses of men to encounter in the female such ferocity and want of mercy.

On the second morn the men found my sister on a shelf of rock some hundred feet above the tunnel mouth. Her wrists had been bound with rawhide, one ankle wedged into a cleft so deeply that the stone had to be split with mawls to crack her free. She appeared emaciated and could not be made to speak. Her horse, Redhead, remained at her side, untethered, having endured the full furlough from Athens, apparently, above twenty days, on drink and rations as meager as her rider's.

Into such a state was Father cast, to behold his darling borne into camp in such extremity, as I feared would part him from his reason. He took up station at Europa's side; nothing could tear him from her. From the burns of her flesh and the tar gummed in her hair, it was plain she had been with Selene in the Underworld. Had she too launched darts upon our men? From intervals of lucidity this much could be gleaned: she had indeed tracked Selene from Attica and overtaken her on this site. Selene had repulsed her, however, ordering her home. My sister would report no more, nor take food or be touched by any save me, and that only after much crooning and gentling. When I looked in her eyes I could not find her.

Where was Selene? No longer beneath the earth, told the swamp people. They had seen her emerge on horseback, immediately after the melee, from an entrance to the grotto unknown to us. She had fled north, they reported. Three skulls clattered from the wale about her waist.

Our party may not resume pursuit without interring the bones of its comrades. Yet the men could not be induced to descend again to that sepulchre of horror. Prince Atticus himself led a picked team, but at the lake of bitumen the resolve of all save the commander failed, and when he sent two back with orders to dispatch others in their stead, none above the earth would obey. Of what account is fear of hell, when hell itself yawns in your face?

At the third evening my sister began to rave. Spasms racked her frame; she writhed as one in labor and men gave back, fearing hell spawn. Only Father, Damon, and Atticus owned the bowels to kneel at her shoulder.

Fresh evils struck the camp. Toads, black toads, infiltrated by the thousands. Their filmy eyes bugged from the slime; they toppled into one's stew and squished beneath his tread. A fellow woke to find his cloak freighted with their myriads; a hundred times a day men flung the loathsome vermin from their flesh. And all the while my sister wailed.

Now the swamp people exacted vengeance for our trespass. Before, they had feared the squadron's numbers. Now they smelled our terror and it made them bold.

They staked a ditch across the single track out of the bog and erected a palisade to defend it. This rampart they manned in hundreds, launching their darts upon the probing parties of our company. Atticus ordered the capture of one of the swampers, that we might parley. But a man could not hang on to these creatures. Their ratskin mantles came apart in his fist, leaving him clamping a garment so fetid he flung it in revulsion to the earth, where it melted, it seemed, into the muck upon whose surface its owner made away, lithe as a waterbug.

The gnomes commenced to snipe. Their weapon was the bow, diminutive as a child's, with which they shot arrows slender as reeds, whose prick upon the skin could barely be felt yet whose barbs worked in with wicked art. The punctures swelled and suppurated, inducing fever, nausea, and convulsions.

Atticus offered our tormentors a ship, horses, gold. Any token of penance the foe required, he would donate to the Womb Goddess, if they would only let us free. But they had grown insolent, these mire denizens, and negotiated nothing. They penetrated the perimeter at will, setting poison stakes beneath the ooze and pricking men, as they slept, with venom-tipped darts.

Now my sister came to herself. She would not heed Father or Uncle or me, but bespoke Prince Atticus directly. Following her, a party located the hidden adit to the cavern and entering there discovered the remains of our comrades. How dolorous arose that pyre upon which their bones were made to ash!

Europa reckoned the company's predicament and pronounced

that we must break out this night or die. Such was the authority of her conviction, reinforced in the men's minds by the scourging they had endured at Selene's hands, that none dared disbelieve. She was given oil with which to bathe, and men uncommanded stood sentry. When her curls could not be governed, tangled from her ordeal, she called for an edge and hacked them off.

Camp had been struck when she returned. What could not be carried was torched where it lay. The party would make to the ships, impelled by dread lest these be already taken. Uncle would send my sister and me home as soon as we got clear.

Europa defied him. She would strike north on her own now, she declared, and hell take all the company.

Father revolted. "You are a child and I your master. By Zeus, you will obey me!"

Europa gestured to the Underworld. "I have treated with the Goddess. Only through me will any leave this place alive."

We must fashion broadboots, Europa directed the men, to trek the mire and shield our soles from poisoned stakes beneath. Two by two we must flee, shields lapped fore and aft, with hide mantles sheathing arms and legs, for every thorn might bear us venom. Further, we must proceed in silence, lest the Goddess hear, and not cry out at the fight, though death wring us by the throat.

She claimed spear and shield and mounted. At the palisade she fought in the van and by her charge broke the foe. At last on the strand, the posse dashed to safety (save three who fled in a longboat) behind a stockade erected by the men guarding the ships. The swamp people withdrew; our company made haste to embark. Again Father ordered Europa and me to make ready to be escorted home.

Again Europa defied him.

"My child, you are but fourteen! Six months hence you shall be a bride."

"Never!"

The posse ringed her, in awe at her temerity, foremost among them Prince Atticus, the betrothed-to-be she now rejected.

"You abhor my bold speech, Father, lest hearing it my prospective husband no more want me. But you think not to ask, Do I want a husband? I repeat: Never. No man shall rule me."

"I shall rule you."

With these words Father advanced upon her, hand raised to deal her a blow.

Atticus intercepted his rush. At once Europa stepped round the prince, soles planted, ready to pitch tooth and claw upon her sire if he willed.

Father gave back in astonishment.

"By the gods," he declared, motioning to include me, "what a pair of hellcats have I spawned!"

Atticus cut this off. There would be no return to Athens for all or any. Too much blood had been shed, of too many good men. The three who had deserted would bear our news home, informing our kin of events thus far, or their own self-serving version, which would suffice. "As for me," Atticus declared, "I will not return to my father or mother, or to those of our fallen, bearing failure."

The prince turned to Europa.

"You followed the Amazon Selene here, didn't you?"

"Yes."

"You sought to join her?"

"Yes."

"And flee with her to the Wild Lands?"

"Yes."

"But Selene repulsed you, didn't she? She would not have you. She called you child and commanded you home."

Europa's aspect told this was true.

"You hate the Amazon for this. You hate Selene."

No answer.

"You know where she went. You would follow. You would demonstrate by your acts that child you are no longer."

Atticus stepped directly before Europa.

"Therefore I put this to you, maiden. Cast your lot with us. Guide us. Instruct us."

Father protested with vehemence. "You would use a girl, Atticus, a child . . ."

"I see no child but woman, Elias. And I make no shame to voice that which stands in the hearts of all. We have faced this warrioress Selene, and that woman-spirit which animates her has struck us through with terror. This same spirit we behold in this maiden, your daughter Europa. I for one want this spirit. I want it with us, on our side. Will you come, woman?"

The prince summoned his master at arms.

"Arm her," he commanded. "Draw her a berth in the fore of our company and a shipboard stall for her horse. Let no one condescend to her henceforth by word or action, but address her with such respect as he tenders me."

Atticus stripped his own shortsword, tugging it over his head by its sheath and baldric, and, crossing to my sister, set it in her hands.

The men cheered.

Father looked on, appalled but powerless to intervene.

Yet Europa, far from being caught up in the sweep of affect, regarded Atticus with cool remove.

"You seek, my lord, to use me for your own designs."

"Indeed I do." The prince made no effort to dissimulate his object. "But by such use you may, as well, use me for yours."

BOOK THREE

AMAZON
LOVE

8

A GATHERING OF
THE CLANS

Selene's testament:

Horse, when she taught the peoples of the plains to live, established for each its own usage. One race was instructed to constitute itself as stallions and harem, another as all colts, still others one way at one season and another at another. Tal Kyrte, the free people, she commanded to dwell apart from men, mares unruled by stallions, and to breed only at one season. Horse licensed carnality within two moons of the year only, but enjoined her daughters to hold their persons apart as children of the sky and of freedom, franchising no rival to acquire dominion over their hearts.

So it is that each spring when the sun enters the Ram, the tribes and nations gather, the Themiscyra and the Lycasteia, the Chadisia, and the Titaneia, the Saddle Mountain, the Yrte, the Yssone, and the Echal, those of the mountains south of the Amazon Sea and those of the steppe to the north; all the clans across all the leagues from the Hypanis to the Tanais, those who dwell in Armenia and

Cappadocia and those who make their homes in the Ceraunian Cau-cacus and beside Lake Maeotis. All assemble at the Mound City of Lycasteia, where the river Borysthenes empties into the Amazon Sea. And a time of rejoicing it is, anticipated all year. Not alone for the occasion of begetting daughters to procreate the race, though great joy is derived in this, but as well to reunite with sisters and mothers, mates and mentors and children. Even enemies of feuding tribes are embraced. One salutes her sisters, *Eto aparchein,* "I have seen your numbers [meaning the horses she leads]," and *Arche kena tal,* "They are many as the stars."

At this season the steppe abounds in herds and cookfires and the cone pinnacles of the *yrtai,* the goatskin tents of the plains nations. The male merchants permitted to establish camps at the Mound City, those Lykians, Phrygians, and Greeks whose associations render tribute to tal Kyrte, are required to provide provender for the horses. One treks beside feed troughs a quarter mile long, brimming with barley and rye and emmer wheat. The earth for miles is paved with straw and fragrant with droppings. Fires break out so regularly as the straw ignites in the sun that special rakes must be laid out at inter-vals, three times normal size. At the cry of alarm, all fall to, children as well as kings, and a grand time is had. Cheers ring each time a blaze is extinguished.

Tribesmen of neighboring nations assemble as well in the season of *Saurasos,* "the Gathering," but may neither bear arms, take food (save in prescribed precincts of the camp) or compete in the games. They may trade however; in fact at that season fortunes are made in horses, furs and hides, gold and copper and iron. Yet lust is a power-ful draw. Many come for this alone. So potent indeed is the attrac-tion of sex that many traders (to keep their men's minds on business) dispatch as their emissaries men of seventy and older, as-sisted by lads under ten, yet even these are dragged forth by the women at the height of the rites and compelled to copulate. Much mirth is derived from this usage. They have a song, the maidens who may not yet participate ("smoke" being their obscene word for the female portion):

God preserve me from these geezers
With their clawing spindly nards
Rather pluck my smoke with tweezers
Than to mount these never-hards.

One of tal Kyrte may not be permitted intercourse with a man until she has either slain three enemies in battle or experienced a mighty vision for the people. A warrior discovering herself with child stints no measure to make light of this. It is a matter of pride to yield to no infirmity throughout the course of one's term and, having birthed, to return without break to the practices of freedom—hunting and war. Among the free people the time of birthing is called *aidos*, "shame," after that Daughter of Night, sister of Hecate and Nemesis, but the connotation is less of stigma than of silence. A warrior approaching delivery crops the manes and tails of her string and strips them of battle finery. The beasts take on such a chastened aspect that their fellows sense it and shun them, even dogs and birds. One of tal Kyrte gives birth alone, at night, beneath the sky, assisted by that herb called mugwort or artemisia, the virgin's plant, and attended by Artemis Midwife and Hecate of the Crossroads. The cord of life the new mother severs at both ends, wrapping it about the infant's waist if a girl and throwing it away if a boy. The afterbirth of a female she feeds to that pregnant mare, called *inakane*, whose foal will belong to her daughter when she grows. A warrior chancing upon a mate delivering will shy apart, not to embarrass her by observation. Pride ordains that the new mother reappear as nonchalantly as possible. One does not employ "infant" or "child" but says, "I have found a bundle," which she hands over without ceremony to her own mother. She may not touch or speak to the child again until she, the daughter, has passed her horse trials at age seven.

A mother of our race may not raise her daughters (sons are either sold or given to other nations), just as she may own nothing, not even the horses and scalps she captures in war, but all are given into the keeping of her own mother, and great pride is taken by this matriarch, not in the possession of much but in the capacity to donate much to the people. One calls her mother by that name, but its import is closer to sister, and of far less station than grandmother, or "mother-mother," as it is said. The concept of immediate family is unknown among tal Kyrte, to whom devotion to the nation is all. A stern and scrupulous protocol governs all intercourse between mother and daughter; pride is taken in disseverance, that a mother train and favor others before her own blood, and a daughter obey and seek approval of all before her own dam. By this practice, the free people believe, the natural love of one for the other is not hoarded "within the tent" but turned outward to all the race. To amuse myself I once counted the names tal Kyrte employs to reckon relation. The tally exceeded two hundred. Our tongue has twenty names for sister, forty for aunt and great-aunt, with escalating multiples for cousins and cousins of cousins, cousins of nieces, nieces of cousins, daughters of cousins' nieces and mothers of nieces' cousins and nieces' cousins' sisters.

By such usage the individual is not only known to all and all known to her, but related to all by blood. As a child if I committed a transgression, say, passing between an elder and the fire, or speaking carelessly of one ill or impaired, I would be taken aside at once by an aunt or sister-cousin-aunt and upbraided, firmly but with love; and growing to majority I in turn schooled those daughters-nieces-cousins whom I called my blood and who called me theirs. So that no Amazon (to employ the Greek term) owns even the conception of feeling alone or apart. All are blood, and all family.

This is a mirror of the society of horses, among whom, even in their thousands, each is known to, and known by, all others. It goes without saying that our horses are known to us, each as an individual, as we to them. Foreigners are astonished to behold a child of six enter a corralled herd in the dark and without even a whisper locate her horse from among hundreds. This is no magic, but the horse-friend recognizes its child-friend's footsteps and halts for her. You will never see a branded or ear-notched horse in the province of the free people. This to us is savagery.

When Theseus came to the Mound City and spoke before the assembled people in praise of Athens and the way of civilization, he pronounced as its cardinal virtue that happiness which the individual realizes within the open marketplace of ideas and experiences. That is, that the citizen of the city may be or become whatever he wishes. Antiope in rebuttal laughed at this and, putting aside the fact that no woman of Athens, save her whores, is free to step even into the street without the leave of her male master, declared such a state not happiness but madness.

"Who is more happy, the storm or the ocean? Such distinction is fatuous, for storm is ocean and ocean storm. I have walked the streets of cities," Antiope declared, "and looking into each stranger's eye felt such despair as may not be recounted. It came to me, moreover, that not only were these city people strangers to me (who was, after all, a stranger) but to each other as well! They knew each other no more than I, a stranger, knew them. How may one know herself, knowing no one? How be sister, apart from sister? Once within the city walls of Iodessa, I came upon a man dead in the street. His fellows stepped over the corpse, without breaking conversation, and continued about their business. You call us savages, Theseus. Yet we have not forgotten what comprises chivalry and gentility, which is that love which binds all to all and makes none a stranger in the name of 'happiness.' "

Among tal Kyrte, girls are raised by no program or elder but by themselves and by Ehal, Nature. She is our book, in whose pages we study as Greek children with tutors and texts. Horse raised me. She taught me silence and solitude. From her I learned how to wake and how to sleep, how to run and how to rest, how to be born and how to die. Horse taught me to roll with joy in the sand, to endure heat and cold and hunger. Horse taught me to dream. All that I know, I learned from her and from sky and storm and steppe. Infants of our race ride on the hips of their sisters and cousins, and because these are always on horseback, it may be said with truth of our babes that they can ride before they can walk. I never knew a moment when I was not part of a horse. To be severed from her, as I was in Sinope as a child, was to be walled off from air and from sun.

Grandmother is the primal and most sacred authority among the daughters of tal Kyrte. Mother-mother, as they call her, owns responsibility for the child. If the child dies or is killed in battle, to mother-mother is delivered her corpse. She must dress and clean it; provide habit and ornament, sustenance, and horses for sacrifice at its burial, and the bronze mirror with which the spirit knows itself in the life after. Mother-mother raises the funeral mound, though in practice of course this is done by the tribe entire, in the rite of *epotame*, "leave-taking," in which trikona mates, lovers, and friends donate to the Underworld those arms and artifacts they love most and that will serve best their departed comrade.

In the rearing of a child, mother-mother provides food, clothing, and shelter, weapons, bridle, and riding stock; to her is awarded the prize in all horse trials and all her daughter-daughter's bounty of battle. Mother-mother inducts her charge into the War Society of her own clan, which marks the child's accession to womanhood and constitutes the deepest blood tie of the free people. Beyond this bond, however, and noblest of all unions, tal Kyrte believes, is that of friend.

Once I died in your arms, Mione.
Find me now, lest I wander
across this lifetime
alone and without you.

At age seven, after passing her horse trials, a maid chooses and is chosen by two friends. With them she forms her first trikona, the triple bond of life and death. In addition each girl partakes of two other trikonai: a second, of which she is a novice apprenticed with another novice to an elder; and a third, in which she is the elder, schooling two novices. Together these constitute the famed "triple-triple" of Amazonia.

Thus Eleuthera, for example, was "seated" (the same word as used in riding) in one trikona with me and the lass Aella, in which Eleuthera was our elder and we her novices; and in another in which she and her sister Skyleia were novices and Alcippe, Powerful Mare, was their tutor; and in a third with her peers ring champion Stratonike and war queen Antiope.

The latter was Eleuthera's first, or High Trikona. This means that under the laws of the free people, any of the three, perishing while holding civil or war command, is replaced by the senior of the surviving two, and no other.

No one not of tal Kyrte, male or female, may penetrate the triple bond. Many have tried. Princes come in the season of heat, seeking to bewitch a daughter and bear her away, prize of their vanity. Her mates slay him, or her. For the forswearing of this bond constitutes the supreme sacrilege among the tribes of the free people.

When Theseus captured Antiope's heart, as the poets claim (or detached her from her reason, in Eleuthera's edition), he broke the central High Trikona of the nation. And when he bore her off to Athens, this act plunged the dagger of perfidy into the hearts of the free people.

There is a rite among tal Kyrte, convoked so rarely that a generation may pass without witnessing its enactment. This is called *tal Mira*, the Disburdening. The ceremony is conducted before the convened battalions or "families" of the Corps of Mounted Archers, when the bonds of the trikona have been broken by one of its members.

The two who have been wronged bare their chevrons, the *matrikonai* carved on their left breasts. The self-incised flesh is reopened and a brew of lye and camphor oil poured into the wound. Acid smoke rises while each bereaved thrice pronounces the disseverment of those bonds which had married her to her mate. That bow and bridle which the offender had dedicated to Ares Manslayer and Artemis Void of Mercy at her matriculation are now sundered and cast into a trench six feet wide, six feet deep and three hundred feet long, which has been excavated for this office and is called *etesta*, the grave of friendship. Down this channel the battalions pass, mounted, brows stone-dashed and bleeding. Three stallions are sacrificed to Ares and their bones interred in the crypt. Each warrior dumps into the ditch every article given to her by the traitor. A mound is heaped up. This is performed upon some site of the steppe which for a year after may not be revisited. All children born that day are put to death, so unwholesome is the date accounted. At ceremony's end the battalions, with the bereaved at column's head, turn their backs and depart the barrow at a funerary walk.

Such was the rite enacted in the aftercourse of Antiope's defection. It was conducted exactly as I have detailed, with this exemption: a solitary adit was left unsealed to the crypt, at Eleuthera's command, in the hope that Antiope's purpose could yet be resuscitated and her heart, poached by this pirate Theseus of Athens, won back to the free people to whom she belonged.

In my lifetime, only two warriors of tal Kyrte have incurred the infamy of desecration of the triple bond. These are Antiope and I. My treason was double and consisted in this: first, the abetting of our queen in her most calamitous defection from the free people (when she took arms against them at the climax of the Great Battle of Athens) and, second, in that battle's aftermath: my failure to take my own life and that of my beloved Eleuthera, who was gravely wounded and in my charge. I knew it was my duty. I had the blade in my hand. But I could not do it. My stroke was stayed not out of my love for her alone (for what could be sweeter than to depart with her to the life after?) but accounting her indispensability to the free people. Without her, who would lead tal Kyrte? All others had been slain or broken. Without Eleuthera, what would become of our nation?

I imagined that these derelictions, once effected, would put a period to my life, as an axe, falling, shears a shoot of pine. But acts of import, I have learned, bear issue of their own and form that field from which other imperatives arise. Destiny begets destiny, it seems, and neither Eleuthera's nor mine, nor Antiope's and Theseus' and our nations' entire, had yet, then, reached its consummation.

BOOK FOUR

THE AMAZON
SEA

9

A PRINCE OF ATTICA

Mother Bones:

❦❦❦❦❦❦

The posse under Atticus now embarked from the River of Fire, bound again for the Amazon Sea. All resolved to think no more of return to Athens, but fixed their purpose upon completion of the mission, do or die.

Heaven now sent fair weather. The ships glided north before a favoring wind. At Phthia the hero Peleus welcomed the vessels. The horses got grain into their bellies for the first time since the storm. Fresh meat for the men heartened the company considerably. Repairs were made, new sails and oars shipped; recruits of adventurous spirit restored the flotilla to its complement. For myself, I reveled in my sister's company; just to have Europa present set the sun back in the sky. The men's blood purged itself of poisons; grief receded for those lost. It seemed that fortune had come round our way at last.

Then on the fifth morn the companies woke to discover Europa gone. She had made off during the night, taking her own horse and another, with rations and arms, despite double watches on the caval-cade and pickets every forty feet. Spirits plummeted. Not that the men had held my sister's recovery as justification for their toil. But it had been a success, the only one they could look to, set against lives lost and perils undergone. Now they must hunt her again, possibly as foe this time, and the start she had would give Selene, when Europa overhauled her, even more warning to rally forces against whom our companies must contend.

Father was devastated. He scourged himself for this dereliction, to lose his daughter not once but twice. For my part Europa's deser-tion had left me heartbroken, not just that she had flown but that she had flown without me. It did not occur to me to hate her; she was perfect and always would be. I reproached myself instead. Something must be wrong with me, or my sister could never have left me so!

One among the company took note of my misery. This was Prince Atticus, who might be absolved, as Europa's betrothed-to-be, for being more concerned with his own bereavement. That first dawn he had led one mounted party and sent two others after Europa, seek-ing sign. All had come back with nothing. I was wiping down the horses of the first company when the prince approached. "You're not going to bolt too, are you, Thyone?" He was aware of my nickname, Bones, but was kind enough not to use it. "I should hate to face you as well," he said, "across the line of battle."

The prince's tone was teasing; I cannot overstate how much this meant. I felt tears and swiped my face that he not see. He looked away. The curls at his neck were held by a silver pin in the shape of a cicada. It seemed the most beautiful thing I had ever seen.

"Are we in the wrong, Thyone? To track Selene, I mean. It is my father Lykos' doing, stirring the hornets' nest to work harm to The-seus. But the swarm, once loosed, is not so easily put back."

How I esteemed him for addressing me thus! I longed to offer something to allay his burden but could not find my tongue. He seemed to sense this. He smiled.

"Give me your word, then, that you will not run. Otherwise I shall have to set a watch over you."

The other who took care for me was Damon. My uncle put me to work caring for the horses, addressed me as "wrangler" and ordered me about in a gruff voice, for which kindness I could never repay him. At his command I slept beneath his bearskin and arose to stand watches at his side. I began to ken his rough-timbered ways. "Consider how warriors of Amazonia ride in their triples," he counseled me. "Not shoulder to shoulder but wide apart, sometimes nearly out of sight across the plain. Yet the slightest chirrup will send each flying to the other's aid. This is how you must think of yourself and your sister. Do you understand?"

The ships embarked from Thessaly on the ninth day, navigating north by Athos, that mountain holy to Zeus, which appeared for two dawns on the port quarter, passed abeam, then at last sank from sight beneath the stern. The vessels coasted western Thrace now, drawing toward the Strymon. This was wild country. War parties of tribesmen tracked our passage from the shore. When we landed to take our meals and to make camp, they approached, demanding drink and baubles and sniffing about the ships, light-fingered. One heard Greek no more but savage tongues.

The sea smelled different this far from home. Light was harsher, nights colder. I had to mind my cheekiness with the men now; they had gone testy and stalked the runway, spoiling for fights. They were scared. They gravitated about those veterans—Damon, Philippus, Phormion called Ant, even Father, irascible as he was—who had experience of these regions and could apprise them of what trials might lie ahead.

Above the shell beach which marks the frontier of Strymonian Thrace, Atticus called the companies together. It was evening, after the meal and hymn. A stockade had been erected, horses picketed, arms stacked, and sentries posted.

"Comrades, the elements have favored us since the River of the Underworld, all thanks to God. It has been my judgment, as the aboriginal tribes have thus far permitted us passage, to concentrate upon making speed east. Now, however, we must recall ourselves to the business at hand. Within ten days we shall strike the Hellespont, or so the natives of this place apprise us. Another ten will bear us into the Black Sea—the Amazon Sea, as it is called out here—from which only Heracles, Jason, and our own Theseus have returned. We younger men know nothing of this country. Our intelligence of the race of warrior women, not to say the other savage tribes of the region, is slender at best, comprised primarily of myth and legend and tales from our fathers of the Amazons' march on Athens. Therefore I have assembled the complement this night, to put forth a call to our veterans."

He turned to Ant and Philippus, Father and Damon, and the other men who had sailed on the first expedition.

"Come forward, gentlemen. Our squadron coasts the same shoreline you sailed with Theseus, twenty years past. Tell us of that voyage. When exactly did it take place? For what ends was it undertaken? What happened when you reached the Amazon homeland? And how may the companies of our current voyage profit from your experience?"

First to respond was Phormion called Ant, who had saved Damon's life at Hell's River; he offered bloodcurdling tales of the women warriors' ruthlessness and ferocity. Next spoke Aristocrates the wrangler, proffering equally mane-blanching sagas.

Then came Philippus. This fellow, a crack cavalryman, was a dear mate of Damon's and, apparently, as wild as a weed. He introduced himself by the nickname he had been given in Amazonia— "Dew Lap"—with which the wild women had tagged him, he swore, upon remarking the scale of his naked manhood.

"Here is no fiction, brothers. For my 'dog' swung between my thighs in those days like the clapper of a watch commander's bell. I was hung like a Prienean ass."

The men roared. This was more like it. Philippus alias Dew Lap had fortified himself with a snootful of Ismar, the dark Thracian wine, and now, nosing into a third and fourth bowl, set to disarm his confederates of their apprehensions. Perhaps no war awaited, but love! Our companies might fend off kisses and not blows! The men clapped their wine bowls in ovation.

Philippus spoke of the horse-derived nature of the societies of the steppe: Amazons breed in one season only, like mares, and as promiscuously. The neighboring tribes assemble, those trolleying globes of iron, in Philippus' phrase, and a randy jamboree is held, lasting two months or more. Yet hold your jism, he counseled his listeners.

"One does not court these wenches, lads, but they you. To mate with a lioness would be as lenient of toil. Should you fancy one above others, a spiked heart will be your profit. For they call themselves *melissa*, 'bee,' and like these flutter flower to flower. Nor do they know the word privacy. Two and three will take a man at once, jabbering in their savage tongue the while. And if you call yourself stud to hoist the tent pole, try it with three wild vixens disporting about you in a tongue you can't savvy, and giggling. And don't forget, bucks, that these bawdy bitches are horsewomen from birth; many's the stallion they've gelded with the flint knife, so that it's nothing to them, a chore of denutting. Recall this as they grapple your globes in passion. I'd sooner mate with a wildcat."

The men whooped and cheered. Many called out that they'd gladly take their chances, so long had this sea trek enforced celibacy upon them. Their mentor wagged a finger.

"Not so fast, lads, for here's more matter to turn over. When in shipboard reverie you conjure visions of these Moon Maids, each floats before you more comely than the next. Now fetch reality. For these 'Daughters of the Horse' may live up to their name! Ough, such faces! And if you meet their eye, out of curiosity only, they take the notion you fancy them. Then, lads, you'd better sprout wings, for they'll run you down afoot as fast as a horse!

"Here came one I loved," Philippus twined his tale. "She set me up against an oak, lifting my skirts and seizing mast and anchor stones in both fists. I fancied this strumpet, by Orpheus' lyre I did, and sought throughout the bout to woo her with amorous phrase. I would make her my bride, I swore, and bear her home across the sea. I extolled her beauty and besought her love. '*Anora! Anora!*' she cried, with such passion I knew I had conquered her heart. '*Anora, anora!*' I bawled in return, and when she had got my seed, not once but twice (aye, I was a younger man then!), and bolted, leaving me spent, I inquired of one passing, what does this mean, '*Anora*'? 'It means shut up,' he replied."

More such lore was narrated, to the delight of all, not least myself. And now Philippus, turning to Damon, made jest that he of all could offer instruction in Amazon love, and summoned him forward. Uncle protested, citing his wounds of Hell's River, yet such was the eagerness of the men, and so vigorously declaimed, that at last Damon must yield and mount to the fore.

"Our friend Philippus' speech proves one thing: the older you get, the more spectacularly hung you used to be." Damon bowed theatrically to his mate. "As to this Amazon romancing, however, I never saw such stuff. Perhaps, my friend, your celebrated endowment provided you entry to a steamier quarter of the camp."

The companies responded with much profane chaffing of their comrade Dew Lap.

"My experience was the opposite," Uncle resumed when the levity had abated. "I never saw an Amazon mate in the open and I challenge any to declare he has. They build bridal bowers, most modest, of willow stalks plaited with limbs of white poplar. They select a grove in a high meadow or vale of the plain and fabricate a sort of arbor, waist-high and open at one end. Upon the floor they set hides of elk or ibex and hang that charm called a *cypridion*, the passion knot of Aphrodite, upon the lintel.

"Nor is such occasion the subject of jest or whimsy to them. Recall, friends, that for these maids the object of intercourse is not carnal rapture but produce of offspring. They wanted female issue, the taller and stronger the better. Nor have they come to this privilege absent adversity, but each must have woven three scalps of enemies into the mane of her pony simply to earn this right. To daunt the foreign suitor further, he must compete against beefhearts of the neighboring tribes, hairy as Hephaestus, many of whom have known these lasses since childhood, or got foals on them heretofore, or their fathers have. They become affianced just like we do, with costly gifts and dowries, and families share bonds over generations.

"But let me reverse, gentlemen, to matter more germane to our present predicament. Our commander, Prince Atticus, has requested that we veterans share our intelligence of the country into which this expedition now advances. He asks that we address business of which you youngsters stand as yet in ignorance. Why was the former expedition undertaken? What was our king Theseus' object and how may we of this present party profit from our predecessors' ordeals? Let me call my brother Elias forward, who not only served on that voyage but earned command by his initiative and valor."

He turned to Father, urging him to speak. Father resisted. The company however, led by Prince Atticus, pressed him earnestly. "You are friend and kinsman of Theseus, sir, and in those days as now much within his confidence. Who can enlighten us more ably than yourself?"

Father rose and came forward. The companies had drawn up on the strand between two beached ships. Bonfires lit the interval, bound by the black hulls glistening with freshly applied pitch. The space, though great enough to contain above a hundred, yet felt sheltered and snug.

Father thanked Atticus first and commended him for convening this assembly. "Atticus, I have had my eye on you since you were a sprout. I judged then that your nature incorporated those qualities which would render you one day preeminent among our race. This is why I accepted service beneath your command on this expedition and, as well and with pride, made compact with your family to betroth to you my daughter Europa. Nothing I have seen on this passage has countered that conviction. Forgive me if grief has estranged me from yourself and this company. And you, gentlemen, permit me to make up for my self-imposed sequestration. I shall obey our commander and, if you will heed me, offer such intelligence as experience may provide."

A bowl was redrawn; Father wet his throat and began. . . .

10

THE BIRTH OF DEMOCRACY

Father's testimony:

⦾⦾⦾⦾⦾⦾⦾⦾⦾⦾

The first Athenian voyage to the Amazon Sea, whose course we now retrace, embarked some twenty years prior to this date. Theseus was thirty or thereabout, I twenty-five, my brother Damon twenty. Philippus, what were you—nineteen? Other veterans among our current corps were surely little older.

Why did the expedition sail? What was Theseus' object? To answer we must hark back to that hour of Athens's chronicle. Now pay attention, friends, and heed this recounting:

At that time, and for the first time, the warring baronies of Attica had been drawn into confederation. This was Theseus' doing. He had made them all Athenians. Such did not sit well with every headknocker. The princes, say, of Marathon or Aexone, held their fiefdoms jealously; when they met in council in the palace they brawled like barn cats. I was then a buck lancer of Theseus' corps and I can tell you, the place was a riot.

Theseus overturned this by a single stroke: he moved the sessions outdoors, to the hill of the Pnyx, where the people could attend and observe their betters. What a revolution this affected!

Before, within the walls of the palace, the knights could comport themselves as churlishly as they wished. Now before the eye of the commonwealth, they had to behave.

Theseus set his council throne on a ledge overlooking the platform and from this vantage governed the debate. Yet when he argued a brief himself, he made it a point to dismount this post of privilege and offer his opinion from the floor, as an ordinary citizen, so to say.

Again this alteration proved miraculous. For though it was clear that no baron could match the prestige of the king or the presence of the man, nonetheless the very fact of Theseus' voluntary condescension acted as a tonic of emancipation. He commanded the herald to convoke each session with the call, "Who comes forward with good advice for the city?"

Thus was rhetoric born, and the art of public speaking. But Theseus saw beyond an invigorated Council of Nobles. His vision forekenned that agency by which Athens would be elevated before all polities of the world: the participation of the people themselves.

In the heat of disputation, our king divined, no faction would limit itself to advocates of noble birth, but call forward all champions possessed of wisdom or skill in debate. This, Theseus abetted by his own hand. For when he spied a landsman, say, or grover daunted to orate before his betters, he set the *skeptron* himself in the fellow's fist and stood at his shoulder as he spoke.

How the hidebound revolted! Yet there is this and none may refute it: when a man, however mean of birth, speaks true, his words ring as gold. And if his counsel prove of utility to the commonwealth, foolish indeed is he who would despise it. So it came about that at Athens and Athens alone, any may speak and all listen.

Friends, I have trod the Lion's Walk of Mycenae and trekked the colonnade of seven-gated Thebes. These are not cities but courts. Royal courts. Nor are their peoples citizens, but subjects. They wait, dumb, upon their masters. "Aye" is their lone rejoinder, save "Milord."

This was Athens too, before our king set her emancipation. Theseus gave her a voice, and this has made her the jewel and envy of the world. At Athens and Athens alone, a new stamp of person was being born, neither baron nor yeoman, but a man of the city. A citizen.

So enamored did men become of this liberated discourse that hundreds, my own father among them, took to overnighting in town, just to be near the action. With such concentration the city acquired a political energy unprecedented. On days when the Assembly didn't meet, the chorus did not tramp back to the farm, but picked up the tune on its own, in the marketplace. This body possessed no official standing; its findings carried no legislative weight. Yet what knight was so witless as to take a position in the big Assembly if it had failed first to carry the little?

The market became a kind of fore-Assembly. Here even saddler and butcher may speak. And speak they did! Parties began to form and these, maintaining cohesion issue to issue, cohered into blocs of influence. Now a new hare had hopped into the stew. This was the opinion of the public. Theseus understood that this game favored none so much as he. For who stands taller with the people than he who has set them free?

Theseus' rivals perceived his object, to elevate the commons as counterpoise to the nobility. Every inch of monarch's space he ceded, Theseus believed, came back to him twice in leverage over the gentle-born. Many princes grumbled, as they do today. And indeed a peril had arisen which even Theseus had not foreseen.

This was the disgruntlement of the younger nobles, the bucks his own age. These bloods, though surpassing all in strength, good looks, and venturesome spirit, yet tolled too callow in wisdom to make a showing in the Assembly. When they orated, catcalls descended; hisses chased them from the stand. They hated this. They abhorred the ascension of the people. And such was their power, this genera-tion soon to inherit the land and treasure of Attica, that Theseus must disarm them with a counter or they might prove the shoal upon which the ship of state foundered.

Thus the voyage to Amazonia.

Thus the great adventure.

I recall our father summoning my brother, Damon, and me. Theseus had put out the call for volunteers. The king himself would sail in command; he wished three hundred as companions. The company would be gone a year, journeying to uncharted shores. I had no interest whatever. I was twenty-five and betrothed to my sweetheart; I had twenty acres I burned to bring under "man's ordering hand." My brother had his own pursuits and felt the same.

Our father sat us down. "My sons, if you do not sail with Theseus, you might as well caulk your own crypts. For none who spurns this call will amount to a heap of dung."

Father cited the champions already enrolled beneath the king's banner. Prince Lykos, the wealthiest and most brilliant youth in Athens; the hero Peteos; the chariot racer Bias and his twin, Tereus the wrestler. Father named Telephos, prince of Marathon; Eugenides the boxer, son of matchless Telamon of Salamis; Stichios, called Ox, lord of Itoneia; and Phaeax of Eleusis. Down the roster Father tolled, hailing champion upon champion. Even our mate Philippus was cited, youngest of four brothers, scions of the barony of Thria.

That buck who stays behind, our father pronounced, will be known ever after as lubber and laggard. While those who enlist in Theseus' company will be our monarch's mates forever, his table companions and lords of Attica.

The expedition, Father made us see, would afford each youth a field within which to display his mettle, and for Theseus to discover the best and brightest as his inner circle. Such was the cunning of our young king. He named his flagship *Silver Seed* in honor of Athena's olive and embarked with her squadron on the sixth of Elaphebolion, one month before the anniversary of that date on which as a youth not yet twenty years old he had sailed for Crete, slain the Minotaur, overthrown Minos the Great, and first set Athens on her ascent to glory.

11

BEYOND THE KEN
OF GOD

Mother Bones:

ᏇᏇᏇᏇᏇᏇᏇᏇᏇ

Father drew up at this point and, turning to Philippus, Aristocrates, and the others who had sailed with Theseus, inquired if his narration stood sound thus far. Philippus ratified with this emendation: that the object of the expedition had never been Amazonia.

"Our king burned to top Jason and the *Argo,* and Heracles as well. His vanity craved to set the mark higher than these rivals had, to sail up the Phasis, or trek, if he must, to where the griffins are said to guard the gold of the North."

Father approved this point as well taken. "Indeed," he resumed, "but such objects were tributary to what the king truly coveted: iron. Iron was dearer than gold. Iron for sword blades and spearpoints, helmets and arrowheads, body armor, and, most of all, iron for the slashing sword. We had bronze. Bronze was nothing. Theseus' goal was the country of the Chalybes, master metalworkers, and their capital, Ash City, where the faces of the chalk cliffs arose hundreds of feet, men said, pocked with smelting ovens and foundries, and the smoke of the smithies hung over the valley in a perpetual pall. Aboard his vessels our king carried eleven tons of olive oil, in hopes of trade, and a hundred and eighty amphorae of Thriasian wine, as cultivation of the vine, so we heard, was unknown in that province, but men dined on meat raw and mare's milk hot from the teat.

"As for the country of the Amazons, the expedition's intent was to bypass it entirely; the inhabitants were too warlike and the place possessed nothing we could use. That we fetched up there in the event was pure mischance—unless you call it fate, or what the Amazons name *netome*, 'new thing' or 'thing of evil.' "

I glanced to Prince Atticus as Father spoke. Clearly he was delighted to have his captain Elias reyoked to the cause and taking pleasure in it. As if sensing this, Father checked his narration. He begged the company's pardon for interrupting "a far keener bard"— meaning Uncle—when his tale was just hitting its stride. Father stepped down. No entreaty could induce him to remain.

"Damon, my friend"—Atticus turned to Uncle—"it seems we must have you again. Clearly the men are eager for your tale. Come forward, then, and pick up where you left off. Remember please that we younger men are understandably anxious about what perils lie ahead. Tell us, then, how it went with you as you sailed these same seas, when you were callow and untried as we are now."

Let me assay a description of my uncle, for he cut at that hour a most singular figure. From his ordeal of the Underworld, both hair and beard had been charred so sternly that he had cropped them off entire; his crown was sheared to stubble. He felt this made him look ridiculous; in fact it rendered him quite dashing, displaying to effect the square cast of his jaw and the noble contour of his skull. He was forty then, and sturdy as a stag. One could not but take pride to call him kinsman. I thought, watching him step forth now into the firelight, that when that day came when I would be presented with a husband, I would favor indeed a fellow as striking and manly as my uncle.

He resumed, recalling his listeners to Athens and Theseus'

seven-ship armada. This sailed north, as our present party, hugging the Magnesian coast. "I will skim over the ordeals of this passage, gentlemen, save to say that we endured two winter storms (as the vessels to reach the Amazon Sea at summer's commencement must depart two months before the start of the sailing season) which, although no more violent than the one this present company most recently survived, yet worked far graver mischief. At the height of the first gale two vessels collided, *Panope*, Prince Alcman's ship, and *Galateia*, gift of the League of Twelve States, shearing the former's steering gear. She was never seen again. At the mouth of the Strymon our companies were fallen upon by such hordes of orange-maned Tralliai, women as well as men, as packed the strand like ants. We lost another thirty there, and *Panegyris*, sister of *Silver Seed*, despite slaying three and four for every man.

"A second tempest succeeded, delivering such a drubbing as to start what few planks remained watertight after the first. Casualties had passed near a hundred now, and we still had not cleared Europe. We could not go home. How show our faces? Despair gripped the companies at our own conceit and want of preparation.

"The tribesmen of the east communicate like cicadas in a meadow; as soon as one hears, they all do. Report of our companies' enfeeblement preceded us on wings. Every sheep-bugger within a hundred leagues descended to take a run at us. No fighter is more cunning than the savage. He spies your vessels making for the spring you have spotted from offshore. Furtively he surrounds the site. He does not show himself, nor bend so much as a stalk, but contains his malevolence; he permits you to land, jug your water, even make camp and commence sacrifice. Then he strikes. From darkness, howling and painted black. Nor will he close with you man-to-man, but unleashes clouds of darts at a distance. If you stand, he flees. But only so far as to outrange you. Retreat one pace and he rushes again.

"Off Strymonian Thrace the ships could land only on the run. Past the Chersonese they could not land at all. We had no water. We must break into the wine, and choke it down neat, which served slender for thirst but hell for acrimony. When we cast the chip to reckon distance traveled, a silence oversettled all, for we knew that each league east was another we must fight our way out of, west.

"The winds hold contrary all summer in the Pontos. The long-shore eddies are wicked; to stand out means advancing at the bare pole into a gale, breaking your back, while to pull inshore, seeking a seam, demands passing beneath bluffs lined with aborigines and points off which raiders may launch. Twice a day, it seemed, we rounded headlands to discover booms of catboats cutting off our passage. One mob of troglodytes even had nets! The only option was to stand out to midpassage, leagues across at this point. Into the brunt we must beat, but with ships incapable of pointing past square to square, it took all day to work a mile eastward. In the end we could make way only under oars and at night when the wind dropped.

"And yet miserable as it was—if you will forgive such phrase, my friends—I was having the time of my life. For the youngster, novelty is the currency of dreams. What could be more novel than this? Then too one stood never unmindful of the illustriousness of the company in which he ventured. To stand with such knights and heroes! Theseus, Lykos, Peteos! Stichios, Telephos, Eugenides! The meanest chap at oars was a prince, it seemed, and when we remembered mates at home, however carefree we conjured their hours, we wouldn't swap places for all the silver of Halizon.

"A youth loathes nothing more than his own callowness. Experience is his object. Experience, however ghastly, for the lad longs before all for the lined face and the chiseled squint of the veteran. Even his submissions to terror, the very shit with which he paints his thighs under fire is trophy to him; he points it out to his mates, laughing in the aftercourse of action as if it were a decoration for valor, which in its way it is, for it makes him a salt, a vet, an old hand. Nor may casualties or deaths, even of those dearest, faze him long. At night he settles, reckoning his accrual of experience as a miser his hoard, and gloats in the knowledge that nothing, not even God, may take it from him.

"The most appalling overthrow occurred on the south-facing coast of the Bosporus, just when we thought we were safe. A camp party had ventured ashore, running-in with one ship first, to clear the site and ring it with a palisade, while the others hove-to out of bowshot. The savages came out of nowhere, seizing three of our mates on the strand. Theseus ordered attack, but as soon as the ships entered the cove, small craft by the hundreds launched from the treeline, slinging darts and fire lances. These were Saii and Androphagi, Man-Eaters. The struggle surpassed in grisliness all heretofore, hand-to-hand along every foot of gunwale, our comrades bashing the skulls of slough-dwellers seeking to clamber aboard, while their mates, axe-wielding and mantled in animal skins, hacked at both oars and hull timbers. There is this to a clash with savages: they attack not in discipline or silence, but hooting and howling. It goes without saying they are shitfaced. They're having fun! Theseus fought like a maddened ox, as did his champions, Lykos, Peteos, Phaeax, Eugenides, Stichios, and Telephos. At battle's climax we lashed the ships together and defended them like a fortress on land. Only the stoutness of Greek armor and the fact that our companies fought downhill, ships against dugouts, held the swarming foe from hacking us to mince. When at last darkness and their own losses induced the tribesmen to give back, our complement discovered itself decimated by wounds and exhaustion, all four ships holed and nearly oarless, stuck a quarter mile offshore, in dead wind, with no means of regaining way. Worse, the savages still held our men they'd captured. What atrocities they performed upon these I shall never repeat, save to say that we must endure our mates' cries nightlong, not alone of affliction and despair, but of our own names, called upon in prayer for the boon of death.

"Theseus passed among the grief-stricken oarsmen, directing them back to work. Collect what axes remain and take down the masts and yards, he cried; shape these into oars. This chore, occupying the men with physical toil, preserved their reason. By midnight way had been reestablished; by watch's end the ships had pulled from sight of land. Not a man spoke, nor met his fellow's eye, with such woe was each riven. Further evil, we had lost our fire. That holy flame which had been kindled at the temple of Athena atop the Acropolis and borne with us across all these leagues, without which we could offer no sacrifice nor even light our brands and cookfires. What could we do now?

"We rowed. All day and all the next, men labored at oars, as if by putting distance between themselves and the site of their overthrow they could flee its consequence. Thunderstorms stalked without letup. The men toiled on in wretchedness. All feared they had sailed so far as to pass beyond the ken of God. Again Theseus sought to recall his cohorts to their manhood. 'Zeus reigns even here,' he proclaimed. 'Behold his bolts of fire!' No one listened. We had no more excrement with which to soil our ankles and no more piss to sluice into the bilges in terror.

"By the third morning the ships had reached new country, torrent-cut and densely wooded, with waterfalls visible at a mile. Atop one stretch a tableland extended, lit golden by the ascending sun.

"Horsemen could be seen tracking the squadron from this eminence. Theseus resolved to land, to entreat clemency of whatever tribe or nation held this country. We would hire out our swords, or our labor, to repay any kindnesses conferred. The vessels entered the haven, heaving-to beyond bowshot, with *Silver Seed* advancing alone to shore.

"Down came the riders at a walk. They were women. 'Is this the country of the Amazons?' Theseus called. But the females could not savvy our tongue, and even the word Amazon meant nothing to them. The leader was about twenty-five, with a reddish-blond plait beneath the doeskin cap of Phrygia. Her companions were attired as she, in buckskin leggings with *gorytus* quivers at their horses' flanks, a bow and brace of javelins across the back. Clearly they were savages, yet with such knightly bearing did they sit their mounts that we who looked upon them were held spellbound and felt trepidation recede, supplanted by awe.

"And their horses! Here were no runt ponies such as one associates with the nomadic clans of the steppe, but strapping battle mounts, sixteen hands high, nobler than any in Attica or Greece entire. The redhead loosed a whistle. From concealment beyond the hill cantered a fourth rider, a girl no older than seventeen. To our relief this one spoke Greek, with a strong Aeolian accent; she called man *maun* and sky *skua* as they do.

"Theseus sketched our plight; our patronesses attended with gravity. The king was permitted to land. He identified himself by name, title, and city, assigning three others only—myself, Euphorus of Oa, and Eteocles of Marathon, all beardless youths, so as not to disquiet our benefactresses or overmatch their number. The warrioresses gave us game, two harts they had shot and bore across their saddles, if such a term may be applied to the frameless wolf-skin pads they made their seat upon, not 'deep' as Greeks will, but high, as speed riders. We might help ourselves to water and forage as well, the huntresses declared, and remain on the site to repair our ships. This was their country, they confirmed; absent their sanction, no one might work harm to us.

"The women would return next day, they pledged, with more game and with *yourte*, fermented mare's milk, the staple of the region, it seemed. They would not approach nearer, however, but maintained their remove at half a bowshot. Nor would they dismount. Last, they left fire in a jar, which they bore with them, lit from no temple but Zeus' own bolt, they informed us. This heartened our company mightily.

"All four maidens, be it noted, possessed a distinct odor of person which cut the nostrils even across such a gulf. The leader, we learned later, was Stratonike, granddaughter of Hippolyta, who later held the post of wing commander in the attack on Athens. The names of the second two I have forgotten. Last, she who spoke and translated, was Selene. The very woman upon whose pursuit our ships today make their errand."

Uncle drew up. The posse attended.

"You have chaffed me, brothers and friends, hearing of my history with these maids." Here he turned to me. "And you, Bones, my niece, no doubt have wondered, with your sister, Europa, as to my actions, both among these women in their homeland and when their army advanced on Attica. Let me tell you if I can how I was struck, encountering these creatures, there, at first, upon that alien shore.

"All the lore of Amazonia we had rumor of, and eagerly antici-pated our first contact with these warrioresses. But nothing could prepare one for their apparition in the flesh. How may I impart it, brothers? As a domestic dog looks a certain way and acts a certain way and yields in a certain way to a man, so does the race of domesti-cated women look and act and yield.

"These females, the ones before us now, were as wolves to such dogs. They were wild. That was the difference. Men may call them savages, and many of their practices, as we have seen, are appalling to the civilized sensibility. Yet the look in their eye, as a wolf encoun-tered upon the high ground, struck one through as never could the glance of a tame woman. It was the look of a predator. Cool and piti-less, absent fear. One felt as he might coming face-to-face with a she-bear or a lioness. I was electrified; thrills coursed the length of my spine."

Damon paused again.

"I confess to you, brothers, and acquit me, please, remembering such savagery as we have seen her perform upon dear mates and kins-men, that when I beheld this lass, Selene, I was stricken through with love. How fair she sat her gallant pony, with her jet mane streaming! Such posture and pride! My eyes never left her, while I beseeched every divinity I could think of, *Let her see me; let her glance find mine.* Yet not once could I discover her eyes upon me. I was stricken with the hopelessness of my passion. I felt my heart swell and fill nonetheless, for just to see such a creature, to know that one such as she existed, opened the wide world before me. I felt as a man feels stepping forth upon a new continent, which was in fact what our company was doing. All we had known had been superseded. Nothing would ever be the same."

12

THE DERANGEMENT
OF EROS

Selene's testament:

﷽

We had known of Theseus' coming a month before his ships touched at the Strymon and two before they reached the Amazon Sea. I have told how Heracles had ravaged our nation two generations prior, slaying in single combat a dozen champions, including my mother's mother. Now these trainbearers, Theseus and his ilk, made bold to emulate the hero's exploits. We would give them, we vowed, a welcome they could pack to hell.

We had learned, two days prior to encountering them in the flesh, of the rough handling Theseus' companies had received at the hands of the tribes to the west, Saii and Androphagi, the Man-Eaters. Our elders feared that these villains had beaten us to the punch; we prayed they had left enough meat on the Athenians to carve up for ourselves. Parties of our scouts ranged the sea bluffs in both directions, seeking sign of the invaders. We meant to take them alive and subject them to *Aremateia,* the saber ceremony, that is, sacrifice them to Cybele and eat their hearts.

But when at last we discovered them, so few and so hard-used by our neighbors whom we hated, we took pity on them as enemies of our enemies. And when the great Theseus approached, unarmed and appealing for sanctuary, our rancor relented, as did Stratonike's, senior of our troop of four. She elected to proceed toward the foreigners with charity.

How grateful they were. And how handsome! Such burnished curls and slender waists! So that even I, who had steeled my heart to savor their slaughter, found my blood quickened by the sight of them in the flesh. They seemed a race of princes, made all the more engaging by the meagerness of their number and the sternness of their straits. It was the season of the Gathering. With our assembled tribes outnumbering them five hundred to one, what harm could come? So we gave them meat and fire.

It was on this bluff, called Walnut Hill, that I first saw Damon. A lad he was, barely three summers older than I, and far the handsomest of the bunch. Or so he seemed to my eyes. I set him apart from that moment and told my sisters, *This one belongs to me*.

Tal Kyrte reckons the year by months as well as equinoxes. Thus on the ninth day of the Moon of the Coursing Freshets, Theseus and his vessels entered the anchorage of the Mound City of Lycasteia, where the river Borysthenes empties into the Amazon Sea.

No end of bards' yarns portrays this occasion: the arrival of Athens's dashing king and his welcome by brilliant Antiope, war queen of the Amazons. This never happened. Antiope was in the mountains on a hunt. Eleuthera was with her. I know because I was sent to bring them back.

Antiope disdained this summons, in part to demonstrate contempt for the encroachers, and as well from heedfulness of Eleuthera's love. I cannot prove this, but I believe that Antiope divined, long before she had sighted Theseus' squadron or even learned of its arrival, that these ships bore her hard fate. I believe Eleuthera sensed it too. This is why both protracted the hunt.

Antiope at twenty-seven remained a virgin. So much the harpers got right. For this she won repute from all, but devotion everlasting from her lover. For Eleuthera (who, with Stratonike, constituted

Antiope's High Trikona) had sworn from the moment of her own accession to womanhood that she would hold herself *anandros*, unpossessed by man. So long as Antiope remained likewise, so long did the pair own love perfect and inviolable.

They were hunting ibex above the timberline when the ships of Theseus came. To stalk such shy creatures, one must dream. The rams tell where they may be found and what exertions must be made to take them. This night all had retired, when Eleuthera sprang awake with a cry. Her mates rushed to her in consternation, for Eleuthera would never loose such a howl even in her sleep, which, among peaks, where sound travels, effectively terminated the hunt.

"I slew you, Antiope."

So Eleuthera spoke, recounting her dream and, for myself, to repeat these words aloud, even at this remove of time, yet sends the gooseflesh coursing.

"We had ringed the peak," Eleuthera continued, recounting her dream, "I and the others of the hunt, and had reached the final outcrop, readying to raise and fire. Only I carried no bow but the iron-cored lance, the horseback javelin. When we made the cry and raised, no ibex stood before us but you, Antiope.

"You were not yourself but a white ram. Yet I knew you, and you me. You rushed, not with horns lowered as they do, but crest high and breast forward. My cast had not yet been made; I could have held. Yet some daimon drove me. I slung and pierced you through. You tumbled, and your blood painted the rock."

Antiope crossed to comfort her lover. But Eleuthera would not be consoled. "The sensation was joy," she reported. "Elation of such sublimity as I have never known."

The party broke off the hunt and rode home.

The Athenians had reached the Mound City ten days earlier. Their arrival had created a sensation. Among our people the sea is a feared god. Many of tal Kyrte could not conceive of a country beyond the water, from which these strangers had come and to which they would return; rather, they believed these foreigners had come from the sea itself, from the Void where the disk of ocean meets the vault of sky.

The word for "new thing" in our tongue—*netome*—is the same as "evil." The free people's ways stand unaltered since creation; they believe that any innovation brought to them from outside their universe is inherently wicked, bearing potential to overturn society. What a Greek might call law or custom, the free people call *rhyten annae*, "the way we do things" or "how it has always been done." Any new thing imperils rhyten annae, for it threatens all we have been and known, who we are and how we wish to live.

When Antiope and the hunting party returned, they rode down to the strand, drawn by the crowds flocking about the beached ships. I held in my post as novice, at Eleuthera's shoulder. She saw the ships and spoke one word:

"*Netome.*"

Thing of evil.

Eleuthera reckoned these Greeks at once as enemies. Yet such privations had the sailors undergone in their passage, and with such uncomplaining industry did they endure, that their condition elicited sympathy rather than hostility. A number ailed with wounds; others tossed, fever-wracked. I became acquainted with the character of Theseus over the succeeding months; it was by no means past him to exploit the distress of his men to gain advantage. This he did now. He quarantined his party. The season as I said was Saurasos, the Gathering; for miles the plain was carpeted with encampments of the tribes of tal Kyrte and of traders and caravan masters, livestock dealers, gold miners, and lovers. You may imagine the riot. Theseus commanded his company to hold themselves apart. It worked. The contrast between the deportment of his young gentlemen and that of the loutish and grog-besotted tribesmen proved irresistible. Our maidens fell for them. They drew us like honey.

I too was stricken with love, for that beautiful youth sighted on the strand at Walnut Hill. I grew ill with this passion. In Sinope as a child I had been compelled to memorize verses of love poetry.

How I abhorred it and its authors. Now, at one stroke, I understood. I too fell before Eros' affliction, base as a slave and as devoid of dignity.

Damon.

Damon!

To learn his name set me dizzy with joy. A thousand times a day I rehearsed it, silent and aloud, as if its pronouncement were a charm by whose repetition I could draw its owner to me.

I loathed myself. How could I be so abject? How permit such folly to overwhelm me? Yet whelmed I was, and no cure for it. When Skyleia and Alcippe, captains of my battalion, called me apart with the command to serve as interpreter to the Greek camp, my heart nearly burst with dread and joy.

What if Eros dissevered me from my sisters?

What if love drove me apart from my warrior's vows?

I went to Antiope, the only one to whom I could confide my derangement and hope for impartial hearing. (Eleuthera would flay me.) Antiope was eight years my senior and seemed wise as the Sphinx. Of course I must serve, she said. I groaned. To her I made this petition: should mania of love cause me to act counter to the weal of the free people, she must slay me herself! I saw her jaw work and thought my distress had touched her heart; I realize now she was just trying to keep a straight face.

"Love is a god, Selene, to whose direction none is immune. Even the immortals, they say, are powerless in his grasp."

"Not you, lady. You would never yield to such base emotions as now besiege my heart."

Smiling, she indicated the grass at her side. I sat; she plucked my dagger and hers and sank them, blades crossed, into the turf.

"Then we will strike an oath, you and I," she declared. "Should you fail the free people, I pledge my thrust shall end your life. However, should it be myself to fall, you must perform the same for me."

My heart leapt at these words. "You will never fail, lady."

She smiled.

"Pledge this then, by Cybele and Artemis Chrysanios, the holiest oaths of our people, and you and I shall be bound by this pact forever."

Thus I swore and felt the weight of distress lift from my heart, such are the devious designs of heaven.

13

THE EQUESTRIAN SQUARE

Selene continues:

Among the clans who gather each spring as allies of tal Kyrte are the Iron Mountain Scyths, spectacular horse warriors, whose territory commences east of the river Tanais and extends for six hundred leagues, passing so close to the Land Where the Sun Rises that none may proceed farther, men say, without sacrifice of his sight. Some eleven hundred of these had come, under two princes, Borges and Arsaces, and made camp in the Scythian Meadow (such is it called), as they had time out of mind. The Iron Mountain clans are constituted of three nations, the Myrina, the Lagodositai, and the Ythe. The latter came with manes and tails cropped in mourning for their prince, Misethantes, slain fending pirates not many days prior. Numbers of tal Kyrte shared bonds of friendship with the Iron Mountain clans; much sympathy was expressed by the warrioresses, no few pledging to join in hunting down the brigands who had committed this outrage. As Borges and his lieutenants elaborated their description of the pirates, however, it became clear that these were none other than Theseus' companies, freshly landed, and that the fight in which Prince Misethantes had been slain was the very one Theseus had reported, which had driven him to our country in such distress.

No host may offer falsehood under the spring truce. With gravity Hippolyta arrested Borges' speech. "The men you seek are in camp now, under tal Kyrte's pledge of sanctuary."

Borges rejoined with outrage, declaring it the act of an enemy to grant asylum to brigands who had murdered a prince and ally. He demanded that these villains, the Greeks, be turned over at once to his justice.

Hippolyta was at that time sixty-one years old. She wore a leopard skin across her right shoulder and a double axe in a sheath upon her back; her iron-colored hair fell in a plait to her waist; upon her flesh were carved scars of battle going back fifty years. She straightened upon her sixteen-hand grey, Frostbite, and repudiated Prince Borges. By now a sizable throng had gathered, including myself and Eleuthera. We watched as our peace queen Hippolyta, at past sixty still half a head taller than her knights and companions, stood firm in rejecting Prince Borges' claim.

"I hate these foreigners more even than you, my friend, for the evil their countrymen Heracles and Jason have brought to the free people in generations past. Yet the honor of tal Kyrte dictates that they may be given over to no one while they stand protected by our pledge of sanctuary. Let the season of the Gathering run its course, Borges, then exact your vengeance as you wish."

This was not good enough for the Scyth. He wanted Theseus' head now.

Word travels swiftly in a camp. Before the prince had finished his harangue, Theseus appeared in person, accompanied by a score of his own champions. By now Antiope had arrived as well. Her post as war queen set her on a par with Hippolyta; she advanced and ordered Theseus brought in.

Let me describe the site. The landward earthworks of the Mound City are monumental in scale (erected not by tal Kyrte but by some prior race, long vanished), with the central redoubt covering above twenty acres, and the inner plaza, the Equestrian Square, trebling that. Great palisades stretch for furlongs, enclosing the site by a grid of elevated causeways from which the slopes, grass-covered, decline to the square itself. Directly beneath are excavated revetments, formerly defensive ditchworks but now used as holding pens for the thousands of horses brought in for trade. It is an ingenious scheme. Buyers pass at ground level to view the stock, with ramps ascending from each enclosure, so that an individual mount may be easily cut from the band and brought up for inspection.

Above these pens, on the earthworks, now settled the antagonists and their onlookers in thousands, as in some vast amphitheater. Theseus spoke. "Before all," he declared, "it was not we Athenians who offered offense. Rather we were attacked without provocation by men who refused water or even a place to land to those only passing through their straits, intending not harm, but trade. Second, we had no idea we were fighting allies of tal Kyrte (how could we, who had never even encountered yourselves, our benefactresses?), but only defended ourselves—and in fact barely escaped with our lives."

Borges disdained this. All that mattered, he reiterated, was that the blood of his kinsmen had been shed.

"Very well," said Theseus, "I will stand up to Borges or any champion he elects, in single combat, here and now—and hell take him who falters."

You may imagine the uproar this touched off. Borges it was who was called Iron Rider, for the armored chariot from which he led the charges of his troop (driven by his brother Arsaces, a fearsome bowman) and from which he had never been unseated. The knights of his Iron Mountain clans, constituted always as a war party, wanted only the horn's cry to inaugurate the bloodbath. As for the Athenians, they, recall, were princes and heroes all, and commanded by one who claimed descent from Poseidon himself, and who owned abundant incentive, beyond even the preservation of his companies, to display his mettle before the clans of Amazonia, in whose debt he stood for his very survival.

Order was restored by Antiope, acting upon her office as war queen. Tal Kyrte, she proclaimed, may under no circumstances permit the blood of guests to be spilled. Nor could the suppliant be turned out, once asylum had been granted.

"The laws of tal Kyrte are clear," she declared. "The free people shall defend to the death all who have been granted sanctuary within their camp."

Antiope called the Scythian forward.

"If you wish to fight, Borges, you must fight me."

A DUEL OF HONOR

A champion of tal Kyrte may not be armed by one of her own trikona, but another at one remove, assisted by the warrior's mother-mother. The lot, as fate would have it, fell to me, as trikona-mate to Eleuthera, who stood the same to Antiope. It was my role, not only to dress our war queen in corselet and armor, but to select and whet the warheads of her arrows, repaint the blood gutters in ritual jet and ochre, and to razor-fletch the flight feathers. She took four only, one for each cardinal point, with three bronze-sheathed javelins, and a single *pelekus*, the double axe. None other may attend, save a priestess of Artemis Ephesia to prompt the verses of the ceremony. I must bathe Antiope, apart in the Willow House, which sat astride the thermal springs of the Borysthenes marsh, and donate from my own trove that mirror of bronze by whose reflection our queen would know her soul in the life after, and which, if she were slain, would be buried yoked to her right wrist. In that event I must bear her body from the field and deliver it to Eleuthera and Stratonike, the mates of her High Trikona, who would bear the corpse to Hippolyta, her mother-mother, for burial. This was the mightiest honor of my life. I would sooner have sliced my own throat than committed an error in the rite.

I had expected to find our lady solemn, and had prepared my aspect with gravity for this chore. But she was gay, and joked away the time, not from restiveness but excess of spirit. Her concern was entirely for a clean kill: that the Scythian be slain at the first blow and require no untidy butchery. My own fear was less of the prince Borges than his brother Arsaces, henchman of the chariot; I urged our queen to remark him with vigilance. I had seen him shoot. To my further surprise, she interrogated me, quite gaily, on the progress of my "affair" with the youth Damon. "Have you kissed him, child? Have you tousled his curls?" When I blushed, she teased me more.

When we were done and she was fully armed, she made me go over her again, twice. "I must be beautiful today," she said.

The harpers have retold the treachery offered by the prince of the Iron Mountain Scyths. That Borges commanded his brother to trade places with him, identities concealed beneath their armor. So that Arsaces, the younger and far superior archer, served not as henchman to drive the team, but as champion, where his skill could work against Antiope, exposed upon her mount, while Borges, shamming as his brother, handled the horses. It was Theseus who smelled out this device, sending an agent to bribe an informer among the Scythian guard. Or, as I have heard as well, a dream may have apprised him. Whichever, he appeared in person, at dawn, seeking entry to Antiope.

She was in the smoke bath, with Hippolyta and the priestess of Artemis, completing her purification. Two of the Queen's Companions intercepted him. Theseus was not permitted entrance but must speak from outside that screen erected for such intercourse, called the Willow Wall. He had acquired enough of our tongue to make a stab, but not enough to get it right. "Borges will fight you upside down" was how the message came. So I had to go out and speak to him directly.

Such an urgency of care informed his voice as confirmed my

blackest fears. Not of the treachery of the Scythian, for this could be faced, but the concern of Theseus, stricken with love for our queen. Two of his knights, Lykos and Peteos, accompanied him. They saw it too.

When could it have fallen, this bolt of Eros? Theseus had never spoken to Antiope alone. No messages had been exchanged, and nothing passed between them beyond a look. Yet he loved her; nothing could be plainer.

I was stern with him, and, pledging that his warning would be faithfully conveyed, banished him from the precinct. How reluctantly he withdrew!

Returning through the Willow Wall I discovered her, my lady, watching Theseus through the withes. She had read the trepidation on his face and heard the anxiety in his voice. I have never seen such joy as lit her in that hour. Of speech she made none, apart from this: that I leave her bow and lances back, arming her with the horseback javelin, the discus, and the axe.

Here is how the fight went. Above the Lane of the Champions, upon the earthworks which face the sea and are called the Paeon Gate, the clans took their places in order. Borges and his brother fought from the iron chariot; Antiope from horseback, atop the chestnut gelding she called Sneak Biscuits. Theseus and his men looked on, as did the Iron Mountain clans, eleven hundred in all, with the other tribes of the East and the nations of tal Kyrte, sixty or seventy thousand in all.

The antagonists rushed at each other down the avenue bounded on each face by the earthworks. This is called in our tongue *ana kessa,* "up-and-back." The skill is not so much in the initial pass, with the discharge of missiles at full gallop, as in the double back or reversion, when the antagonists come about and for a moment present their vulnerable flanks and heels. Two cypress posts stand here thirty yards apart, in a space called the Runway. Beyond the poles neither foe may strike, but both must withdraw to commence a second pass. Within this gantlet, however, anything goes. The gallant champion disdains the pole and slugs it out here.

Three times Antiope made her pass and each time took the pole, much to the displeasure of her partisans. With each rush she endured the shafts shot by her rival from behind his iron wall. This vulnerability Antiope had set for herself, fighting from horseback without armor save the crescent shield on her left forearm, designing to make up for this in agility between the posts, cutting back to the chariot's vulnerable rear and striking from there. But the henchman, the masked Borges, was no novice and employed the slopes of the earthworks to make his wheel-about, churning up great storms of dust and sand, with Antiope at the gallop hard behind, yet unable to get directly astern, so to say, as the car continued to double with terrific dexterity, descending the bank, wheeling across the lane, and mounting the opposite as it made its escape. All the while the masked Arsaces loosed his bolts rearward with fabulous speed and accuracy, while Antiope picked out the shafts in midflight and batted them aside with the flat of her shield.

Three times more the antagonists thundered down the chute. Now at each pass Antiope slung one of her trio of iron-freighted javelins, rising upon her sole planted on her horse's belly-band and slinging at the gallop, the missile's moment augmented by the sleeve extender. The bolts slammed into the iron facing of the car with such violent concussions as made the multitude cry in wonder. Each time the plate buckled and caved, yet no cast pierced the bunker entire. The chariot master loosed his bolts through embrasures on both sides and rear, standing shoulder to shoulder with his brother, who held the team, and so swiftly did one shaft follow another that it seemed not one man fired but three. Such was the prowess of the youth Arsaces, feigning to be his elder, that the thousands watching from the slopes cried out and even gasped as each bolt screamed toward his rival. Yet Antiope each time fended the hurtling death.

Six passes had been made, which Antiope had deliberately protracted that the onlookers might begin to suspect, by the skill with which he handled the bow, that beneath his armor the champion was Arsaces, the younger brother, and the henchman Borges, his elder. Now on the seventh rush the queen wheeled her mount so swiftly onto the rear of the slewing chariot that she drew hard alongside, into that shadow of vulnerability created by the relative stations of driver and champion, and from this vantage loosed point-blank the iron discus. The twelve-pound missile, slung at the rising gallop with all the champion's weight and strength behind it, struck the bowman upon that amber device of a griffin which he bore at his helmet's prow and, staving at once both helm and skull, dashed the latter and tore off the former. Arsaces' bow dropped; the prince pitched sidelong from the car. The helmet bounded end over end in the dust, describing an arc which terminated, at last, adjacent the corpse of its owner, which, unmasked, revealed itself to be not Prince Borges, but his younger brother Arsaces.

I looked to Theseus in this moment, then to Eleuthera, who had sensed as well the Athenian's passion for our queen. His aspect altered only an instant. Yet in that moment, as Antiope's foe rolled vanquished in the dust, I read upon Eleuthera's face such foredoom as compassed not just herself and Antiope but our nation entire. For as our queen here won Theseus' heart and gave hers to him, by this act she severed herself from the people, whose right arm was Eleuthera, which means freedom.

Now Borges' chariot fled. So swiftly did Antiope overtake it that her horse's forehooves actually mounted to the platform of the car, as she swiped with the axe, first at one flank, then the other, while Borges, slacking the reins and cringing to the floor planks, diced and dodged. When Antiope's mount spilled from its perch, the prince recaptured his team and resumed his flight, now out of the lane entire.

The yet-masked Borges fled down the earthway to the corrals where the horses for trade were penned. Into these excavations he lashed his team, with Antiope on his heels at the gallop, so that the onlookers in their myriads had to vacate their stations and scramble up and over the earthworks so as not to lose sight of the spectacle. Now could Antiope have pursued Borges into the pen and cut him down. Yet such an uproar of levity saluted the Scythian's comeuppance that she reined in, a javelin cast shy of where Borges found himself impounded among the milling herds, while from a score of ramparts the scorn of the nations pelted upon him.

Antiope tore her helmet back, revealing her flushed and triumphant face. With her axe she gestured to the Runway, where the corpse of Arsaces lay sprawled in the dirt.

"The challenger Borges has been slain. This fulfills the law. Therefore let his brother Arsaces live!"

Thus Borges the swindler fled with his servitors, never putting off his helmet to reveal his fraud. By the measure of his disgrace did Antiope's renown enlarge.

Men have asked what it was that Theseus loved in her. I answer with this story.

There is a tree in my country called the Weather Ash, which stands yet, by the river Hybristes, of such antiquity as to bear the lightning strikes not of Zeus but of Cronos, his father, and this tree has a legend. For two boughs grow from her, curved like the horns of a ram. Who could string these and draw them as a bow would rule all "beneath the Bear" and claim whichever bride he chose.

Many came. Bellerophon and Jason, and Heracles himself, but none could budge the horns. Now, in the aftercourse of this challenge of the Runway, Antiope took Theseus there and bade him make trial. Two thousand rode and witnessed. He strung the bow but could not draw it, though he offered prayers to Apollo and the Muses and promised each a temple if they would grant him victory.

Now Antiope stepped forward and in the name of love restrung the Horns.

"Try again."

Theseus feared to, lest he fail. But she set his palm against the bole where the horns conjoined and begged him, as he loved her, to draw. And with as little effort as a child bends a reed in play, so he worked the Horns in their draw, and so distant flew the bolt.

Antiope laughed. "Now you have won your bride."

For fairness of form and feature our lady was peerless among women, who could ride and run and knew no fear of beast or man, and none of Theseus himself. For other women desired boons of him, if only his seed or his name, or to claim place as his consort. Antiope wanted nothing. Only the man himself, to ride at her side and take his pleasure of her and she of him. At Athens in later seasons he brought her jewelry of ivory and gold; she laughed at it. Nor could her head be turned by fine linen or precious stones or houses or even horses, which she loved beyond all. She wanted only him, and this with all her heart. And what may a man resist less than to be loved for nothing but the fall of his curls and the sound of his voice? Thus Theseus, who had known women before as prizes or competitors, now fell into this wild creature as into a bottomless well, his delight in her society overmastering all other pursuits, so that he forgot his ships and realm and even to eat or sleep.

But our tale runs ahead. Let us return to the flight of Borges and his eleven hundred.

There is a rite of the Gathering, a night sacrifice to Ares called the Hecatomb, which comes after the Games of the Moon and inaugurates the final nine days of the season, during which the tribes reconstitute themselves and the novices, horse trials behind them, are enrolled in the clans and the orders.

The occasion of this ceremony chanced to fall four nights after the duel of Borges, while the camp yet rang with Antiope's triumph. In these rites the tribes, and all guest nations, are invited to select one of their number to offer an address in praise of that people's ancestors. This is an occasion of gaiety and fellow-feeling, with each tribe licensed to hoot in derision at the self-congratulation of its neighbors, with none taking offense but all delighting in the give and get.

A number spoke this night, the Maeotians and Cappadocians, Taurians and Massa Getai. Someone called the Athenians. Theseus stood and started toward the stand.

Three of tal Kyrte intercepted him. These were Eleuthera, Stratonike, and Skyleia. Eleuthera accused Theseus of bringing evil to the free people. Blood has been shed, she said; we have made enemies on account of this man.

"To what purpose has this outlaw been given leave to speak?" Eleuthera addressed Hippolyta, Antiope, and the Council of Elders. "Every other nation attends the Gathering at tal Kyrte's invitation; these Greeks alone have descended out of the sky. Are they pirates?

Why have they crossed oceans, except to rob us? A prince and ally has been slain in their cause; war may follow. Beneath our shield they cower, these foreign mice, while our valor preserves them. Yet now they have found their tongue and presume to make speeches on the superiority of their ways!"

An uproar ascended, seconding the speaker. I glanced to Antiope. Her gaze held fastened upon Theseus, revealing nothing.

Theseus begged leave to reply. I recall his words because I was summoned to interpret.

He did not rebut Eleuthera. Rather he directed his defense to the queens and the elders. He acknowledged the straits in which he and his companions had stood on their advent to our homeland. Absent tal Kyrte's clemency, all would have perished. He thanked the free people for making his men welcome, and Antiope for so valiantly defending their honor. He had heard much of our nation, he declared, but nothing had prepared him for its greatness and magnanimity. He proclaimed himself, and no few of his men, smitten with our young women, not alone as comely females, but as exemplars of the warrior ethic and champions of a proud and noble race.

Acclamation saluted these sentiments; the people began to warm to the orator. Nor did his good looks work to his disadvantage. You who have known the man only in his middle years may not account his beauty as a young king of twenty-nine or thirty. As he stood before the tribes of tal Kyrte, few could look upon his grace and manliness and not find themselves favorably disposed.

Eleuthera cut this off. "Sisters, here is the seducer! He sets honeyed words before us as a vendor plies cakes in a bazaar. In just this way is *netome*, evil luck, brought to the people."

More clamor erupted. Theseus clearly sensed the gravity of the charge; he requested that the term be translated, that he might know what he was accused of.

Tal Kyrte, I informed him, has an evil god, Netosa, who is the lamprey, the succubus. This creature works his mischief at night, to overturn the order of the world. Anything which makes its apparition uninvited is mistrusted as alien and possessed of malign intent.

"I will not sit to hear this man extol his ancestors," Eleuthera declaimed, "and I call upon you, sisters, to drive him by your outrage from the stand."

More cries reinforced her. Theseus held till the tumult had abated.

"If it displease you, Captain," he spoke, addressing Eleuthera, "I shall not speak of ancestors. However, with your exemption, I propose an alternative. I will praise my nation's issue. Will you permit this? Will you let me speak, not to Athens's past but to her future?"

Laughter greeted this. The people approved the novelty and responded with enthusiasm. Eleuthera reluctantly acceded.

"My city is young," Theseus began. "In might and fame she stands in the shadow of such courts as Corinth and Mycenae, Elis and Thebes, not to say your own nation. Yet of all these, I propose, she is the only one whose political virtue will enlarge with the passage of the years."

Again Eleuthera sought to interdict. This time, however, the people had been caught by the speaker's theme. "Let the man say his piece!" they cried and compelled her to give back. Theseus thanked his hearers and resumed.

"Once, my friends of tal Kyrte, all of humankind lived as the nations of the plains do now, keepers of stock, great warriors and raiders, as yourselves. Clans owned no more than they could carry, but lived by their wits and skill at arms. Death skulked about them in the dark. At night the tribesman lay down with weapons to hand; even in sleep he held vigilant, fearful of attack by beasts or men.

"Then came the city. Her walls of stone held out the enemy; behind her ramparts man might live free of fear. He learned to cultivate the land. The gods taught him domestication of grains and fermentation of the grape; he had bread now, and wine. The potter's craft and the smith's provided him with tools and weapons; the mariner's art extended his reach across seas. He learned to trade. With time, wealth accumulated. He need not merely subsist, but live. For the first time humankind possessed leisure for the gentler pursuits of music, poetry, and the arts. Agriculture banished famine, for the husbandman might lay up from one year's plenty reserve for the next.

"In the city man enjoyed protection of law. He might walk abroad unarmed. In his prior, tribal life, all property had been held in common. Now in the city, he might call things his own—land, home, implements with which to procure his livelihood. By hard work one could make a better life. What energy and innovation this released! Community multiplied the individual's reach and moment, for the knowledge acquired by one might be set at the service of all. Now, each individual need not contain within himself the sum of all experience, but concentrate, if he will, upon a single art, as goldsmithing or physic, viniculture or sailbending. The singer may sing, the weaver weave. Each prospers in happiness and imparts prosperity to all.

"An individual need no longer be a warrior, whose every hour is spent in war or readiness for war, but each has leisure to think and talk and pray, to participate in politics, travel to the wonders of other lands, erect temples to the gods, and lay out a beautiful city, where the wealth of the world's goods and wisdom is available to all to enrich his soul. In the city, man's years are extended by the medicaments of the physician's art. He need not expire untimely, beneath the blows of the elements or wild beasts, but live out in health the measure of his days."

At this point Eleuthera could contain herself no longer. "Ha!" she cried and, calling upon the assembled tribes, sought their permission to rebut, in her phrase, these lies and calumnies. The multitude roared its approval.

Eleuthera mounted to the stand of cypress hewn into the stone outwork. And it must be told that she matched her rival both in physical stature and presence of person; of such surpassing comeliness was she that the antagonists, standing little more than a spear length apart, seemed struck as two sparks from the same ember, peers and equals in every way.

"Our visitor," Eleuthera began, "declares the way of the city superior to our life of the steppe because it produces, he claims, a nobler being. Hearing this, it was all I could do to keep from hooting aloud, which I would have, were I the rude savage he styles us to be."

She hailed the life of the plains. The openness of spirit, the equality of station, the rigorousness of person its demands instill in the hearts of all. "I have seen men of the city, with their paunches and spindly hams. They could not last an hour beneath God's sky. Agriculture! I would sooner carve furrows in the flesh of my mother than rend the earth with the hideous beak of the plough. For what? To prize a mealy legume from the dirt and call it dinner? God made humankind to hunt, as the lion and the eagle, not graze upon straw like cattle and sheep. The chase inculcates vigor and fortitude. It leaves Mother Earth as God intended, unriven and undefiled."

Acclamation resounded. The tribes of tal Kyrte, seconded by the male Scyths and Cimmerians, Black Cloaks and Tower Builders, clashed their spearshafts against the bowls of their shields and roared to heaven. I glanced to Antiope, whose eyes still held fastened upon Theseus, himself enduring with patience this rebuke of Eleuthera.

"Our Athenian guest," the champion resumed when the tumult had subsided, "claims that cities produce leisure. What rubbish! Who has more free time than the hunter and warrior, whose very work is sport? We of the steppe do not know the word labor, for all we do is engaged in with joy, reverencing the ordinance of our Maker. Our days are passed in God's play; at night we lie down with the healthy fatigue of activities well shaping to body and soul. Property! What is its produce save misery and estrangement from one's kind? In the city discontented man toils beneath the lamp, lest his neighbor get the jump of him. The blacksmith becomes slave to his bellows, the musician to his lyre. Each reviles his fellow as rival and foe. City man returns from his day jaded and debilitated and rises to the next dreading his own self-indenture. Tal Kyrte turns to the east with joy, saluting the dawn in wonder and anticipation. For us the day is that to which we surrender, not like the city man, who seeks to shape it to his will. Blasphemy and arrogance! Walk his streets, sisters and guests. Inspect his grotesque spawn. Whores infest his doorways, rogues and mountebanks pack his courts, cutpurses and pickpockets his marketplace. And don't preach to me of law! What need have we of it? Education? We require neither proctors nor pedagogues to tutor youth in our ways but each maiden bursts her heart to master them, unbidden. We could not stop them if we tried! And as for the arts, which our guest cites as proof of city man's ascension to nobility, I ask: Why attend an imitation of the nightingale when you can hear the real thing? Why render sky in art when you have but to look up to behold heaven itself? This sermonizer Theseus has praised physicians and their arts of tendance upon the sick. Ha! We know no illness on the steppe. With the city comes unnatural extension of days. When it's time to die, die!"

Yet mightier ovation saluted this. And Eleuthera, borne aloft as an eagle, elevated her impeachment to a yet more truculent pitch.

"Our guest in his oration praises the city for its gentility and restraint. Between the lines he calls us savages. Are we, sisters? Consider our pass:

"We are women unmastered by men, yet hemmed on all quarters by those who would inflict this wretched state upon us. Do you wonder at our ferocity? Other nations fight to preserve their native soil; only we must defend our flesh and souls, which men would enslave if they could, as they have in every other quadrant. Your own wives and mothers, Athenians, once held the franchise, I have heard. They could vote and owned an equal voice in affairs of state. You stole this from them—your king Cecrops did—immuring them in servitude and silence. Never will tal Kyrte endure this! We are bound by our resistance to those who would make chattel of us. We as no other people stand isolated and apart, with none to count as allies save our own spirit and resolve. Do we defend ourselves like wild beasts? You would too! Do we spurn quarter? You would too! Enemies envelop us and more come, as yourselves, across oceans to steal our freedom."

She faced Theseus directly now. "And if you think to thieve it from us, thou pirate, remember this: in other societies, willingness to die for the nation is a virtue which must be inculcated. Not in ours. Among the free people allegiance unto death arises as immanently as in a pack of wolves and endures, as impossible to eradicate. I will embrace my own slaughter this moment, and so will every woman and girl here, to preserve our freedom. And if the free people must fall, then nothing of us shall remain, for we will bathe the earth in our blood and yours before surrendering this liberty we love so that we call ourselves by its name, tal Kyrte: the Free."

Further uproar ensued, with thousands acclaiming Eleuthera's fervency, while others cried out that such excess was exorbitant, no proper way to address a guest. And Eleuthera herself, perceiving that her rancor had waxed immoderate, stepped aside and abated her harangue.

Antiope stepped in. She proposed to Theseus that the Athenian resume his panegyric and carry it to its close, at which point Eleuthera might respond. All approved.

"I commend our most excellent friend," Theseus resumed, with a bow to Eleuthera, "and her heartfelt encomium of the life of the steppe. I make no brief in opposition. But she has closed her discourse upon the subject of death. Let us pick up there, and carry on.

"Beyond all which divides nation from nation, one lot unites us: our mortality. Death's mill makes grist of us all. This before all elevates humankind above the beasts: we alone foreken our mortality. We alone know we must die.

"The nature of our species is savage. The imperative of predation resides as deeply in our bones as in the wolf and the lion. Yet the foreknowledge of our extinction not only dissevers us from these brutes, but imposes upon us an obligation. For beyond God's statute of slaughter rises another, mightier decree.

"Humankind is commanded to ascend from savagery. This is God's mandate, which cries out from the epicenter of our being: the imperative to mount from the base to the noble, from the savage to the civil, from beast to human.

"In earlier eras men knew no law. He slew those even of his own family, and when he vanquished his enemies, the savagery of his vengeance exceeded even that of wild beasts. How brutal and appalling have been his acts of atrocity!

"But let me not try your patience, friends. Only hear and consider. There exists a universal law, before which even the gods must bow: the higher supersedes the lower. As the Titans and the Sons of Earth have been overthrown by Zeus and the Olympians, so must the race of men and women continue to progress, toward humanity and apart from bestiality, toward reason and apart from passion, toward love and away from fear."

Theseus concluded by praising the clemency of Hippolyta and Antiope, yes, and even Eleuthera, and of the nation of tal Kyrte entire. In granting sanctuary to him and his men they had acted as Zeus Who Protects the Stranger would have them act and thus sided with the higher impulses of humanity, not the baser reflexes of beasts. He thanked them and stepped down.

Now the people called for Eleuthera to respond. But she had observed the closeness with which Antiope had attended Theseus throughout the debate. She saw her mate moved by the foreigner's eloquence and bending to his case. For this reason and others she declined to respond, declaring herself no orator, but called instead upon Antiope, as war queen, and bade her pronounce the rebuttal in the people's name. For Eleuthera hoped, by setting her lover as antagonist to the Athenian, to crush in the shoot any affinity budding between them, or, if Antiope would not take him on, then compel her to demonstrate this before the people. I stood immediately to Antiope's left and could see her face throughout this summons. Though she perceived her friend's motive, yet the acclamation of the tribes could not let her slip this call. She came forward and began:

"Sisters and mothers, daughters, allies, and friends, I have not mounted to this platform prepared to rebut our Athenian guest's panegyric. I accede only at your command and speak, not from my reason, as this Greek would say"—here she nodded, but did not look, in the direction of Theseus—"but from the ground of my being and all being, which is God, which is all that is and all that will be. This my heart commands me to speak:

"Humankind may not ascend to God by evolution, as our guest warrants, but only fall from Him. Our guest looks upon God's creatures and calls them brutes. I say it is we who deserve that name. Let us make them our teachers—the earth and her elements, her children of four legs and her winged captains of the air. They have come straight from God and speak his tongue direct and untutored. Only we have fallen, and by those very arts which our friend from across the sea acclaims as evolutionary. He looks upon sky and steppe and sees that which God has created. I look and see God Himself. Let us enroll ourselves in His academy of wind and sky, birth and death, of seasons ordained eternal. Here is our Teacher; in His book is all we need to know.

"The city, our friend declares, is man's creation, the produce of his reason, by which he may ascend from the state of savagery. I answer by calling his attention to this rock. I bid him look to that sea. Has man made either? So long as sun rises and rain falls, man can make nothing. Not the sky nor the earth, nor seeds nor horses nor stone. Man has not so much as seen or spoken even these thoughts which blaspheme His name, save by the Almighty's grace, or drawn one solitary breath absent heaven's license. Moons and stars God makes and throws away. With but a puff He blows out the lamp of our lives."

As she spoke, Theseus studied her. And though he made his face a mask, yet this was plain: the words with which Antiope refuted his testament arose with such purity from her heart that as each fell upon his flesh, as the blow of a lash, he received them as they were kisses. He had not been felled, one saw, by Eros' bolt. Rather he had encountered in his antagonist that which he had never known before, or even knew existed—a mind and spirit equal or superior to his own—and before this he genuflected, not so much to her, whose gifts struck and illumined him, but to that greater Spirit in whose name she spoke.

And Antiope, perceiving, submerged herself in that stream whose power guided and animated her speech, so that her words beat upon him as combers upon a strand, and he endured them, casting each back with his silence and acceptance, that it in its retreat might assist to form that next crest, which broke upon him and enlarged his joy.

"Our guest in other contexts," Antiope continued, "has employed the word 'barren' to describe what he perceives as the 'emptiness' of the steppe. Look again, my friend. Her seeds and grasses feed us, her wind animates our spirit, her mantle swathes us gently in our sleep. Shall we 'cultivate' her? I will never let my people farm, for she who farms cannot dream, and who cannot dream cannot live. Husbandry of the earth does not ennoble man but degrades him, for it sows within his breast the blasphemy that earth belongs to him. Nothing belongs to us! Not even ourselves and our lives, which are God's and have been since our birth. To call a thing one's own is madness. Such thinking engenders greed and avarice, acquisitiveness and niggardliness. It rends brother from brother, making men to count and measure everything. Is this 'progress'? Progress to what?

"Does our guest imagine that the nations of tal Kyrte have stood, for want of intelligence or industry, incapable of building cities? We don't want cities! To dwell within such a press of humanity deforms the soul. Give us silence and solitude, which purify and concentrate the spirit. Shall we build temples to God? Why, when His cathedral compasses us day and night! Preach to us not of reverence, for we tread in God's footprints every step of our days, and account no trespass graver than to stray from His path.

"The life of the city has made men less than they were, not more. And as for your women, I have seen them, I am sorry to say. Is even one as beautiful as these? They are painted whores, your wives, who have bartered their souls for a place out of the rain and not even sold them dear. Your women are shells of what God intended and you know it, or you would not have crossed oceans to trail after us, moonstruck as calves!

"Those gods to whom you erect temples, Theseus, are in my view but reproductions of yourselves, and laughable ones at that. Here is heaven before you! Seek no further, only hold still and annul the yammering of your 'reason.' I despise reason if it severs me from my soul and from God.

"But the greatest proof of the rightness of my argument (and the mightiest refutation of your own) arises from you yourself, Theseus. For if you truly believed what you preach, you would be home now, trudging behind a plough. But you are not, are you? You are here, with us!"

Such acclaim greeted this as made the very earth pitch and tremble. Spearshafts resounded upon shields, soles smote the plain; even the horses stamped and nickered as if they understood. Antiope elevated her arms to still the tumult.

"And if you would gainsay me," she addressed Theseus, "declaring that the men you have brought with you from Athens feel bereft upon these shores and pine in their hearts for home, I challenge you to command them now, before the witness of this host, to form again into their companies and embark upon their ships. They will revolt and you know it! They are happy here, as you are."

The multitude burst into laughter, Amazons and allies first, then Athenians, when I had translated. Theseus replied, in like tone to his men, that in at least one of civilization's arts he and they had been bested—that of oratory.

Antiope grasped the meaning of the Greek before it had been translated, and leapt upon it.

"Not oratory has vanquished you, my friend, but you have fallen beneath your own weapon, which is reason. Is this not your god, Theseus? Then admit that even we who are untutored and uncivilized possess insight from which you may profit."

The king acknowledged with a bow. Cheers resounded, as much for his concession as for Antiope's triumph.

At this instant a rider galloped in through the gate between the earthworks. This was my own trikona-mate Aella, "Little Whirlwind," a lass of twelve, whose post at this season lay on the northern steppe with the great breeding herds being moved to summer pasture. She thundered now onto the square, her horse lathered and tongue-sprung, and reined-in before the speaker's stand. Before the maid had caught breath to speak, the nation had divined what evil news she bore.

Borges and his Iron Mountain Scyths, the girl reported, had appeared without warning, two nights past, at the ford of the Hybristes, where she and the novices of the White Mountain clans tended a herd of three thousand. Borges had approached the camp, proffering signs of friendship. He had been welcomed. His men had gone so far as to unyoke the oxen from their women's waggons and even laid out their bedding for the night. But at a signal they rose and attacked. Their numbers were above a thousand; the lasses' under two hundred. Those Borges did not slaughter at their posts, his men ran down and butchered on the plain. He rounded up the herd, three thousand prime stock, and drove east toward the Scythian homeland.

Uproar erupted. Theseus advanced before Antiope, Eleuthera, and the other captains. "This is my fault. Let me make it right. I am not without ability and my companions are heroes and champions all, eager to prove their mettle to you. Give us only a guide and horses and we will set out this night and come back either with your stolen property, to restore it intact to you, or not come back at all."

15

REFLECTIONS IN
GOD'S MIRROR

The avenging brigade was on the move in the time it takes to gallop ten furlongs. Of course Theseus' Greeks could not be licensed to requite an outrage against the free people. They were permitted to accompany the troop as auxiliaries only. Tal Kyrte supplied horses. I gave Damon three from my string. I had assumed sponsorship of him, as they say in our tongue, *yste arran*, to "stand at the shoulder." This meant I was responsible both for his safety and his comportment. In battle I would defend his life; in society I would make sure he behaved himself.

My first duty was to teach him to ride. This proved no trifling chore. For though he declared himself a prizewinning equestrian in his own country (and though I mounted him on my cleverest and most tractable horse, a gelding named Knothole), not only did he prove incapable of fight riding, to hold a line in assault, say, or execute an up-and-back, but he could not even trot in a straight line across dry level plain.

The novices called him *Motanis*, "Stone Hands," and trotted in his train, giggling. In his defense, few of his compatriots did better. They were all hopeless. They insisted upon "ruling" their horses, attempting to "handle" them as they would a Greek beast. "Your horse knows how to trot, Damon. You don't have to teach him!"

In truth I was charmed to witness my sweetheart's frustration. I could see he was in love with me. He wanted so badly to appear competent in my eyes. I could not respond, of course. I *would* not, particularly in the stern circumstances under which we rode. But in my heart I felt the sweetness of answered love.

The army pressed on. Damon was keen to acquire our tongue; I practiced my Greek on him, explaining where we were and what would happen.

The Tanais River flows northeast to southwest, I told him, three hundred miles ahead. From here to there is Amazon country; on the other side the Scythian lands begin. Borges must cross the Tanais to get home. We would overtake him at the ford and cut him down.

There was danger on the way, however. For, to reach the Tanais, Borges and his eleven hundred must pass through the territory of the Titaneia, the Eastern Amazons. Within this expanse grazed more of tal Kyrte's herds; the Scyths might attempt to seize these and slaughter the girls who watched over them, as no warning could reach the maids in time.

"How many days' ride?" Damon asked.

"Four or five."

And what would Borges do with the stolen horses?

"Keep some for his own wealth, bestow others as rewards to his princes. The best three hundred he will keep aside, to sacrifice over his brother Arsaces' barrow. They will constitute Arsaces' fortune in the life after."

Tal Kyrte does not picket its horses at night but permits them to graze, protected by outriders. I watched Damon's pleasure as he wandered out among them. The bands responded to his approach. They are fearless and full of mischief. The boldest noses up first; he sniffs the man all over, nuzzling between his legs, under his arms, against his ears. Now the whole band packs in. They surround the fellow, picking his wallet for treats, taking his fingers and hair between their lips; they nip him and butt him and jostle him. At times Damon appeared lifted off his feet by their merry press. I could see him weep. I knew this ecstasy. He was being swept up by the wild ways.

"Will we fight the Scyths, Selene?"

"Oh, yes!"

"What will happen?"

I explained that the foe could not outrun us, trailing the stolen herds. He must tarry for pasturage, spend hours crossing rivers, nor would the thirsty beasts be easily driven off from a good stream, once they had gained it. Further, the steppe across which Borges must flee was carved by washes and ravines called "breaks," whose walls may plunge sixty feet below the level of the plain. To double these without a guide, the Scyths must track laterally seeking a crossing. This could be miles.

Damon asked how the fight would go.

I anticipated a sharp skirmish, followed by a rout. We would slay between thirty and a hundred. The rest would flee. We would take back our herds and avenge our daughters. Equally important, each warrioress would acquire scalps, prize mounts of the foe, not to say fame, glory, and wounds of honor. How many would we lose? Damon asked. I told him none. When he questioned this, I laughed.

"Look around you."

It was the third morn of the pursuit. The army radiated across that pan called in our tongue *Tamir Nut,* "God's Mirror." The day itself had come up splendid, as if hatched by heaven for this occasion. It had rained at dawn and the animals, made frisky, capered and bucked along in joy. Upon every quarter arose sights of color and exuberance, not alone the pageantry of the companies of warrioresses, got up in their most brilliant kit, but the cavalcade of reserve mounts, which trailed in hundreds, ruled by the novices, the lasses of ten to thirteen years. Rivals who would demean tal Kyrte have made much of her warrioresses' height and muscularity. Indeed our nation, from the severity of its life, stands second in physical vigor to none of man. But what tenders the race its fearsomeness is not muscle but heart. Though the object of the corps' pursuit, Borges' eleven hundred, eclipsed the brigade both in numbers and armor, not one deemed the foe a match on the open steppe. So preeminent did the mounted warriors of Amazonia account themselves in the type of fighting at which they excelled, on the kind of ground to which their arms and tactics were most suited, that victory in our sight stood foreordained. The air shimmered with the warrioresses' conviction, as did their own persons, resplendent with the iron of their arms, the gilt and platework of their outfit, the electrum and ivory of their horses' caparisons. The observer's eye took in cloaks of lion and wolf skin, leggings of elk hide and buckskin, and helms of silver, cobalt-bossed. A number rode bareheaded, with feathers of eagle and osprey in their hair, one for each enemy slain; others wore the doeskin caps of Phrygia, banded with elk horn and bears' claws.

At the van rode Antiope, in the black leopard cloak and boar's-tooth helm by which her figure could be picked out among hundreds. At her shoulder tracked the mates of her High Trikona, Eleuthera and Stratonike, without peer across the Wild Lands, while at the fore of the companies advanced the champions: Alcippe, Powerful Mare; Skyleia, "Mistress of the Family"; and Glauke Grey Eyes; Tecmessa, called Thistle; Bremusa, called Blur; Rhodippe Red Mare; Xanthe Blonde; Arge, "Fleet"; Leucippe, "White Mare"; Aridela, "Illumined"; and Lyssa, "Battle Fury." Hippolyta commanded her own war society, the Black Wings, whose totem was the raven and who painted their faces jet.

Fabulists report that the race of Amazonia dwells apart from men, an all-female society. This is not so. Numbers of males live among us, as camp husbands and muleteers, smiths and wrights, workers in wood and leather and iron. Many pack wives of their own (of nations other than tal Kyrte), which society exists within the greater nation yet apart from it, much as so-called service birds accompany the crocodiles of Libya and the hippopotami of the Nile.

These trailed us now, a score of gaily painted waggons drawn by mules and the half-wild asses the Lykians call clover bellies, which once bolted cannot be caught even by the fastest horse. They speak their own language, these fellows, called *kabash* ("stew"), which even tal Kyrte cannot understand, and are renowned as diviners, of both dreams and omens, as well as bird sign and the reading of entrails. While alive they will not peek in a looking glass, believing the reflected image their otherworld self, yet are buried, as the warrioresses of tal Kyrte, with a bronze mirror at their right hand, through which this spirit-double escorts them to the next world. The *kabar* (as they are called) believe that life is lived not forward but backward. They ask not where are you going but where you have been. To them each hour has been lived before; that which they learn, they only remember, having known it heretofore. They believe that at death (or birth, in their lexicon) a man must be naked both of goods and cares to pass to the Happy Isles. Thus avarice is unknown among them, as is ambition, niggardliness, and jealousy. Their god is Apollo Loxias, the Trickster. They weep when happy, laugh in grief, and are the most hale and carefree of fellows. They make weapons but will not make war. None will fight, even to defend hearth and children, or flee to preserve his life, but each offers his slaughter to the foe of his own will. In consequence, tal Kyrte defends them with unwonted ferocity.

The greater brigade of tal Kyrte totaled six hundred grown warrioresses, with double that in novices, two to each champion. Theseus' Athenians, a hundred and fifty, constituted a sort of infantry on horseback, with volunteer clans of Gagarians and Shore Scyths, heavily armored males, bringing the total under arms to about nine hundred.

The army trekked on, trailing the sundered turf left by the Scythians' passage. The plain teemed with antelope and gazelle. Hunting parties brought in fresh meat, which was roasted over bricks of dried dung. This stuff starts hard but, once caught, burns clean as charcoal and twice as long. Streams rising in the mountains produced draughts superior to wine. The brigade encountered no opposition, only coming upon the paunch fires of the foe, in which the gut sack of the slaughtered beast serves as vessel to cook its flesh, and its own bones as fuel.

I watched Damon when he didn't know I was looking. He was

fascinated by the silent tongue of tal Kyrte, which so mimics the language of horses in its signs and postures, advances and retreats, that, as he expressed it to me, marveling, "Your people communicating do not switch from 'human' to 'horse' but speak and breathe in 'horse' the whole of their lives."

I approved this. Horses offer love without condition and must be given it in the same terms. They are curious, I instructed Damon, and easily bored; they enjoy adventure and human companionship and are never happier than when learning something new.

"Among tal Kyrte is a type of horse you will find nowhere else, what we call *kal ehal*, 'volunteer,' a wild horse come in to us on its own. This friend"—I indicated my sorrel, Daybreak—"appeared like that. Out of the sun, walking straight up to me."

On the steppe the passage of any herd or cavalcade attracts great flocks of prairie hens, as the tread of the beasts stirs up the insects upon which the birds feed. This produced great sport among the army, as the high-spirited novices love to give them chase. It goes like this. As the girls drive the flocks into the air by their rush on horseback, one or two birds fail of flight, incapacitated by a broken wing or other infirmity. These turf-skimmers become the prize; after them the troop gallops.

One of Eleuthera's novices, and mate of my second trikona, was a maid of twelve, Aella, Little Whirlwind, granddaughter of the legendary Aella who was first to take on Heracles one-on-one, who had raced into the Gathering with the report of Borges' attack. This young champion at once flew to the fore. Across the field the feathered prey scooted with dizzying speed, while the girls, first twenty in number, then twice that, gave chase, hanging off their ponies' flanks seeking to snatch the hen as it flew. How smartly these birds changed direction! Rider after rider nearly spilled in her pursuit, yet so lithe was each maid that she had remounted, it seemed, before her feet even touched the earth. The girls trailed a dragline from their horses' necks for just this purpose, so that even in the moment of their tumble they were already hauling themselves back aboard. To further color this entertainment, the plain was pocked with dens of the steppe marmot, not only a terrific hazard for the horses but an avenue of escape for the birds. Into one such burrow our gallant hen dived. Too late! The lass Aella snatched her up, a hair's-breadth shy of the getaway.

Across the field the conqueror cantered, holding her prize aloft, while the column acclaimed her along its length, even the rivals she had bested. At the fore Aella drew up, plucking a feather for her own hair and one for her horse's mane, then, dedicating her hen to earth, sky, and the four corners, offered this prayer:

"God gave you to me, nimblest of birds; now I give you back to Him. In requital for the gift of your life I pledge to send a man's soul to hell, for you to feed upon."

With that she slit the victim's throat, gulping the blood as it spilled down her breast and belly. Her reward was assignment, with the older girls, as forerider, to relieve those ahead in tracking the foe.

I turned to Damon as the column resumed its march. He no longer stood apart from our ways, studying, but had surrendered to them, transfixed in ecstasy.

BOOK FIVE

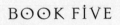

THE WILD
LANDS

16

OUR SEA

Damon's voice resumes:

꙳꙳꙳꙳꙳꙳꙳꙳꙳꙳꙳꙳

The third day ended; the fourth began. The Amazons trekked now, no longer mounted but at the foot trot to spare the horses, which were swapped, jaded for fresh, five times a day. The country had gone from level pan to rugged plateau, cut by great washes and ravines. You could see where these breaks had checked the foe's flight by the boulevards churned in the turf as he drove his herds, hunting a path to get round them. Now the track became stony. The Amazons wrapped their mounts' hooves in ox-hide and packed their kit on their own backs.

To have known women of Athens, my own mother and sisters cloistered within the fold, and then turn to these specimens of the steppe was to behold not different cultures but different species. Do you imagine you can trek with these daughters of the plains? Give it up, my friend. They will run you into the dirt. As for strength, I adduce this incident with the captain Alcippe, Powerful Mare, to whom I had been assigned one noon as liaison. In a stand of sycamore she discovered an infant wren toppled from its perch. Cocooning the fledgling in her right hand, she grasped the bough above with the left and hauled her entire weight one-handed, eye level to the nest. This, with ten pounds of axe and sheath on her back, as well as a fore-and-aft cuirass of leather and bronze. On a bet I called out Selene to a javelin cast. I could not come within thirty feet of her. As to the current trek afoot: I have never suffered as on those two days, and they who were my companions may testify now: Theseus himself must summon every reserve simply to keep up.

At the fourth noon the dust of Borges' rear guard was spotted, twenty miles ahead. At once a hundred took off in pursuit. Amazons run their prey down in relays, with fresh mounts trailed up under the care of their novices. I straggled far to the rear, with my brother and several others, arriving at dusk on our spent horses to find Selene's sister Chryssa and a party of six just scalping two Scyths whose mounts had played out beneath them. To the nations of the steppe the hairs of the head are receptors of divine *aedor*, soul; to take a scalp is to possess the foe's essence—and to prevent it from finding rest in the life to come. To our party Chryssa presented the grisly sheaves. We withdrew, appalled. The women eyed us with incredulity. These fellows, they clearly concluded, are madder than we thought.

We were picking up a feel for Amazon life. The males of the *kabar*, the smiths and mechanics, are granted by their mistresses all freedoms save two: they may not speak in counsel and may not ride. They are permitted mules and asses for their waggons but may not learn horsemanship. This is for warrioresses alone.

Like their horses, Amazons take no bread. Wine too they will not touch. Meat and mare's milk, from the teat when they are children, in the fermented form of *yourte* when they are grown, comprise their diet, with goat's milk and cheese, honey, berries, and the marrow of reeds. When depleted, they tap their herds' veins and gulp the blood, patching the incision as insouciantly as a tailor mends a tunic. They gnaw clay and chalk, and think nothing of devouring an antelope or aurochs, bones and all.

The depth of their intimacy with their horses may not be overstated. Each beast is known to each woman, across herds of a thousand, and each knows his station within the string and the band. Primary mounts lord it over lesser, while night horses hold themselves apart, haughty as barons.

Amazons of different ages take differently to the horses, the elders with matter-of-fact ease, warriors with proprietary dash, young girls deliriously in love. Not all the gold of Babylon may detach these maidens from their mounts, and this love is returned thrice over. On the trek the girls seem more like horses than people. Their language is sign and posture; they communicate by whistles and squeals, indistinguishable to Greek ears from the sounds made by the horses themselves. The concept of "breaking" a horse is inconceivable in such an environment, as the animals seek the society of the girls out of love alone and may not be parted from them by fire or flood.

On the army trekked. The Wild Lands, one came to understand, were to our patronesses not featureless wastes but peopled across every league with gods and ghosts. Descending to a course unexceptional to civilized eyes, the brigade breaks into a hymn. I query Selene. There, she points to a depression, Mother Horse first struck the earth with her hoof, bringing forth water. Farther on, we mount a plateau pocked with chunks of black pumice. Here the bolts of Zeus drove the race of Cronos under. The corps puts up "Fall of the Titans":

Now the hour of their passing.
Younger wait to take their place.
Even they weep who have them vanquished,
Never more to see their face.

On the trail Greeks and Amazons share scant intercourse; at night they pitch their camps apart. At that season the heat of the steppe is fierce, but plummets with darkness. Nights are frigid. The Amazons sleep with their kind, by pairs and trios, under the ground-hugging elk-hide shelters called "downwinders," pillowed on the wolfskins and fleeces which make triple duty as saddle cloths and blankets.

Of all Greeks and Amazons, beyond myself and Selene, only two took pains to acquire knowledge of the other's tongue. These were Theseus and Antiope. I saw them converse directly no more than twice a day, governed by a self-imposed reserve, but each independently sought out those like Selene who had proficiency in both tongues. My brother and I were present in the Athenian camp, the third night, when Theseus and Prince Lykos got into a row on this account.

The company had settled about fires of bricks. Theseus was observing that the Amazon word for acorn is "nut small hand," as the oak leaf to their eyes seems to have five fingers. Our king was charmed by this simplicity, remarking it direct and pure.

"Rubbish!" declared Lykos. He proclaimed the Amazon language the tongue of savages, "the speech beasts would make if they could."

"Exactly!" replied Theseus with animation. "The Amazons tread lightly with language, not to rob a thing of its spirit by the magic of giving it a name."

Around the fire, looks were exchanged. "Indeed the woman is beautiful," observed Philippus with a laugh.

"The charm of these bitches lies between their legs," Lykos declared, "the same as with all women, and we are drawn to them for this and no more, the same as all men."

Theseus regarded his countryman with patience. "I asked the maid Selene what her people meant when they said they 'dream.' She indicated the steppe, which she called *aral nata*, 'Our Sea.' I could see she meant not plain and sky alone, though these comprised the physical expression of the term, but rather an inner plain and sky, save that to her, I believe, inner and outer were indivisible. 'All that we do and speak arises from this sea. We listen to its voice. This is dreaming.' "

"This is twaddle!" snorted Lykos.

Theseus: "Have you seen them stand beneath the sky, these women, the way horses do, motionless for hours? Is it not a marvel?"

"They are dumb as stumps," declared Lykos, "and stand so."

"Two will stand," Theseus continued, "wordless and motionless, neither touching nor regarding the other, yet clearly yoked. Now a third approaches. She greets neither, simply assumes station, beside her sisters yet apart. The first two have taken no notice, it would seem, yet clearly they welcome the third. All simply stand, as they are."

"They are daft!"

"They are 'dreaming.' "

"Mackerel may dream, my lord."

"Yes, and leviathans. They swim in this sea, these braves, and wish to be plucked from it no more than a cetacean seeks to be beached upon dry land."

"And what is this sea, Theseus, but the sea of ignorance? The ocean of barbarism and benightedness. They are a race of savages, however shapely their hips. It sits not well upon a king of Athens, my lord, to yield to such sentimentality. The language of Greece is mankind's glory! It has raised us from the slough, and its reflection, reason, has elevated us above the base and the bestial. What would you have us do, Theseus? Lie down in this sea of 'dreaming' as a hog in a wallow? If you want to have your way with this wench, take her! Pack her home as your bride, for all I care. But spare us the humbug, if you please!"

All this was reported to Antiope, one may be sure. Little took place that she didn't know of. Did it cause her distress? I chanced to approach Selene that morning as she groomed her mount; I failed to notice Antiope, standing on the further side. From the queen's lips I heard, "Are we savages, Selene?"

Antiope saw me now. I flushed and stammered an apology. She did not curb her query.

"Are we savages, Greek, as your captain, Lykos, contends? Is Selene? Am I?"

That morning male riders joined the column from the north, Caucasians from the mountains on the track to the Gate of Storms. They brought reports that Borges' men had taken another herd and butchered the lasses defending it. The Scyths, the new arrivals told, had scalped a number, and taken the heads of most. They would make drinking cups of the skulls and pend them as trophies from their war belts.

All lightheartedness now fled the column. The pace redoubled. Warriors began to paint themselves and their horses. Now the names changed of every weapon and item of kit. They became war names. This was new to me. That battle-axe called a *pelekus* was now named *arapata,* "soul slayer"; horses became "eagles," shields "walls." Each item became personified. One observed Amazons addressing lances and ironheads aloud, as if these possessed reason and the capacity to respond. Each arrow had become a living thing; the warrioresses made compacts with them, beseeching their favor, and sacrificed strips of skin and lines scored in their own flesh.

An Amazon referred to herself now in the third person. Selene had become *Mela,* "Black," and painted her face, breasts, and shoulders with a substance made from elk grease, chalk, and charcoal. If you addressed her as Selene, she did not hear, nor could you call her "Black" in the first person, but must put it in the third: "Will Black answer a question?" "Is Black hungry?" Speech, of which the Amazons had never been prodigal, was now cut near to nothing. The women conversed by signs, and these curt and warlike.

Among our Athenians, numbers began to ape the women, binding their curls in aboriginal fashion, even scarifying their flesh. It became necessary for Theseus to forbid such barbaric practice and, when several defied him, to make examples of them.

Late on the fourth day, the corps came upon paunch fires of horseflesh. The foe no longer hunted but butchered the beasts he drove. He knew fear and stepped up his pace. Amazon foreriders shot ahead, no longer in twos and threes but platoons, and not novices but grown warriors.

Elias and I rode ahead too, with Philippus and others under Prince Peteos. We pressed on till dark, alternately trotting afoot and riding. We had long since lost sight of the Amazon foreriders. Our mounts were worn to a nub; they must rest and be watered. We came upon a dry wash and scooped sand till the muddy wallow showed.

From the rear came a lass of the Amazons. She reined at a distance, uncertain if we were enemy. We waved and shouted in Greek. From her throat ascended a cry of woe. She elevated her lance, pointing north as to some theater of horror, then wheeled and spurred in that direction.

With the dawn our horses could travel. We followed the girl's trail. Our party was still ahead of the main body; their dust could be seen eight or nine miles to the rear. The lass's prints led over a rise. We crested it to a bend in a dry course, backed against chalk bluffs. Such a scene spread before our vision as to brand itself in recall, unspeakable and ineradicable.

At first it seemed only that a great fire had scourged the basin, as if burned-down cookfires had been abandoned, pocking the earth. Then one realized that each pit had been a person. Each had been a young girl.

We dismounted, at no officer's order but impelled by horror. On foot the doughtiest advanced. One sought to look away, yet the ghastliness compelled him. Beneath the bluffs, horses had been slaughtered, disemboweled and decapitated. These were arranged in a ring, fifty-seven in all, when they were counted later. Before each were the incinerated flesh and bones of a girl. Every one had been beheaded. In the center, crucified upside down upon two crossed timbers, hung the corpse of a lass. Her skull too had been taken. Such desecrations of person as bear no profit to recount had been perpetrated upon her flesh, as no doubt they had before their immolation, on that of all the others.

This was Aella, Little Whirlwind, trikona-mate of Eleuthera and Selene, the courier who had made a prize of the prairie hen.

The girls' bones had been pounded into the chalk by the hooves of their murderers' horses, then the mass spaded up and heaped in piles, the remains of each confounded with all others. The arena entire was scored with foot strikes and slathered with evil-looking signs and symbols.

The corps of Amazonia arrived not long after. As in all columns the forward elements appeared first, then the main body, company by company. Each time the same drama was enacted. The warriors broke into a wailing. Grief overwhelmed them. They did not know what to do. In anguish braves sliced off pieces of their ears and incised gashes in their legs; others seized sharp stones and beat their flesh or scooped ashes and heaped them upon their heads and shoulders. Numbers ran off into the washes, where they simply spun in wild woe, while yet more writhed upon the earth or beat their elbows and knees into the stony bluffs. I saw one warrioress race up a face and fling herself down. The plunge must have been forty feet; across its fall, rocks flayed her flesh; again and again she performed this flagellation, uttering such cries as even to hear became unendurable.

With each increment of daylight receding, fresh companies arrived and made discovery of the holocaust; these too broke down, appending their ululations to the general dirge. Some drove arrow points through the flesh of their palms; others scored their scalps with knives; the blood of grief matted their hair and sheeted down their brows. They carved their horses as well, lancing the flesh and cropping manes and tails. Throughout, such a plaint of lamentation arose as may not be described. Across the scene warriors by hundreds writhed in affliction, their flesh painted with their own blood, onto which the chalky dust of the site adhered, rendering them, as darkness descended, wraiths of horror. At one juncture I came upon Selene, blood-masked beneath lacerations of her scalp. In her eyes I saw no person or even a beast but a force of nature, as impervious to reason as fire.

At dark Eleuthera appeared. Aella had been her novice, junior of her third trikona. As Eleuthera rode in, others of the corps made to take the corpse down. At once they broke off. Eleuthera advanced to the gibbet and reined in at its side. There she remained all night.

It was explained to us later that the Scyths had offered such outrage to the persons of these girls as to take not just their hair and heads, that the souls might not enter the life beyond, but had confounded the bones of their corpses so that their shades might not even be reconstituted in the afterlife but must exist, sundered and particularized, in some unspeakable netherworld of despair.

All night the requiem kept up. The most extravagant of Greek rituals were as nothing beside it. Its excess was appalling. I could not endure it. I found my brother and Philippus. We rode onto the plain, until the pitch of the mourning and its exorbitance abated enough to be borne.

Another rider could be seen, solitary beneath the moon.

This was Theseus.

He recognized us and motioned us to him. We drew rein alongside. "They are invoking Hate," he said.

At first I did not understand. Then, turning toward the precinct of grief, I apprehended an alteration in its tenor. The Amazons summoned Hecate now, and Nemesis and Aidos, Daughters of Night, and Artemis Void of Mercy. We could hear the "elelele" they put up. Their prayers ascended to gods and goddesses unknown, to Phrygian Cybele, Great Mother, Womb of Creation; to Demeter and to Black Persephone, Mistress of Hell. As these wails ascended, a correspondent anthem broke from the wilderness beyond: wolves in their packs, bloodcurdling and primordial.

"What do you think of this, brothers?" the lord of Athens inquired in a voice dry as the chalk of the plain. We turned toward him. Theseus' features appeared gray beneath the moon and animated by such a cast of woe as I have never conjured before or since. He elevated his crop, gesturing back toward the theater of blood.

"Here is how one lived," Theseus observed, "a thousand centuries gone."

17

MASSACRE AT THE
PARCHED HILLS

The Tanais is a great river, the boundary between Europe and Asia. Its breadth at the nearest ford, the one Borges and the Scyths must flee to, is six hundred yards. Here the Amazons would fall upon their enemy. Here they would exact their vengeance. The sequence of events went like this:

Two hours before dawn the corpse of the child Aella was taken down from its scaffold and burned. The bones were painted with ochre and swathed in the wolf-skin pallet that had bound Eleuthera's war bundle, that kit of tokens and amulets which constitutes a warrior's holiest and most potent possession, and laid out upon a stand of chalk elevated calf-high above the plain. Fifty-seven such biers had been erected, one for the ashes of each maid, as best as such could be determined. Atop each packet an axe of battle had been laid. Around the ring, horses and riders formed up, painted death colors. One Amazon stood at the head of each pyre, enacting the office of priestess. All affect had been drained from the corps by the nightlong riot, replaced by such resolution as transcended hunger and exhaustion. That fearsome emotion that animates the female in all-female groups (called *outere* in Amazon and *gynekophoitos* in Greek) could be felt now, palpable as the predawn chill. Before each crypt a platoon of warrioresses advanced, single file, and drew rein. As each rider came up, the priestess elevated the axe, whetted to a razor's keenness, and split the tip of her mounted comrade's tongue. This was the Invocation of Ares, the "iron rite" that few males had ever witnessed, by which each warrioress tastes the salt of her own death, so that no enemy may claim he drew first blood.

> *Blood to iron,*
> *Iron to blood.*

Two further scorings were incised upon each cheek, while the corps chanted a hymn of such antiquity, Selene later confirmed for me, that not even she understood the whole. The bundles of burned bones were rolled within their wolf-skin packs and stowed in the waggons of the auxiliary. The priestesses mounted, joining the company. The brigade ascended from the wash and formed up on line, awaiting the sun.

Now the first scouts returned. They reported an axle-split waggon of the Scyths fifteen miles on, abandoned where it had broken down. This was sign that the foe was in full flight. More foreriders appeared. Dust had been sighted ten miles beyond the junked waggon, fifteen from the Tanais. The war council convened, from which all Athenians were excluded save Theseus and Lykos. If orders were passed, I never heard them. I fell in beside Selene, and, as no one made move to repulse me, stayed.

The sun is to the Amazons what the Muses are to the Greeks. He who sees all and recalls all. In silence each warrioress now prayed to Him, that He witness her valor on this day and remember it for the free people for all time. The instant the first beam cut the skyline, the brigade broke into that yip-yip ululation that makes the hair stand up all over a man's body. Selene shot forward beside me. A thousand yards across, the line whooped and catapulted into motion. I spurred my mount and hung on for dear life.

When Amazons advance in force anticipating battle, they employ the trikonai, the bands of three, in the following fashion: the foremost companies, those first to set out, are constituted of the eldest of the third triple, riding her secondary warhorse while trailing her primary and advancing at the best speed she can make without jading the mounts. The elder novices comprise the succeeding element, each on her own horse leading the main of her champion's string at a modified pace. Last to kick off are the most junior, trailing the remainder at a yet more abated gait.

The Tanais was forty miles ahead, a day's ride across that broken country. The Amazons aimed to cross it in a morning. The corps made speed into the ascending sun, at such a hard canter as had the snot sluicing from my nostrils like water. On the steppe one never pisses; every drop you drink passes out in sweat and spit.

By midmorning the brigade had passed the abandoned Scythian waggon and covered six or seven miles beyond. Here was a cold stream; a halt was ordered, as even the primary battle mounts, carrying nothing, had gone fagged. We would never overtake Borges by midday. The second string caught up; the corps got fresh (or fresher) horses under them. The line kicked off again.

Noon came. The river was within ten miles. We could see Borges' dust clearly now. The line of advance broke into columns as each rider dodged rises and breaks, seeking the smartest path. Amazon captains transited, holding the eager bucks from the canter. I stuck with Selene and a platoon of about thirty. The steppe was dry grassland, chest-high on the horses. Suddenly a brave galloped across the front, calling out a word I did not recognize and pointing with her lance into the postnoon wind toward the clouds of dust raised by Borges and the herds seven or eight miles ahead.

At once alarmed cries pealed down the front. Amazons stood on their horses' backs, full height at the trot, squinting ahead. Whatever her comrades had seen, Selene saw it too. She whistled rearward to alert the novices. "What has happened?" I called.

"Follow me!" Selene cried and laid the quirt to Daybreak with more violence than I had ever seen. I turned back to the front.

Flames.

Borges had set the dry grass afire.

The Amazons thundered north, perpendicular to the line of pursuit. I called to Selene, declaring the corps' agitation excessive. I was congratulating myself on my cool head. Then I looked back.

The fire's front, which had been a smudge ten heartbeats earlier, had doubled in breadth and vaulted a mile closer. I turned for Selene; she was half a furlong gone. When I looked again the blaze had redoubled.

A tributary of the Tanais twined back, six or seven miles north. This was what Selene and her mates were running for. Fresh horses might have made it. Mounting out of a wash, my Knothole buckled into the clayey face; he keeled so slowly I was able to step off, as from a boat to a dock. The conflagration roared behind. You could smell it now and hear it.

Other mounts had played out beneath their riders; now their comrades came back for them. I saw Hippolyta, at past sixty more vigorous than the bucks. To my astonishment Selene wheeled in above me. She had come back for me.

A mile east the fire had got ahead of us. We were cut off. With five or six others, Selene and I plunged into a wash. Half a foot of water stood in a silty pool. The captain Alcippe, Powerful Mare, ordered all to dig in, which we did with fingers, knees, and toes, burrowing furiously into the bank, that the blaze might pass over. The Amazons had got their mounts prone, laying their bodies across the horses' necks to hold them down. With both hands the women slathered muck on themselves and their animals. Cloaks and buckskins they tarred with mud, to mantle their own heads and those of their mounts.

The fireball passed over like this. First came a wind, not from the direction of the blaze but opposite. It was not hot but cool. This was air at ground level being drafted into the fire by its greed for combustion. In moments this mounted to a gale. Selene and I had our breasts pressed together, with sludged buckskins over our heads and a pocket of muddy air between. "Do what I do!" she shouted. She meant breathe through the buckskin, to keep out the fire. The wind built to a pitch, scouring plain and wash, then cut abruptly. The lull lasted moments; then the gale resumed, roaring skyward. One felt his breath sucked out as by a blacksmith's bellows. Our cowls went dry in instants, then heated like parchment to ignition. From our foxhole I peered back to the pool of the wash; in moments the earth was seared to ceramic.

The heat hit. Sound vanished. One entered a vortex. To say one held his breath would be fantastic. Nothing could hold. Your guts down to your asshole were sucked up and out, and when you gasped for air, flame flooded in instead. Selene clung to me. We were lifted bodily with the horses beneath us. The gale dashed us like dolls. I came to myself amid a cyclone of soot. Something was whipping me. It was Selene, tearing at my cloak. This was afire. She slung it to the earth, every yard of which was charred and smoking. I heard Alcippe's voice crying, "Rise!" Somehow we did.

The fireball had passed; through eyes gummed to slits we could see its hinter wall sweeping northward. In its wake soot tornadoes churned; before our feet spread a wasteland of ash and smoke; we clutched at each other, just to know we were still alive, and spread our stances to keep from being bowled over in the aftergales. The horses rose and the company hauled them by their draglines up onto the flat in the direction from which the conflagration had come. Every inch of dirt was sizzling. One trod as on a griddle. My footgear was ox-hide, thick as a thumb; the heat scorched through as if it were tissue. The Amazons peeled the hide of their leggings to make boots for their horses. As far as sight could carry, the plain smoked like an anvil. We had to get off. The heat drove us.

The captain Alcippe commanded. We must learn the fate of the main body, she declared, those that had gotten away toward the tributary. Two riders were dispatched to report our condition and find us again with orders. Meanwhile our party would make all speed toward the Tanais and the foe.

Cries came from the soup. Hippolyta's band materialized, charred to a crisp but still eager for action; our troop fell in with them. Across the cinderland this outfit trudged, perhaps forty in all, men, girls, older warriors. The sun could not be seen, so dense was the canopy of smoke and ash, not even a glimmer to get one's bearings by. But the horses knew. They knew where the water was. I glanced at Selene and her comrades; without a word all were roused to exploit the smokescreen, to close on the foe from the quarter he could least anticipate. I set one sole before the other, purblind and suffocating. A mile passed. Two. From the smoke arose a waggon of the Scyths. An arm of the fire must have turned back on it. The rig was charcoal, including its women and children. Nothing remained of the oxen but the cages of their ribs and their skulls with the great horns, pitched forward onto the earth.

We heard a whistle; more riders broke from the murk to the west. Amazons coming up from the rear. Within minutes three companies had materialized, reinforcements who had set out from the Mound City a day after the main body and whipped their mounts to a lather when they saw the smoke. These were tribes of the White Mountains, under the war leaders Adrasteia, "Inescapable"; Enyo, "Warlike"; and Deino, "Terrible," who had arrived tardy at the Gathering on account of an oracle. The novices of our own brigade followed as well. Fresh horses. In moments our party had enlarged from two score to two thousand, superbly mounted and armed to the eyeballs. The reinforcing companies had discovered the scene of slaughter at the bluffs. Every woman's blood was up. They were painted and ravenous for revenge.

Meanwhile the main body of the Amazons, the companies who had bolted north fleeing the fire, had managed to escape by means of an upper fork. They had crossed this, raced east, and swum the Tanais at a deep ford north of the one Borges was fleeing for. In other words, they had gotten ahead of him, though still a distance to his north. They were laboring south right now, on the opposite bank of the Tanais, driving themselves and their exhausted horses to beat Borges to the ford. Their numbers including novices were eight hundred, all mounted archers.

Borges didn't know this. Neither did the brigade I trekked with. Our leaders broke into the open a mile or so west of the river, thinking we were the only ones left alive. Ahead Borges and his Scyths drove the herds into the ford. The total must have made four thousand head, with a quarter already in the crossing. We could see the Scyths' whips and the flash of their "flies" in the sun.

The Amazons under Hippolyta, Alcippe, Adrasteia, Enyo, and Deino deployed into a thousand-yard front. The elder spurred to the fore on her big grey, Frostbite, her leopard-skin shield somehow intact through the conflagration, with her iron-colored plait falling down her back. From its sheath she snatched the *labrys*, the double axe sacred to Zeus, Hurler of the Thunderbolt. Hippolyta elevated the weapon before her, blade and spike extending toward Borges' Scyths, the river, and the horses.

"Sisters! Take back what is yours!"

I had never witnessed a charge of massed cavalry before, and certainly not one constituted of riders of such prowess, mounted on such stock. The Scyths themselves were magnificent specimens, warriors whose command of the steppe stood unchallenged across a thousand leagues. Yet these bolted in flight before the Amazons had closed within half a mile. My position was near the fore, trailing the captain Alcippe, who advanced, as the entire corps, at a hard canter. The Amazons, responding to no command I could detect, formed on the fly into that front that comprises the famous "crescent charge." One felt the *outere*, the wildness of females in all-female groups, crackle between them like heat lightning. At this stage they still held their mounts in check, conserving them for the final burst.

Here came Selene alongside me. "Keep from the foe!" she commanded, indicating the mass of the Scyths now plunging into the ford. "These are not for you." I could see her scalping knife strapped to her thigh. Her pony lengthened stride; in an instant she had shot clear. A tide of hooves and hindquarters surged in her train. I strained to glimpse the Scyths. This was impossible for the clouds raised by the Amazon horses' passage, not to say the hoof-slewed clods and divots which beat about me in such density that I had to seat my face like a jockey into my animal's flying mane, and even then the broadside nearly bowled me from my seat. The corps of Amazonia thundered ahead. I have never heard a sound of such power or felt the earth shudder with such violence. And above all, that war cry which turns men's bowels to liquid.

You could see the river now, the actual crossing, which had been obscured from the plain by lines of alder and sycamore. It seemed leagues across. There was an islet at midchannel; in its shallows, horses in the hundreds milled, abandoned by their drovers. The Scyths had hauled their waggons over first, to preserve the women and children; the van of these could be seen laboring up the far bank. The main of the horsemen, above seven hundred, surged into the jam at midchannel, parting the milling herd with whips and rods and the flats of their great iron slashing swords. On the near shore, stranded parties of the foe rallied into a defensive front. They were overturning their waggons to form a palisade. They slew the oxen right in the traces, hacking their necks through, to add the beasts' bulk to the rampart.

Now the Amazons shot to the gallop. Across the front one saw rider after rider release her reins, clamping only the slack ends in her teeth while she filled her left fist with the great horn-and-ash bow, containing as well three secondary arrows, fletched ends skyward; from the belt-mounted quiver drew that foremost shaft, whose warhead she had honed to razor keenness and whose death-seeking flight she had dedicated to Ares, Hecate Dark Moon, and Artemis Void of Mercy. Far ahead I glimpsed Selene and the captain Alcippe. At Hippolyta's side they plunged among the foe. When I reached the site nothing remained but mounds of flesh and armor and Amazons straddling them, slicing scalps. The river frothed with Borges' corps in flight.

In the accounts which have been circulated of this battle, and the songs by which it has been made known, the substance is that the Scyths were overhauled and massacred at midriver. This is not how it happened. The slaughter took place beneath the cut banks of the far shore, where the foe in his hundreds sought to mount the bluffs into the teeth of the Amazon blocking force. The women had got ahead of them. The companies commanded by Antiope, Eleuthera, Skyleia, and Stratonike, those which had swum the Tanais via the upper ford, now made their appearance, thundering into position atop the river bluffs. I was at midchannel, my poor Knothole having played out utterly, where I drew up into the shallows of the islet. Here is what I saw:

Across two fifths of a mile of bluff, the warrioresses of Amazonia massed on horseback and afoot, blocking Borges' flight. The Scyths bunched up in the eddies below. From above, the Amazons loosed volleys of shafts and darts, point-blank and by hundreds. The enemy returned fire with bows and lances, maces and pikes and slung axes. They fought with whips and bare hands. At some sites the cut banks held the foe ten and fifteen feet below the Amazons. Here they were being slaughtered like fish. At others, where the bluff stood less sheer, companies of the Scyths sought to mount and duel face-to-face. The broadsides of the women beat them back. Steed after steed of the Scyths upended and foundered, pitching rearward upon their mates.

Now Hippolyta's two thousand closed on the foe from the rear. Breast-deep in the channel, this corps rained iron on Borges' eleven hundred trapped beneath the banks, while from above Antiope's battalions slung shafts and bolts without letup. Missile after missile beat upon the Scythian cohorts. Above the cries of men and horses, one could hear the thwocking concussion of shaft piercing flesh and the metallic ping as warheads caromed off armor and shield. One saw men shot five, ten, fifteen times; their chests, arms, and legs bristled with shafts, yet still they struggled.

Into this melee the daughters of tal Kyrte plunged, driven by *outere* and *lyssa*. Not content to offer slaughter at a remove, they dismounted and pressed upon the foe hand to hand, with axe and saber, spear and thrusting sword, fashioning a front that extended, helmet to helmet, shield to shield, across nearly half a mile. The whole thing looked like some colossal frieze of marble: the twined forms of horses, women, and men, pressed so proximately upon one another that the observer could not tell where one warrior's limbs left off and another's began; individuals conjoined into one seamless mass, depicting by their postures every aspect of strife imaginable. Nowhere on the field could cowardice be descried, but both sides, dying and dealing death, contended with fathomless valor. I saw Theseus, blood-slathered, and Antiope and Eleuthera, insatiate of slaughter, as the poets say. Both women scoured the field for Borges, seeking the trophy of his head. It seemed none of the foe could escape the pound into which he had been driven. But the river had been in spate only days before, it turned out, such that a fresh channel had been gouged downcourse, where the banks were not so steep, and in the initial scrimmage a number of the enemy had gotten clear, with their women and children, into the ravine country on the far bank known as the Parched Hills. Borges apparently was among them.

I got across. Theseus was calling for cessation. I looked to the warrioresses of Amazonia. These resided in such a state as I had never seen beings of human kind. Led by Antiope and Eleuthera they wheeled, seeking Borges' fleeing waggons. The Amazons were after the skulls of their daughters, which the Scyths had taken as trophies to ring the barrow they would raise over the corpse of their prince Arsaces.

There is a trace between cliffs, there at the Parched Hills, along which, I was told later, the sheep and goat traders trek their flocks in season. On this track the Amazons overtook their quarry. The women's numbers were three thousand; the surviving Scyths a tenth of that. The warrioresses fell on the column as it bunched up entering a defile. They slaughtered the rear guard of male defenders, who stood with spectacular valor, then overran the body of the column as it massed in terror midway through the strait.

Borges had fled, marooning his dependents. The Amazons ran these down on horseback, slaying men, boys, and women indiscriminately, taking scalps or simply decapitating all who fell within their grasp. Theseus and the Athenians reined-in amid the carnage, requiring no injunction to contain their fury, so appalled were they by the extravagance of the slaughter, while the Amazons, at first in blood madness, then coolly, unhurriedly hunted down the last living thing. They butchered every beast of the foe, even his draft mules and pack animals, hacking their necks through with the *pelekus*, so that the blood pocked the earth in pools and the parched dirt drank it.

I saw Amazons, gore-mantled and so exhausted they could no longer ride or even lift the axe, yet staggering among the baggage train, dragging forth children and even infants, which they stuck like pigs, disemboweling even the girls and bathing in their blood. But what horrified one most was the mien of these maids as they enacted their evisceration. They were cheerful. No other term may tell it. One was stricken mute at their capacity for horror.

At the junction of two ravines was a sinkhole. Across this, some half dozen of Antiope's cohort had strung the hide cover of a Scythian waggon, four-cornered, so that the midpoint, pending of its own weight, formed a sort of tub or vat. Above this a rude gibbet had been erected. Upon it, women and children of the foe were being strung up and gutted. Their blood spilled in great sluicing gushes, like hogs meathooked in a farmyard, while the yet-living victims cried to their gods and bawled for mercy. When I came upon this, the pool stood calf-deep.

The Amazons had found the skulls of their children among the baggage train. Within the bath of blood they laved now the bones of their daughters. This was the justice they had come for. As I looked on from atop my mount, too horror-stricken to turn away, a youth of the Scyths burst from hiding and fled toward me, crying for clemency; before I could bend, he was snatched apart and scalped, so swiftly I thought his head had been pared off, by a silent black-maned warrioress who then hauled him to the bath of blood to be drained of his fluids.

Everything was red. Not a stone of the ravine, it seemed, had escaped its slathering. Even the canyon walls were painted with the prints of hands and the sole marks of those butchered while attempting to flee. At the center of this theater stood Antiope, an axe in one hand, the severed head of a Scyth in the other. Blood painted both her legs to the hip; fluids dripped from the blades of her pelekus; her hair and even her teeth showed black with clotted gore.

Straight to her face advanced the Athenian Lykos, and it must be said that it took no slender spirit for him to do so, such was the light of slaughter in the Amazon's eyes.

"What do you call this, thou savage!" The prince gestured to the broth irrigating the walls and floors of the canyon. "Are these 'God's footsteps'? Is this the 'path of holiness' in which your race treads?"

Theseus hastened forward, reining-in at his countryman's shoulder.

"This is not war," Lykos bellowed to Antiope. "It is butchery!"

Theseus sought to speak, as if to offer extenuation for the actions of the Amazons. Lykos cut him off with a curse. "You cannot defend the indefensible!"

The prince spurred off, leaving Antiope and Theseus alone at the epicenter of the massacre. The Amazon met Theseus' eye. Such horror stood graven upon his features at this spectacle of barbarity that she, perceiving, came to herself, surfacing, it seemed, from that primordial state into which her warrior's heart had descended. In Theseus' aspect she read this indictment: "Savages."

Behind Antiope, a paean broke from the corps of Amazonia.

Now it is done, now it is done
Look, all, and behold it
Now it is done.

The Amazons bayed now, a cry which was not the hymning of humankind but the howling of beasts. Antiope peered at her sisters and beheld herself in their reflection. Her stricken glance returned to Theseus. The Amazon sought, it was clear, to summon some defense or grounds of extenuation; to make appeal to him, by sign or idiom, that his verdict was excessive. No speech came. Only, from behind and in compass of her, that ungodly wail.

Night had descended and with him his daughters, Hecate of the Dark Moon; Nemesis, "Righteous Retribution"; and Aidos, "Shame," to whom the Amazons shrilled as wolves. Theseus read in Antiope's aspect the grief of this awareness. He sought, one could see, not to impose judgment but to exonerate her heart, absolve it somehow, out of his love, not so much for her as a woman, though this was abundant, but as a fellow regent, lord of a people, who so vividly desired that events had transpired otherwise, yet who knew, as Antiope did, that as commander she alone bore responsibility.

At this moment, as Amazon and Athenian stood across from one another, monarch to monarch, a cry broke from beneath a waggon, where, somehow undetected, a girl-child of the Scyths had survived. From this covert the maid dashed like a hare, seeking a slope too steep for mount and rider to scale in pursuit. The lass did not know the Amazon horse. Three warriors flew in her train, running her down in moments. The first snatched the child at a dead run and, up-ending her bodily with a cry of joy that ascended alongside the wailing of the dirge, cleaved the babe's skull with her axe.

BOOK SIX

THE RAPE OF
ANTIOPE

18

THE OVERTHROW
OF ANTIOPE

Selene's testament:

◉◈◈◈◈◈◈◈◈◈◉

It is common belief that Eleuthera came to be called Molpadia, "Death Song," subsequent to the siege at Athens. This is not true. It was the Scyths who gave her this name following the massacre at the Parched Hills. It came about like this:

In the immediate aftermath the victors galloped back to the Tanais, where the corpses of the main force of the foe, those who had been slain in the river fight, lay tangled by hundreds in the shallows.

We wanted their scalps.

I myself may testify to the elation of the hour. Here awaited our prizes, which we had won by the valor of our arms and which we coveted for our glory, each and all, that none be accounted less than her deserts, and, for myself, to display before Damon and claim him as my lover. Only the unconventional nature of the fight, that is, the urgency of breaking off to overhaul those of the foe in flight with the bones of our daughters, had conspired to swindle us of the moment for proper prize-taking. It was time to make this up. In a body the corps swept back to the river.

Among the tribes of the plains dread of water eclipses all other terrors, and in this aversion no nation exceeds the Scyths: they abhor lakes and the sea, and will not even bathe, fearing that the liquid conducts apart their *aedor,* their soul. To perish in a river as these foe had, and then lose their scalps, as we intended, was desecration upon desecration. Tal Kyrte burned to inflict this.

But at the bluffs Antiope hauled the corps up. She held the battalions at the brink, and there ranged horseback before the line, exhorting her countrywomen to turn apart and leave the bodies undespoiled. "Enough!" she cried. "We have exacted vengeance sufficient!"

Outrage greeted this. Indignation howled along the line. Why should we not claim these prizes, which Ares Manslayer has granted us? Heaven has exalted us with this victory! It is sacrilege to spurn God's grant! In fact our intent, merely to carve the hair from these bags of guts, exhibits excessive forbearance, for the Scyths, had they gained the day, would have visited unholy desecration upon our flesh, as they had on that of our maidens.

I was at the left of the line. I could no longer hear Antiope, who ranged now at the center. But her intent was clear from her posture, galloping across the front with her axe of war held horizontally above her head: *Hold back! Do not enter the river!*

From the brigade broke Eleuthera. I was too far away to hear the rebuke she addressed, first to Antiope, then to the squadrons as a whole. I saw her surge forward, breasting Antiope's mount with her own, then bolt past with a cry, down the bank and into the river.

As one the corps followed. I too churned down, the hooves of my pony ploughing furrows in the slope, already ground to muck by the foe in his doom. We fell upon the prizes indiscriminately—for how could one tell which had been hers?—each seizing that number she knew she had won.

Tal Kyrte has a word, *anoxe,* which has no equivalent in Greek. It denotes that overthrow which occurs in a wolfpack when the leader fails to make his kill, or in a pride when a lioness hesitates on the hunt. The monarch's fall is instantaneous and irreversible.

This fate Antiope had now brought upon herself. She had offered outrage against God's primal decree: Clemency may never be proffered to the foe. To do so violates Ehal, holy Nature, in whose lexicon the word quarter finds no citation. Doubly infamous, such an act was *netome*, thing of evil, for clearly its expression was the fruit of our lady's corruption by the Greeks and her consorting with Theseus. In one instant she was finished, and the whole nation knew it.

That night when camp had been made and the brigade had assembled sated with glory, to Eleuthera was awarded the prize of valor. Not only for her deeds in the fight but for her overturning of Antiope's mad summons of leniency for the foe. Two dawns later, when the kinsmen of the Scythians arrived to reclaim the corpses of their fallen and beheld the spectacle that Eleuthera's hate had prepared for them, they out of their bereavement bestowed upon her that title by which she came ever after to be known: Molpadia, "Hymn of Slaughter."

Among warrior nations, supreme honors may never be accorded by one's own people but only by enemies. To receive such a name, and from so warlike a race, catapulted Eleuthera to the firmament. Her perduring state as *anandros*, unpossessed by man, reinforced her stature as an icon of implacability for all foes of the people. Nor was it lost on me, even then, that the elevation of my friend would redound spectacularly to my own prestige. I was drunk with the glory of our triumph. By our might of arms, tal Kyrte had requited the iniquity of our foes and, by bathing the bones of our children in the blood of those who had offered them outrage, had reconstituted their persons for the life beyond.

Further, this slaughter, far from rendering the nation vulnerable to the reprisals of our enemies, though such may come, had—as Eleuthera stated, addressing the corps that first night—buttressed the people and vitiated our rivals of the will to attack. With one blow tal Kyrte had revived her flagging fame, establishing the rising generation as no less than those champions who had gone before, but mightier and more to be feared. This victory will give pause, Eleuthera declared, to all who would presume to test us. And it will work us no harm, even among the Iron Mountain Scyths, whom we have so ravaged, whose fear of us, enlarged by this victory, will render them more tractable to accommodation, should the Council elect to seek it. This is the only peace that lasts, Eleuthera proclaimed before the corps, one fashioned upon a foundation of fear.

As a vessel which overflows, I could not contain my joy, but felt as though all I had ever hoped and dreamed had at one stroke leapt to fruition. I burned to make for the Athenian camp to display my prizes before Damon and to claim his love.

But as I withdrew following the Hymn for the Fallen, a girl intercepted me, named Teardrop, who was cousin to Antiope and novice of her third trikona. In distress the lass imparted this message: I was to come away to Antiope at once, apart on the steppe, informing no one. Further, I was to bring a number of my horses, whom Antiope specified by name. I groaned at this, such is the heartlessness of youth. For I well understood that Antiope's star had fallen; I feared that association with her would work harm to my ambition.

Reluctantly I rode out to the site. Antiope waited alone beneath the moon, dismounted, apart from her horse Sneak Biscuits. I had never seen her in a posture of such impotence. This horse as a colt had been named Thunderclap and acclaimed superlative of all the northern steppe, but he had been an incorrigible thief and nuisance, so much so that the elders had summoned Antiope for discipline. Defending her colt, she had likened him to a camp goat who loves to haunt the cookfire, compelled by his rascal nature to sneak biscuits. The council rewarded this with laughter and decreed that the horse may stay but must give up his proud name and take this silly one. Silly or not, Sneak Biscuits had proved his mettle on a hundred fields.

Now he stood apart from his mistress and would not come at her call. Antiope signed me to approach. I trailed the four mounts she had requested. Her horse, she demonstrated, would not hold at the approach of her step. She signed to me to let her try mine, Daybreak, who was also her friend, and the others I had brought, with whom she was acquainted. None would let her on his back uncompelled, nor heed her commands absent application of the quirt.

Antiope had lost her *hippeia*, her mastery of horses.

Loss of *hippeia* is an omen of surpassing evil. It means heaven has withdrawn its favor, in condemnation of crimes against the people.

Antiope staggered beneath this. She instructed me to return to camp, to communicate to the corps the indictment Mother Horse had pronounced upon her. May Eleuthera, she said, as senior of her High Trikona, succeed her as war queen.

Antiope would enter exile this night, she declared, retiring to the mountains to fast and pray.

Would she return? I asked.

She made no answer.

I watched her ride off, compelling Sneak Biscuits by bit and whip. The sight of horse and rider, who had been for as long as I could remember so leagued as to appear a creature of one flesh, now proceeding estranged and disunited sent dread through my heart of evil to come.

In camp Eleuthera formalized her accession by binding about her the war girdle, which Antiope had given me for her. The Song of the Underworld was offered for Antiope, by which rite the corps absolved itself of culpability, should their deposed queen elect to take her own life.

To my shame I countered nothing. Not a breath did I offer in Antiope's defense, but hailed with all her ouster and excommunication. My blood still ran high with my return to Eleuthera's favor and the anticipation of taking Damon as my lover. I sought him out that night among the Greek camp and showed off my four trophies, pended from my battle staff, expecting him to respond with pleasure and pride. Instead he withdrew, repelled. I was baffled and moved to fury. I insulted him, viciously, then spurred away, hot tears coursing.

The roundup and drive home began. To my consternation, and to that of many others, Damon's reaction, or something like it, was repeated across the company of Athenians. They had gone cold and remote, the Greeks, and regarded with aversion those whom days before they had adored. I witnessed one clash between lovers. Glauke Grey Eyes slung an amulet of ivory in the face of her sweetheart. "You used to show a bull's dick for me, now you're limp as a stalk. What has become of you? You have put on women's skirts!"

I had not reckoned how many of tal Kyrte had taken Greek lovers. Now on the homeward trek these unions came to light, if only by their disintegration. The Athenians had become stricken with that malady all wide-voyaging sailors know: of being too far from home too long. They rued their excesses and yearned for familiar skies. Theseus must embark them soon or they would mutiny.

As for Antiope, it was as if she had never existed. No one asked after her; no one offered remembered tales. On the move, her station at the fore of the column was taken by Eleuthera. In camp our new commander occupied that promontory which had always been reserved for her predecessor. The revolution had been effected without a ripple. So it seemed on the surface. Underneath, however, the people moved unsettled. The nation was not the same without Antiope. Order was awry; a color had gone from the day.

Eleuthera as war queen lacked nothing of martial virtue, and Hippolyta as peace commander was more than wise. Nor did either want for political cunning, particularly Eleuthera, who had already dispatched couriers to the nations of the Massa Getai and Thyssa Getai, the Chalybes and the Copper River Scyths, summoning them to council at the Mound City. Eleuthera had schemes for new alliances, a new war to exploit the victory over Borges and the Iron Mountain clans. Yet the pair lacked some element—Eleuthera for all her valor, Hippolyta for all her sagacity—that Antiope alone brought to the people, and without which the nation stood disfigured and diminished.

Perhaps I alone perceived this. All day trekking home my gaze scoured the mountains, seeking the dust of a lone rider, sign of Antiope returning. Days passed. The train took its time, allowing the herds to graze and regain their strength.

One other accompanied my watch. This was Theseus. Though he never approached me, I remarked him day after day, scanning the northern slopes. Dawns and sunsets he watched, the hours one sees farthest on the steppe. He would ride apart from the column, often three or four miles, there mounting to the loftiest eminence and remaining till dark or, if morning, till the column began to move. I knew his coming had brought evil to the free people, as Eleuthera repeatedly professed, yet I could not but feel pity for him. He loved Antiope. It was plain as that.

On the tenth day he let his mount drift in my direction. He had learned our ways by then. He fell in a distance to my flank and indicated by sign that he wished to approach. By sign I acceded. Theseus had learned not to plunge in impatiently, as a Greek will, but to speak of other matters first. Several times he stood on the point of blurting the inquiry which burned like vinegar on his tongue, yet to his credit he contained his impatience.

"I will take you to her," I offered.

That evening when the herd had been settled, I rolled my kit and mounted. I had sent no word to Theseus, nor even glanced in the direction of the Greek camp. Yet as I departed, at a walk, I could hear his horse, whose gait I recognized, move off, parallel to mine and at a seemly remove.

We rode into the foothills two days. Clearly he burned to interrogate me. Yet again he mastered his tongue. "We seek a col," I told him on the second noon, meaning a natural bowl in the mountains where prayer would be concentrated by the configuration of the rock. "That is where she will be."

It is cold in the mountains at night; I could see he suffered. He must sleep under my cover, I instructed him. It was comical, his abashment. "You have never slept beside a woman?"

He writhed in his slumber. Twice he called Antiope's name and once clamped me so tight I had to elbow him, hard, to shake him awake.

"Antiope believes she has committed some crime against the free people, doesn't she, Selene?" Then: "Will she take her life?"

Theseus rose before dawn, fearful for her and anxious to overhaul her. "If I were to offer my own life," he asked, "would your gods accept that in trade for hers?"

We found Antiope on the fifth morn, as day broke. She descended across a meadow of white poplar, a thousand feet above us. "Do you mark her?" When I turned to see if he had heard, his eyes worked as though stung by the wind, though the air was so still a feather would have dropped to earth like a lump of lead.

I left him then, not staying to salute Antiope. I should have backtracked down the slope, ceding them their privacy, but instead traversed at an angle, mounting even higher. Turning back on a ridge I could see them, woman and man, cross toward one another within the bowl of the meadow.

The man reined and dismounted. The woman came up to him, still on horseback. The man crossed to her side and, standing beneath her, embraced her about the waist, burying his face in the buckskin legging of her hip. Only after some time did the man release the woman and remount. The two tracked down together.

This sight cast me into consternation, for I saw, and credited truly for the first time, that Antiope, bulwark of the people, had lost herself. She was like that space which is neither battle nor advance to battle, but that no-man's-land between. And I the same. For although I knew my duty, which was to gallop to the new commanders and inform them of all I had seen, I could not overrule my passion, which bound me to the same mystery as had bewitched our queen: a man to whom my heart had surrendered.

How I scourged myself for this! I abhorred my spinelessness and stood upon the point, more than once, of taking my own life. What had become of my warrior's constancy? Would the gods rob me too of *hippeia*, exposing the treason of my heart as they had our queen's?

Yet the alternative—never again to speak to, or even catch sight of, this youth I loved—was unendurable to me.

At last at the Mound City I went to Damon by night. Beside the ships, where the Greek camp was made, I called him away and declared the holdings of my heart, weeping at my own deficiency and dreading more than hell his spurning of my affection. We had moved apart to a space adjacent two vessels a-building. The ships stood hull by hull, with a shack of unplaned timber between them to shield the tools from the elements. Into this hideout my lover tugged me and, once within, broke down as I had, reciting his own anguish at his actions at the Parched Hills. Yes, I had scared him, he said, by my *lyssa*, battle rage, and my countrywomen's *outere*, the emotion of women in all-female groups. Yet he had never intended by his retirement to cause me grief. He loved me, he swore, and had from the moment he first saw me. To hear such words, my heart seemed to dissolve as the ice of winter streams when the spring sun brings its warmth. The smell of his skin, the tenderness of his touch . . . he sought to take my maidenhood there, in that barn, but I would not endure it. I made him ride onto the steppe and there consummate our passion, with none to witness but the sky, who was made by God and is God.

Never had I experienced such despair as in the aftercourse of that act. For as a part of me idealized this youth as if he were a young god and held, as a jewel in my palm, all that he would grow to and become, yet at the same time another part saw him for what he was, a boy bursting with the sap of youth and on fire for me, perhaps, only as one in the grip of such fever for any who fell within his frame. And I knew, hearing my heart in his arms, that I would desert the free people for him, yes, even work treason against them, if he so commanded.

I mounted and galloped away. I drove Daybreak till his lather frothed my thighs, fearful at every step that he would revolt from my rule.

Days passed. Antiope and Theseus did not return. I vowed never to speak to Damon again, or even present myself in his sight. Yet each night my tracks returned to our bower on the steppe. I could bear this loss of self-sovereignty now, I told myself, when its cost to the people was nothing. But what would I do when my beloved's captain called him and he mounted to his bench aboard the ships? How would I live, never again to hear his voice or feel his touch? Such joys as had sufficed my heart before he came, to ride and to hunt, now had lost all savor. My lover's farewell would steal the moon from the night. I would give up earth and sky for him; yes, and sun and stars! I declared this to him and he to me. I would sail with him! No, he would stay, make his life here with me!

One dawn Theseus was at the ships. Antiope was not with him. I rode in to the Mound City. She was there, on the Runway, training alone. Later she took the baths and attended Council. The camp had become a hive which buzzed of nothing but her reappearance.

The people had turned from Antiope in a way I had never seen. Had she been conquered by simple heat, I believe, tal Kyrte would have exonerated her. To mount a man beneath the sky, this could be indulged or made light of. Even had her passion been spurned and she mooned about, lovestruck, this too could have been acquitted. But what Antiope had surrendered to Theseus was different. What belonged to the people, she had ceded to him. Tal Kyrte hated this, and hated her for it.

Among the herds of the steppe, mares will form up in phalanx to expel one "struck by God's axe," a cripple or misbegotten. So did tal Kyrte now exile her who had been their queen and champion.

None confronted Antiope directly. No harsh words were offered. Rather each pair and trikona turned apart at her approach. None would give her fire. When she knelt to draw from the stream, those on both sides withdrew. Even the horses shied from her. I too held apart, I am ashamed to confess.

Antiope bore the people's ostracism in silence. She did not go near Theseus, nor alter her regimen, but each morning trained on the steppe, alone with Sneak Biscuits and the others of her string, and in the evening made her camp solitary and apart.

One night within the Hexagon Court she and Eleuthera fell out. This was the first open clash between them. The people attended raptly.

The Athenians, Eleuthera declared, prepare their ships now for departure. Will you, she demanded of Antiope, sail with them?

Antiope: If I do, sister, you for one will not stop me.

Eleuthera: Those are your thighs talking, wench. I smell the mare stink on you, and it makes me sick.

Antiope: Whence your rage at me, sister? My love for you may never abate, nor is it threatened by what I feel for this man you hate for no reason other than jealousy of him.

Eleuthera: I reckon the object of your love, sister. It hangs between the legs of this incurser. What is love, I say, but madness? And what its issue but disseverment from one's wits? You and I have sworn as warriors to remain free at all times, never yielding to fear or anger, which are forms of possession, undoing the valiant heart. Love is the supreme form of possession. I behold its mastery of you, Antiope, and I abominate it.

Antiope: What is this "freedom" you so venerate, Eleuthera? How are we free, you and I and all of tal Kyrte, except to live as exiles from our humanity, freaks of nature as deformed as satyrs and centaurs? God made man and woman as halves of one whole . . .

Eleuthera: Yes, halves. You said it.

Antiope: Will you make me your enemy?

Eleuthera: Will you betray me?

The people clamored, hearing this. Not one sided with Antiope, but each sway and cry seconded Eleuthera.

Eleuthera: This barnyard stud has bewitched you, sister. Wake up! Do you think love animates his purpose? What he wants from you flows between your knees. This he scents as a stallion and counts you another mare within his herd, as Ariadne and Phaedra and scores before and since. You are this season's filly, Antiope. He loves not you but the possession of you. How I hate his pride! When I see him strut about . . .

Antiope: Will you take arms against me, Eleuthera . . .

Eleuthera: Will you stand with this foreigner against your people?

Antiope: . . . for I count my skill not inferior to your own.

Eleuthera: Answer! That the nation may know you for what you have become.

Antiope's silence spoke for her.

Eleuthera: Go to him then! But know this, thou whore: from that moment thy sole treads the planks of this villain's vessel, thou art mine enemy.

And plying upon her heel, Eleuthera strode from the chamber, never turning to look back.

19

ACROSS THE
FRONTIER OF LOVE

⟨⟨⟨⟨⟨⟨⟨⟨⟨⟩

Was Antiope pregnant then? I do not know.

Did she herself know? I cannot say. That she gave birth at Athens well within the year to that boy-child she named Hippolytus, any who can count the months may confirm.

For my part I recall the days following the clash between Antiope and Eleuthera as a term of unsettlement unlike any tal Kyrte had endured. The tribes' blood was high. Games and sacrifices proceeded in the wake of the victory at the Tanais. Many trophies had been taken; their influx into the body of the nation acted as an inflammatory. Those who had tasted glory were hot for more, while they who had missed out burned to "paint their blades" in emulation of their scalp-wealthy comrades.

Theseus and his men were packing up fast, to sail home, or at least get quit of Amazonia before the people's caprice took it in mind to make prizes of them as well. Already bands of mounted warrioresses had taken to running speed drills along the strand where the Greeks' ships were beached. They built up bonfires, these hot-bloods, amid nightlong chanting and agitation, producing such an incendiary atmosphere that the Greeks must keep arms to hand as they labored, even erecting a palisade, while they redoubled their ex-ertions to make ready for sea.

My own heart burned with little save fear for my Damon. How soon would this squadron cast off? Theseus might embark on the in-stant, compelled by some sally of his besiegers. I could not go on liv-ing without my love. I would flee at his side, I signed to him across the space between us. He replied that he would stay with me, jump ship to make his life among the free people. At worst we would fly to some far country, there to reconstitute ourselves as something wholly new.

At that time, in the aftercourse of the recovery of the herds, all warriors who had taken scalps were giving away horses. This rite is called *tal Neda*, "the Repayment." It works like this: A warrior's mother-mother has the herald cry through the camp the names of those to whom she will present horses and arms. These are usually women between thirty or forty whose daughters have not yet reached majority, honored veterans whose role has evolved to that of dam or mother and who possess slender means of acquiring wealth. These, hearing their names, make their way, convoyed by the lasses they are raising, to the Islet and the Needle, the twin yokes of the pens that form the buttressway to the Mound City. Here the horses are awarded. These will become the mounts given to the recipients' charges, the young maidens in training, or used to pack their kit, or for trade or sale. The Sky Song is sung and the Hymn to Mother Horse, then the individual war songs of the women. Each of these veterans has her own, of her exploits in battle, and the girls in her charge sing this to honor her, as does the warrior donating the horses. Tal Neda is an occasion of joy, in which the generations are bound—the elder honored, the middle honoring, and the younger feeding upon the interchange.

This time it was different. Rumors flared among the horse pens. The Greeks, it was said, hatched a plot to assassinate Eleuthera and reestablish Antiope. Theseus would seek to extend Greek power by his bewitchment of our deposed queen, to rob us, as the pirate he was, and turn our enemies upon us. So detailed was this report as to include the watch of the attack and even the names of the conspirators.

You may imagine the outrage erupting in this train. At its peak Eleuthera herself appeared. She forbade the rumor's further circulation, but stopped short of denying its substance. When she saw me, she called me to her and commanded me to break off the round of tal Neda. I was to bear a message to Antiope.

"Our friend is in danger, Selene. You have heard the people; you see their state. Bring Antiope to me. I will protect her."

I asked Eleuthera why she did not go herself.

My mate regarded me queerly. "Let me not be seen approaching her; this will only further publish our break. Rather let the people see us together, bond reaccomplished, as though we had never been estranged."

I found Antiope at the Runway, training alone, apart from the seven or eight score who also drilled on the site. She was running the stop-and-go exercises in which one races at full gallop toward a stake or post, to accustom her horse to shy from nothing. Mastery of this skill is fundamental; a girl trains her horse to it before she is six. That Antiope ran these drills now with Sneak Biscuits told she had still not regained her *hippeia*. But what struck one most was that the lane she had chosen was the most remote from the city, with nothing but open steppe beyond. It was a place where a warrior could not be taken by surprise—and from which she could flee with no obstacle intervening.

I did not ride directly to Antiope, as that would constitute unseemliness, but drew rein at a distance, held for a time, then trotted off around the shoulder of a rise. I did not have to wait long before Antiope appeared.

She rode Sneak Biscuits and trailed two more of her string, one pack-laden, the other rigged for battle. Her eye scanned the site for treachery.

"Eleuthera has sent you," she spoke by sign.

I acknowledged this.

"To assure me it is safe to come to her."

Again I confirmed.

Antiope smiled, rueful.

"We must cross frontiers now, Selene."

I dared not inquire what frontiers she meant, though my heart knew: those borders which separate innocence from necessity, on whose far side one's dearest love may betray her or use her for infamous ends.

"Tell me, my friend," our lady spoke, "have all the people turned against me?"

"Not all, but . . ."

She smiled again.

"Ah, Selene. You are incapable of perfidy. Would that to preserve you thus would hold you from peril."

I read fatigue on her. Care lined her face.

"Do not wonder, child," Antiope continued, "that I address you so plainly, as though we were closest of friends, for fate has called us to this juncture together. Do you fear me? That association with one so fallen will work mischief to your ambition?"

My look must have answered. Antiope acknowledged with sorrow.

"My years are twenty-seven," she said. "This is ancient among our people, where many by twenty have donated issue and by thirty have put aside their bridles of war. Yet I have held myself till now *anandros*, unpossessed by man. Do you know why?"

I did not.

"Because I had never found one worthy of me."

She laughed.

"In this you have bested me, Selene, and have not had to tarry so late."

I understood. Because love had claimed me, as it had her, I might, when others could not, apprehend the conflict of her heart.

"Do you remember when we crossed daggers in the earth, Selene, and swore a mighty oath, each to take the life of the other should she fail, through madness spawned by love for a man, to put care of the people before all?"

Our lady regarded me gravely. "Theseus is a great man, Selene. Not alone for his triumphs as a warrior, which place him second among mortals only to Heracles, but for the flame he bears and the destiny he has been called to champion. Do you understand, my friend? Theseus has taken a nation on his back and embodied in his flesh its ideals and aspirations—and no rude or savage nation, as those that surround us in the Wild Lands, but one whose charge is epochal and noble and unmade heretofore, this thing called Athens and *democratia*, rule of the people, which Theseus has invented by his own hand and bears as a herald a brand in the wind. The gods are with him in this, Selene. It may be true that he is Poseidon's son, in that mighty forces stand at his shoulder and that he must bear the burden for their manifestation, unsustained by a single ally who comprehends his office and his isolation, but compassed by enemies, devoid of vision, who would snuff this flame and him with it for no cause but their own fear of the brave and the new. Perhaps I was made for him because I too know what it is to bear a nation upon my shoulders, to surrender all that is private and personal and live only for the greater whole. In any event, I am swept up in this destiny. Do I frighten you, Selene? You were charged only to impart a message. Do you wish to fly?"

What could I say? I understood then and believe to this day that this soul, with whose course fate had caused mine to intersect, was the noblest ever produced by our nation. I knew her too to be what her war name called her, *om Kyrte nas*, "Bulwark of the People."

She held me with her eyes. "The warrior bound for battle crosses a frontier, Selene, which tal Kyrte calls *ahora pata,* 'to abolish the ordinary.' We honor this passage so highly as to give it its own language, do we not? On its far side we call our horses by different names, and our weapons and even ourselves. We call things by new names because all have been made new by the proximity of death.

"The same holds true of love. In love we cross a frontier, upon whose far shore all has altered. We have altered too. Beneath love's hand I am Antiope no longer but some precedentless creature, spawned afresh, as my lover is new, reconfigured by my love and by his own. You understand this, Selene. You too have been transfigured by love. Therefore I beseech you, standing in for the people: be my witness. Do not forsake me because I have been made over into that which you have never known me to be."

At this word her speech broke off. I heard hooves approaching at the gallop. Into view thundered Damon, racing from the city.

If he had bolted the ships it could mean only calamity.

"Two hundred are coming for you!" Damon cried to Antiope in Greek, using the feminine to denote warrioresses of tal Kyrte. She knew. One saw she had no fear. She saluted Damon in gratitude and commanded him to get clear, before harm came to him. His eyes shot to mine in urgency. I heard Antiope behind me: "Go with him, child."

I should have known this was the moment. I must flee with my lover, now or never. But to abandon Antiope as I had done before, even now when she commanded it—this I could not do. I could see the dust of the two hundred approaching. If they discovered a Greek bearing warning to their queen, they would tear him to pieces. "Go! Go!" I heard my voice cry to him I loved, and felt my heels drive my horse at his, to put him to flight.

Our lady held her own mount in a grip of iron. I turned back to her. A peace possessed her, as one who, worn with dread of the worst, hears it acclaimed and breathes at last absent apprehension, knowing she has no more to imagine but only to endure.

"Your fate has held you at my side, Selene," she spoke, her eyes tracking with mine my lover's reluctant withdrawal. "May God preserve us both."

THE WILES OF
THE GREEKS

≈≈≈≈≈

The two hundred broke into view and reined across from Antiope. They were young, buck warrioresses my own age, the same who had harassed the Greek camp. I recognized Glauke Grey Eyes, Tecmessa Thistle, Xanthe Blonde, and my own sister Chryssa. All were armed and painted. What was their object? Perhaps they had hoped to discover their queen in flight, in which case they could either drive her out of the country or overhaul and murder her. Instead they found her facing them, one against two hundred. Antiope called for a champion to stand forth and state the two hundred's errand. No one budged. Awe of her held them paralyzed. "Follow when I get clear," Antiope commanded me.

She spurred straight into the mob's teeth. Not one stood to check her. The front parted, permitting her passage, then wheeled and fanned in her train, blocking any reverse toward the steppe but initiating no action to attack or arrest. I found myself at the rear of this formation. Antiope made for the city at the canter. What did she intend? To call out Eleuthera and face her down? To try the people and make them choose? Did she seek some worthy death, knowing herself foredoomed? And her pursuers; what was their aim, now that their prey had faced them down? We will never know. For halfway to the Mound City Theseus arrived at the gallop, backed by two score of his own and a number of mercenaries who chanced to be in the city on other business. A skirmish ensued in which Theseus' company, now shielding Antiope, broke from the two hundred and fled back to the ships. Warrioresses had been wounded. Blood had been shed.

The plunging sun cast the scene into further disorder. I found myself racing flat-out beside my sister and Glauke Grey Eyes, pursuing the party of Theseus and Antiope. I was among the two hundred. Chaos reigned, and the sense of events catapulting out of control. What did I hope for? To stand with Antiope and meet my death? To overhaul Damon and flee with Theseus by sea? I glanced to Chryssa and Glauke. They knew nothing of my turmoil, only that I had delivered Eleuthera's message as ordered. In their eyes I was one of them. Yet should I try to bolt, to join Damon or Antiope, they would slay me as a traitor, as they should. My heart hammered; I could not catch my wind or command my reason.

Where the northern earthworks of the Mound City extend into the plain, the Greeks turned the corner and got out of sight. Darkness had fallen. Suddenly from the west appeared riders of tal Kyrte. They were hundreds; Eleuthera rode at their head. Antiope and the Greeks were fleeing for the strand; the host of our squadrons galloped after. At the Lion's Gate, Eleuthera commanded the two hundred to break to the west, cut off the track that Theseus must take to the sea. I kept with this corps. I could not tell if the brigade pursuing Antiope intending her slaughter or to preserve her from abduction. This I know: I never saw cavalry in mass move so fast. Three miles remained for the Greeks to cross. They would never outrun this pack.

The two hundred galloped in double column across the tidal flats between the Aryan road and the Barrows of the Champions. The companies ploughed through the slough at the gallop, sending cranes and plovers wheeling into the dusk as they swept toward the promontory of Cynoscephalus, Dog's Head Point, upon which the Athenian ships were beached. Cresting the inner causeway, the column could see ahead to the strand.

The ships were gone.

The two hundred slewed up in confusion. We could see Eleuthera's division, which had taken the shore road to trap the Greeks should they seek to reach Dog's Head by that route; they thundered into view out of the gloom. Their mass too reined in in consternation.

Theseus had moved his ships earlier, undetected. His riders compassing Antiope had not fled to Dog's Head, where the vessels had been beached as recently as this postnoon, but to another launching site called the Flat Iron, two miles east, which both pursuing divisions had overrun in their haste. The corps of Amazonia wheeled back now across the marsh, spurring all-out toward this second strand. Night had fallen. One glimpsed ships' lanterns in the distance, rising and falling—that motion produced only by vessels already on the sea.

A score of horse squadrons ascended from the bottomland and pounded onto the strand at Flat Iron. Eleuthera had the lead. Across a mile of front, mounts were reined-in, lathered and steaming. From where I found myself, at the center right, I could make out four hulls in the channel, already beyond bowshot, yet close enough to hear the steersmen's cadence, even above the hammering of one's own heart and the heaving and stamping of the horses, as the vessels rowed seaward by surges and the deck crews stepped the masts and ran up the yards. Behind me the last of the riders emerged from the lagoon, their horses' coats steaming from the run and the slathering of salt sluicing from their muzzles and barrels. Along the front the corps brought itself to line. In the last light one could see Theseus' sails drop and, drawing against their brails and sheets, fill before the wind.

Hope is a stubborn goddess. Could our lady yet be with us? Had

Damon jumped ship to stay with me? I knew his vessel and bench by heart. I peered to sea and found the mark. Alas, there was no gap in the oar bank, but all shafts pulled in strength and unison.

At once all animation fled my heart. Fatigue crashed on me like a wall of stone. Had the world ended? Was I in hell? My bones seemed to come unstrung; teeth chattered; my limbs quaked as if palsied. I could reckon nothing but that I was wet and cold and hungry. My horse was drenched. I must rub him down, I heard my voice instruct myself, and get something into his belly. I must look to the care of his feet.

The squadrons were keening now in agitation. Something had caught their eye down the strand. I looked. Two horses, the latter riderless, transited before the front at the hard canter, coming from where the Greeks had launched, hastening toward the rise on which our commanders now marshaled. The rider was a maiden named Sais, Eleuthera's favored courier. She spurred past my position now, sitting her own mount and leading Antiope's Sneak Biscuits. Our queen's saddle was empty, her *gorytus* quiver gone.

AMAZONS AND ALLIES

Selene's testament continues:

〰〰〰〰〰〰〰〰〰〰〰

Where the foothills of the Taurian Caucasus descend to the Amazon Sea lies that strait known as the Cimmerian Bosporus. Upon the Asian shore two and a quarter years later, the hundred and twenty-nine clans of tal Kyrte assembled for the march on Athens. This was the mightiest massing of horse warriors in history and the only occasion on which all four nations of tal Kyrte, the Themiscyra, Lycasteia, Chadisia, and Titaneia had united beneath common commanders.

The corps of Amazonia was reinforced by male allies of the Rhipaean Caucasians, Chalybes, Issedonians, Cicones, Aorsi (the "Whites," or "Westerners") Arian, Sindic, and Alanic Scyths, as well as our own male auxiliaries, the *kabar,* with additional brigades of the Strymonian Thracians, including the fierce Saii, Tralliai, and Androphagi, "Man-Eaters," who had attacked Theseus' ships. This host was further augmented by detachments of cavalry of the Lykians,

Phrygians, Mysians, Cappadocians, and Dardanians; mounted infantry of Mariandyne and Hyperplakian Thebes; plus two tribes of the Mossunoikoi, called Tower People; horse warriors of the Massa Getai and Thyssa Getai, lacking of their own only the Ptyregonai, the Eucherai, and the Tetyai (for reasons of tribal feud); with further battalions arriving unsummoned from the Maeotians, Gagarians, Taurians, the Royal and Copper River Scyths, and the clans of the Armenian Caucasus known as the Black Cloaks, who spoke a language so savage it could be comprehended by none save their immediate neighbors, the Tisserandic Alans, and who were mounted not on horses but wild asses of such swiftness that when they spooked from the cavalcade, nothing and no one could run them down, but riders must be left on the plain to secure them when they returned of their own, which they invariably did, once they had shaken the gallop out.

The entire force of tal Kyrte were mounted archers; of the allies, the steppe nations and those of the Troad were heavy cavalry; the mountain clans archers and light infantry, slingers and javelineers. The Royal and Copper River Scyths were both horsemen and foot bowmen, firing the heel-braced bow, which can propel a warhead a third of a mile. Tal Kyrte's mounted corps totaled thirteen thousand primary horse, supported by thrice that in the cavalcade, the novices and elders herding the strings. In command rode Hippolyta and Eleuthera sharing equally, the former now sixty-three, the latter twenty-four. The post of peace queen had been abolished; both served as war queens. As Eleuthera had foretold, the Scyths of the Iron Mountains, despite our massacre of their women and children at the Parched Hills, proved not only tal Kyrte's most ardent allies but the most extravagant donors of foot and horse, providing four thousand of the former and twenty-five hundred of the latter. Their commander was Borges himself, seconded by his son, Prince Maues, at seventeen holder of three prizes of valor, and his nephew Panasagoras, son of Sagillus, Overlord of all Thrace, who did not ride in person but sent three waggonloads of gold, his personal seer and physician, and a suit of armor for the first fighter to plant his standard atop the Athenian acropolis. Borges had been brought over to our cause by a private embassy of Hippolyta (upon which she had donated a thousand horses to ring the barrow of his brother Arsaces) and by the prince's own hatred of her who had shamed him, Antiope, and his greed to exact vengeance upon her. The grand total of the forces, excluding the general crowd of sutlers, whores, slave dealers, camp wives and children, stood between ninety-five and a hundred and five thousand. The citizen population of the Athenian foe, not counting women, children, and slaves, could not exceed thirty thousand. Estimates for the size of the army which might face our brigades, once the Athenians had applied to the Twelve States and other allies across northern Greece, Crete, and the Peloponnese, were between fifty and sixty thousand.

This would be, if such proved true, the greatest war in history.

The date of the army's departure was the Moon of the Iron Frost, the dead of winter, that the straits might be crossed south to north on the ice. The central corps of tal Kyrte had summered at Themiscyra, on the southern shore of the Amazon Sea, recruiting allies from among the nations of Anatolia and the Troad, Armenia, Paphlagonia, Bithynia, Cappadocia, Mysia, Lykia, and Phrygia. The army would cross to Europe via the straits, transit the Wild Lands to the Mound City, there to link with the allies of Maeotia and the Scythian plains; the host would provision in the European Chersonese at the Hellespont, then proceed by shore and inland routes across Thrace and Macedonia, turning south and entering Thessaly just as the land greened up with spring. Thessaly was horse country, rich in pasture. The force would lay over a month or more, permitting its stock to fatten and recover from the march, while assembling further allies. From there it would strike Athens.

Victory, tal Kyrte believed, was foreordained. What individual warriors seeking glory feared was not that the foe would resist, but that he would turn rabbit before our army had even struck his frontier, abandoning the country entire, to recolonize on some site across the sea. That the Athenians would stand up to us seemed a hope beyond imagining. In fact, the main of Eleuthera's diplomacy was directed toward this end only: to estrange from our cause as many of Athens' allies as possible, incenting them to combine and stand. She sent no spies with bribes or offers of alliance. She wanted a fight. To tal Kyrte, one Greek was the same as another. They were all city-dwelling, sea-ranging pirates who spread the contagion of *netome*, evil luck. Time to gut them all and be done with it.

As to the princes through whose lands tal Kyrte and her allies must pass, these were approached in the following manner. First were dispatched embassies of six and fewer, under the protection of the herald's staff. These missions were composed of nobles and war-rioresses of distinction, when possible daughters and sisters of the army's commanders. Celia, Antiope's mother, headed a number of such deputations, as did Eleuthera's sisters Clonie and Paraleia; as well, Stratonike, Skyleia, Alcippe, Glauke, Tecmessa, Arge, Rho-dippe, Adrasteia, Enyo, Deino, and Pantariste led others. I myself served. Male allies were included in these legations, often promi-nently, to mitigate the shock of our corps' apparition upon the wild chieftains, to whom all females were chattel. We brought gifts; mag-nificent war mounts and weapons of iron, bridles and helmets of gold, charms and amulets in silver and electrum, copper tripods and stocks of amber and cobalt and bronze.

Succeeding the embassies came light cavalry. These were picked companies of the tallest and best-looking warrioresses, mounted upon the most superlative stock. They were unique in that they in-cluded both older knights, past fifty, who had served their seasons as dams and matriarchs and wished now to return to action, as well as maidens as young as ten and eleven, chosen from among the bright-est and noblest-born, to expose them early to great events and fire their hearts with aspirations for preeminence.

Last came armored corps, heavy infantry, men, to stake out pas-turage, if it could be found, silage if not, and water. These established camps for the main body, cut firewood or acquired it by goodwill or purchase. Often Eleuthera and Hippolyta accompanied these brigades in person, for their presence accorded honor to the princes upon whom they called.

It is no mean skill, treating with such wild barons as held the provinces through which our multitude must pass. Their gods must be reverenced; one must know their conventions and not offer unwitting offense. Days were spent rehearsing such missions. But what nothing could prepare one for was the sensation ignited among these tribesmen's women by the apparition of our corps.

The sequence never varied. The dames of the villages gaped first, huddling along the roadsides, sullen and mute. This state was succeeded by disbelief, as if they could not credit the sight of free women, armed and autonomous; then came a species of anger, at our liberty or their slavery, one could not say. Next they wept. At last they broke into cheers, these chattelwomen, and, bursting from their places, thronged about the column, clutching at our trousered legs, stretching up to touch our hands, burying their faces into the flanks of our ponies, as if to confirm by this the reality of our existence, while tears flushed their cheeks made ruddy by the frost. The lads and buck warriors tracked us too in awe. At each tribe hundreds recruited themselves to our adventure, so lifted out of themselves as to offer all they owned, bronze and silver, arms and horses and oxen. Among the Thracian Dii, one lass stood out. This was Dosteia, whom the corps came to call "Stuff." Thrice in one departure this girl was rousted from the waggons of our commissariat, each time returning to stow away again. At her last ejection she flung herself before Skyleia, captain of the column, with a flint knife at her own throat, threatening to slay herself there in the road if we would not take her. "What will your father say?" Skyleia confronted the maid through an interpreter.

"Let him salute this!" cried the child, lifting her skirts. The corps howled.

Skyleia indicated the baggage train. "Pack yourself among the stuff!" The girl did not wait for the translation. "Stuff!" she cried. From then on, that's what we called her.

The army breasted the Strymon in cold so bitter that dagger blades came undone from their hafts; touch iron and your flesh peeled away in sheaves. Still, recruits poured in. My pony fell in step beside Eleuthera one gale-scoured noon. Why, I shouted into the blizzard's teeth, did these tribesmen permit us passage? We claimed no alliance with them; the treasures we bore them were but baubles to these lords, who held lands in leagues and herds by tens of thousands. They had suffered no ills at Athens's hands; most had never ventured within two months' ride of the place and never would have, except for us. They should have fortified the passes against us and blockaded us in force on the plains. But they didn't. They opened their highways and storehouses. They showered us with provisions and permitted their noblest youths to march off with us to war. Why?

"Because," Eleuthera answered, "they fear Theseus more than they fear us."

At once I knew she was right. These rude princes understood in their guts that tomorrow lay not with them and the free life of the plains, but with the city and its walls and ships and, before all, the engine of its ascendancy, the masses of its commons.

"The army of Amazonia passes over these princes' lands and moves on. Theseus' army, the army of the city, comes and stays. It will efface these clansmen and their way of life as surely as it will us and ours." My friend whose name means Freedom turned to me, her breath pluming upon the air. "And nothing we can do will stop it."

But our story has gotten ahead of itself. Let us reverse two years and address how the march on Athens came to be conceived and put into action.

On the night of Antiope's flight aboard the ships of Theseus, the corps of Amazonia, which had watched in impotent fury as the vessels glided from its grasp, repaired to the Mound City in a state of dismay and dislocation. All sensed that an epochal overthrow had taken place, yet none knew what to think of it. We were lost. We did not know what to do.

Rumors raged through the assembly. One declared that Antiope had dueled at Theseus' shoulder beside the ships; she had fought against our own people, this report proclaimed, and taken flight of her own free will. Another story said she was dead, slain by Theseus, her corpse borne to Athens as his prize of war. A third restated the calumny that Theseus and Antiope had conspired to assassinate

Eleuthera but, this treason discovered, had been forced to flee for their lives. Such profusion of hearsay cast the congress into chaos. I recall my own novices, Kalkea and Arsinoe, so beside themselves with agitation that I must apply the quirt just to make them obey me.

The Mound City has only one square great enough to accommodate the nation entire, the Grand Avenue beneath the outer earthworks, the site where Antiope had dueled the princes Borges and Arsaces two months previous. Within this plaza the host now assembled. The hour was past midnight; rumor and slander continued to whipsaw the throng. From the same platform on which Theseus and Antiope had jousted so brilliantly during the Gathering, lesser orators now offered hearsay and humbug as to what had driven them forth. At last Eleuthera and her Companions, among whom I took pride to number myself, succeeded in clearing the stand and restoring order. The host hailed its new commander, crying her forward to rally the nation, inform it of the truth. Eleuthera addressed the corps from the Stone Palisade.

Our Lady Antiope had been raped, she declared.

At swordpoint and employing a force of men at arms, the pirate Theseus had ravished Antiope in the mountains (so Eleuthera swore), where she had gone alone to seek counsel of heaven after the victory of the Parched Hills.

Theseus had caught Antiope, Eleuthera proclaimed, unarmed and at her prayers. But such was the least of the evils inflicted by this villain, for he had stolen not only our lady's virtue but her wits. Among his company stood warlocks and sorcerers, who had drugged our queen and made her turn against her people. Antiope fought these potions with all her strength, Eleuthera now reported. But Theseus' magicians, in league with Hades and those gods who hate the free people, had overcome her. Torn with grief at her violation, our lady sought to return to us, her people, but in our blindness—here Eleuthera included herself among the blameworthy—we had spurned her. At last, helpless beneath the alien's evil draughts, Antiope fell.

Raped and kidnapped!

Borne in bondage across the sea!

Of course I knew this to be rubbish. Yet the people devoured it as fact. The host thundered in approbation. At one stroke all trepidation fled the corps, supplanted by hate and *lyssa,* war fury. The nation clamored for vengeance, shrilling Antiope's name as its battle cry, and calling upon Eleuthera to lead it in avenging her abduction.

Over succeeding days, reports corroborated Eleuthera's story. Drudges who had served the Greek camp were produced and tortured; they repeated her account word for word. Eyewitnesses came forward of our own people, swearing mighty oaths that they had been present upon the strand where Theseus' ships lay beached; they had seen Antiope dragged from her horse by a mob of men whence, her will vitiated by the narcotics with which her predator had enfeebled her, she fell resisting to the last.

More troubling to the people was this dispatch from the east: the pirate Theseus' vessels, far from sailing west toward home, had beyond sight of shore put about toward Colchis and the river Phasis. There even now, the report declared, the Greeks traded for iron with the Chalybes, grain with the Royal Scyths, and gold with the Rhipaean Caucasians. In each land (so these reports told), possession of our queen had elevated Theseus' prestige spectacularly, while painting us as impotent and vulnerable.

North of the Mound City is an eminence, the Hill of Ares, upon which the Council convenes, in a pavilion erected for such occasion, to debate and declare war. To this site Eleuthera and her Companions made, myself among them, ten days subsequent to Antiope's flight. We purified the ground and set up the Council tent. Past dark on the eve of assembly, chance set me at Eleuthera's shoulder within the pavilion. My heart was afflicted and she saw it.

"Spit it out," my friend commanded.

I obeyed. "You have spoken falsely before the people." From my breast burst this indictment: "Antiope was not raped and you know it. She fled willingly. You compelled her with your two hundred. You meant to murder her!"

The Companions drew up in astonishment at this outburst from me. Eleuthera responded for all to hear.

"Do not confront me, Selene, with the fatuous indignation of a child. We are women now. Antiope had to die. I took the step to effect it. I miscalculated one factor only—the power of her presence. Two hundred I sent, and she cowed them all!"

My mate met my eye with a look I had never seen. "Understand this, Selene. From the moment our lady sought clemency for the foe at the Tanais, her doom was sealed. She knew it. All that wanted was the site and the hour. Let her be slain by her sisters; this would be well. The nation may grieve and grant her honor. An orderly transition of power may take place. More important, our enemies will perceive no crisis. One outcome alone could not be permitted, the very one which has eventuated: that Antiope flee or be stolen alive by such pirates as the Greeks.

"Nor is this the worst of it, my friend. But Antiope has abandoned us, not for love of a man (which I could admire, after all, as it is founded on passion and ecstasy) but because her heart has rejected the way we live and who we are. She has named us savages. Our society she abhors as unnatural and condemned."

Two pages chanced to enter at this moment. Eleuthera banished them with a glower. She turned back, not to me alone but to the others of her circle—Stratonike and Skyleia; Alcippe and Glauke Grey Eyes, Tecmessa, Xanthe, and my sister Chryssa, as well as Electra, Adrasteia, and Pantariste.

"Antiope believes Theseus superior to us. She warrants his way worthier than ours. And here is a further truth, Selene, since you prize candor so highly: if the people learn this, it will crush them. Do you doubt? Then tell your tale. Tell the people there was no rape. Tell them our lady flew, uncoerced and unabducted. And while you're at it, tell them she is with child. Theseus' child. Tell them that knowing herself to be impregnated, she fled to bear her babe at Athens. Tell them that. Do you know what will happen? They will not believe you. They will take your life on the spot for offering such slander, which in their hearts they know to be true but cannot bear to hear spoken."

Eleuthera addressed the Companions. "Understand, my friends.

Tal Kyrte's ways are pure but they are also vulnerable. The stainless heart is most easily corrupted. As Antiope fell, so others may, and by the same contagion. So I keep it simple for the people. I tell them the foe has forced Antiope's flesh. This is enough. This they understand."

I sought to protest. Eleuthera cut me off.

"You have imbibed too much of civilization, Selene. Your sojourn among the shopkeepers of Sinope has estranged you from tal Kyrte's simple ways. This is why you take Antiope's side against me. It is why you have found a lover among men, as she did, and surrendered yourself to him as she to Theseus. Your devotion you have withdrawn from me, Selene, whom once you loved beyond all others."

Eleuthera turned away. I saw that the loss of Antiope's love—and perhaps mine as well—had stricken her to the quick. I would have felt pity for her had she been less formidable. One might as well dole leniency to a lioness.

Voices could be heard outside the tent. The elders entered for their convocation and, discovering Eleuthera and her Companions in the posture of conflict, held up at the portal, preserving our dignity by affecting not to see. In moments we had hustled the site into shape. The council reentered and took their places, seventeen in all, including male chieftains of the Maeotians and Gagarians, the body as a whole presided over by Hippolyta as peace queen and ranking elder.

A page attended each councilor. These set before their mistresses the low four-legged altars tal Kyrte calls "smokers." The pages piled sweet herbs atop each, lit the mounds and withdrew. The elders, sitting cross-legged, plied the ascending vapors with their palms and their raven and eagle wings, drawing the wisps over their crowns and shoulders, inhaling. None spoke, but each convened with her own spirit, while the priestess chanted the invocation and call for counsel. The chamber thickened, blue with smoke. At last, by a look Hippolyta indicated Eleuthera, directing her to begin.

Eleuthera spoke from her seat, cross-legged, within the circle. She did not plunge at once into matters as a Greek would, but offered first prayers for the free people's well-being. She acknowledged her own shortcomings as a commander, praised the elders for their forbearance, and supplicated heaven for guidance in the days to come. The council looked in every direction except hers; they seemed barely to attend her. Yet they missed nothing. Observing, one marked only the graceful plying of palms and raven wings, and the smoke passing over each listener in purifying purpose. Eleuthera spoke of Antiope and the loss the nation had suffered. She remarked the consternation into which the people had been cast and assailed those who sought to underportray its moment. Then, speaking calmly but with emphasis, she arrived at the meat.

"In the absconding of Antiope, I perceive an epochal overthrow which threatens the very survival of the nation. Here, my heart tells me, is the most critical reverse since the champions fell before Heracles, not only for the blow it deals the people's self-certitude, but, far more gravely, for the evil it will inspire in our enemies. The nations of the steppe are superstitious. They will perceive in Antiope's flight evidence of heaven's disaffection. With her has perished our *aedor*, they will believe, our soul and power. The princes of the plains will be emboldened to make trial of us, perhaps not at once, perhaps not in force, but by degrees they will be nerved to step up their aggression along our frontiers, to poach more aggressively upon our herds. Nor may we except our foes across the sea, Hittites and Armenians, Medians and Cappadocians, not to say Pelasgians and Greeks, who will be drawn like wolves smelling blood.

"Our enemies reckon us vulnerable. They will test us. If we are slow to respond, they will strike with greater boldness. Remember, they hate us as no other nation, for we are to them that which they fear beyond all: women unmastered by men. We need not attack to elicit enmity. Our very existence makes them abominate us, for it calls their own wives and daughters to aspire to freedom. They would drink our blood if they could. Only one thing prevents them: our strength at arms.

"As the days pass and Antiope's loss is felt more keenly within the tribes of tal Kyrte, those qualities which she accorded us will be missed more and more. I reckon my limitations. I am no Antiope. I am a fighter not a queen—and we need a queen. We own none Antiope's equal, save you, Lady Hippolyta, and if you will forgive the harsh finding of my speech, your years prevent you from acting as a war queen must. Hear, sisters and elders, what my heart tells me:

"The nation of tal Kyrte possesses many strengths but also weaknesses. Most pernicious is this: we do not act but react. It is our way to tarry and dilate, awaiting signs of heaven and the ancestors. Our enemies don't. They act!

"Theseus acts.

"He beyond all our foes hatches schemes and lays designs. He strikes with vigor and audacity. Tal Kyrte must learn to fight as its enemies do, behind a commander unafraid to employ cunning and art, and whose will is iron to drive the people to victory. When we played at war as girls, did we rehearse ourselves as deer? No, lions! I would rather have an army of deer commanded by a lion than an army of lions commanded by a deer!"

Here Eleuthera drew up, perceiving that the fire of her speech had distressed the elders, that they read it as a strike for more power, even absolute power, for herself. Reining her zeal, Eleuthera addressed this head-on:

"Hear, sisters, what my heart proposes. Let me not stand alone as war queen but be yoked with Hippolyta as co-commander, abolishing the office of peace queen, and making two mistresses of war, peers and equals. By this stroke, lady," Eleuthera addressed her elder directly, "your vision may be coupled to my passion, in that way which may best serve the free people. Perhaps together you and I may make one Antiope, until that day when our arms restore her and bring her home."

This motion found approval. Eleuthera followed up, urging war on the Iron Mountain Scyths and their allies, not alone, but in concert with other nations who hated Borges and wished to see him fall. "This has been coming since Heracles. Let it be decided now, while we are still strong, and by blood, which alone our enemies understand."

Others of the Council spoke, some seconding the course of militancy Eleuthera urged, others counseling restraint. At last the staff came round to Hippolyta. The peace queen had then sixty-one years; her hair, iron-colored, fell in a plait to her waist. As eldest her word bore the most weight. No motion would be passed in the face of her resistance; conversely, few causes she championed could fail to prevail.

Hippolyta elected to speak now, not with words but by sign. She indicated Eleuthera.

"I have watched our sister, whose name means Freedom, since she was so small she could be set within the bowl of this smoker. Always my heart has shown me: she beyond all of her generation craves honor, setting it before love, happiness, life itself. In warlike virtue none is her equal. She bows to no man, but ever sets the weal of the free people before all."

As Hippolyta's hands spoke, the elders acknowledged. Eleuthera held, still as stone.

"Yet," Hippolyta continued in sign, "I discovered our sister deficient in temperance and self-command, rash and easily provoked to anger, headstrong, stubborn, and violent. Like a racing colt she bolts to the gallop and bites the bit at every stride. In times of peace, one of her nature must be reined by wiser heads, or her love of strife may lead the people into reckless adventures."

Hippolyta shifted now and spoke in words.

"These, however, are not times of peace."

The lady Hippolyta rose. From around her neck she unbound the raven's wing, signalizing the priesthood of Ares, and, crossing before her younger compatriot, cinched it about Eleuthera's throat. Tears stood in the younger woman's eyes. She dropped upon one knee before her elder.

"I second your accession, child," Hippolyta spoke, "and accept your proposal of joint command. Take this Raven Wing, which has marked the Society of War time out of mind." She set one hand upon Eleuthera's head and elevated the other, palm upward, to heaven. "I thank thee, Ares, god of war and progenitor of our race, and thee,

Great Mother, Hecate Dark Moon, Black Persephone, and all lords and ancestors who stand sentry over the free people, that they have brought forth at this hour such a champion as this."

The Council assented with raps and murmurs. The co-commanders resumed their places, Hippolyta retaining the staff. Long moments passed; the councilors made smoke and held silence. At last Hippolyta straightened and resumed.

"Captains of the rising generation," she spoke toward Eleuthera and the Companions, "I honor your war plan with this sole reservation: it has not gone far enough. Let tal Kyrte not content herself with skirmishes against the tribesmen on her borders, but carry hell's bane to that state and its monarch which has set our survival at hazard.

"I mean Theseus.

"I mean Athens."

Citations of approval growled from the gorges of the Council.

"It was my folly that brought this necessity upon us." Hippolyta meant the surrender of her virgin girdle to Heracles, which act decades prior had prompted the bloodbath of the champions. "By my appeasement of the Greeks, two generations gone, has their aggressiveness grown wanton and inflamed. To this offense I own. I ask you now to let me make it good.

"Let us enlist hate now, as we should have then.

"Let us invoke Ares now, as we should have then.

"Let us make war now, as we should have then!

"Athens!

"Let us strike there, at the belly of the beast, and bring it low!"

At once cries burst from the Council: *Aii-ee! Ai-ee!* Even the sober elders whooped. Outside the chamber the tribes had massed in their multitudes. Hippolyta could hear the pages and heralds relaying her words and the roars of approval ascending in rejoinder. The queen rose, drawing the Council in her train, and emerged beneath the dark moon whose face is Hecate of the Crossroads, mistress of the track to hell, and, mounting the stand before the people, pronounced for their hearing all that had been debated and proposed within. The nations roared in approbation. Eleuthera looked on, watching the spark she had struck ignite to conflagration.

"As to the male nations of the steppe," Hippolyta addressed the daughters of tal Kyrte, "let us not make war upon them but enlist them to our cause. I will treat with these myself, the Massa Getai and Thyssa Getai, Taurians, Maeotians and Gagarians, Mysians, Carians and Cappadocians. I will approach the Colchians and Chalybes and Issedones, Phrygians and Lykians, Trojans and Dardanians, Saii and Androphagai, the Black Cloaks and the Tower People, Saiian, Trallian, and Strymonian Thracians, the Royal Scyths and the Scyths of the Copper River. They will come for plunder and glory. Even those of the Iron Mountains will fight at our shoulders. They will be swept up as wildfire on the steppe!"

Acclamation saluted this. The cry of "Antiope! Antiope!" rang beneath the cresset flare of Hecate Dark Moon.

Two years it took to forge the alliance. But at last, at the floe-mantled straits of the Cimmerian Bosporus, the hour of departure had arrived. Two hundred thousand marshaled on the shore; the crossing buckled with drift ice gale-borne from Greater Scythia. The order of march called for the army to cross as a body following the night sacrifice to Cybele and Asia, but numbers of high-spirited novices, and particularly the horse troops of the Fox River clans, could not be held. They bolted onto the floe field, driving their mounts in that sport called *macronessa*, which is played with a stuffed skull wrapped in ox hide, and which they contested by torchlight all the way across.

To the brink of the ice the main body advanced. I rode Daybreak, trailing Knothole and Thrush, the first laden with bedding, armor, and spare arms beneath a bearskin mantle lapped across his chest to protect on the headwind marches. Kalkea and Arsinoe were my novices, trailing a string of eleven. Thrush bore a shell like Daybreak's but of elk and sable, atop which rode a pack frame balanced with sacks of parched oats and rye, as well as horsehair blankets, picket stakes and lines, windbreaks of ox-hide and ibex, which would be rigged each night to shield the stock. Both mounts wore hood-winks, as did Daybreak, as cloaks against snow glare and gale-driven ice. Cured and fresh meat were sealed in bags of badger gut and stowed beneath the pack shell.

As to kit, I rode upon a half-frame wolf-skin saddle, with my crescent shield slung from the cantle behind my left thigh. On its face was my war totem, Selene Bright Moon, in ivory and gold, ringed with those annals, the celts and amulets commemorating each raid and fight, which comprised my history since girlhood and simultaneously shielded me from hazard and called forth by their placement and power further glory. I had crafted none, as was tal Kyrte's law, but each had either been won as a trophy or made for me (as I had for others) by lovers and friends. Quiver and bow case hung at Daybreak's right shoulder, both of doeskin with flaps of fox fur, quill-embroidered and trailing bands of ermine and mink. I packed twenty-seven primary shafts, straight and true, which had taken me two years to fashion, and another two score with Knothole in the spare kit. My bow was a four-footer of ash and horn with a grip of boar skin trimmed with amber and jet. In my right hand I bore the death lance of my "stick," or fighting unit; six feathers of hawk and osprey, for comrades gone to the life beyond, pended from its tip. A buckskin trophy-fall hung at my back, with more glyphic annals, and seven scalps woven to tassels, which whipped and snapped in the wind. My boots were fireproofs of ox-hide lined with sable and fox; atop these, wolf-skin trousers with the fur on the in-side, overmantled by leggings of buckskin. Twenty charms of elec-trum and silver were woven into a stripe down each leg, talismans of the gods and heroines into whose care I had surrendered my soul during the Gatherings of my youth. Around my waist I wore a star belt of seven windings, gift of Eleuthera. My breast was mantled with a vest of fox fur and fleece, thick as a hand, with an overcloak of bearskin, tightest against the wet, and a hood lined with the fur of white marten. Over my right shoulder rode a black panther skin, with the head still on, draping my back to form a pouch in which I carried my moon bundle. On my head I wore a Phrygian cap of doeskin lined with otter; its flaps shielded my ears, while through its forestall of horsehair, bound across my mouth and eyes, I could see into the sternest glare. My battle-axe I wore not as others in a scabbard between my shoulder blades but loose, across the tops of my thighs, in an antelope case lined with fleece. Daybreak's coat was shaggy with winter, a pile so thick it swallowed both fists to the wrist. You could hang by it at the gallop. On all sides warriors advanced in such pride, numbers, and brilliance as surely heaven had never looked upon before.

Hippolyta and Eleuthera had meant to leave a third of the nation behind, to safeguard our lands and herds. In the event, half of these could not be contained, but veterans and novices in thousands swept upon the column, leaguing with its squadrons and refusing to be driven off. I was there when the clans of the Titaneia marshaled before the strait. Uncommanded they set fire to their tents and waggons. Everything they owned beyond what could be borne to battle, they torched and good riddance. The Lycasteia followed, and the other tribes of tal Kyrte; even the Scyths and Taurians, the Massa Getai and the clans of the Caucasus were caught in the fever. As the storm of smoke sheared skyward, the corps as one put up the Hymn to Ares Manslayer.

Victory or death
Victory or death
No outcome other
Victory or death

What treasure was going up in smoke! The merchants who tracked the army could not bear it, but dashed in among the tents, seeking to retrieve items of value. The column burst into laughter, succeeded by cheers. In and out of the flames the vendors shuttled, cloaks smoking and beards scorched, to snatch the prize of a copper skillet or emerge triumphant bearing a Mysian carpet.

The horn sounded. The column stepped off onto the floe. At its head advanced a picked company founded by Hippolyta's order:

Antiope's company, with Sneak Biscuits led, riderless, at its fore. Before Athens's walls this corps would be drawn up and our lady summoned to step down and assume its command.

I fell in between Stratonike and my sister Chryssa in the battalions of our nation, the Lycasteia. Never had my heart swelled so; I must bury both fists in my horse's coat simply to keep from pitching faint. My glance found Eleuthera at the column's crown. She was right: tal Kyrte had gone too long without war. War is what we were born to, daughters of Ares. We had drifted apart from ourselves by falling away from war. Let us return to it and to the ground of our greatness!

Ai-ee! Ai-eee! The column spurred onto the field of ice. An image of Damon ascended before me. I banished it with hate. Who was he to me but that demon, as his name, who had bewitched my heart and estranged me from myself and from my people? Let him fall beneath my axe and hell take him!

The army swept in lines onto the frozen strait. It was impossible not to look right and left; we all did, and when we saw what a magnificent body we composed, an emotion of awe and humility overcame us. I glanced to Stratonike and saw she wept. I said nothing then; not till the far bank, which took all morning to reach, when the army doubled and redoubled, linking with the clans of the Taurians of the northern steppe and the massed companies of the Rhipaean and Iron Mountain Scyths.

I fell in at Stratonike's shoulder. "Why did you weep, sister, back there when the corps first advanced onto the ice?"

Chryssa rode at our friend's other flank; remarking my question she too drew in closer to hear the reply. Stratonike's gesture swept across the seabound plain, indicating the spectacle of the massed armies of the East.

"It struck me," she said, "beholding this host and reckoning the scale of its daring, that none of tal Kyrte will return to this place the same as we are now. Even if heaven grants us victory, that life we knew is over."

Stratonike's words chilled me, as I saw they did my sister. For moments we three rode in silence. Then Chryssa spurred and straightened, facing into the gale.

"Then may hell take me in battle before the walls of the foe, for I wish to remain above the earth for no life other than this I love."

BOOK SEVEN

ATHENS

THE USES OF ECSTASY

Damon:

⬡⬡⬡⬡⬡

The first tribesmen into Attica were Fox River Thracians. Their numbers were about three hundred. They torched farms at Aphidna and Hecale and swept round the shoulder of Parnes into Paeonidae and the outer boroughs. At the same time troops of Sindic and Alanic Scyths punched south out of Thebes, cresting Cithaeron at Eleutherai and Oinoe, breaking through to Acharnae via the Parnes-Aegaleos gap. The date was Munychion thirteen, two years and seven months since Theseus' ships had made their forced decampment from the Mound City, bearing Antiope home as the bride of our king. One might imagine, reckoning the scale of the army marshaled to take vengeance upon us, and the hundreds of reports of its advance received at Athens over the succeeding two years, that no exertion would have been spared to prepare the citizenry and to fortify the state. On the contrary, accounts of the plains nations' mobilization were dismissed as fiction and fabulation. Tall tales arrive with every ship, so Athens believed, and poets routinely send children quaking to bed with bugbears of centaurs and Amazons. The very scale of the foe's undertaking confuted its credibility. Who could believe the unbelievable? That a ragtag confederation of savages, indeed savages perpetually at war with one another, could summon the cohesion to pack up and vacate their homelands, trekking three months across hostile territory, in the dead of winter, no less, and toward a site that was, to them, the extremity of the earth, all in the cause of repatriating one lone absconded female . . . this was preposterous. It could not happen.

Indeed, my friends, I anticipate your next query. Reports from fifteen hundred, two thousand miles away in the Chersonese, even five hundred miles off in Thrace, yes, you say, such could be dismissed, citing the remoteness of their sources and the hyperbole common to all tale-tellers arriving from foreign lands. But the Amazons had been within a hundred miles for days! Was no alarm received, even then, at Athens? Had no warning come from our allies at Thessaly or Thebes?

I answer thus. A Greek commander might have held his forward elements until the main body could be massed for the attack. Amazons and Scyths did not think like that. Once their advance parties struck the frontier, no curb or injunction could hold them back. They went after every stick of loot they could lay their fists on.

Why had no warning come from Thebes? Simple: the main body of the foe had not even reached Thebes! Her vanguard shot past on the fly. Why assault walled cities on the way in? Cut them off to starve! Pick them clean on the way home!

By the second day Athenian cavalry had got out into the countryside, if you can call an undermanned posse of ring riders and parade prancers by such a name. I rode with Philippus, keeping on our own. We identified Rhipaean and Ceraunian Caucasians later that day and, toward nightfall, the first clans of Greater Scythia. These were all males. And not in mass but small groups, raiding parties. My mate and I fled from them at first. But they had no interest in us. They were after fatter kills—cattle and farms and estate houses. Each gang competed with its cronies. One band would set-to, torching a farmstead; another would gallop past, whooping in derision. The first, fearing its fellows would beat it to choicer pickings, now jilted the original kill and made off at hot spur to overhaul its rivals.

This was no joke. For the foe's numbers and the astonishing swiftness of his assault had put him in command of the countryside before the citizen populace could be alerted, let alone evacuated. Our compatriots must flee to the city now, not over secure roads in Athenian possession, but across country already overrun by the foe.

Now a more perverse crick arose. This was the farmers themselves: they would not quit the land. You know north Attica, my friends; the yeomen live on leeks and poached hares; they are mean as dirt. They would not budge. All day Philippus and I lurched from hold to hold, crying the peril. Will you credit: no one believed us, or if they did, told us to take it to hell. They would dig in, to stand or die.

What mule is more stubborn than the bumpkin? Philippus and I bullied and pleaded, invoked Theseus' name, not to say every local god and hero we could think of. No use. These garlic-grubbers had set their bowels. They would defend their miserable patches, they and their sons, with stones and meathooks and bare hands.

We reached my brother's farm around sunset. The place had been razed to bare stone. The raiders, Copper River Scyths, had scalped two of the hands and chased Elias' bride into a dry well, raining rock and rubble upon her until they tired of this sport. She was all right, but cut up pretty badly.

The second dawn we saw Amazons. Not clans of the Lycasteia and Themiscyra we knew, but Chadisia and Titaneia. They swept south, seeking what? the city? the southern passes? Where Philippus and I remained, at Acharnae rallying the crofters, one encountered not Amazons but Scyths. The natives believed now. But a new pig-headedness had taken them. They would not make for the city proper (too newfangled for them) but fell back on the upcountry keeps, the strongholds of the local barons. Countrymen breaking for town now paid hell for their tardiness. On the road the Scyths overran them in mass; cross country they rode them down one by one. The Scyth is an impaler. He spikes skulls and nails hides to trees. Numbers of our own sought to hide in garners or root cellars. This is raw meat to the Scyth. He sights a likely covert and falls upon it with fire. He spits the first bugger he flushes; this one gives up the rest. We saw men scalped and still living, disemboweled and staggering with the spool of their guts in their fists. To prize off a finger ring is not the Scyth's style. He hews the hand entire and frees the band with his teeth. He will hatchet a head to gain an earring, scattering the pulp to his dogs, or that army of curs, self-recruited, which scavenges the banquet wherever he treks. Nor will you cheat the Scyth by stuffing goodies up your bum. He carves this as a house dame a goose and buries his arm to the elbow. God help those matrons who sought to stash treasure anywhere but in their purse.

As for me, I had my own problems, namely evacuating my father and his kith. These codgers had dug in, intractable as goats. I had to truss the old man hand and foot, he spewing oaths the while, and pack him in on a two-wheel cart. Next my uncles and their people, who at least acceded to reason, not to say the sight of a troop of Thracian Saii torching their neighbor's barns. Then my own poor patch. I owned only one item worth an iron spit—a colt named Tanglefoot I had hoped to race. Two sisters of the overhill farm, Gaia and Maia, had been my jockeys. They were twelve, twins, superlative riders. I set Gaia on this horse and her sister on another, ordering the lot to town. But at Holm Oak Hill, so I was apprised later, the lasses' party drew up across from a cohort of Amazons. Gleaning but one glimpse of these warrioresses (and that at above a quarter mile), the twins fell smitten. At once they forswore allegiance to nation, hearth, and gods, and flew to the foe, who welcomed them, as clearly they had scores and hundreds of others. Nor would these maidens come back.

To war's wonted horrors had been added such grotesque inversions. A state of hysteria gripped the populace. The defenders beheld their assailants driven on by *lyssa* and *outere*. It was this ecstasy that struck the deepest terror, for it called our own wives and daughters like the horns of the moon. Men's slumber was riven. Children sensed this upending of order. They wailed nightlong and no remedy could pacify them.

No one slept the next three days. A man rode to exhaustion, collapsed where he stood, then got up and went at it again. Our troops defending the city could not be called an army. They were militia. Farmers and shopkeepers, grovers and vineyardmen, many armed with only billhooks and mattocks. The knights of the baronies alone could be called warriors. These at least could ride and fight. But the more desperate the peril became, the more pressure each prince felt to defend his own stronghold, city be damned, so that numbers of nobles, even those who called themselves companions to Theseus, balked in the event and could not forsake elders and retainers and ancestral lands. In the end barely fifteen hundred knights rallied behind the city walls.

Philippus and I linked with these on the third day. Theseus led the troop out. The riders were all good men, stoutly armed and organized into companies. The Amazons toyed with us. I was with a cohort of three score on the plain near Thria when two wings of thirty warrioresses fell upon us. We formed a skirmish line, armed with saber and javelin. The enemy were Titaneia Amazons, holding our corps in such contempt as to send even their novices. They attacked with the bow and the battle-axe. We could not touch them. Three shafts each the foe loosed, the first at range as she approached, the second at the rush, the third point-blank as she ripped past. If one found its mark, the shooter wheeled upon her prey, sinking shaft after shaft, and when he dropped she fell on him with axe and scalping knife.

In the city men toiled without intermission, throwing up walls and breastworks, packing in rations and materiel. Shore roads teemed with evacuees bound for every cove and strand between Phaleron and Marathon, where husbands packed wives, children, and stock aboard smacks, bumboats, galleys, lighters, barges, any bucket that would float, to be ferried across to Euboea. Night and day the armada shuttled. On the shingle Theseus' paladins detained those able to fight and confiscated the treasure of all evacuating. Every bauble and trinket must be recruited to the city's need, to bribe the foe, fortify the ally, buy our way out if we could.

On the sixth night the citizenry, or what ragged portion remained of it, rallied in the city before the Temple of Hephaestus. A downpour had turned the square to mire. I arrived at the tail of the opening motion. I had never witnessed such a riot.

The throng called first for Antiope's surrender. Turn the bitch over to the foe! She was the cause of this calamity! Pack her off and hell take her!

Theseus confronted the multitude. Antiope was his bride, the mother of his son. If she went, he went.

Panic now seized the assembly. The people dared not call their king's bluff; without him they were cooked and they knew it. Their posture reversed, dropping all notice of Antiope, demanding instead an end to democratic assembly and the accession of Theseus to supreme command. With one voice the mob called their king to the post of *autokrater*, commander without appeal.

Theseus refused.

The square seethed like a cauldron. The mob, above six thousand densely packed, no longer conveyed its convictions by speech, but swept in mass from one bank to the other. Men did not vote by show of hands, rather migrated physically from shore to shore within the square, crying their posture. Theseus put this question to the people: Fly or stand? The riot redoubled. Men literally seized one another, citizen seeking to convert citizen by brute fervor. I saw my cousin Xenocles with his claws about the throat of some hapless bugger, who choked back with matching zeal, while two others sought to lift both and bear them bodily across the square to where the adherents of their own position had taken station.

Three times Theseus set the motion before the people. Three times the mob refused to respond, calling instead for his accession to supreme command. Take over! Tell us what to do!

The king would not do it.

He would compel the people to rule themselves.

Remember at this hour it was by no means certain that the city would be defended. Half the citizenry, even those now within the walls, were loading up to flee. The enemy had not yet sealed Attica. You could still get through. You could still get out.

Theseus reconvoked the debate: Stand or fly?

The downpour continued to pelt the square. Men were torn; some who had lost farm and family wished to quit with their lives; others in matching straits burned to fight, believing they had no more to lose. Some who retained lives and property wished not to hazard these by resisting the foe, while more in the same case shouted that to fly was to give up life and property both! Meanwhile numbers, perhaps two fifths of the state, had decamped to their home baronies, the upcountry holds. Two thousand had taken refuge on Mount Hymettos; more camped at Ardettos and Lykabettos, and in strongholds on Parnes. Others aimed to ferry to Salamis or Troezen, or shoot the isthmus to the Peloponnese. No few hoped to fly to Sicily or Italy, even Libya and North Africa.

Past midnight couriers came in. The foe had captured the last passes over Parnes and Cithaeron. Eleusis had been taken; the enemy held the Thriasian highway. Further terror was produced by the arrival of a runner from the Isthmus. This too had fallen, eliminating all escape by land.

The invaders had sealed Attica. Athens was surrounded and cut off. Had Theseus anticipated this? Had he stalled the Assembly till the foe had done his work for him? Many have asked in subsequent season; he has said only, "The people voted aright."

Indeed they did, now they had no choice.

Stay and fight!

Defend the city!

But Theseus would not settle for this. He insisted the vote be tallied not by show of hands or acclamation but that the electorate take station bodily on either side of a line, which he scribed himself with the butt of the *skeptron* into the muck bisecting the square. This was so that all could see who stood where and, more important, that none reverse except in infamy.

Theseus had the Knights awakened before dawn; the corps mar-shaled in the Horse Square on the Hill of the Muses. Allies had come in overnight: from Thessaly, Pirithous and Peleus with a hundred cavalry and four hundred pikemen; from Crete, the boy-prince Trip-tolemus with three hundred famed archers; from Sparta, the spear-man Amompharetus with eighty armored infantry. The apparition of these heartened the defenders mightily. Theseus spoke, address-ing all:

"Knights and Companions, you are the champions of the state, the scions of her noblest houses. You she may count upon to do or die. Yet, if I read you right, another question disquiets your hearts.

"What of our comrades, you wonder, the farmers and craftsmen who constitute our corps? They are not fighters. Many own neither armor nor weapons; the only thing they know of battle is how to run from it. Look in their eyes. They are terrified before this foe and her unprecedented numbers and savagery. Will such troops hold? How shall we command them? Hear, brothers. I will tell you.

"Men in fear crave order. Give it to them. Tell them where to sleep and where to shit. Make no appeal to lofty ideals of patriotism or self-sacrifice. They are too dread-stricken to hear. Just tell them what to do. Keep it simple. 'Stand there. Hold this. Do that.'

"Your job now is to quell your men's terror. Get proper food into their bellies and proper arms into their fists. Bind your fellows with sweat, for who builds a wall builds valor, and who whets his bronze whets his courage. Let your men grumble; it makes them feel like sol-diers. Let them joke, for none can fear and laugh at the same time. Remember that each man's concern is for his own family now. This is natural; do not seek to quell it. Unity will come. The foe will force it upon us.

"A word about arrogance and impatience. Some of you fancy yourselves favored. You offer smart remarks of the husbandmen who comprise our army, naming them rubes and yokels. You err, brothers. For they know something you don't. They know how to endure. Rude, flinty, hard-bitten? These are the qualities Athens needs in this hour, more than heroism, more than brilliance. Therefore, bear your command with humility. Lead, do not condescend. Remember, these are great events and men will rise to them. Treat every man as a soldier. He may surprise you and be one."

He indicated Peleus and Pirithous, Triptolemus and Amompharetus. "If you fail of inspiration, brothers, look only to these knights who have with such honor crossed seas and mountains to stand at our shoulders. If they will shed their blood for Athens, how may we, her own sons, offer less than our all?

"Lastly, my friends, recall that the worst that can come—death and extinction—may not be robbed of honor unless we so consent. God Himself cannot take this from us: to fall with valor, if fall we must."

Theseus had barely finished when a cry resounded from the west-facing lines. Men were gesticulating and running. I fell in beside my brother; we mounted the bluff, still chill in shadow, toward the wash of the ascending sun. You know the summit of the Muses' Hill; the Acropolis mounts at its hip while across the laundry-hung rooftops of the Weavers' Quarter, sliced through by the Ceramic Way, arises the Hill of Ares, mate to the Acropolis and stark with its bluff side facing.

Along this crest now horsewomen of the Amazons ascended. A hundred first, in helmets and armor, then another hundred, and another and another. Now with a sound such as no man had ever heard appeared battalions in such numbers as to obliterate the ridgelines from the Ceramicus to the Itonic Gate. A thousand, and a thousand more, and three thousand, and five and seven and ten. These did not charge but walked, absent haste, one hoof set before another, in such myriads as made the stone tremble beneath their tread, and ourselves, observing at range, quake with palsy from sole to crown.

To the fore advanced the enemy commanders. One saw knights of the Scyths and Issedones; horse cohorts of the Massa Getai and Thyssa Getai; Ceraunians and Cicones and Aorsi; Tower Builders and Black Cloaks; Macrones and Colchians, Maeotians and Taurians and Rhipaean Caucasians; cavalry commanders of the Phrygians,

Lykians, and Dardanians; brigadiers of the Chalybes and Mysians and Cappadocians; Gagarians and Thracians of the Strymon and the Chersonese; Saii and Tralliai and Androphagi; black Sinds and blond Alans; nation after nation and, at the center atop the Hill of Ares, the Amazons of Themiscyra and Lycasteia, Chadisia and Titaneia.

Eleuthera and Hippolyta advanced before the corps; you could see the former's triple-crested helmet and her elder, bareheaded, with slung *pelekus* and iron-colored plait. Behind them into view ascended rank upon rank. The rising sun shot flares and diadems off their bronze, burnished to incandescence, so that the front they presented was not one of figures individual or human to whom appeal might be made, but an unholy wall of glare and dazzle, blank and faceless and implacable. The line of the foe extended north across what had been the marketplace and cemetery but was now a martial plain, already called by our men the Amazoneum, out of sight round the shoulder of the Acropolis, and south an equal measure, two deep, three, five, seven, until the defenders stared out, it seemed, not upon lines or ranks but a solid sea.

Across from this our poor few hills projected like islands awaiting the flood. It was a queer moment. On the one hand, one could not but stand in terror of this colossal show of arms. Who could stand against such a host? Yet at the same time the spectacle was of such brilliant stagecraft and brought off so impeccably that one felt struck with awe and admiration and appreciated it, apart from its malevolent design, just for the showmanship. No trumpet sounded. No Amazon commander bawled attack. The foe did not start or stir, only stood, across from those she held besieged, a tide of bronze and iron before which no bastion, not even the Rock of Athena, could hope to stand.

23

STARFISH AND
SEA HORSES

No assault came at once against the city. The invaders contented themselves for the moment devastating the countryside. Attica is a big place; even the hordes of Amazons and Scyths must take time to sack it all. From atop the Rock one took in the entertainment. For the first days you could make out individual farms as the invaders razed them or, later, watching the smoke ascend in the distance beyond the hills, speculate upon which estate or vineyard now succumbed to the torch. Soon this sport expired; the landscape receded into murk. It was summer and no wind; a pall of smoke hung from Eleusis to Decelea.

That quarter of flats and tenements directly beneath the Acropolis was called then as now "the city." Its citizen population was about ten thousand, crammed into a maze of lanes and alleys clinging to the slopes at the base of the Rock. Beyond this the boroughs fanned out. "The town." As today, one went "up" to the city and "down" to the town.

The town was both more populous and more open then. The great houses of the wealthy dominated the hills of the Pnyx, the Nymphs, and the Muses; the wide squares of the Museum, the Palladium, and the hero shrine of the sons of Pandion provided meeting places for citizens and staging areas for troops; while the three great Ways, the Sacred, the Ceramic, and the Panathenaic, facilitated movement from quarter to quarter. About twenty thousand (fifty thousand including women, children, and slaves) inhabited the town in those days. Beyond, the sprawl of suburbs began, and, past this, the countryside with its farms and estates.

The city was walled then. The town was not. An ancient fortification of Pelasgian origin, called in our time the Wall of Aegeus, ringed what are now the town wards of Melite and Itoneia, but this bulwark had fallen down in so many places over the centuries and been rebuilt in such slapdash fashion as to be unserviceable, not to say unfindable, along a third of its length. Along the other two thirds, houses and tenements had been built flush abutting, incorporating the wall itself into the dwelling places. Doors and pass-throughs had been cut, even lanes and carriageways. Theseus had sought to rebuild this ancient circuit, even funding the project from his own purse. But who believed there was need for it? The scheme languished, progressing spottily if at all.

The appearance of the Amazons and Scyths changed that overnight. Beneath the lash of terror, men bricked up alleys and shuttered lanes, threw up breastworks and erected battlements. Brawls broke out over where the new wall should stand, each boroughman seeking to preserve his own kennel while lobbying for the demolition of his neighbor's. Theseus' officers, myself among them, must draft the line. Brick this house up. Tear that one down. Fields of fire had to be cleared. An open space must be made outside the wall or the foe would simply mount from the contiguous rooftops and overrun us. Stones and timbers were recruited from the razed homes and used to reinforce the spared, which now fused beneath the mason's trowel and mortarman's hod into a rampart of bricks and rubble and timber, wicker and stone and hides, with stacked baskets of sand atop the rooves, manned by every able-bodied buck, urchin, dame, and pensioner who could scrabble up a ladder and pull it up after him. The outer suburbs were left to the foe; the town and city would be defended to the death.

The permanent walls of Athens were two: the Lykomid or Outer Wall, which embraced the full circuit of the city (but not the town), and the Half Ring, the monumental bastion protecting the Acropolis itself. Both were double walls with sallyports at intervals. At the western base of the Rock squatted a system of defense works called the *Enneapylon*, the Nine Gates. These were courtyard-type bulwarks, one behind the other; they defended the Acropolis on its least severe and most vulnerable flank, directly beneath the Three Hundred Steps. The inner wall was called the Half Ring because it enclosed only the western waist of the Rock. No battlements protected the faces east and north. These were unscalable.

The Rock itself was walled massively at the summit by those great stoneworks called "the Fortress." Eleven towers studded this circuit, each sited to provide covering fire for the towers on its flanks. Embrasures for bowmen notched the circumference, with an additional forty-seven artillery ports, the "beaten zones" of whose drop ramps covered every quadrant by which the citadel could be assailed. Within the Rock the central cistern, the Deep Spring, captured drinking water year-round; steps ran down to it broad enough for two water bearers to pass abreast. Stockpiles of grain could hold out thirty-six months. Nor was there any shortage of stone to hurl down upon the foe, and if there were, the defenders would break apart the Rock itself to extract more. Theseus' chief of artillery, a transplanted Thracian named Olorus, estimated that with all forty-seven ports firing, gunners atop the Acropolis could dump thirty tons a minute, with a fall of between ninety and a hundred and forty feet. This was moot for the moment, however, as the city and its dwellings squatted directly in the path of such a barrage.

I had found Selene, among a unit (or "stick," as the Amazons call them) in the suburbs south of Coele, and would call to her across the lines. It heartened me tremendously to see her, despite the malevolence of her people's designs and her own manifest enthusiasm for them. I saw that she had steeled herself against all tender feeling toward me, yet, will you believe it, I felt confident I could overcome this if given the chance. As for my own feelings, I loved her with all my heart, more even than in Amazonia. Was this madness? I knew only that the malaise that had borne me down for two years, since the expedition's return from the Amazon Sea, had dispelled like magic at the sight not only of my beloved but of the women's army entire. Life had begun again. Though I might perish defending the nation, and in fact fully expected to, I felt not downcast but exhilarated.

Selene herself was in high spirits. All the Amazons were. They were taking the suburbs block by block and leveling them. They scorned our chockablock cottages and coops. "How can you live in these pestholes?" The warrioresses would yoke a team to a lintel and send a housefront crashing. "There, now you can breathe!"

The Amazons hated every doghouse of the metropolis. While the Scyths looted for trophies and plunder, the daughters of Ares seemed bent on eradicating the city entire. They tore up paving stones and razed pediments to the nub. Nor were their depredations confined to Attica. Selene vacated for ten days, fighting at Thebes, a great battle, we heard, at Chaeronea on the river Haemon. A corps of the Titaneia lost hundreds in Thessaly, between Scotussaea and Cynoscephalai, before making off with half the prime stock of the nation. A brigade under Hippolyta and Skyleia laid waste to the Peloponnese from the Isthmus to Patrae. They captured Nisa intact, with both ports of Nisaea and Cenchreae, as well as Troezen, Sicyon, and Orchomenos, and occupied all of Corinth except its citadel, the Acrocorinth. Amazons are not looters. They care nothing for gold, slaves, or property; the only wealth they prize is horses. They had so many now that no nation of Greece could pasture them. Certainly Attica couldn't. Selene came back from Thebes with six new animals. Her string was now seventeen. Other warrioresses had even more. These must be rotated to pastures at Marathon and Thria, in cavalcades of thousands, or driven north to the plains of Boeotia in great dust-trailing herds. The Amazons dammed the Ilissus and Cephisus and turned the Eridanos, such drizzle as it produced, into a watering trough. The Haymarket they made a racetrack. They occupied all the outer boroughs now. At night their fires blanketed Market Hill and the Hills of Ares, the Nymphs, the Pnyx, and the Knights. We camped across from them on the hills of the Muses and Ardettos; we still held the Cemetery, East Melite, and the full quarter of Itoneia.

At this early stage of the siege, the bulk of Athenian companies at arms was still quartered in the town. Horses of the cavalry units were picketed on the slope south of the Museum, others before the Palladium and Ioneum. Astonishingly, the defenders' morale held high. Now that the women and children of Athens had been gotten safely across to Euboea, the men settled to their duty. A refreshing equality suffused the site, as knights and yeomen found themselves recruited to the same chores: the erection of defense works, the clearing of fields of fire, and the humping of quarry baskets of rock up the Three Hundred Steps of the Acropolis, there to be loaded onto counterweighted booms that the engineers would crane to freight the magazines that fed the citadel's artillery. The companies labored at this task in two-hour shifts, twice one day, thrice the next. Everyone worked, including the king.

One such noon, perhaps twenty days after the invasion's onset, the lady Antiope called me to attend upon her. A page brought the summons, just as I dumped my hundredweight at the summit. "Next time hail me at the bottom!"

The lad led me to the king's palace, called the Crooked House for its inclined foundation, on the south pediment of the Rock. One could not wash up. No water for that. At the lady's door a second page waited with a broom. He beat the chalk off my back and plastered my mane with oil.

The lady received me in the nursery, which was outdoors, high up, a gallery open on two sides, screened from the sun by that type of marine canopy called a topsider. The day was high summer but the space beneath the fly remained breezy and cool. A vantage gave toward Ardettos and another to the Nine Gates. Painted dolphins disported themselves across two walls; the floor was tile made to look like sand, with sea crocuses and starfish underfoot, the whole ingeniously contrived to create the illusion of treading on ocean floor, safe beneath the waves. It was a babe's room, and a delightful one.

The lady was dismissing two knights as I entered. I recognized them as horse couriers, employed by the Council of Lords as well as by the king. "Welcome, my friend of the plains! Come in, Damon. Forgive me for not sharing an hour with you before this time."

The lady motioned me toward a child-sized bench. There was no other place to perch, save a rocking horse or a smiling-sun drum. "Don't be shy," Antiope teased. "Court ministers have parked on that hobby colt. Besides, we are all shorn of dignity in the play attic of a child."

I was struck as ever by the lady's beauty, and by an aspect I had never seen on her—sorrow. She seemed a figure of poignancy, speaking Greek, with her flesh made over by maternity. She sensed my perception. She asked if I remembered, from her country, the custom of the two cats.

"During the season of the Gathering, two felines, one black and one white, rule on alternate days. A woman is one person on Ulla's day and another on Narulla's." She smiled. "I have become in your country a different cat."

I asked what kind. I meant it lightly; to my surprise, the lady drew up with gravity. "I am no longer who I was, but not yet who I must become."

She rose from her bench, gently detaching the babe from her breast. He was a rugged tyke. Did I wish to hold him? I demurred, citing the clumsy paws of bachelorhood.

"Do you hate me, Damon?" the lady asked of a sudden. "So many do," she observed, "of your people and my own. Better I were dead, for the woe I have brought to both our nations."

Antiope set the infant in the crook of my arm. Below we could hear the couriers' horses departing. Antiope crossed the toy-littered carpet and stepped out upon the gallery. I followed.

"Do you count yourself friend to Athens, Damon?"

She meant Theseus. Most emphatically, I declared.

"You sailed with him to the Amazon Sea and have taken his part in the seasons since. Do you love him?"

I stammered something.

"I do," she swore. "More than I imagined I could love anything. More than my own people; more than this babe, flesh of my own flesh."

She squinted down toward the Half Ring, upon whose ramparts Theseus labored, somewhere, even now.

"When I departed my country at his side, I judged him a great man. But now that I have come to know him as only a wife and friend may, I realize this estimate was far too slender. Kings before him ruled by might; he governs by restraint. Who has shown such greatness of heart? Theseus dares that which not even the gods have assayed: to elevate the race of humankind. To endow each individual with sovereignty over his own heart and to lift the state as a whole to govern itself. Every hand is against him in this, even his own nature, which loves the wild ways, as you have seen. You do not appreciate what you have here at Athens, Damon. Such a thing has never existed and, once extinguished, may never come again.

"What is new too is what has been born between this man and this woman, between my husband and me. I know it is right because so many hate it. It is the hope of the world. Yet it must fall, and I must make it fall. Do you understand, my friend?"

I did not.

"My people have come for me. I must go to them. Dead or alive, they must possess me."

She had crossed back within now, to a chest whose outlines I could just make out in the sudden gloom, and, employing the key she wore on a chain about her neck, opened it. She withdrew her *pelekus*, the double axe with which she had slain Prince Arsaces in the duel at the Mound City.

"Only one deed can stop this war: the slaying of Eleuthera. She is the invading army's heart. Kill her and the host packs up for home."

She regarded me. "Yet who is a match for this greatest of warriors? Not Theseus, for all his strength and valor. Eleuthera is too quick for him. She will not let him close with her, nor is he her equal, for all his prowess, in mastery of arms. One-on-one she will beat him. And his pride will make him duel her one-on-one."

Antiope had not spoken in my direction throughout. Nor did she now, rather offered this address to herself or some unseen token, myself present as witness alone.

"Only one champion is a peer for Eleuthera."

She meant herself.

"Yet my husband forbids this. He has exacted this pledge from me, never to offer such action, even if the city fall or he himself be driven down beneath the onslaught of my countrywomen."

The Amazon turned at last in my direction.

"Do you know why I summoned you, Damon?"

I did not.

"To kill you."

She lifted the *pelekus* in its sheath of oiled fleece. "You are my size. Your tunic will cloak me. I bind my hair like yours and mask my face within the shadow of your helmet. I walk out the gate and take my place among my people. Nothing less will make them withdraw."

She met my eyes.

"But I cannot do it. This is how weak I have become."

She regarded the axe within its sheath. Here was no mean instrument, but a two-hander, stout as a woodsman's oak feller. I have seen many heft such a weapon. None held it like this Amazon. She turned from it to me.

"There is one other way this war may end."

I waited.

"If I am dead."

I begged her not to speak so.

"If I am dead, the object of the invasion no longer exists. Yet I must not perish by my own hand, for none would credit this, nor by homicide, which would inflame my people's wrath the more. Only in one way will my death produce a period to this conflict. I must fall in battle. In battle against my own."

With a tug she released the thong which bound the axe's sheath.

"My husband has divined this. It is why he has commanded that no man arm me, nor place me at hazard in any way. Do you know why he does this?"

I did not.

"To preserve my soul. Which will be lost, he believes, if I raise this arm against those who love me."

The lady forced my eyes to meet hers.

"The hour will come, Damon, when I must break the vow I have made to my beloved and arm to fight against my own. I will call you then. Will you come?"

The lady read the query which must have shone like flame in my eyes. Why me? Why not any page or squire?

As gently as a mother tugs the caul from her infant's curls, so did the Amazon slip the sheath from the double axe. "A warrior of tal Kyrte may be armed only by one who loves her. This is why I summoned Selene before the duel at the Mound City. And why I call you now."

At these words my brow flushed.

"You love the wild ways, Damon, as you love Selene. That love has twinned you with her and me and our lord the king. And with this child."

She advanced before me. With a shock I realized I yet held the babe. Before his face the lady now extended the axe, side-on and gleaming like a mirror. The child gurgled in delight; his chubby fist extended. Antiope tugged the blade clear.

"In the name of that love and of both our peoples, I beseech you, Damon: come when I call. Wrap me, I beg you, in my death armor."

Stone steps descended from the palace to the Square of Erechtheus atop the summit, congested now with bivouac tents and outdoor kitchens, facing the precinct of Athena Polias, Protectress of the City. A page was waiting when I came out. He conducted me down the Three Hundred Steps, past the sanctuary of Aphrodite Pandemos and Persuasion, the goddesses by whose aid our king had united the warring baronies of Attica, and across the sprawl of defense works to where Theseus now labored atop the Enneapylon, reinforcing the breastworks of the Seventh Gate. Gangs in hundreds sweated in the sun; the king labored too. This was how one was granted audience with the lord of Athens. You picked up a stone and toiled at his side.

Theseus offered only a glance in my direction, but in it I read plain: the couriers had reported my reception by the lady Antiope. "To what did she make appeal, my friend? Love of Athens or of Selene?"

"Both, my lord."

Before I could incriminate myself, the king eased me from the scaffold.

"I cannot let Antiope arm for battle, Damon. Not only for reasons of her honor, to avert the treason that such an act would constitute in the eyes of her people and of herself and of the world, nor for my own self-interest, the loss of her love, which I could not endure. But for the preservation of the state. And more: of the ideal of self-governance that Athens has come to embody and exemplify."

He regarded me, grave as a ghost.

"I should never have taken Antiope from her people. Some god must have addled my wits. But once taken, she must be defended to the extremity. This is the canon of kings and the ordinance of sovereign states."

His look inquired if I understood.

"If the king cannot defend his house," he said, "he cannot defend his kingdom. He fails—and Athens fails with him. Even victorious, the city's ideal falls. This cannot be permitted! Let me die defending my beloved, let the city herself fall—yet Athens's ideal lives on. But for me to survive, for the city to endure, losing Antiope? This is the solitary outcome which cannot be countenanced. Do you understand, Damon? May I have your oath, you will not arm her?"

I pledged. The king set his hand upon my shoulder.

"You imagined we had entered unknown country, my friend, when we voyaged across the sea to Amazonia. Yet that was nothing beside the frontier I cross each evening with this woman who is my equal. Each dawn new continents are sighted; each night one alights on shores where no man's sole has trod."

He laughed and squinted toward the Hill of Ares, barely a bow-shot away, upon which sprawled the central camp of the Amazons. "Have you found Selene yet?"

Several times, I replied, at Coele and south beyond the Temple of Herse and Pandrosos.

"My lady summoned you this day," our king instructed me, "because of your love for Selene. She sees you two as a set to herself and me, like pairs of fire dogs in a hearth." He clapped my back with a laugh. "Give thanks you have only to duel Selene, my friend. God help you if you must love her."

It is a terrible thing to be a king, especially a great one, for one must serve ideals of spirit at the price of lovers of flesh and blood. Who profits from a king's fidelity save generations a thousand years unborn, and which of his works will they recall at that remove, or care?

BOOK EIGHT

SISTERS IN ARMS

24

AN ARMY
OF CARPENTERS

Selene's testament:

⦿⦿⦿⦿⦿⦿⦿⦿⦿

For another month the Athenians fought us. If their manner of warfare could be called fighting.

Skyleia broadcast her outrage in night council. "God has birthed
these Greeks from his ass! Have they no shame? I have run out of insults, seeking to draw these rodents from their dens. Who has seen
this? Not even a rat fights with such want of chivalry!"

Roars seconded this. Stratonike spoke: "Where is the honor in
dueling those who huddle behind walls and within holes in the
ground? They sally to daylight as beetles, trundling their shields before them like balls of dung!" That day, the ninth in a row, our companies had routed the foe in the open, only to have him tuck tail and
scurry behind his battlements, from whose heights he launched
stones from ramps and machines. Stratonike howled at such abdica-
tions of honor. "I will not fall, crushed like an insect! Where is the
fame in this?"

The Scyths and Massa Getai added their outrage to the chorus, though for another reason.

"No gold in this country!" This was Borges' complaint, himself blind-soused three hours before midnight. His men could find neither horses nor cattle on this godforsaken promontory, he proclaimed, but only leeks and goats.

Prince Saduces of the Thracians arose, attempting a case for siegecraft. Our army must build walls of circumvallation, set sappers to dig tunnels, construct siege towers and rams. He was shouted down by knights of all nations, despising this vocation of drudges.

Glauke Grey Eyes seconded her sister Stratonike's contempt for the foe. "Who would display a scalp from men of Athens? Behold their potbellies and spindly shanks. We duel not knights but carpenters!"

Makalas, prince of the Chalybes, backed Saduces, emphasizing the strength of the enemy's position and urging that we, the allies, make study of siegecraft.

Alcippe Powerful Mare told the army's answer. "I know all I need to know of siegecraft. It is warfare shorn of honor."

Ecstatic citation acclaimed this.

"At home," Alcippe railed, "if someone ordered me off my horse to root in the muck like a sow, I would flay him on the spot. Now I do it all day! What are we becoming, protracting this siege? We will turn farmers, or worse!"

"Indeed," Skyleia picked up the tirade she had initiated, "we came to this war as innocents. We imagined we could shame the Athenians, as any warrior people, either compelling them to face us and be defeated or, by driving them behind their walls, heap upon them such ignominy as to render them impotent forever.

"We were wrong. The Athenians have no shame. I despise them! Their land is so poor they have no deer or lions but only hares, and scrawny at that. What kind of people inhabit such a country? Who elects to gnaw green berries and dry crusts? I hate this place!"

When the army had cheered itself out and had at last, it seemed, spent its outrage, Eleuthera rose.

"Sisters, no act would afford me greater satisfaction than to show my backside to this sump hole. I squat over it! I piss upon it!"

Clamorous acclaim saluted this.

"I would load up this instant and leave these catamites to steep in their own offal. But hear me, sisters and allies. If we pack up now, the very shamelessness by which our enemies confound us will be invoked by them to claim victory."

Howls of outrage ascended. Eleuthera signed for silence.

"Yes, victory. For what is victory but the driving of the foe from the field? Give Theseus this: he is a genius. And his discovery consists in this debasement of virtue—to prevail at the sacrifice of honor. This is the Athenians' invention, by which they will overturn all that is free and noble in the world."

The throng roared, indignant.

"Therefore I say: We may not pull out. We may not permit these vermin to claim victory by boring us to death or stupefying us from want of action!"

Riot acclaimed this.

"Further, we must not content ourselves with besting these mechanics as we would knights upon the steppe—that is, by counting coup and allowing them to live. We must wipe them out utterly, as an abomination upon the earth and an affront to heaven! Exterminate them to the last man! Enslave the last child and woman! Burn all to the ground! For the crime these reptiles have offered is that most abhorred by heaven, to degrade not only themselves but all who hold to honor and the warrior's code!"

For ten days attacks redoubled. Our cohorts overran the last suburbs. The foe fell back to the town. The wall defending this was unfinished. It was nothing but the facings of houses (so squat one could vault to its summit with a leap from her horse's back) with alleys and lanes bricked up in between. Sections were not even breastworks, but palisades of hides and wicker. We must storm this and root these swine from their sties.

Eleuthera attacked at the thirty-second dawn. Before the Rock had emerged from shadow, Theseus and his champions broke in disorder. Companies of tal Kyrte punched through the ramparts in a hundred places. Taurian and Lykian infantry swarmed into the borough of East Melite. The clans under Borges cut off two thousand of the foe on the Hill of the Muses; the Scyths swept into Itoneia. The enemy reeled rearward on every front; it seemed the assault would drive him all the way back to the base of the Rock. But pockets of resistance held. The maze of the town frustrated horse tactics. How could one fight in such a labyrinth? Past noon the Athenians, resisting with unwonted stubbornness, recaptured two key salients—the Temple of Herse and Pandrosos and the Square of the Return—from which, when these companies linked with their cut-off troops on the Hill of the Muses, they were able to mount counterattacks on vulnerable flanks of our allies' advance. Give the foe this: he would not quit. It took till the descent of darkness to root him off the Muses' Hill and drive him back into the city. Eleuthera ordered the town razed to its paving stones. This was more easily said than done, however, as the knights of tal Kyrte would stoop to such labor no more than Borges' Iron Mountain Scyths or any of the mounted clans of the steppe, to whom such toil is degrading and abhorrent. Yet it must be done, for without leveling the town, the camps of our army, now throttling the city like a noose, remained vulnerable to counterattack. If Theseus elected to break out in force (and he was canny enough to see that he must), we would be dueling his shield-trundling rabble within a rabbit warren of streets that could not be defended on horseback. We would find ourselves back where the day had started: clashing in a maze of lanes and alleys, within which the might of our mounted cohorts was, if not overturned, then at least neutralized. We must attack. An assault must be mounted at once against the walls of the city, behind which the foe had been, for the moment, driven—that is, the Outer, or, Lykomid Wall and, behind and above, the Nine Gates and the towers of the Half Ring. All must fall. We must drive the enemy to the summit of the Acropolis itself.

Among tal Kyrte, the unit of cavalry is called a "stick." Its complement is eleven (though some in raids are small as four or in sweeps as great as thirty). A stick's string is forty-four, four horses for each woman. Its trikona is twenty-two, maidens and novices in support, each with her own mount in addition to those of the string, and as many more as she can carry, meaning feed and find time to tend.

These were the warriors of my stick on the day the divisions under Eleuthera assaulted the Lykomid Wall: Anthea, called "Torch"; Arge Fleet; my sister Chryssa; Bremusa, "Blur"; Hesione, who fought with the *macerra*, the ten-foot pike; Calliste, "Beautiful"; Euippe, who had taken seven scalps at the Tanais; Theodora, past forty years and strongest of the lot; Scotia, "Dark"; Rhodippe Red Mare; along with our eager recruit of Thrace, Dosteia, called Stuff.

My own horses were Daybreak, Knothole, Thrush, and Snakebite, the last my night horse though Knothole, so named for his toughness, moved surefootedly in the dark as well.

This was one stick. Above a thousand comprised the corps, with seven hundred more, give or take, of our male allies. With this, my own, I would take on twice its number, the cream of any nation.

The attack came on the forty-first day. Here was how it went:

The buildings of the outer town had been broken up, as much as one could such a hive hewn of stone, isolating the city behind its Outer Wall, the Lykomid. The wall was no unbroken rampart, however, but the foe had erected redoubts and salients before it at sites of vulnerability. Staked ditches broke up the approaches. The defenders' outcamps at the west were three, at the crown of inclines fronting the Sacred and Panathenaic Gates and at the outer bastion which shielded the Nine Gates. Each was manned by about two thousand, protected likewise by staked ditches and palisades. The slopes north and east of the Acropolis had been quit by tal Kyrte. Too steep to attack. The assault would concentrate on the south and west, beneath the Hill of Ares. The northernmost redoubt fronting the Nine Gates was called the Ravelin. This was the bulwark my stick would attack.

The honor of comprising the first wave went to the Themiscyra, Hippolyta's tribe, and to prince Saduces' Trallian Thracians, all mounted archers, reinforced by elements of the Saii, armored as shock troops, with knights of the Massa Getai and Thyssa Getai fighting on foot. My unit was in the third wave, with six others of the Lycasteia and eight of the Titaneia. The plan was to assault with male infantry first; the wings of horse would follow when these had punched through. It looked good sketched in the dirt. We painted up and made our prayers. Mine was this: that should I encounter Damon across the line of battle, I would own the courage to cut him down. Between the Hill of the Pnyx and the Hill of the Muses, Eleuthera drew up four thousand horse, a mixed company of Lykians, Dardanians, and Amazons. These were to sweep the field once our assault had initiated the rout.

The battle was preceded by Eleuthera drawing up the cohort of Antiope, with Sneak Biscuits riderless at the fore, and calling to the foe's camp for our mistress. Volleys of obscenities came back. Before the line, the priestess sacrificed a black ram to Hecate. The hymn to Ares Manslayer resounded. The attack began.

I had never commanded before, that is, been responsible for lives other than my own. The experience was excruciating. How can one take care for even her own survival, let alone that of others? I ranged the line as the corps marshaled, exhorting vigilance. "Don't look so serious," my sister called. "We won't fall off!"

With a cry the male infantry charged out. I have never seen men so drunk. The line was littered with discarded skins and "nosefuls." Still they were magnificent, the Getai with their fox-fur shakos and ten-foot pikes, the Saii pushing fire waggons with tinder prows bigger than warships. Our cavalry squadrons were supposed to hold till the foe had been engaged. But riders and horses became so excited they could not be contained. Sticks of the Titaneia, the two foreranks, bolted onto the field, overtaking the foot troops before these had got within a furlong of the walls. Within ten heartbeats the trick had broken down to fiasco.

The course was all uphill, white limestone crazed with fissures, the worst footing imaginable for a mounted charge. The horses' hooves skittered on the stone; mounts spilled, fouling the squadrons laboring up the slopes behind. Attacking uphill the horses presented their breasts to the missiles of the foe, who had the advantage of slinging from above, so that our troops in the assault entered the beaten zone of their artillery a hundred feet before they could bring their own weapons to bear. A hundred feet is an eternity under fire. The Athenians bawled from the heights and let fly. Neither Scyths nor Thracians succeeded in breasting the works nor even attempted to, but beat across on the oblique, launching their volleys and coming about amid wild but empty whooping. Not one shaft in a hundred found its mark. All that prevented calamity was the terror of the Athenians. These were either the rabble of the city, or their betters performing as rabble, the main so addled with liquor they could barely stand. I saw man after man make to sling his stone and literally drop it onto his toes, so pissed or terror-befuddled was he.

Three times the lead units of Amazons and Scyths hurled themselves into the assault; three times they fell back. My stick still hadn't budged. We had actually dismounted, lashing ox-hide shoes about our mounts' hooves for footing, when a cry came from the slope to the left. The lines began moving. I could see nothing. "Strap up!" I bawled, more to inspirit my own outfit than from any intelligence of what was going on. We spurred up the stone.

The face was in natural stair steps, hurdle-high, so that the rider must scissor heels, knees, and thighs with all her strength, while with each vault and leap, her seat made to skid over her mount's hindquarters. I could feel my arrows jamming like jackstraws in their quiver; I had to take my bow in my teeth; my axe slammed so hard between my shoulder blades I could feel its whetted edge bursting the sheath and dicing into my flesh.

The bastion our stick attacked was in three linked sectors. The primary was a stockade of oak and ox-hide, at the crown of an eminence, with staked ditches below. Above and left arose a stone salient, which the Athenians called the Nipple, jutting from the slope below the northernmost wing of the Enneapylon, the Nine Gates. Fire from this covered the flank of the outwork. A third position, forward, reinforced this.

Foot troops of the Saii had breasted the trench that defended the

Nipple. They had hauled a fire waggon to the lip, a feat of stupefying valor uphill under a barrage of stone and lead. At the brink, however, we learned later, they were foiled in setting it ablaze. Someone had dropped the fire jar. In frustration the troops rammed the truck un-fired into the ditch, where it overturned among the stakes. Miracu-lously: a causeway!

Over this the infantry swarmed. Our stick and others spurred after. On the steppe one fights with speed, slinging fire from behind her horse's bulk while making herself the smallest and fastest-moving target she can. Not here. The Saii were assaulting the Nipple. The oak stockade protected this position; fire poured from it upon our al-lies. It was our job to take it, and this could only be done, we saw now, by foot assault.

The tower was two stories, hexagonal, with bunkers at three corners. The timbers were uprights. The gaps formed embrasures. Through these the foe fired bronzeheads and thrust outward with the ten-foot spear and the marine pike. Oak will not burn and is too tough to be hacked through. The only way was up and over.

Nimblest of our stick was the maiden Stuff. She taught us a new trick. She drove her mount tight to the stockade, springing from his withers with an axe in each hand; she drove these into the timbers above her head, hauling herself up hand over hand with a swiftness I could not have believed if I hadn't seen it. At the brink she van-ished. The next instant a brute of the foe appeared, clutching his guts and pitching face-foremost from the peak. Stuff was in! She hauled up Anthea and my sister, packing fire. I and four others went against the wall on foot.

On the southern wall of the stockade a stick of the Titaneia had got a line down; they were going over on that side. The fort had no portal; the defenders got in and out by ladders. I shouted to Stuff to find one and lob it over. She could not hear. We were at the north wall. Defenders thrust through the embrasures with ten-foot pikes. Rhodippe hacked one to splinters with her axe; I seized the shaft of another with both fists and hauled with all my strength. The spear-man inside pulled back. I was stronger; I wrenched it from his grip. Bremusa and Hesione had dismounted too. We beat back the foe's spears with our axes, then pressed against the stockade wall, firing ironheads through the gaps. Such elation cannot be told. We hacked through the ties of the timber and hauled the wall down with our horses. Above us the Saii whooped atop the Nipple.

We were in the city. The breastworks of the Outer Wall, the Lykomid, dropped behind; the towers of the Half Ring loomed above. The place was a neighborhood, a civilian quarter. The foe had been clever; he had walled up lanes and alleys at random, so that attackers could not tell, spurring into one, whether it led onward or into a dead end. Our horse troops fell for this trick more than once, chasing gangs of the foe into bystreets, only to find ourselves penned on three sides, while he, in squads of ambushers, scurried from house interior to house interior, through whose party walls he had punched passageways, emerging to sling darts from alley grates or unleash fusillades of stones from the peaks of rooves.

We galloped onto the Ring Road. The defenders had broken it up with pitfalls, staked ditches, and leg-breakers. The tents and shacks of his camps fouled the track further; I saw Hesione's horse pitch into a trench at a gallop, shattering both forelegs and hurling her rider like a doll.

Breaches had been opened all along the Lykomid Wall, and through these Saii, Trallian Thracians, and Amazons surged. But the defenders, in addition to their other ploys, had erected cross-bulwarks, firewalls, at right angles to the Outer Wall, with secondary walls cutting off the go-round, and to these they now retreated, hurling stones and missiles, so that our companies had to fight from pocket after pocket, each of which was too confined to permit cavalry tactics and each of which ran exposed to artillery from the Half Ring above. The layout was a labyrinth; all that saved us was the muddle of the foe. The Greeks were mazed with terror. The first crosswall we rushed was of wicker filled with stone. Horses and women jammed up prime for slaughter, but when artillery began raining from above, it was the foe who panicked and not us. We swarmed the wicker hand over hand. Stick after stick punched through the seams. Before us the enemy stampeded for the next wall. "No trophies!" I bawled. "Just cut them down!"

At each rupture the foe broke before us. The bow was useless. Over such ground no one can ride hands-free. The axe. We fought with the axe and our horses' hooves, trampling every man we could get under us. The Greeks fought back from trenches and cavities, on their knees, ramming at our mounts' bellies with pike and spear and the sundered stubs of their one-handers. Artillery rained from the Half Ring above. Chunks of limestone the size of field balls burst at our feet; rebounds caromed, wreaking havoc on the horses when they hit and sowing panic when they didn't, from the animals' innate terror of something sharp and fast-moving beneath their vision.

I cannot say how many walls we assaulted. The hive seemed to go on forever. Our climax came at the crown of an incline. The crew our stick dueled was a dozen, their fort a bathhouse, which stood at the crook of a lane, demolished and afire. Three had mounted to the roof; the rest made their stand behind the court wall. A noble olive rose in the center. Chryssa, Anthea, Stuff, and I took our mounts over the partition. Within the cloister the struggle reached its crisis.

The three on the roof hurled bricks and tiles. In the court others stabbed with butt ends of splintered pikes and lances. One with great chin whiskers swung a mace at Daybreak; I drove him under the eave and took half his shoulder with the axe. A runt on the roof made to return the favor. His foot slipped; he slid down the tile, on his back like a child on the ice, to plunge right over me, landing on Daybreak's hindquarters, spilling hard to the stone of the court. Stuff fell on him with a cry; I saw her smash a heel into his temple, then dive on him with the sickle blade the Thracians call a "nut-cutter." From the wall others of ours, with allies of the Scyths and Lykians, poured bow fire onto the trapped Athenians. The foes' last missiles had been spent. I saw one, their captain, apparently, seize a dry cheese and hurl it in despair at Hesione as she rushed at him on foot. Another Athenian attacked, wielding an oak table. They never had a chance. Our stick sparred with the Scyths over the scalps.

Ten minutes more and the day's fight was over. The foe's artillery, firing from towers atop the Half Ring, protected his companies as they scurried like rats for the safety of the inner gates.

I rallied my stick. I cannot overstate my dread that one or more had been lost or maimed. Here came my sister with Scotia and Euippe. Stuff, she told, had chased off afoot, harrying the foe. I vowed to scourge her when she returned, but in the event forgot and embraced her in tears. I assembled the remainder, with only wounds that would heal, thank God, and sent them to gleaning, meaning to scour the field for reusable shafts and missiles; the balanced lance and unwarped arrow were dearer than gold. For myself, my nerves were wrung to tatters, from fear for those I commanded. Even my horse was more exhausted than the others.

Prisoners of the foe were being rounded up. My stick had washed up among clans of the Iron Mountains. The Scyths went after the enemy wounded like drovers on cattle, noosing the wretches to haul them off to the slavers' block. This was in violation of Eleuthera's and Hippolyta's orders, who had commanded all captives be segregated for interrogation. But since when did a Scyth care a whit for the orders of an Amazon?

Before the lines, our allies massed, wrangling their prizes as if they were steers. We had wrested a few to safety; more now bolted in fright. The Scyths ran them down and hacked off their hands. "Here, now you can have them!" The butchered Athenians bawled in horror; their mates cried for ransom. They had gold, they pledged, in the citadel, and named preposterous sums which their mates would hand over if only their captors would spare them. Gold is honor to the Scyths. Now these went after the captives who had bolted to our lines, demanding them back. Our front dug in. A bloodbath stood imminent, ally against ally.

At this moment Eleuthera thundered onto the site. She took in the fix at a glance and, dismounting, advanced upon the Scyths, striking with her whip. Others of ours followed, likewise plying the lash. The Scyths fell back dumbfounded. Such was the brilliance of Eleuthera's instinct, knowing that these liegemen, accustomed to being treated as vassals themselves, would retire before the presumption of the lash, when they would have repelled in pride an advance at arms.

My stick got away to our horses. In a raid of a hundred on the steppe, perhaps one animal will fall. Here in this war an hour's toll was four of eleven, splendid mounts all, and a fifth, Hesione's Anare, "Keen," legs broken in agony. Hesione ended his misery, strangling him with her riding wale while her eyes held his in death. Fallen mounts we dragged from the field by teams, not across the stone, which would have constituted desecration, but lashed aboard litters of hide and wicker. Heartbroken, our stick fell back to the stockade below the Nipple. A cloudburst had broken; rivers sluiced down the slope; in the pall beneath the stormheads the foe's artillery at last broke off. We stumbled to the remains of the first camp, the one with the stockade of oak.

Dead and dying horses were everywhere, their riders seeking them in anguish to end their torment. Many had broken legs and backs. No sight is more heart-scoring than that of a riven beast, thrashing to rise on two legs or three. "I cannot endure this!" Rhodippe cried, meaning stand by out of honor, waiting for each animal's rider to find it so she herself could put it from its misery. I released my stick to this work. They doled their deliverance as swiftly as they could. Rain sheeted down. The stone where the enemy had bivouacked squatted grimy with wine jars and sacks of poppyseed, lentils, and peas. Refuse spread in a welter, bread in flat loaves, ropes of garlic, wallets of onions and radishes and leeks. One saw shields cast aside, and even stacked arms, which the defenders had abandoned, fleeing. Excrement mounded beneath straw in the slit trenches, steaming in the downpour. Upslope we could hear the Scyths, still brawling over the prisoners.

"Is this how it will go?" Chryssa put into words the revulsion each of us felt.

I ordered all to shut up and look to their arms and horses.

25

THE MUSICIAN'S REPORT

~~~~~~~~~

I was summoned that night to assist in the interrogation of prisoners. This was at the main camp on the Hill of Ares. They did not need torture, these captives of the tent, just one peek at the Scyths outside.

Eleuthera did not oversee the interviews personally, being called to more urgent business. Her needs, we were told, were intelligence of the foe in three areas: water, food, and morale.

The fourth prisoner I questioned was a musician. This man, more even than his fellows, had been struck with horror by the chopping off of hands. He began to speak with such obvious truthfulness that I sent for the commanders to hear him. Glauke Grey Eyes and Skyleia arrived first, then Alcippe, and Hippolyta with Eleuthera, who took over.

By now the musician had recovered his courage. You could see him steel himself for torture and death. He would supply, he declared, no intelligence that might work harm on his countrymen.

To her credit Eleuthera resisted the application of terror. The musician had not been apprised of her identity and she did not volunteer it, introducing herself only as a captain of cavalry and friend of Athens. She admired the captive's spirit, she testified, and would honor the limits he set to his interrogation.

"Impart this only, my friend. What does Theseus tell the people? I admire your king and wish to make myself his student. Answer, please, and I will ask no more: By what arguments does your lord keep up the defenders' spirits?"

The musician balked. Not from fear, one felt, but delicacy, even chivalry. A faithful recounting of the king's words must offer insult to the foe, he said, meaning us. Sooner slay him now and get it over with.

Eleuthera ordered wine brought for the man and, taking the bench at his side, pledged impunity by Hecate and the Great Mother. The musician would not be harmed if he spoke the truth. Nor would he work injury to his country, merely by relaying its king's assessment of the foe.

It took some coaxing, and no lone noseful from the store of wine, but at length the fellow relented.

"Theseus tells the people first to have faith in our fortifications. The Acropolis is impregnable, he declares. He cites his travels throughout all Greece and the Eastern seas and proclaims our citadel the mightiest natural fortress on earth, unscalable and irreducible."

No axe fell on the man's neck, no slivers were inserted beneath his fingernails. He settled, gaining confidence, and plugged on.

"With the Deep Spring, Theseus tells us, we draw water from an inexhaustible source. We have grain in abundance, and more coming in each night from Euboea through the porous lines of the foe. The Amazons and their allies cannot cross in force to the island, to which our wives and children have been evacuated; the foe does not have ships, and she fears the sea. The channel may be narrow, Theseus acknowledges, but our war vessels, even our ferries and scows, can beat back any ragtag armada cobbled together by the enemy."

Eleuthera absorbed this soberly. "What else does Theseus say?"

The musician hesitated, fearing, he declared, to offer offense.

"Speak! We want truth, not flattery."

"Theseus says those who besiege us, excepting the Lykians, Phrygians, and Dardanians, are wild tribes. They possess neither discipline nor patience, he contends. They cannot sustain a siege. Further, Theseus tells the people, the contingents of the Scythians and Thracians, Massa Getai and Thyssa Getai, are not the nations entire under command of their kings but wild young bucks, enlisted for plunder and adventure, and unofficered by any but themselves. Though born fighters, they are proud, fractious, and ungovernable. They can endure anything but tedium and will make any sacrifice save cooperation with an ally. They possess valor in quantities unquenchable, and when worked to a pitch of intoxication (as they invariably are, entering battle) will die three times before they fall. They are great fighters, Theseus tells us, but a bad army. We Athenians, on the other hand, may be poor fighters but a good army."

The musician's throat grew dry. Eleuthera wet it.

"Further, our king attests, the wild tribes who besiege us despise one another. Their foremost delight is to steal each other's horses and carry off each other's women. To them the assault on our city is but a diversion in which they indulge for booty and novelty before returning to their habitual round of warfare upon one another. Further, the Amazons, though technically at the head of the alliance, are in fact hated by the other tribes, who are jealous of their independence and covetous of their lands and herds. The Scyths and Thracians would fall upon them in a heartbeat if they thought they had a chance to prevail.

"Theseus adds, of the Amazon commander Eleuthera, that she is the least likely to control such headstrong troops, as she is just like they are—rash, intemperate, given to impulse and overhaste, constitutionally incapable of compromise or coalition-building. She is the kind of leader, Theseus assures the people, who by her willfulness and arrogance will drive her allies apart from the Amazon cause. We defenders need do nothing to cleave the corps arrayed against us. Eleuthera will do it for us. The Amazons, Theseus declares, have only two leaders capable of commanding allegiance and obedience

from all: Hippolyta, who at past sixty years lacks Eleuthera's war prestige, and Antiope—who stands with us."

This testimony was received soberly, so true did it strike to the
mark. "The besiegers' forces," Eleuthera continued to the musician,
"outnumber yours five to one. What does Theseus say to this?"

"He assures us the foe's numbers work against her. We need not
fear their multitudes, Theseus says. The root of the Amazons'
prowess is their horsemanship. He declares he has not seen the horse
yet who can scale a wall or leap a twenty-foot battlement. The enemy has thirty-five thousand animals. How can she feed them? Not
in Attica, that is certain. She must range afield, across the Isthmus
even, while each raid she makes outrages more nations and converts
more allies to our cause. The Amazons must find pasturage for their
herds, not ranging over leagues of grassland steppe, but stuck here all
year on fields of stone.

"But the enemy, Theseus declares, cannot remain in Attica
another year. Her mares at home will foal in the spring. Even now
foes encroach upon her lands. For the Amazons the war must be won
by summer's end. Remember too, Theseus tells the people, that this
country of ours is to these besiegers the ends of the earth. They don't
want it. What can they use it for? They abhor it. They only wish to
destroy us and go home.

"In sum, Theseus proclaims, the defenders need only hold pa-
tient to prevail. Athens need not defeat the enemy in battle. We
need never set foot off the Rock. The foe will grow weary of this kind
of warfare, to which she is not suited and within which her strengths,
however magnificent on other fields, are neutralized. In the end she
will give up and go home."

The musician finished. His knees, even his ankles, quaked, so
certain was he that this report would incite his captors' wrath. Nothing of the kind. Rather the acuteness of Theseus' understanding of
our weaknesses and those of our allies struck the company mute.

"Your king owns a canny head, my friend. And you have done
well not to seek to deceive us."

Eleuthera ordered the musician fed and returned to his comrades
in detention outside, but given no especial care that might draw at-

tention to him and thus set him at peril of reprisal from his country-men. He would be ransomed with the others and returned to the Athenian lines.

An expulsion of breath conveyed the prisoner's relief. Eleuthera had risen and turned to depart.

"One thing more . . ."

At the musician's words our commander turned back.

"They're scared," the man appended.

Of what?

"Of you. Of women. Of women such as you.

"My countrymen are dread-stricken," the musician explained, "by the Scyths and Thracians, who to them are beasts taking form as men. But of you their terror exceeds even this. Men fear to die at your hands as they would being devoured by wolves. You are mon-sters to them. You cannot be human, they believe, for how could gentle mothers, as must be the same in all lands, produce daughters like Gorgons and Hydras? Theseus, when he seeks to stanch the peo-ple's fears, makes this point alone: that you breathe air and bleed blood as we do. Few believe him. They think you have fallen from the moon, which you worship."

Eleuthera inquired how Antiope was received by the Athenians.

"They approach her in awe, those who dare," the musician an-swered, "and study her every move when she appears in public, which is seldom, so wretched does she seem at the woe she has brought to Athenian and Amazon alike. Yet men marvel at her; they ape her walk and speech. Many urge that she be armed to fight in our cause, thinking her the equal of Theseus and worth battalions on her own."

Last, Eleuthera asked how much Antiope contributed to the counsel of Theseus. The musician answered that he could not know what passed between the pair in bed, but in the city it was well known that Antiope would not so much as step forth onto the bat-tlements but remained in the citadel's innermost cloister, as if she could not bear to hear the fighting or receive report of its floods and ebbs.

The Scyths and Massa Getai returned past midnight. For hours

Eleuthera wrangled with them and the other allies. We had won a mighty victory today. Yet our comrades chafed for want of plunder. I and others must produce prisoners, to bear witness to the gold held by Theseus on the Rock, nor were Borges and his fellows satisfied till several of these had expired under torture, so testifying.

Among the Scyths and Thracians, three commanders had emerged—Saduces, lord of the Tralliai; Hermon of the tribes east of the Strymon; and Borges of the Iron Mountain Scyths. They all wanted gold.

"You have sacked Attica entire," Eleuthera replied in exasperation. "What of that?"

"It is gone," declared Borges.

Eleuthera had already promised the allies half the treasure of the Acropolis. What more did Borges want?

"The men to kill. The women and children for slaves."

They are yours, Eleuthera vowed. "But you will take my orders and fight the way I command."

Borges wanted the prisoners, the ones taken this day. It was his way to demand and demand, and nothing but blood would make him stop.

"The prisoners go back to the Rock." Eleuthera put a period to the debate. "Take more and I will send more back. For each is a belly Theseus must feed and a soul whose terror he must quell. Do not lose sleep, Borges. You will get them all in the end."

When the session had adjourned, near dawn, I approached Eleuthera alone.

"And what is your complaint?" she demanded.

I took hurt at this tone. My friend saw it.

"Forgive me, Selene. This is the state to which I have been reduced by this relentless politicking."

We walked together. She wanted to hear of the army. How were their spirits?

I told of my eleven. What had unnerved them most this day was not the unwonted manner of fighting, nor even the casualties among our comrades, but the fearsome toll this type of combat inflicted on the horses. The sacrifice of these noble beasts had broken our hearts, particularly in the fight's aftercourse, when we must destroy those shot and maimed and leg-broken. Interring our beloved mounts this night, I informed Eleuthera, many sisters had experienced a keener grief, it seemed, than for mates of womankind.

Eleuthera, I saw, shared this anguish.

"A warrior, however grievously slain, may be made beautiful in state," she observed. "But a dead horse just looks dead. What sorrow cuts deeper than to raise the barrow over innocents fallen? No love, we think, may be greater than ours for them. Yet ours is nothing alongside that which they return. Tenfold they repay our devotion. They give and give, till their hearts burst beneath us, and, dying, seek only to give more."

Our commander's voice broke. I felt her hand clasp mine. We drew up where we stood. She had become again the friend of my girl-hood; love for her flooded my heart.

"Will you stay with me, Selene?"

She wished me to detach myself from my unit, serve with her in staff command.

"I need one at my side who loves me. I cannot bear this weight alone."

Of course I would.

We walked farther, mounting the Hill of the Pnyx, overlooking the Athenian lines. I told her of a clash in camp this evening, with my sister. This was after the Fire Ceremony, the inhuming of the horses, when grief had left us all lacerated to the quick.

"I had given Chryssa an order," I recounted. "She refused it. She challenged the whole conceit of giving orders. 'It is not *rhyten annae*. Not the way we have always done it.'

" 'There must be discipline,' I insisted.

" 'Nobody ever bossed me before. And certainly not my younger sister! To appoint us officers over one another is *netome!* It is Eleuthera's doing, who hates the Greeks so much she has become just like them!'

"I flew at my sister; our mates had to pull us apart. Afterward I told her she was right. Giving orders is not *rhyten annae*. It is not 'how we have always done it.' "

Eleuthera flared at this. "So our warriors do not like taking orders. Too bad. I will ram orders down their throats."

She seized my arm and marched me to the crest.

"Look there, Selene. The camp of the Strymonian Thracians, five thousand men at arms. There the Tralliai, seven and a half thousand. Lykians, Phrygians, Dardanians, Cappadocians; see, south, the horse nations of the Massa and Thyssa Getai, the Royal Scyths and Issedones, the Chalybes, Gagarians, the knights of the Rhipaean Caucasus, and, most numerous, Borges and the clans of the Iron Mountains. How many? Forty thousand? Sixty? You stood in the tent this night. Borges champed to eat us raw. One breath of weakness and he would have."

Eleuthera gestured to the Rock. She would have broken it apart with her teeth, she hated it so.

"Understand one thing, Selene: we must come away from this place with victory. If we fail and try, then, to get home, these same tribes we call allies will man every pass and bar every river crossing. Perhaps we should not have made this war. Its undertaking may have been madness. But we have stepped off the precipice, and nothing will break our fall till the bottom."

Eleuthera had not slept, I knew, in at least two nights. Yet here at dawn my friend stood annealed by such fire as would drive her unfailing, it seemed, this day and the next after that.

"Tell this to your sister," Eleuthera addressed me, "and those other knights whose necks are too stiff to fight this war the way it must be fought. I will break their necks! Who resists shall perish, beneath the foe's hand or my own, by Artemis and Ares Manslayer, I swear. The people's survival comes before all, victory or death!"

26

NIGHTS AND DAYS

〰〰〰〰〰

I left my unit in command of Chryssa and Euippe and, packing my novices, took my place among Eleuthera's Companions. The siege had passed its fiftieth day.

Borges, greedy to capture the Athenians' women and children to sell as slaves, had defied our commanders' injunction and mounted a seaborne assault on the island of Euboea. That is the charitable way of putting it. In truth the mob of clansmen launched upon the channel in log rafts and scows. The Athenians made dice of them. Three hundred drowned, that fate most hideous to a Scyth. The host fell back on the city in grief and rage. They tore apart the Lykomid Wall, which had been captured at such terrible cost, and which was indispensable now in keeping supplies from getting in to the enemy and, more critical, keeping their appeals for aid from getting out. The tribesmen leveled it at one go, with our own rioting to join the entertainment.

Siege warfare now began in earnest. There was no other way to assault thirty-foot walls; even Eleuthera could see this. The Chalybes, master ironsmiths, and the Mossunoikoi, the Tower People, took the lead. The latter inhabit the densely forested foothills of the Ceraunian Caucasus, a terrain impossible to defend by conventional means, as any encroaching foe can close without being detected, concealed within the timber. Thus the great towers these people build. I have never seen them, but they are said to comprise whole towns, carved of unfireable hardwood and elevated a hundred feet above the forest floor. Roundabout these stockades the Tower People clear the woodland for miles. They hunt and fish and are, so they claim, the happiest of men, invulnerable within their forest forts.

These fellows now became our siege engineers. Here is the art they employed: They first erected masts, with armored bunkers atop, overtowering the walls of the Half Ring. To these stations mounted archers of the Copper River Scyths, experts in the foot-braced bow, which can fire an arrow a third of a mile. With these shafts—which were of such length and girth that the Athenians used them as javelins when they recovered them—our allies hurled fire over the enemy's walls and sowed terror along his lanes, as no site within the city was too remote to be struck by these long-range missiles. Many of the foe's houses had thatched rooves. These he himself tore off. Every street corner, we heard, sprouted its mounds of sand and pumice, with shovels and paddles plunged aboard, and pots of vinegar and birdlime for the brigadiers to snatch up against the conflagrations ignited by our archers' incendiary darts.

Alongside the masts our champions next set up towers, sheathed with hides and felt to retard the "fried eggs" (firepots of flaming pitch and sulphur, made to shatter upon impact) and "scorpions" (brands of burning tallow with iron spikes extending, meant to hook onto a surface) which the foe hurled and launched in salvos of a hundred. We countered with volleys of tow and frankincense gum. Six, eight, even ten of our Scyths could launch at once from the towers. With twelve such turrets firing in unison, the barrages cleared the foe's walls at one swipe and, judging by the clamor within, terrified the defenders all the way back to the face of the Rock.

The foe countered our broadsides by stringing sails, hides, carpets, and even ladies' wicker dressing screens across the crowns of his walls. He ran these up on lines and pulled them taut with windlasses. The place looked like a harbor lane on laundry day. But it worked. The enemy also made his battlements taller by erecting towers of baskets filled with sand and brick. These would not stand against troops in the assault but they did the job stopping missiles.

Our engineers next built rams to assault the gates. The enemy parried by lowering great bags of chaff and inflated ox-hides to damp the blows. He lassoed the rams or poured blazing pitch and sulphur upon them. In gangs the foe would roller a great stone atop the besieged gate's lintel, then a boy would creep out on a beam with a plumb bob (the lad himself shielded by a rolling carapace of iron maneuvered by his fellows atop the wall, while mighty fusillades of arrows, stones, and sling bullets hailed upon him) to set the ram within the gunners' sights. Then they'd drop the stone. Hit or miss, one had never heard such a racket of cheers and groans.

The foe rigged counterrams and sham walls. He erected walls behind walls and gates behind gates. When our sappers sought to tunnel under, the enemy countered, releasing bees and hornets. He even set a bear loose; God only knows where he got it. By the sixty-first day our Chalybes and Tower People had rigged a colossal siege engine, forty feet high, with rollers as tall as a man and overheads of oak two feet thick. The machine had bunkers atop for sixty archers, whose fire would clear the foe from the parapets, while a bronze-faced ram a hundred feet long, housed beneath the engine's overhead and propelled by two teams of forty men each, would assault the gate. The contraption was sheathed in iron and warped up the slope by teams of horses, four hundred strong. The entire army massed, whooping and bawling encouragement, while the foe's complement, absenting no one, it seemed, returned the clamor from atop the walls.

Up the slope the colossal engine trundled. The foe hailed scorpions and fried eggs upon it. These salvos rebounded harmlessly off the iron. What a machine! Even the knights of tal Kyrte had fallen in love with it. We whooped ourselves witless as it beetled, like a moving city, up the incline. I could see the great ram beneath the sheathed mantlet. Our army was massed in its battalions, awaiting only the staving of the gate. But Theseus, that serpent, had outwitted us again. He had sent his sappers beneath the walls in the night, undermining the earth over which our engine must approach. The Chalybes were wise to this gambit, however, and had sent a bold fellow before the machine's passage, shielded by its brow. This stalwart set a shield bowl-downward on the earth, which he then sounded upon, rapping for such hidden voids. Alas, an unlucky shot (lucky for the foe) took him in the foot. By the time his mates had hauled him to safety, the machine was within forty feet of the wall. No one would call hold now. I was behind and to the left when the forward rollers crashed through the hollowed-out earth. Thirty warp lines snapped as one; the teams of horses at the base of the slope sprawled like spindles. The tower's rollers punched through the voids. Men were spilling from its upper bunkers like wasps from a hive, some shinnying down the timbers of the face, others mounting to the penthouse, more calling upon the gods and vaulting from the heights. On the walls the Athenians put up a cry. The machine wallowed in its trough. Timbers cracked with a sound like thunder. When it finally toppled and crashed, even our own could not restrain their cheers. It was the most spectacular fiasco we had ever seen.

Such was the day's work. At night the army amused itself with a different diversion. This was the hectoring of those bunkers and outworks of the foe that had been overrun when we drove him back behind the Half Ring. These pocket forts still had men in them. Several stood as close to the wall as two hundred feet.

It became a sport after dark: the defenders dashing to bear food and water to their countrymen, the besiegers sprinting to intercept them. We called their runners "rabbits." Clouds of missiles flew at these speedsters while their compatriots in the island forts trailed harnesses over their battlements, into which the racers sprung and were hauled up hand over hand. From the citadel the foe in thousands cheered his champions, while, spurred by corresponding stanzas of the Amazons and Scyths, our own youths galloped the gantlet of protective fire, trying to bag these buggers in midbolt. Boldest of the foe were two lads who came to be called "Spider" and "Scooter." Bounties were offered for their hides. Everyone took a run at them. Most reckless was my novice Stuff. Going after Spider one night, she foozled her shot point-blank. The host hooted in derision. Stuff was beside herself. She vaulted from her mount, overhauled the youth, and dived onto his back just as he leapt into the haul rig. The pair here snatched airborne jerking like shot eels, the lass seeking to rip her rival from his cinch, the lad kicking to shuck his attacker. Stuff hung on to the top, so close that defenders were piking at her fists and dinging stones off her helmet. At last her grip was beaten apart. She plummeted thirty feet, tumbling another hundred down the slope. Cheers erupted from both sides when she sprang to her feet unhurt.

The siege was going nowhere.

I had moved to the main camp on Ares' Hill. Eleuthera did not call me to her bed. That honor had gone to the maiden Stuff. I was content with this, though bewildered by my friend's insistence upon my close attendance. Days would pass without Eleuthera addressing a word to me, yet if I made to slip apart she caught at me in alarm. Once, alone with her, I asked why she wished me so near if I were to be neither lover nor counselor. "You are a champion," she declared, as if nothing could be more obvious.

Another night I walked the lines with her.

"Do you see that wall, Selene? No siege engine will take it. We must do it ourselves, by frontal assault." The Half Ring loomed directly across, so close we must take care for Theseus' Cretan archers, who had nailed more than one of ours with a potshot. "Yet how do I initiate it?"

She meant casualties.

"I spouted bluster the other night, raving about breaking necks." She laughed. "One cannot enforce discipline on warriors such as ours. They must be led, as children or horses. Speech will not serve. Sign and action they understand. I must produce a spectacle for them."

For ten days Eleuthera drew up the cohort of Antiope before the walls. This was the special battalion, whose commander's berth had been left vacant—awaiting Antiope's return to her people. To the fore of this company Eleuthera set our lady's mount, Sneak Biscuits, riderless, in armor. No proclamation was offered, no herald dispatched. A thousand simply took station, silent, beneath the walls.

The Athenians did not respond. They manned the battlements, at places shoulder to shoulder, but did not launch stones or, more remarkable, abuse.

Antiope did not appear the first day, or the second or third or the fourth. The cohort held, dawn to dusk. Other than sluices of urine or mounds of apples from the horses, no sound or action came. The odd rider swooned, overcome by the sun; she lay on the stone where she had pitched, till she recovered or till night's descent dismissed the troop.

The rest of tal Kyrte were free to look after their own business. None did. All were held by a tension approaching the unbearable. One dozed and woke and dozed again.

The allies hated this. They did not understand. It bored them. They continued their raids across the Isthmus and north into Boeotia and Phocis. Their greed had reduced every croft within fifty miles. Their horses and ours had cropped the country to whisker.

Within the walls we could hear the Athenians working. From the hill we could see them. They were breaking up the residential quarters enclosed by the Half Ring, using the stone to reinforce the wall and to fortify positions within.

Theseus was keeping them busy.

For our part, we had dammed the Ilissus, the Cephisus, and the Eridanos. Cisterns had been founded to contain the flow of these miserable streams. In the exhilaration of the initial overrunning of Attica, our companies had demolished springhouses and wells. Now these must be restored, stone by stone, as thirst began to torment the besiegers.

The sixth day passed, and the seventh. Still Antiope did not appear.

Watch discipline of the Scyths and allies remained atrocious. With the outer wall torn down, Theseus' couriers came and went all night, bearing dispatches to the baronial strongholds upcountry, to the camps on Ardettos, Hymettos, Lykabettos, and out of Attica entirely. They got supplies from Euboea and, worse, correspondence. Letters kept up the defenders' spirits, while no measure of threat or blandishment could seal the sieve that was our lines.

Then one evening Antiope appeared.

There are two main gates of the Enneapylon—the Sacred and the Aegeid. It was upon the latter that our lady stepped forth. She was clad in mixed attire, Greek and Amazon: a white quilted jerkin beneath a bronze cavalry breastplate and a russet overcloak, with a bear-claw clasp, emblem of Artemis Who Assists at Childbirth, which all recognized as a gift from her mother, Celia, passed down from her mother-mother Hippolyta.

Within moments of her appearance the entire army had mounted, Scyths and allies included. Atop the Half Ring not a space remained, while the parapets at the summit swarmed with defenders.

Eleuthera and Hippolyta spurred to the fore of our formation. The allied commanders Borges, Saduces, and Hermon, with Skyleia, Glauke Grey Eyes and Stratonike, took their places on the flank.

Theseus had not appeared.

Antiope's cohort saluted with her war song. She elevated one hand in response. In the stillness succeeding, a child's cry pealed.

In the crook of our queen's arms was her infant.

With both hands she held the babe aloft. The troops murmured. This ascended to a rustle, then to a sort of rolling anthem. Antiope addressed Hippolyta, directly beneath her on Frostbite, with her leopard skin across her shoulder and her iron-colored plait falling to the middle of her back.

"Hippolyta, best of the people, I show you your great-grandchild, whom I have named in your honor Hippolytus."

From the host arose a rumble, yet inarticulate, but boding of wrath and indignation.

"Will you accept this innocent, Mother-mother, as blood of your blood?"

From where I stood I could see Eleuthera's face. A look shot from her to her elder which clearly warned: Take care, sister, for acts now contain the fate of the people.

Eleuthera herself spoke first, addressing Antiope:

"Make no more of this child, lady. Leave him with his father, where he belongs. I call upon you now. Come down and take command of your cohort. And I pledge before God and this host that if you do, I will yield my office. What you order, I shall obey. Only return to your people, sister and friend. Lead us again."

Now Theseus appeared. Not at his bride's shoulder, in such position as would indicate he stood as her lord, but set back several paces upon the battlement. Antiope neither turned toward him nor acknowledged his arrival.

"If I descend from these walls and take command of the free people," Antiope's answer rang down, "my first order will be to withdraw. Will you obey me?"

"We have made this war for you, lady," Eleuthera answered. "You restored, we turn for home."

Cries of outrage rose from the Scyths and allies. Across the faces of the hills the multitude beat spear shafts against shields. Even the corps of tal Kyrte picked up the tattoo.

"If I come, I bring this child. Will you accept him?"

Indignation ascended. From every quarter arose cries of "Never!" and "Take him to hell!" Antiope elevated the babe again, addressing Hippolyta.

"Look on this babe, Mother-mother, whose blood is yours, and issue of both our nations. How can I hate him? I may not carve him down the middle, giving my heart to one half while warring upon the other. I must love all of him."

More outrage from the army. Antiope's response rang from the battlements.

"I repudiate these leaders who have used me as a pretext to make this war. I want no part of it. I will resist any act which promotes war between us, and embrace every undertaking which bears our nations toward peace."

Antiope finished. Hippolyta spurred forward. Her speech sounded for the whole army to hear.

"You dare hold up a boy-child, Antiope. Then hear what my heart tells me. Boys grow to men!" She gestured with her axe in challenge to Theseus. "Will the scion diverge from the stock? Will the heir stand with women against those who would bind them in chains?"

"Sisters," Antiope cried, "here is your chance for peace!"

"I give you peace!" Eleuthera bolted forward onto the flat beneath the bastion. "Fight me! Settle this now!"

The throng thundered in ovation.

Antiope held the child close. "You want no peace, sister. You come for hate, which is your anthem and that of tal Kyrte. I fear you and grieve for you."

"Keep your grief. Face me!"

"I will not!"

"Fight me now!"

"Never!"

Antiope's glance darted to Theseus.

"Is he your master?" Eleuthera roared. The army clamored its endorsement. Before the host Eleuthera spurred to Antiope's riderless horse, Sneak Biscuits, who was held by a groom at the fore of the cohort. Without dismounting, she stripped the animal of his armor. His war bridle she dashed; headstall and trappings she flung to the dirt. With a lash of her quirt Eleuthera drove the beast upslope to the Aegeid Gate, from whose battlements Athenian and Cretan archers drew down on her, point-blank. Yet such was the violence of her will that none dared fire. Eleuthera beat on the bronze plate of the gate with the flat of her axe and when the bolt was cleared and the portal cracked ajar, she drove Sneak Biscuits through.

She lashed back into the open, crying up to the towers. You could not hear above the uproar. You did not need to. The army saw Eleuthera elevate her axe and point it at Theseus. She held this posture, then swept her blade toward that level ground fronting what had been the Athenian marketplace, an arena capacious enough to stage a bout of single combat.

Every eye swung toward Athens's monarch. Theseus offered no response. Eleuthera repeated her challenge and, when again it was refused, wheeled to face the armies of the besiegers, elevating both arms as if to say, I have tried and been repudiated.

Now ascended the mightiest roar yet. Jeers and insults were flung at the walls from a hundred thousand throats. Before this storm Theseus withdrew, and Antiope trailed after him.

I watched Eleuthera spur back to resume her station before the corps. Though she made her face a mask, yet in the cast of her jaw one read plainly that she had got the spectacle she wanted. By sign and action she had fueled the fever that would drive the army in assault on the walls and had turned the nation and the alliance, even those who feared and hated her, to her will.

BOOK NINE

UNDER SIEGE

27

THE TOLL OF VICTORY

Damon:

〰〰〰〰〰

Here was how Eleuthera came against the walls. She picked out weak points, where the thickness of the stone was under ten feet and the slope least severe. Against these she sent her Chalybes and Tower People. The foe advanced behind mobile stockades, foretimbers faced with iron. Fire and stone could do nothing against such dreadnoughts. The sappers worked their way flush to the walls. Here they dug in and commenced their boring.

The besiegers' tunnelers were miners of the Copper River and stonecutters from the Rhipaean Caucasus; the defenders were masons from the Ceramicus and quarrymen from Pentelicon. Now the duel began. The foe trucked out stone on his side; we dumped more in from ours. He cored out his burrow; we packed it full again. The enemy dug mines; we undermined his mines. He bored at angles; we drilled at angles to his angles. He attacked our tunnelers with fire; we countered with smoke. He released wasps into our lodes; we loosed rats and snakes into his. Night and day our crews broke up shops and houses inside the city, recruiting the rubble to throw up secondary walls to defend when the primary fell. Between these we erected crosswalls, breaking the space into defensible compartments. We mastered the architecture of trap hatches and ambush ports. But the foe kept coming. And though the Amazon knights would not stoop to such drudgery as mine-boring and wall-building, still they possessed abundant labor from the *kabar* and the general crowd, not to say the battalions of aspiring pillagers who had flocked in from all Greece. We fell back, street by street; the foe advanced, alley by alley. Under ten acres remained, the strangled perimeter at the base of the Acropolis.

Reports declared that the enemy had commenced a causeway to Euboea. If this was true, it put our women and children at peril. The foe, scouts claimed, used sleds and teams of oxen to draw great stones to the water's edge. They floated these offshore on rafts, sinking them to found the track, then packed the voids with rubble and built the road atop. In this task their ironsmiths the Chalybes proved spectacular, so we heard, fabricating fittings to bind the work together. They were a hundred feet out now, with four hundred to go. Could the foe actually complete this labor? If she could, we would have to abandon the Acropolis and fight in the open.

Behind the walls, the hours had inverted. One fought at night and slept in the day. Knights caught winks beside their horses, infantry alongside their stacked arms. The month was Metageitnion; blistering, suffocating summer. Men hunkered breathless beneath tent flies and sought shade in the mouths of sappers' mines. My spot was a dandy; a bench beneath a beetle on the west face; it got a breeze after noon. I shared it with my brother and our cousin Xenocles. He was a boxer, hard as horn, and a wit besides. Elias had sought him out for just these qualities, which, under fire, are dearer than ivory.

I was shaken awake late on the seventy-first day. The Amazons had breached the wall at the Callirhoe Road. They had got horse in, our criers were shouting, and threatened the entire southern face.

Artillery atop the Acropolis could not loose barrages for fear of hitting our own men. My brother rallied with the infantry, Xenocles and I with the knights. I had imagined, before the actual experience of it, that defenders under siege would fight only from behind or atop their walls. This was not how it worked in action. Let the foe punch through anywhere and all bets are off. You must go out and meet her. Infantry and cavalry poured from sallyports, taking the enemy from the flanks and rear. Earlier in the siege the foe had suckered us, drawing us out into ambushes. Blood had put us wise. One must not burst forth in undermanned and disorganized gangs, we had learned, but hold until a stout company could be assembled and set in order by officers. Then you can go—and bring every ounce you've got. Nor are such stunts derangement only (though no terror exceeds that of a breached wall) but may be sound tactics as well, for the enemy is never so vulnerable as when her forces bunch up, seeking to force a constricted passage, and thus present their unarmored backs and right sides to the defenders' counterattack.

This day was no different. As the massed foe—Scyths, Taurians, and Amazons—poured through the wall north of Callirhoe, Athenian cavalry and infantry swarmed out to draw the fight away into the field. The arena was that quarter that had been Itoneia, a charming neighborhood of shops and residences. It was all rubble now. Our cavalry galloping onto the field numbered four hundred, well mounted and fighting with the desperation of survival. The Amazons carved us up. Their captains issued orders not by shouts, unavailing in the din, but by whistles, which they produced without pipe or bone but by passing air sharply over the tongue and teeth. That sound alone could break us in terror, signaling some fresh feint or attack against which our numbers could not stand and our horsemanship not prevail.

Most fearsome were their individual champions. We had no answer to an Eleuthera or a Skyleia. The enemy's mounts were stronger, faster, and better trained; their iron weapons beat our bronze to splinters. It is one thing to defame the foe as "fighting on emotion" and another to stand before her *lyssa*-driven rush. For these Amazons were not madwomen but skilled professional cavalry, who knew how to fuel that war fury when they needed it and throttle it back when respite called. Further, their cohesion was such that no champion rushed unreinforced, but troop succeeded troop as the blows of the sledgehammer drive the woodcutter's wedge. Before the notorious "crescent charge," numbers of our outfit bailed off their mounts and fled on foot. Others were shot down or unhorsed or simply pitched to the dirt from exhaustion, terror, or want of horsemanship. In minutes our four hundred had been halved and halved again. For myself, I found the better part of valor to fight dismounted, clinging to my animal's reins, I confess, partly out of shame, not to crawl home horseless, and partly to have some means of flight when strength and fortitude failed.

Our company had carved out a sow's wallow on the slope below the Palladium and had formed into what we imagined was a sturdy front, lambda-shaped, of infantry and dismounted cavalry, two hundred strong, facing west toward the altar of the Hersephoria, or what was left of it after our crews had bashed it apart for artillery stones and the foe had finished the job for fun. Suddenly in the lane appeared Eleuthera. A score of Amazons thundered in on each flank. All bore crescent shields on their left forearms, with a bow, arrow nocked, in the fist, and two more beside, fletched ends up, ready to load and fire. They formed on line. You could see them take the reins between their teeth, freeing both hands for action. Eleuthera whistled. Within moments two more troops emerged, one on the bridge side, the other where the footpath led down to the Ilissus. On our rampart every bowman drew and elevated. The field was dense with dust raised by the stamping hooves of the Amazons' mounts, eager for action and ours balking in terror. Through the haze I could make out the crest of Glauke Grey Eyes and the shield of Tecmessa Thistle. Each commanded about forty. More barks and chirrups flew from Eleuthera. At once a maiden of Grey Eyes' troop shot alone from the flank and streaked across our lines, hanging off her horse's right side so that only her left heel showed, shooting beneath the animal's neck. Our fire discipline was appalling; above half loosed their bolts.

At once Grey Eyes' troop charged from the left. Thistle's cut in echelon across our front. Their first volley hit as our archers reloaded.
Men were falling like wheat. I looked up and there was Eleuthera,
breaking our ranks from the left. How could she know our leaders?
None wore sign of rank. Yet infallibly her bow cut down Telecles,
captain of a hundred, then Memnon and Alpheus, his lieutenants.
We were routed now and stampeding in all directions. I did not see
her axe slay Demaratos the coppersmith and Eucles, called the Bald,
Androtion, who could lift a calf above his head, and Ariston the tutor. The corpses of these we recovered, scalped with her sign; the first
two taken down from the front, the last pair in flight.

Our officerless corps, or that part to which Xenocles and I yet
clung, fled farther out onto the field. We were among the foe's camps
now, being shot at by cooks and baggage bearers. Twice I glimpsed
Selene. She did not see me. We were hundreds of yards outside the
Half Ring. The field had broken down to chaos. You could see units
ratholing like we were; that is, staking out an unscathed patch and
hunkering there, hoping to escape notice. What unmanned us, beyond the foe's superiority, was fear of getting cut off outside the walls.
So fluid was the battlefield, with Amazon and Scythian horse ranging
at will, that the possibility of donating your skull as some savage's
boozing bowl was far too substantial. Men kept turning anxiously
toward the southern gates, the Callirhoe and the Melitic, and to the
lesser sallyports through which one could wedge if he must, while the
"All return" flag flew and we could do nothing about it. We transited
the field like sheep in a storm. Coming upon the enemy in a gaggle
less numerous than our own, we nerved ourselves to action; the instant she held her ground, we fled. The battle seemed dispersed over
miles, no single clash dominating but scores of lesser frays, all within
sight of one another. At one point our forty pulled up on the brow of
the Muses' Hill. Between ourselves and the Pnyx could be counted
half a dozen melees, hundreds dueling in each, with a score of subordinate scrimmages at intervals lapping the faces.

Our troop's end came on the Street of the Cranes. This was an alley only, where the foundations of the houses had been carved into

the cliff, as all in that quarter. Every property had been demolished, leaving a warren of open cellars with partition walls between. Two troops of the foe cut us off in this impound, Titaneia Amazons from the fore, Copper River Scyths at the post.

Here is how superbly disciplined the Amazons are in action. They did not rush on us in mass down the narrow lane, but sent only two, at the gallop, armed with the throwing axe, which they whirled over their heads to sow terror by sound and sight while they loosed that war cry that turns men's blood to water. Under attack a poorly trained horse in an enclosure will turn, seeking to flee, thus presenting its vulnerable flank to the oncoming foe. This both our leaders now did. You could hear the Amazon axes end-over-ending. Both Athenian mounts bowled like dishes in an earthslide. Two more warrioresses rushed; two more of our horses fell. From the rear the Scyths pounded in behind a cloud of darts. They drove us into the compartments excavated from the hillsides, while enemy infantry, Dardanians and Lykians, swarmed upon us from the slopes above. A hundred of ours were shot down amid the most horrible cries. I bolted with Xenocles and two others up an incline so sheer a man on foot must mount it hand over hand. Yet such was our terror, and that of our horses, that we flew as on wings. My mate had just cleared the crest when a horseback javelin struck him beneath the left nipple. The word "struck" gives nothing of it, for the missile, iron-freighted and as long as a man is tall, hit with such force as to pierce him clean through. He bowled rearward, the great pole transfixing his breast and emerging a full arm's length out his back. I goggled in horror, experiencing that shame all soldiers know: I should help, I must . . . but to what end?

"Don't let them!" Xenocles cried in mortal travail. Let them what? I heard hooves at my back. Two Amazons thundered up, helmetless and painted, one black and white diagonally across face and breast, the other red from the nostrils down, eyes ringed in white gypsum. The striped one went after me with the axe. I thought: I will die at the hands of painted savages. She was left-handed and attacked underhand in rhythm with her horse, which had been trained to this art, so that the stroke swept at belly height toward me. Simultaneously, the gypsum brave wielded an Athenian cavalry saber; she was right-handed, so that both strokes came at me between the mounts. I dived like a rat beneath the left-hander's horse. I was aware of my cowardice and cared not a whit. I could see the left-hander's heels above me; I clutched at one with both fists, seeking to bite the tendon through. Her mount skittered sidewise, leaving me again in the open; she fetched me such a blow with the flat of her axe as nearly severed my spine. I pitched face-first to the stone; both horses' hooves beat about me. Then came this sight, impossible of conception save within the derangement of war: my cousin Xenocles, shot through with the horseback javelin, had somehow worked to his feet. He rushed upon the left-hander with the lance still impaling him breast to spine. She shivered the shaft with one swipe of her axe and with the next, backhand, sliced through the hero at the neck. His head bowled rearward like a field ball, wide-eyed and gushing marrow at the base, and quashed on the stone with the sound of a dropped melon. I scrambled crabwise in such terror as I had never known, plunging beneath a welter of timbers and demolition scrap. Both Amazons went after me. I was under a stack two or three boards thick; I could feel the grain splintering as the animals reared and plunged. Lefty had gone to the bow now. A gap of two thumbs'-breadths yawned open in my shelter, exposing my face and breast. I snatched a plank into this breach just as the first shaft struck, severing my middle finger. A second ripped through the flesh beneath my arm. Both braves snatched to reload. I seized the interval and, lurching to my feet, began swinging the plank two-handed at my assailants and their horses. The ludicrousness of this spectacle preserved my life. I could see both Amazons grimace beneath their paint, deeming me a duck not worth drowning. They fell back; I wheeled and bolted.

Down streets gone to rubble I raced on foot. Riderless horses ranged everywhere. Twice I clutched at bridles, only to be driven off by the snap of teeth nearly taking off my hand. At last I came on a Scythian pony trailing a dragline; I caught it and managed to claim a seat. Below where the houses had been excavated, the last of our troop were being butchered like geese.

I was at the head of a lane. Though the foe had felled every tree of the quarter for fuel and timber, somehow a lone olive had been spared. I had never seen anything so beautiful. I stared, absorbed in wonder. Then from behind its silver bole emerged Selene.

She held, as in a dream, mounted upon Daybreak. I could see the horse's breastplate of ox-hide lapped with bronze. Selene wore no helmet. Feathers of eagle and osprey adorned her hair; her face was painted vermilion and black. She came on the run. My bride, I thought. I longed only to fly to her arms. I saw her elevated axe and heard her war cry. The blood drained to my soles.

I wheeled, flaying my pony such blows of my bare hand, since I had neither whip not quirt, as to start both his blood and my own. I knew the quarter. The notion occurred that I could fox Selene by fleeing down lanes unknown to her. But in my derangement I forgot the blocks had been leveled. Careening into the Street of the Weavers, I glanced over my shoulder; Selene had shot the angle, cutting me off. I nearly unhinged my horse's jaw, wheeling him into the facing lane. At the corner he lost footing; we slid sideways and crashed into the wall. I could feel my hip and knee give way as the weight of the beast drove them into the face; my head and shoulder whacked with such force that my helmet, cinched with an ox-hide thong thick as two thumbs, snapped clean and went sailing.

Here came Selene at my heels. I whipped up to the Square of the Return. The temple of Hephaestus had dominated this eminence, but now only its steps remained, fronting a maze of trenches where the treasury had stood. Selene chased me down one side and up the other. At the crown was the threshold stone, double high, where the coffer door had set. My pony hit this at the knees. Mount and rider spilled in a tangle. Selene reined-in above. I was down, wedged between the pediment and my thrashing, kicking horse, who frantically sought to right himself on the stone. His hock hit me, hurling me into the wall. The animal pounded to his feet; I hung from him by the mane like a climber from a cliff. I could see Selene's knee drive Daybreak into position to butcher me. Her weapon was not the *bipennis*, with one blade and counterfacing spike, but the *pelekus*, the true double axe. A fan of raven feathers pended from its crown; I could see them twist in the sunlight as she elevated the warhead to open me from craw to gut sack. I thought only: Take the blow from the front. Will it strike you strange, brothers? In that instant, awaiting the blow of my lover that would send me to hell, all I cared was not to prove unworthy in her eyes.

The raven quills stayed. The axe did not fall. "God help me!" I heard Selene bawl. "Help me to strike!"

Some force stopped her. I did not stay to find out what. I vaulted to my pony's back, beating so furiously with my heels I could feel his ribs bow.

How long does a battle last? Who can tell, in the soup of it? I found myself afoot amid a huddle of infantry. Amazon cavalry in hundreds drove us in a rout. We fell back to the Antiochid district, directly beneath the Acropolis. Here stood the mansions of the great families, the court dwellings of Cecrops and Aegeus and Erechtheus and the ancient bastions of Erichthonius and Cranaus and Actaeus, constructed of stones so massive they could not have been set in place by men but only giants. The foe had not been able to wreck these citadels when she leveled the surrounding shanties. As our companies fled into this province, a miraculous revolution took place.

The stoneworks of the great manors broke up the enemy's pursuit. Mounds of rubble offered us ammunition. A wall stood under construction bisecting the Hoplites' Square; our masons had thrown it up before Borges' Scyths had overrun the quarter. Our corps now poured over this in flight. Inspired by heaven, or only the serendipity of the magazine, men snatched up stones and hurled them in fusillades upon the horsewomen. It worked! If not at first upon the Amazons themselves, who smelled victory and ravened for our blood, then upon their animals, to whom blows about the chest, legs, and head, and especially the barrages of stones beating about their feet, broke their order. The foe's rush split apart in the face of these broadsides.

The square had been carved into trenches by our defenders earlier in the siege, and these now worked further mischief to the enemy, for when her reinforcing companies burst onto the site, their rear elements, blinded amid the dust and smoke, pressed unwittingly upon the fore, driving them onto the excavations. The floors of these lay spiked with a jumble of fittings, debris, timbers, and stakes, onto whose jagged ends horses and riders now plunged at the rush. Was this luck or a god's hand? Who cared? For the first time our companies heard the foe cry in anguish and saw her bleed red blood.

The quarter itself proved wonderfully defensible. For these ancient estates had been strongholds in their day; their construction, of walls enclosing courts, acted like a series of forts. Often two or three commanded a square, their proximity producing interlocking fields of fire, so that one house protected another. Our men mounted to courtyard walls as if to battlements and from them slung stones and bricks. Here too the prowess of our Cretan archers proved miraculous, for, given an elevated platform, and a stationary one, they could shoot like gods.

The fight, which had started as a sally, turned into an all-day war. Our side began to discover its courage. Singing the Hymn to Athena Promachos, our men, first in tens and twelves, then in platoons as great as forty, braved rushes upon the foe. The trick, we learned, was to lap shields into an unbroken wall, projecting from this the shafts and warheads of the eight-foot spear. Again it was less the Amazons who were unnerved than their horses. The creatures seemed to perceive the phalanx as a single beast of bronze. They spooked and shied and, once spiked, needed the whip to be induced to charge again.

The defenders had learned to knit a line of houses into a wall. We had got the knack of throwing up barricades between buildings or even between mounds of rubble, binding a block or square into a defensible redoubt. We knew too to punch holes in the party walls between the houses, fighting and retreating from one to the next. As the foe advanced, our fellows bolted through one mousehole to the next, sealing each with rubble and timbers as they went. It did not require mason-built walls to repel cavalry, we learned, but only a pile of stones too high for a horse to leap and pocked with too many voids to overrun. Better yet, walls and ammunition were the same. Had you shivered your eight-footer? Grab a stone and sling it. A two-pounder can knock out a jawful of teeth. A fiver will stave a skull.

Since each lane mounted in elevation toward the Acropolis, the defenders discovered they could retreat uphill from one position to the next. For the foe, taking one fort made it no easier to take the next, but each exacted its toll on warriors and horses. This was not how Amazons fought. They hated it. It was unknightly. Worse for them, in those lanes beneath the overstanding Acropolis, artillery of stones could be called in from above to cover a beleaguered position. A wing of Taurian infantry had backed a platoon of ours against the face of the Rock. Tons thundered upon the foe from above, knocking half to hell in a single bombardment, breaking their charge and daunting all enemy units to try again.

Yet again they came. Toward evening I saw Hippolyta thunder into the Square of the Basket Bearers. She led a hundred upon our corps of forty. We hunkered, shields lapped and spear points projecting, while they flung shaft after shaft upon us. Yet the wall of shields did not break, and when the horse rush receded, we found courage to pursue, putting up a clamor. We had learned to honeycomb our lines, so that the second rank of spearmen could thrust through the gaps left open by the first, thus doubling our front of pikes, and to maintain this cohesion in retreat as well as attack. Again, it worked. If we kept together, it worked.

There is this too about an army of disunited allies, as our besiegers were. Each is jealous of his turf; he fends his own patch like a staked cur, but will not donate a gob of spit to preserve his fellow's. Our companies found seams between the foes' camps. Here we could fight. Within such pockets Athenian squadrons could take ground and even fortify it.

Theseus fought with superhuman valor, migrating from battalion to battalion across the field. It seemed he knew every countryman's name, and his wife's and children's too, and to each standing at his shoulder infused tribute and resolve. Or perhaps it was a god taking our king's form.

Lykos too displayed courage commensurate to his rank. He had come back through the lines from the bastion at Lykabettos, with two companies led by the heroes Peteos, called "the Tower," and Stichios, hailed as "Ox" for the ferocious rush he employed in wrestling, which proved of even more terrific effect in close fighting. With this guard Lykos joined Theseus, Pirithous, and the hero Peleus. These, seconded by Menestheus, Peteos' son, Pylades the boxer and Telephos, champions of the city, thrust on foot into the teeth of the enemy advance. You could see down the hill the pockets of resistance created by each principal. Where the channel of the Ilissus divides is a footbridge called the Girdle, because in ancient times condemned men were led across it, by their belts, to their executions. Here Lykos, fighting with only Peteos, Ox, and their squires, held back half a hundred horse, enduring clouds of missiles, then rushing with their spears upon the foremost riders. Theseus and Pirithous fought with matching valor, holding first the crossroads before the shop of the barber Timaeus, then the mouth of the Street of the Saddlers. But such a defense of champions could not hold. Each pocket drew more and more gallants of the foe, fired to make a famous kill. The heroes fell back, making a wall of their shields, into which the shafts of the foe affixed in such numbers that each face bristled like a hedgehog's back.

In the end the foe's numbers were simply too many. Pocket by pocket, Athenian resistance broke. The exhausted remnant fell back toward the Rock. The Enneapylon still held. Hundreds reached safety through the Sacred and Aegeid Gates. This was on the west. I was on the south. These were the companies under Theseus. Our only way in was through the Callirhoe or the Melitic, and we were cut off from them by an eighth of a mile of field. We could see the ramparts and our countrymen lowering lines and ladders, crying, Hurry brothers! Fall back!

The companies outside the walls were down to a thousand men, half of whom were wounded so severely as to be unable to fight, with another quarter incapable even of getting off the field under their own power. About these swirled horse troops of Amazonia and Scythia and tribesmen on foot in numbers ten times theirs. The hero

Pirithous had fallen to wounds, beaten by Borges the Scyth. He had been evacuated to the summit. The knight Peleus had likewise succumbed, driven down by Eleuthera. Theseus and the surviving captains rallied the mass into a perimeter, shield to shield. Two hundred feet separated us from the wall and deliverance.

We could not get across. Eleuthera, Borges, and their champions had massed in our way. They could have overrun the walls, so great were their numbers, but for the fire of our artillerymen on the summit, who kept up barrages of stones, some as massive as fifty and sixty pounds, to keep a lane clear between ourselves and safety.

The foe soon got the hang of dodging these rock falls. She reckoned how far she could advance and how long each battery took to reload. Each time our pack bolted into the no-man's-land between ourselves and the walls, the foe's companies hurled themselves upon us. Our countrymen above were forced to break off their volleys, lest they pulverize us along with the foe, and in this interval the enemy ground our rush to mince.

Night was falling. Four times our corps sallied; four times we were beaten back. With each, more of ours fell wounded. Worse, when we abandoned the safety of one position, Scythian and Amazon cavalry seized it and launched from it yet more terrific volleys.

Eleuthera ranged before the Callirhoe Gate, barring our entry. "Coward with the heart of a deer!" she bawled to Theseus. "You should have fought me when you had the chance! Your corpse would now feed crows and dogs, but you would at least have fallen with honor!"

Our pack had strength for one more rush. We knew it and so did the foe. All vaunting ceased. I could see Eleuthera prowling the front, mounted on her long-legged Soup Bones. The champions of Amazonia massed at her shoulder. Hippolyta and Skyleia; Alcippe and Stratonike; Glauke, Enyo, Deino, Adrasteia, Tecmessa, Xanthe, Evandre, Antibrote, Pantariste, Electra, and Selene. And Borges and Saduces and Hermon of the allies. Here was their chance to cut out the living heart of our corps, and to do so before the eyes of the last defenders. Across the field, infantry and squires of the foe scurried in hundreds, hauling off all impediments to cavalry, clearing the field for our slaughter.

Our company formed into a hollow square, meaning those on the right had to advance backward, so that their shields would protect that flank. Theseus passed among the company. No speeches now. "Athena Protectress!" he cried, cinching up. "Athens and Victory!"

With a shout the mass pushed off. Scythian foot troops immediately swept in to seize the heights of our vacated position. The foe began pouring bowfire from there. Amazon horse attacked from both flanks. We huddled in our moving square, men falling and tripping, particularly the side I held to, the right, which must advance backpedaling. The Amazons shot their bolts across the tops of our shields, right firing on left and left on right. A man hit may not fall but must make his way as best he could, for to drop underfoot would impede his mates, who were already burdened with wounded. The Scyths fell upon the rear in waves, attacking not only with spears and axes but with great stones, twenty- and thirty-pounders, which the tribesmen bore in two hands over their heads and hurled in a howling rush upon the shields of our rear ranks. When these buckled, the savages flung themselves bodily upon the facings, clawing at the shield rims and pulling them down by the weight of their flesh. The foe attacked clad in mantles of bearskin and bull's hide, many with heads and horns still on, which rendered their apparition even more beastlike, and against which the thrusting sword was worthless as a wand. The brutes poured flush among us. The Amazons fired indiscriminately into the mass; one found himself employing as cover the torsos of the very tribesmen beneath whose onslaught he reeled. So many sprouted arrows, foe as well as friend, that men began stumbling and fouling on the shafts which jutted, numerous as seamstress's pins, from shields and breastplates and living flesh. Artillery stones continued to plummet from the chutes two hundred feet above, keeping clear the last fifty feet before the walls. The sound these boulders made as they shattered on the stone was appalling, not to say the blast of shards which mowed men down like sling bullets, and the choking clouds which roiled upon all, enlarging the theater of terror.

Now came the final push. The artillery atop the Acropolis ceased firing. Across no-man's-land our swarm surged. Our object was a front of wall between two turrets, perhaps a hundred feet across, atop which hung our countrymen, lowering ropes and ladders. As the foreranks reached this face and began to scale it, the center compressed against them, driven by the terror of the foe at the rear, who cursed their countrymen for mounting so tardily. The mob bunched up like bees. In its midst an undigested clot of Scyths went after us with short-swords and bare hands. From all sides pressed Amazon cavalry. As our fellows mounted rung to rung and hand over hand, the foe fired into their exposed backs or, upon those who had draped their shields turtle-style, into their legs and arms. Bodies plummeted from the face; blood and piss sheeted down the stone. I found myself at the foot of a ladder and confess I kept sending others up before me. If I could have burrowed into the rock, I'd have done it and traded places eagerly with a worm. The ground at our feet was strewn with splinters of the boulders already dropped from above. When you lost footing, which you did again and again in that mob, shards ripped your knees and palms. Thighs and arms grew lacquered with blood, to which the stone dust adhered, bleaching all to an unearthly pallor. The sight was ghastly beyond recounting, as it seemed not men but shades dueled, and not aboveground but in some sun-forsaken netherworld.

Eleuthera led the rush upon us. At her side pressed Stratonike and Skyleia, Alcippe and Glauke Grey Eyes; Evandre and Pantariste; Enyo and Deino and Adrasteia. Theseus massed the stoutest of our corps but the Amazon horse punched through. Their weapon in close quarters is not bow but axe, which they wielded overhand, staving shields and helmets, hacking men through at the neck and cleaving arms at the shoulder. They hauled our ladders down with grapnels and buried their blades in the backs of men mounting the walls. I was flush against the face when a wedge of the foe lanced across, driving us out into the open. More Amazon horse poured in behind. We were cut off. Enemy volleys swept the ramparts above. This was the finish. In moments, all would be lost. Then from the melee arose such a cry as surely none save gods and titans had heard heretofore.

This was Theseus, bellowing to the gunners overhead. His call ascended not in words but in some idiom primordial. "Upon us!" his cry commanded. Meaning, Loose your stones on us and the foe together!

My father's kinsman Talos served among the chute gangs on the summit that day. He told, later, of the despair atop the Acropolis as the artillerymen released their fusillades upon the commingled masses of Athenians, Amazons, and Scyths. With terrible prayers our gunners winched up their drop ramps, while along the brink of the Rock, wives and comrades peered down in horror, beholding their countrymen obliterated alongside the foe. Where I hunkered, flush against the face, was a pocket of safety. Yet such sounds and sights assaulted as none may bear and stay the man he was. Boulders plummeted weighing fifty and a hundred pounds, in salvos across two hundred feet of face. Where this tonnage struck, the concussion was titanic. Fragments as big as a man's head blew in every direction. I saw Diognetus the weaver sheared off at breast height. One moment he was a man, the next a tower of sundered guts. Stones plummeted in such quantities as to annihilate a square ten yards by ten. Yet pairs of men still contended. Nor did one cry for cessation, so desperate had become the struggle, but each, convinced of his own end, fought only to take his enemy with him to hell.

Atop the Rock the woe of the artillerymen was amplified by their awareness of that pollution, monstrous and ineradicable, which they brought upon themselves by this slaughter of their countrymen. Men understood, Talos recounted, that this iniquity would haunt them to the end of their days. Numbers defied the order, deeming no fate worth an action so abominable, while others denounced these as traitors. All sacrifice must be borne, however horrible! Your king commands you, at toll of his own life! Men lamented the bitterness of their fate and cried out to the gods to witness their reluctance to perform it. None owned the stomach to look down, my father's kinsman said, but, weeping, loaded truck upon truck and levered these into the chutes and over. Talos himself did peer from the brink and rued this felony all his days. To see your tons of stone plummet, he declared, while gauging with the eyes, as one cannot help but do, upon which province the mass will fall; then the impact itself, the shrieking slivers and detonating dust . . .

Gunners dumped chute upon chute. What else could they do? Their king had commanded, and commanded still. In anguish the men redoubled their salvos, as if by this intensification they could bring the slaughter to a swifter close. Bystanders uncompelled, and even women, seized stones and slung them, amid the most baleful imprecations, upon the foe and on their own.

The enemy fell back. Our men waded to the walls. Their comrades lowered ropes and poles and even bedding straps. I saw Theseus beneath the eastern turret, defending a patch so that others might climb, before he himself took the tether and was hauled clear. For myself, I mounted the face with my bare hands, securing purchase on such nicks as would not support a lizard, so compelling is the impetus of terror and so mighty the imperative of self-preservation.

28

A TRIAL OF AEDOR

Damon continues:

〰〰〰〰〰〰〰

Where the marketplace had stood, on the flat beneath the Hill of the Nymphs, was the only level ground that had not been appropriated for camps (the Amazons and Copper River Scyths had rigged it out as a racetrack). Here at the second dawn succeeding the fight, Theseus met Eleuthera in a duel of honor.

No formal stakes were established, that is, there was no deal that if Theseus won, the Amazons would pack up and go home, nor, should Eleuthera prevail, would the city tuck tail and quit. Nonetheless the freight of the outcome was monumental. The duel would be viewed by both sides as a trial, not only of their champions but of their gods. Who owned the magic? Who had the power? Indeed among the tribes of the East no event, down to the declination of piss in the wind, is accounted innocent of supernatural import. This is why they love to gamble. In the savage's eyes such sport is no vice (the conception would be absurd to him) but a finding of each man's soul power, or *aedor*, as he calls it. A tribesman will bet on anything, from the whorling of leaves in a doorway to the agony of a captive under torture. Let him call the wager right; he is flushed with esteem. Wrong, he plunges to despair.

The savage does not see the world as a man of reason might, that is, an entity discrete from heaven, governed by laws of cause and effect. The clansman cannot conceive such notion. In his view, this earth is but an adumbration of the Otherworld, whose surface he sounds for the apparition of the Almighty. Existence is a gaming board to him; he casts the bones and awaits their revelation. The savage knows sorrow; in his tongue birds do not sing but "cry"; babes weep not but "mourn." The tribesman is a slave to superstition. For all his valor he will cower at the advent of a hare and break off mighty campaigns before mischance in a flight of sparrows. The Amazons are little better and, truth be told, our own countrymen advanced by barely a midge. It was lost on few within Theseus' command, and certainly none within Eleuthera's, that the morrow's bout would be read by both sides as nothing less than the judgment of God. Whose champion triumphed would be seen as insuperable; whose fell as doomed. Thus in each camp no measure was omitted, however preposterous or barbaric, to secure the favor of heaven for the coming affray.

My brother and I, it chanced, were among those detailed to retrieve the dead from the previous day's battle. The Amazons and Scyths had already claimed theirs. When we passed out the Nine Gates that evening we could see them, in their camps on the hills across from the Rock, laying out the coal trenches over which they would spit our captive countrymen and erecting the gibbets upon whose cross-ties these poor wretches would be flayed. This is how the savage entreats heaven's favor.

The tribesman wagers on how his victim will endure. One who has not witnessed such an orgy cannot conceive the ecstasies to which such a brute may ascend, applying iron and flame to the flesh of his foe. Nor are these acts cruelty in the savage's eyes, as they would be, performed by a man of civilized station, but rather a trial of the captive's *aedor*, his magic. The prisoner too participates. By an equation incomprehensible to the emancipated sensibility, the clansman acclaims his victim even as he impales and vivisects him. For the captor's object is the acquisition of the *aedor* of his prisoner; the victim's, to prove his magic superior to his torturer's. The more nobly he endures, the greater his power. He suffers, does the captive, not for himself (for the savage cannot conceive of himself apart from his gods and tribe) but for the grantors of his luck, those Otherworld guardians who have endowed him with his soul magic. He seeks to prove his power mightier than his foes' and, expiring, wring the last drop of renown. I have seen victims spit their terminal breath in their tormentors' faces and dive to hell with a laugh.

The Scyths had tortured Athenians in the early stages of the siege but found it so unsatisfactory that the practice was discontinued. To the savage our woeful performance was proof of Athenian gutlessness. Their contempt for us redoubled. They came to deem even the happiest outcome of the war, victory and plunder, as beneath their dignity. They even gave up taking our scalps. Our hair had no *aedor*. No respectable warrior would hang it from his belt.

This night however, my brother and I saw, the art of torture had been resurrected. Atop the Hills of Ares and the Pnyx, the first fortune-forsaken were being trundled to their ordeal. Soon their cries would ascend in choruses hideous and appalling, to mingle with timbrel and tom-tom and the orgiastic ululations of the foe.

We could hear the Scyths and Amazons scarifying themselves now. They perform this rite in pairs as they dance. An instrument like a carpenter's chisel pares strips of flesh from legs and backs and bellies. By such ceremony, the savages build up power for the duel of champions to come. Elias and I could see their stewards beneath Market Hill, preparing the runway where the champions would meet. On Ares' Hill the Amazons were sacrificing horses in the night rite they call *Nikteria*. Bonfires blazed along the summit. Below, on the field of the slain, we used the light to work by.

The savage strips every rag from the foe he has vanquished. He takes ears and noses, looping these onto strings, which he wraps about his midriff. The foe no longer took scalps, as I said, or heads; rather he hacked off limbs or cleaved the skull clean through, to rob the soul of its magic in the life after. Can there stand a chore more dolorous than this: to collect the corpses of one's countrymen, hewn in two, naked and mutilated, impossible to identify? We heaped the dead atop blankets, two and three to a pile, and dragged these to the base of the Three Hundred Steps. No mules remained to haul them topside; all had been butchered for meat. From here each corpse must be shouldered, intact or otherwise, and humped to the summit.

That night Theseus made no speeches. "If I fall, return the lady Antiope to her people." This was all he said.

Antiope was there that night when our retrieval detail quit. She had come out at last from her cloister. I passed close by her on the battlement; she did not see me, nor did I seek her attention. Her gaze stood fixed upon the pageant of horror being enacted on the hills across.

My duties took me away for the watch. When I returned, past midnight, Antiope had not budged.

The lady stood alone at the embrasure south of the summit gate, compassed only by the pages and guardsmen Theseus had assigned to protect her. I had forgotten what a specimen she was. She wore Phrygian boots with trousers bloused and an Amazon riding wale about her waist. A quilted *spolas* jerkin bound her torso. Over her left shoulder was draped the panther skin she had worn defeating Borges at the Mound City. Her right breast was bare, revealing the starfish scar called *tessyxtos*, produced by the searing of the breast in childhood, and the chevron slashes of the *matrikon*, the ritual self-mutilation Amazons perform on the eve of battle.

The foe's orgy went on all night. Antiope never left her station. Would she join the battle? On whose side? Theseus had forbidden her to arm, as I have told, and set death as the penalty for him who aided her. Would he rescind this? Would it take his own death to annul it?

Two hours before dawn the king withdrew to the citadel. Antiope preceded him. She bathed and armed him, so we heard (for she debarred all entry, even to the King's Companions), and dressed his hair. Her own spear she set in his grip.

The fight took place on the grounds of the marketplace, beneath the foremost of Athens's last untaken portals, the Sacred Gate of the Enneapylon. The King's Companions defended this. Behind, the Three Hundred Steps had been spiked and crosswalled, should the foe offer perfidy. The last houses and treasuries had been fortified; upon and above these massed the final four thousand able to fight. It was dawn. Wounded lined the Fortress at the summit.

Eleuthera's seconds—Stratonike, Skyleia, and Glauke Grey Eyes—rode onto the flat from the north, in armor but not painted. Their hair had been dressed. They were helmetless. Three posts had been erected at the far end of the chute; each rider reined-in beside one. Stratonike came forward alone. At the south waited Theseus' seconds—Lykos, Peteos, and Amompharetus, chief of the Spartan spearmen. They too wore dress armor. The orders of combat were rehearsed by Saduces, prince of Trallian Thrace, speaking flawless Attic Greek. Killing may be done only within the ring, which admonition was moot, as neither rival would forfeit honor to preserve his or her life.

Theseus slewed forth in a chariot, the royal car of his father Aegeus, driven by his cousin Iophon. He wore black armor, a breastplate with a bull's head and matching shield, a twenty-pounder, bronze sheathing atop an oak chassis three thumbs'-breadths thick. His helmet was black with a crest of white kestrel feathers. He had shaved his beard and shorn his forelock to afford his rival no berth of purchase. His weapons were three javelins, in an ox-hide quiver on his car, two eight-foot spears, ash tipped with iron; and the thrusting sword in a baldric at his hip. The chariot drew up at the southern posts. Theseus did not dismount. His seconds crossed and spoke briefly with him.

Eleuthera entered from the north on Soup Bones. She made no show at all. No chariot. No conference with her seconds. She carried a small bronze target shield and one horseback javelin. A *pelekus* axe rode in a sheath between her shoulder blades. In a case at the small of her back nested an iron discus. She carried no bow and no sword.

"I am Theseus, son of Aegeus—"

"Enough! I know who you are!"

Horses on both sides stamped and snorted. You could see the chariot wheels rock, rolling a trace in the dust, and the leather-gauntleted forearms of the henchman restraining the team.

Eleuthera did not drive Soup Bones forward, only let him surge, reining after ten paces, yet a hundred apart from her rival. Her right hand rose to the cheekpiece of her helmet. "Kill me if you can!" she called. With a snap of her neck, she dropped the iron plate before her eyes.

A cheer shot from the throats of sixty thousand as chariot and horse churned from the standing start and gathered way, hurtling toward one another. Theseus elevated his shield, lapping its convex bowl over the prow of the car, and seated his shoulder within the hollow of its rim. His right arm held the first javelin, a five-footer; he set his left foot foremost upon the platform, right planted at the rear to push off into the cast. Eleuthera came at him with the horseback javelin. In instants the antagonists were upon one another; Theseus threw, Eleuthera held. The king's lance would have taken her full in the chest had she not plunged to her horse's flank, hanging on by her heel only and a loop through the mane. In a heartbeat she was astride again. Theseus' javelin had been hurled with such force as to pass on, clear of the arena, and fix among the spectators of the Thyssa Getai, striking a luckless fellow in the foot. He yowled. A great cheer arose. Chariot and horse slewed at the terminal of the runway and wheeled to return.

The second pass, Eleuthera made on the left of the car, veering at the last instant in front of the team. Again she did not throw; again Theseus' cast slung wide, as his rival spurred unexpectedly so that his second lance deflected off her target shield, sailing across the arena to fix into a stake at the far rail. As the chariot spun for the third track, one could see the king strip helmet and shield, so as not to impede his throw, wedging both into their nests on the car. He knew he had been bested twice and must hit home with this cast or fight on foot against a mounted foe.

Again the rivals dug toward one another; again Eleuthera held fire; again Theseus' shot screamed wide. As his car slewed again about the turning posts, the king sprang to the sand; henchman and team withdrew; Theseus advanced on foot, helmet re-seated, with shield and spear. Eleuthera wheeled at the far end of the chute, reining Soup Bones, who was already lathered beneath his armor, slinging spume from his bridle; his jaw worked furiously at the bit. From beneath Eleuthera's faceplate spit shot in a plume, pink with blood from her tongue, bitten through in the excitement. The Amazon took the reins in her teeth. From its sheath at the small of her back she extracted the eight-pound discus, seating it in her left fist, counterweight to the horseback javelin in its sleeve extender in her right.

Cries for blood ascended from every quarter. Among the clansmen watching from elevation, wild fellows could be seen pounding each other's shoulders and backs. Faces crimson, they bellowed in their savage tongues, making the veins of their necks stand out, while clashing spear shafts against shield bowls in a thunderous cacophony. The Amazons loosed such yip-yipping as made the stadium keen like a pine copse in a gale.

On foot Theseus dashed forward to the center of the ring, seeking to shorten his rival's run-up. He worked in fast shuffle steps, at a half crouch, the bowl of his shield before him at an angle, lower edge leading, with its ox-hide skirt skimming in the dust. He canted the shield sidewise as well, to deflect Eleuthera's shot when it came, with the nasal of his helmet set against the sweat stain on the leather of his shield's upper rim, leaving visible to the foe only the eye slits and the kestrel-plume crown. My eye found Selene among the champions; she trembled, it seemed, like a bowstring at the catch.

I searched the battlements for Antiope and could not find her.

Now came the rush Eleuthera had saved for. Seating her right sole within the loop of her horse's belly-band, she drove Soup Bones forward. The steed accelerated to the gallop as only the chargers of the steppe can. The horseback javelin looked lengthy as a tent pole, iron-freighted shaft spanning from its sleeve extender at the terminus of the Amazon's drawn-back right arm to its warhead nearly between the horse's ears, above Eleuthera's counterweighted left hand, clutching the discus, and beyond.

Theseus dropped to a crouch as horse and rider thundered upon him. His helmet pressed against the crown of his shield. This was the royal *aspis* of his father, Aegeus, of oak so strong that a waggon could be driven across it and it would not bow. The king skimmed the lower lip of the frame across the earth, canting the bronze sheathing skyward. His eyes peered over the rim. His right hand clutched both eight-foot spears, flat on the earth so that no blow of axe or disk might shiver them, drawn back beneath the shield's cover, that no hoof strike stave them to splinters. The front he presented to his rival was what infantrymen call "shadowing up," meaning the foe saw the bowl of the shield alone, with all vulnerable flesh tucked beneath. The king crabbed right and left, making himself a moving target. His hand on the dirt felt his rival's closing gallop, seeking that instant either to hunker and endure or to plant his right foot and elevate the thrusting spear to take the charging foe head-on.

Eleuthera gave him no chance. She slung from beyond his range. So violent was her rush and so powerful her cast that her sleeve extender struck the crown of Theseus' helmet as she hurtled past. Warhead and shaft drove through the shield entire, passing so close to the fatal mark that a splinter of ash severed the ox-hide thong which bound the cuirass beneath the king's ribs. The missile seated into the earth like a pavilion pole. The great bowl of the shield stove upon Theseus, pinning him beneath. Eleuthera wheeled and drove back. She had shot her only lance; she must dismount now and close hand to hand.

The Amazon scissored off Soup Bones at the gallop; her feet struck the ground running. The horse, trained for this, bolted clear. Eleuthera rushed upon Theseus from the rear. His shield remained nailed to the earth by her tent-pole javelin. The king owned only two options: expend precious instants wrenching the shield free, or dump it and face Eleuthera's onslaught naked.

The Amazon had the discus in her hand. One saw it swing wide, the eight-pound stone ringed with iron. Eleuthera was twenty paces from Theseus now, coming low and hard. The king at last wrested his shield free of the earth and wheeled to face her. Eleuthera drove, erect now, into that one-two-three spin that throwers of the disk employ; her hurling arm extended wide, moment magnified by the furious rotation of her torso; her right foot planted at the peak of her spin; she loosed the disc point-blank. I have never heard a sound like that iron made upon the bronze.

The shield's face sundered; its frame cracked like a walnut. Theseus' arm fell limp. Eleuthera had hurtled past him in the violence of her rush. She wheeled now and brought herself under control. If you have never seen an Amazon draw her axe from the sheath between her shoulder blades, it goes like this: as the right hand elevates, reaching back over the shoulder to clasp the honed iron, uncinched already within its scabbard, the left hand reaches around to the small of the back, catches the butt of the shaft, and pushes up. In a tenth the time it takes to tell, the weapon has sprung clear of its nest and leapt into the fighting fist of its mistress. Eleuthera rushed. Theseus met her shield-on, seeking to pierce her with the thrust of the great ash spear. In midstride her axe head bashed the killing point aside, slipping the death it bore as it entered the linen facing of her corselet, opening a gash across her ribs.

In two score tongues clansmen cried, "His arm is broken!" Eleuthera saw it. She gathered. With all her strength she drove upon her rival's buckled shield such a blow as made the field resound. Theseus' forearm was imprisoned in the bronze-and-leather sheath that supported the weight of the shield. He cried in agony as the impact drove him down. Eleuthera forsook the axe for the instant; instead she seized Theseus' shield rim in both hands and drove against it with all her weight, seeking to snap her rival's bone or wrench it from its socket. The king dropped to a knee and an elbow, slashing side-long with his spear. A second slice opened across Eleuthera's thigh. Had a housefly lit upon her it could not have affected her less. The defenders clamored from the battlements, summoning their champion to his feet.

Now in Eleuthera's fist reappeared the *pelekus*. Theseus lunged with his spear from the dirt; she dodged and hacked the ash shaft through. He sought to bring her to grips, to overcome her by brute strength. She slipped his rush with ease. Two more blows of her axe and Theseus' shield split in half. A third two-handed swipe sheared the crown of his helmet. His scalp dangled in a flap; blood sheeted over his undercap and his fore-cropped hair.

Now from the Amazon's throat arose that war cry that turns men's knees to jelly. She went for the kill. The king toppled rearward, seeking with his last strength to preserve his vital parts.

Suddenly from the south end of the ring burst a wedge of King's Companions. With a cry this corps flooded upon Eleuthera, beating her back from Theseus with their spears and swords; the Companions lapped the king within a wall of shields, behind which they sought to haul him clear. Eleuthera howled in outrage, hacking with her axe at the picket of bronze.

To her aid rushed her seconds, succeeded by the squadrons of Amazonia; then the Scyths and Getai and the floodtide of the foe.

BOOK TEN

IN LOVE
AND WAR

29

RATS

Selene's testament resumes:

〰〰〰〰〰〰〰〰

When Horse first hoisted the free people to her back she established ordinances of honor by which compacts between nations and individuals were to be prosecuted. Foremost among these stood the sanctity of single combat. Who won, won alone. Who lost, lost alone.

Theseus had lost. Yet he lived, preserved by the arms of others. What kind of war was this? One conquered but could not prevail, took trophies only to be shamed by their possession. I was among those that day who overran the Athenian Enneapylon, tore down the Sacred Gate, and drove the last of the foe to the summit of his citadel; I had three scalps and more weapons and armor than my ponies could carry. I dumped them to the dust in contempt.

The last fight had cost horses and women in the hundreds, including both my novices, Kalkea and Arsinoe. Yet it was not the numbers, however exorbitant, but the want of honor with which the foe contested. I summon memory of it now, that hour of infamy when Theseus' Companions lapped shields and hauled him from the field, and my gut turns in revulsion.

Already traitors of the Athenians had begun slipping through the lines to us, pledging to betray the city in return for eminence beneath our rule. Borges impaled them in disgust, not, however, before extracting intelligence of the quantity of gold Theseus held on the Rock, and what more had been evacuated to Euboea with the women and children.

For once the prince of the Scyths was not drunk, or not so as to slip on his own spit, as usual. "There is no honor in defeating a people such as these," he declaimed in council the night succeeding the duel. When Eleuthera pointed atop the Acropolis and said, "There is your gold; take it," the lord of the Iron Mountains met her eye and affirmed, "It is not enough."

The allied camps now ringed the Acropolis entire. Everywhere lay our wounded and dead. Here was the most grievous woe. In raids upon the steppe one rarely lost a comrade; never beyond two or three, save in the gravest action. Now a hundred, two hundred melted away each night. In ninety days a third of the nation had perished, while another third bore wounds from which they would never be made whole. Beyond this stood the suffering of the horses. How many had we lost? Five thousand in battle, thrice that to falls and affliction. Even our captains' mounts, accorded the choicest feed, could not last ten minutes in action. A rider went through four and five in one fight. All must be rested for days after, and even then they grew more gaunt and cadaverous.

Borges was right. We must take the island. Only that would make the Athenians come down and fight. And we had to get grain; our horses were emaciated; Attica had been cropped dry.

I dropped all subordinate duties to hold myself available to Eleuthera. I learned to step in among petitioners and detach her from their press. I picketed her catnaps and set my cloak as shade when she dozed midday. My body I planted across her threshold, not to slumber, but to debar from access those who would steal her sleep or tear her, for their self-interested ends, apart from the cause upon which all depended.

Each night, and night succeeding night, Eleuthera made her rounds from camp to camp, stopping at fires to lend a word, share a jibe, or simply to let our knights and novices feed upon her presence, she who had vanquished the great Theseus in single combat. A hundred times I sought to break off these junkets. Rest! The flesh can only take so much! "No," she rejected all such calls, "our sisters on the line labor harder, for the weight I bear is rendered lighter by my office and the honors accorded me."

Casualties had sapped the corps' resolve to such extent that warrioresses, in the exhaustion after action, could barely find the strength to bury their horses—not in this shingley marl which must be mined with pick and mattock and even then yielded only stone beneath stone. At this chore again and again Eleuthera shamed her compatriots. Taking station beside a fallen mount, she commenced spading the trench with her own hand, and by her exertions compelled all to emulation. The army ached for the steppe; Eleuthera knew it. We feared for our children, our mares and foals, in peril even now from enemies emboldened by our absence. Eleuthera sought not to throttle such grief but shared it. I watched the bucks and troopers as she passed among them through the camp. Their eyes shone, feasting upon her apparition. They would tell their daughters of this hour, when the great Eleuthera spoke to them, took their hand, smiled at a jest they had made. One read in the eyes of all the readiness to die for the nation. It shamed you and made you humble.

I had sensed as a child the scale of my friend's ambition; I feared that such adulation as she now received would turn her head. Instead, it transfigured her. A hundred times a night one witnessed this exchange: our commander kneeling at a crippled novice's side or clasping the hand of a mutilated veteran. The faces of the wounded lit beneath her touch; their eyes went liquid with love. And they read this in hers: that she would donate all to preserve the nation.

They began to call her *Parthenos*, the Virgin. For the people meant by this that she lived for them and them alone.

Of all our race, Antiope, I believe, was the noblest. But Eleuthera was the greatest. The love she bore for tal Kyrte transcended all passion of woman for man or woman for woman. It was a love not of flesh but of spirit, whose expression was not self-assertion but self-abnegation. From the most proud of warriors, Eleuthera had become the most humble. I marveled to behold her. In my own heart I still yearned for Damon. I experienced shame to feel this. In the end, what is erotic love but vanity and the wish to submerge and surrender? Even to produce a child, I scored myself in secret, was self-interest and conceit alongside this love which Eleuthera bore like a flame for the people.

Envoys of the Athenians now began coming over. Rats deserting the sinking ship, they delivered their messages, then slipped away through lines made porous by our allies' intoxication or their decampment to complete the causeway to Euboea. Word came to Eleuthera from the Athenian general Lykos: he would deliver Theseus' head in return for being spared and made regent. Others pleaded for their families, pledging ransom from overseas holdings. More simply made a run for it, roping down the cliffs and bolting into the dark.

The seventh night Damon appeared with an embassy sent by Theseus. The king still reigned, the legation testified. The proposition they bore was for tal Kyrte's ears alone.

I studied Damon as he addressed the Council. He was gaunt. His cheeks were hollow, the bones prominent beneath his beard. Never had I admired him more. He wore that look which declares, I have no fear of you, I am ready to die. My heart felt love for him as never before.

One saw he loved us. He was one of us. As he recited the proposal his king had charged him to convey, one read between its lines the same of Theseus. He loved us too.

The king, Damon informed the Council, offers five hundred talents of gold, an enormous sum, all the city possesses, if tal Kyrte will cease hostilities and ally itself with Athens. Together, Theseus proposed, our nations would turn upon the Scyths, Thracians, and Getai.

"Tal Kyrte knows her enemy is not Athens," Damon recited, "however grave the grievance she bears. How can our distant city harm the free people? Only those can whom she now calls her allies. Borges and Saduces own designs upon your homeland. The casualties you must suffer to unseat us from our hold will only waste you for the trek home, which will be marked by battles against those who hate you for what you are and who covet your lands and stock.

"Say that you despise us. Say you abhor our ways. But acknowledge the wisdom of having it out with your real foes here and now, while you still have strength and may employ us as allies, fighting from the stronghold of our citadel. We will fight hard, for your enemies are ours, and we wish to drive them out as much as you wish to deplete their capacity to work you harm in the future.

"Consider this alliance, Theseus, king of Athens, beseeches you. By mighty deeds tal Kyrte has proven her preeminence and achieved imperishable glory. Now, Theseus urges you, secure your survival. See prudence and make us your allies against those who seek only your extinction."

Damon finished. The deputation was dismissed. All withdrew, save him. He refused to depart, but held, alone, at the portal of the pavilion.

One could see his fellow envoys turn about in bewilderment, seeking to draw him away with them. He would not go. The Council looked on, puzzled.

Damon addressed them. "The words I have spoken are those of my king and people. What I say now comes from my own heart."

He straightened.

"I will not return with my comrades to the city. I wish to stay with you."

Skyleia snorted in ridicule. "As what?"

Damon balked, as if command of our tongue had deserted him. Eleuthera stepped before him.

"You have been the lover of Selene?"

"I have," Damon answered.

"What is this you make now? A gesture of romance?"

Further derision poured upon him from my countrywomen. Damon maintained his resolve. "What then?" Eleuthera demanded.

"As I have spoken," he said.

I stepped in. "His heart loves the wild ways."

Scorn greeted this, from all and in abundance. Damon was accused of being a spy or assassin, a coward seeking to save his skin, and worse.

My lover bore this abuse without rejoinder. Eleuthera studied him hard. She glanced once to me, deadly sober, then elevated her palm to stay the excoriation which continued to be heaped upon Damon by our sisters in arms.

"Stay tonight," she commanded him. "Decide tomorrow."

To me she signed: Show him the causeway.

30

AT THE THRESHOLD
OF VICTORY

⌇⌇⌇⌇⌇⌇⌇

The straits of the Euripus separate the mainland from the island of Euboea. The narrows are a quarter mile. I rode out that night with Damon.

I had long rehearsed this hour. I knew how I would touch him, take him again as my lover. I had worked out what to say and how to say it.

In the event, all fell out otherwise.

It was dark when we reached the straits. Cressets flared; the site seethed with industry. Progress was spectacular. Where the channel had been looked now like dry land. The causeway spanned three hundred fifty of the four hundred yards needed. This was the least of it. The Tower People had taken command; they had founded not only the central axis of stone, wide enough for a span of oxen, but built out trestles at each flank, along which riders could advance three abreast. Sidescreens protected against seaborne counterattack;

the span bristled like a fortress. Drawn by bounties, adventurers had swum the straits at night, holing numbers of Athenian craft and incinerating others. On our shore the Tower People and Chalybes carved finishing touches in a great rolling drop bridge. This would be warped into place for the attack. The Athenians had erected a palisade where the ramp would crash. But what would this serve, manned only by old men and boys?

Damon and I passed among the host. Here were more troops, and of keener spirit, than besieged the city itself. No captain of Amazonia contributed. These were Scyths and Thracians and Getai, under their own.

My lover and I drew up, overlooking the channel.

"My mother and two sisters are there," Damon said. "Their children are with them. My brother's wife. I have aunts and cousins and grandparents."

With this, I saw all hope had ended for us.

"Theseus must come down now," Damon declared. "Eleuthera will get the fight she came for."

He meant the Athenians would descend from their bastion atop the Acropolis. They had no choice. They must break out, do or die, to breach our lines and destroy the causeway.

We returned to the city around noon. The camp on Ares' Hill thrilled with some fresh crisis. The Council convened; slopes teemed with warrioresses in a state of agitation. I hailed Glauke Grey Eyes. "What has happened?"

"Follow me," she commanded.

She spit the tale as we mounted to Eleuthera's command compound. Antiope, Grey Eyes said, had come down from the Acropolis. Our lady had appeared at the head of the Three Hundred Steps an hour after dawn, mounted on Sneak Biscuits, and been permitted to cross, with an escort of King's Companions, to our camp.

"Antiope came before Eleuthera," Grey Eyes narrated, "bearing her war shield. She set her knee to the earth and her shield at Eleuthera's feet. These were her words:

" 'Our two sides are locked in an impasse which neither can win;

all that remains is a bloodbath, destroying both—Athenians now, tal Kyrte later. I know no way out but swear to you, sister, and pledge my holiest oath upon it: I will do anything to procure peace. Name the sacrifice and I will bear it: my life and that of my child, if you so command. You have won. State that price you need to satisfy your honor and I will pay it.' "

Among tal Kyrte the shield represents a warrior's pride; her victories and wounds are recorded upon it; it is synonymous with her soul; it may never be relinquished. Even in death the warrior's shield lies at her shoulder, emblem of her integrity, in this life and the next.

Eleuthera's wrath dissolved before Antiope's gesture of submission. Who had shown such greatness of soul? Her love for Antiope rekindled.

Eleuthera addressed the Council. "Let us withdraw," she proposed. "We have received our queen's capitulation. We have conquered Athens's king. This is victory. Let us go home!"

Of all people, it was Hippolyta who debarred this. She banished Antiope from the camp and reproved the people, declaring that if they returned to their homeland bearing some imperfect or conditional victory, their rivals of the plains would eat them alive.

"You understood when we embarked upon this war, sisters, that the stakes were all or nothing. You may not back off now. The causeway complete, nothing will stay the cataclysm. We must bathe in blood. Prepare yourselves. I will not let you act otherwise!"

So contrary to expectation are the workings of fate. For now, at the terminal hour, it came Eleuthera who called for peace and Hippolyta who demanded war.

Damon champed to return to his people now, to tell what he had seen at the straits. Eleuthera would not let him go. Past midnight she addressed the Council. She rejected Hippolyta's interpretation of events. "Victory is victory! We have it. As for allies who may protest, let them take it to hell!"

The following were the terms she proposed, which, if the Council so ratified, Damon would carry to Theseus and the Athenians:

"Abandon your city this night. Accept safe passage through our lines. Our allies will not be informed. Each man of Athens may take his arms and one garment. Antiope may depart too; we will not prevent her. Take to your ships with your women and children. Settle elsewhere, in Italy or Iberia, anywhere you wish. Cede us possession of the city, all gold and treasure, and the fame of having driven you forth. This will suffice for our honor. With this we can withdraw. Later you may return and reoccupy your country. We don't care what you do once we are gone.

"You have as much time to answer as it takes one brand to burn down to ashes. For our allies' ears are long and they will never permit this, should they learn."

The Council approved, Hippolyta dissenting. Damon committed the proposal to memory. I was sent with him, to translate and to ensure there was no miscommunication. I rode in armor, on Daybreak. Stuff accompanied me as my novice.

31

THE WATCH
COMMANDER'S TOWER

⊚⊚⊚⊚⊚⊚⊚

Theseus accepted.

The Athenians packed up in the dark. The mobilization went with remarkable swiftness, considering the stakes and the risk of discovery. Stuff and I were held at the watch commander's tower. For the first time we could see the enemy close up. He was a mess. Nearly every man was wounded; the maimed and blinded made a third of the ranks. Rations were exhausted; the foe had neither wine nor bread nor splints to bake it with. He gnawed grain raw and the leather of his own shoes. I felt revulsion to observe this, not out of compassion for these beleaguered wretches, though God knows they deserved it, but for the degradation of spirit inflicted on both sides by this honorless war.

Our site of detention was the eastern bastion of the Fortress, the great defense work that ringed the summit of the Rock. Directly beneath our battlement the summit square seethed with the press of men (and the women they had kept with them to cook and clean) massing before the portals by which the mob would make their getaway.

At once a murmur came. Clearly its sense was alarm. Athenians were pointing in agitation to the camps of the besiegers below. Stuff and I peered over the parapet to the lines of tal Kyrte. Other troops could be seen hastening up in overwhelming numbers, moving in behind our lines and on the hills beyond. They lit great bonfires. A second ring of besiegers took position to the rear of ours.

An Athenian corporal passed. "Betrayed," he spat.

Men seized and bound us. We must kneel at swordpoint; a guard was posted over us.

The troops streaming in below, we were made to understand, were Borges' and Saduces'. Give these buggers credit: they had not only sniffed out the double-cross Eleuthera and Theseus had planned for them, but got ten thousand back from the causeway, across miles in the dark, and into blocking position, annulling for the Athenians all possibility of escape.

The Scyths put up picket fire after picket fire, making a show of it, while those clansmen who had acquired snatches of Greek bawled up to the defenders, taunting them that their scheme had been sold out.

"Make out your wills, men of Athens!"

"Leave everything to us!"

The causeway would be completed tomorrow, the Scyths called.

"Your wives will be our chattel!"

"Your daughters will be our whores!"

All night they kept it up. They detailed the crucifixion that awaited the old men and boys on the island and the fates of the matriarchs and maidens when their captors had wrung the last amusement from them.

Stuff and I were not permitted to speak or to vacate our kennel, even to heed nature's call. The Athenians had taken our weapons; clearly they would slice our throats when the morning's fight began.

I asked if I might get a message to Damon. The watch sergeant laughed in my face.

Two hours before dawn, Damon came on his own. He had water for us, even a heel of bread. He convinced our jailers that we were no spies but as much victims of Borges' stroke as the Athenians. We were freed at last and our weapons returned. Damon himself was in armor. Within the hour, he informed us, the defenders would make their break from the Rock.

Theseus would lead. Damon had seen him. His fractured left arm had been splinted and bound to his chest with straps of ox-hide. A half shield, bronze over oak, had been riveted to his breastplate. His scalp, torn in the clash with Eleuthera, had been stitched back. He bore two score other wounds, Damon reported, including a broken foot (bound now to a stump), ruptures of both groins, and half his jaw sheared away. When he crossed this night to address the commanders, every man on the Rock stood, wounded included. All would arm, even the blinded and concussed; men who could not walk would limp on staffs or crawl on their knees. Boys and women armed in the panoplies of the dead and strapped up to move out. One had to admire them: they showed a kind of nobility, these carpenters and mechanics, unbred for war.

Couriers, Damon told me and Stuff, had slipped from the citadel bearing appeals for aid. Six had been dispatched to the Athenian camp on Ardettos and five to Parnes, in the hope that one would get through. Runners had been sent to Thebes and the Isthmus, and more to Marathon and Phaleron Bay, where lay offshore those fisher boats and barges which comprised the evacuation fleet. These would be sent with calls for aid to Aegina and Salamis, the islands which the invaders had not yet touched.

The watch relief came while Damon told us this. The commander was Philippus, "Dew Lap," the same carefree chap who had been with us in Amazonia. He was in hale spirits, bearing news. The citadel's forges, he reported, which till now had worked only bronze and iron, had this night been assigned a more illustrious task.

"Gold."

Theseus was melting down every anklet and earring on the Rock, Philippus reported, casting them into ingots the size a man could carry. "The king will pack a bar with each courier sent out, promising the haul entire to any ally who comes to our aid."

He and Damon exchanged a glance. Clearly they anticipated no takers. My lover turned to Stuff. He could sneak the lass out of the city, he proposed, even if the guard ordered me detained. "Can she speak Greek?"

My novice would not leave me.

Damon grunted. "Another hero."

Philippus let us rise and look out. Night fog had settled; it was too dark to see. We could hear besiegers rousing and arming for the final fight. I asked my lover what he thought of this.

"I have given up thinking."

Stuff watched him with iron eyes.

"I hope you die," she said.

Damon turned to her, not unkindly, and set a hand upon her curls. "In that petition, my dear, I fear you shall soon be satisfied."

BOOK ELEVEN

THE BATTLE

32

THE BATTLE, MORNING

Damon:

〰〰〰

The companies of Athens massed on the summit two hours before dawn. The plan, such as it was, was to attack with everything we had, seeking not to retake any position but only to punch a lane through the foe and drive down this, as swiftly as we could, with as many men as we could, striking for the straits and Euboea. Beyond that . . . what? Could we even reach the causeway, let alone tear it down? Would our force simply be swallowed by the hordes of the foe? These were questions none owned the bowels to ask, but each man huddled in his armor in the predawn chill, steeling himself for this trial whose outcome would be victory or death, not only for himself and his wife and children but for his country and his gods.

Theseus moved among the troops, seeking to inspirit courage. I had found a space beside Elias, against the Fortress gate; I studied the faces of our countrymen. They had indeed become soldiers, these carpenters and masons, vineyardmen and shopkeepers and weavers.

They bitched and spat and hammered each other's leathers tight to their shoulders; men bound each other's shins and passed the whetstone down the line, cinched corselets tight and farted and pissed and blew snot onto the stones. This at least could be said for the scale of our casualties: so many had fallen, there was armor for all who had not. And for our defeats: so many had been wounded, the mob looked a veteran corps. Theseus prowled among the platoons. Messengers, he said, had reached the camps of our countrymen on Hymettos and Lykabettos; their companies would rally at our signal. Close in, our brothers at Ardettos armed now to fight at our sides. The upcountry barons would come on the run; the allies of the Twelve States had sworn this time to honor their oaths. Amazons and Scyths have lost all trust in each other, Theseus swore. He himself had laid intrigues with critical commanders; our feuding foes might yet prove their own ruin. Darkness was our ally; the omens promised glory. Trust in the gods and strike hard!

The initial rush we never even got down the Three Hundred Steps. The foot troops of Trallian and Strymonian Thrace were massed in such multitudes, and so hard by the summit, that a greased hare could not have wriggled through. Nor did darkness impede the Amazon horse. They rode their night mounts, sure-footed, these warrioresses raised on mare's milk and starlight. Slinging brands, they thundered upon us. I was in the third rank at the right, with my brother and two uncles in the division commanded by Menestheus. Our corps had been a thousand on marshaling; under two hundred got through the summit portal before it boomed shut beneath a storm of iron and fire. The Amazons fell on our unshielded right. Behind us pitch shafts turned the face of the gate into an inferno.

No option remained but to elevate shields, lap edges, and endure. I seated the crown of my helmet beneath the upper rim and dug all ten toes into the clay. Stones and sling bullets rang off the bronze. One felt the concussion of ironheads and heard mates fall fore and aft. The left arm and shoulder cannot bear the weight of the shield alone under such onslaught but the right must assist, seating the spearshaft upright like a tent pole behind the shield's right-hand rim, yoking ash to bronze within the gripcord in one's fist and pressing the unit forward as if into a gale. Drop to one knee, use the other to post the facing rim, plant crown and trapezius, and pray. I could hear Elias at my shoulder, crying the names of the gods. I thought absurdly, So long as he calls, I shall live.

Now came the Amazon rush. "Stay low!" I heard someone bawl, and then the foe was on us. Animals feel terror too and, like men, evacuate themselves in the teeth of peril. I was slipping in horse shit. I felt a hoof ring off the bronze at my temple, dropping me nasal-first onto the stone. The beast, or another, trod on my shield, which splayed flat on the dirt, inverted, spread-eagling me with my left forearm pinned in the sheath and the limb half wrenched from its socket. I felt my spearshaft splinter as another hoof punched into the stone. Horse piss sluiced on me as if poured from a bowl. I rolled left, to keep my arm from breaking, simultaneously thrusting with the broken butt of my spear. It hit something but I couldn't see; my helmet was smashed over my eyes. No hope is too ludicrous in such an exigency. I recall repeating to myself, *Hang on, it has to turn.* Of course nothing would turn. Why should it?

We learned later that our countrymen, the last three thousand, who had fled back behind the summit gate and left us to perish, were confronted at this extremity, not by their officers, who quailed as dread-stricken as themselves, but by a shoemaker heretofore called Finch, so inconsequential a fellow had he been judged to be. Now in the ultimate hour this cobbler strode not only to the fore of his countrymen but into their annals of glory.

"Why do you shrink behind gates of oak, men of Athens? Do you imagine you will be granted quarter by the foe? Our brothers are dying while we cower like dogs!"

The shoemaker raised his spear and strode for the gate. Incredibly, the men followed. The portals groaned apart; with a cry our fellows surged forth, filling the void behind us. The mass swelled to our deliverance. We clambered to our feet.

Fighting long enough in these mobs, one acquires a feel for their currents, as a sailor for the sea. They own much in common, these oceans of salt and of men. Both have waves and tides, and both can turn. If you can start the enemy's front ranks pedaling backward, even a step or two, their weight will press upon the shields of those to the rear. The second-rankers can no longer project their spearpoints over the shoulders of the first but must pull their shafts back to vertical, seat them within the rims of their shields, and push on the backs of their rearward-pressing mates. You can feel it when this happens. The experience is elation. Now the foe's third rank starts to buckle too. Cohesion breaks down. The formation becomes a mass, then a mob. You can hear the enemy's curses and feel his knees giving way beneath him. Your blood surges. You enter a state which is primarily relief from fear but owns as much of rage and exaltation. "They're falling back, men! Push, brothers! Heave!"

Theseus broke now to the fore. The mass of our companies drove the foe down the hill. The individual could see nothing, only hear the cries of his mates amid the din. Ahead lay the Enneapylon, the Nine Gates at the foot of the Rock. "Press on, lads! Break through!"

Here the foe's commanders had miscalculated. Had they left the Gates and Half Ring intact, they could have fought from atop the battlements, hemming us in as we, before, had held them out. But in their hatred of our city and their zeal to wipe us from the earth, the enemy had torn down the walls, leveling the field for cavalry. Our mass rolled over their razed remains and swept toward the marketplace.

Here fortune aided us further. Outside the Nine Gates are a number of wells. Prior to the siege, these had fed fountains in the courts of private homes; the Amazons had first demolished both homes and wells, then rebuilt the latter when their horses began to fail from thirst. The wells sat so close beneath our towers, however, that the foe seeking a drink must run a gantlet of Athenian bowfire. Countering this, his Tower People carved aqueducts in the stone and erected penthouses and mantlets, a regular thicket of them, to shield his thirsty troopers from our bolts.

Into this obstacle course Theseus now drove the foe. As our

massed infantry heaved forward, aided by the downslope, the Thracians and Scyths and Getai backstriding before our rush suddenly
found their footing fouled by the channels and aqueducts, and their
formations broken apart by the forest of timbers and overheads. A
slaughter ensued. For the first time, the tide ran in Athens's favor.

Even in the purblindness of the clash, the soldier senses which
units of the enemy are weakest. He calls these *trogalion*, "candy."
Who fights hardest on the field? One trying to get through to candy.
The foe's Thracians and Getai were brilliant horsemen but worthless
on foot. Many had been made infantry by the starvation of their
mounts. They felt shame to fight this way, and this made them candy.

Theseus found them and went after them. The foe fell back. Our
companies punched through. For the time it takes to count to five
hundred, I thought we might even conquer. For now the mulishness
of the Athenian soldier-farmer, the pigheaded refusal to yield which
had at first been scorned by his betters—now this shone to the fore.
By the gods, these clodkickers had learned to fight! The alternations
of terror and elation, which had unmanned them in the early stages
of the siege, had now become familiar. They had learned not to be
downcast by the one or carried away by the other. They no longer fell
apart at the apparition of cowardice among their comrades or themselves, but had come to understand that the same man may play the
craven in the morning and the hero in the afternoon. Give them
this: they were tough. Tougher than the Scyths and Getai, for all
their savage valor, and tougher than the Amazons, despite their dash
and dazzle.

The company I was with, under Menestheus, had broken all the
way out through the Nine Gates now. We were on the flat at the base
of Ares' Hill, straining north toward the Cemetery and the Haymarket. Battalions under Theseus fought on our right, the forest of wells,
while further platoons, squads, and catchalls under Lykos, Peteos,
and the Spartan Amompharetus comprised the far right, flush against
the Rock. Our total made perhaps four thousand. Against this stood
nearly fifty thousand of the foe, Scythians, Thracians, Taurians,
Caucasians, Maeotians, Armenians, Cappadocians, Issedonians,

Rhipaeans, Colchians, and Ceraunians, horse tribesmen dueling afoot, with additional companies of Lykians, Mysians, Phrygians, and Dardanians—true armored infantry—blocking the northern go-round of the Rock, across which, we learned later, three thousand of our countrymen from the pocket fort at Ardettos had struggled without success to reinforce us. The Amazon stronghold on the Hill of Ares was directly above us on the left. From these heights descended a rain of iron. Men of both sides were being mown down like barley beneath the scythe. I looked up; the Amazons were so close you could see the irises within the painted grotesqueries of their sockets. They shot and shot. A man could do nothing but jack his shield above his skull and promise heaven every payback he could think of. The storm drove down around our ears. Amazon war cries fused with the screams of dying men in a cacophony of ungodly ghastliness. Yet within the pandemonium, some god took Athens's side. For as the squall of Amazon iron cut down our men at the clash's fore, it worked the same murder upon the Thracians and Scyths massed against us. Which side wanted the win more? As the front ranks fell, Theseus and Menestheus seized the main chance. They led the charge; our battalions punched through.

We had reached the marketplace now, the flat where Theseus and Eleuthera had dueled just six days prior. The press of bodies defied depiction. From the Hill of the Nymphs to the Eleusinion, every yard of dirt stood packed with contending agonists. By now men of both sides were so exhausted that overhand blows could no longer be struck or fended. One simply fell against the foe and humped his guts upon him. The spear is useless in such a mob. The shortsword— that's the ticket. No need to plunge it hilt-deep. Just poke your man. Make him leak. Leave spear and longsword to heroes. Hang on to the pig-sticker.

Our fathers had taught us the shield was a defensive weapon. We had learned better. When limbs turn to lead, a shield fights fine. Back your man against something and bash him with your bronze. Kick him. Smash the bones in his feet. If he falters, drive your shield into his face. Use the rim. Uppercut him. Onion-chop him. Break his spear arm. If you can't move, fall on him. Use your heels. Go for his temple. Punch his shins and knees. Break his nose. If he gets you in a chokehold, chomp a steak out of his arm. Spit blood in his face. Drive your knee where his fruit hangs. When he falls, stick him. Just once, that's enough. Now get out. Find your mates and form up. If you face the foe alone, don't play hero. Call for help and take him two-on-one. If he flees, let him. That is called victory. Thank the gods and get the hell out.

By sun's rise we were beaten. The foe was just too many. Four times, thrusts under Theseus and Lykos broke through. As many as five hundred got past the foe and formed up for the push to the causeway. But each time Amazon cavalry cut us off; each time our companies were forced to fall back. Enemy horse was near its extremity too. The Amazons were fighting at ten mounts for each rider, so emaciated had their strings become and so swiftly did the animals wear out in action. From the floor of the marketplace I could see their reserves atop the Hill of Ares and the novices riding them down, ferrying the jaded ones out. Though the foe struggled, she still had enough.

We fell back to the Nine Gates. The enemy's champions now drove upon us. I saw Eleuthera at the head of a squadron; Skyleia, Stratonike, Alcippe, and Glauke Grey Eyes led more into the fray. Every inch we had won had been surrendered. We were back where we started. Hundreds bunched up before the First Gate. You could not get through; our keepers wouldn't open; you had to clamber up the timbers, hauled by your mates on rat lines and shafts of pikes. Before the bolted face, the foe pressed in such numbers as to mount upon the bodies of his own slain. Scyths and Taurians and Rhipaeans poured over. We fell back through the zigzag works, second gate, third gate, fourth and fifth and sixth. Cretan and Athenian archers poured fire on the foe from above, then withdrew higher on the face to regroup and launch again. Before the seventh gate is that terrace sacred to Aphrodite Pandemos and Persuasion, where the choruses marshal on the eve of the Anthesteria. A score of Amazon horse under Enyo Warlike, had got into this court; they rushed the gates, slinging grapnels. Our bowmen could not plant their feet to fire, so many were their own countrymen—myself among them—scrambling over the works, dislodging them. The Amazons sunk hooks into the timbers and hauled on the lines. Forty horsewomen packed the court now; every one, it seemed, had buried iron into the beams. Their teams strained; the doors warped and started off their hinges. I had scrambled topside now. Iron grapnels were ringing off the stone like bells. The wall was only fifteen feet at that point; from a standing spring off the backs of their horses, the Amazons and Scyths needed but three hauls on the line and they were over.

I found Elias rallying a dozen to defend a stretch of wall under assault by clansmen of the Copper River. There is this about the Scyth: he is perpetually shitfaced, not only when he goes into battle but in council as well, where he trusts no finding unless it be made numbsoused. Further, these savages' mode of drinking, guzzling liquor neat, renders them insensate not only to fear but to pain. My brother and I took on one such fellow mounting the wall. He wore a headstall of bull's horns with the ruff still on, while his own greasy beard protruded beneath face mail of iron. Stone for stone, he made Elias' weight and mine together yet vaulted up the line as nimbly as a goat, planting one bearskin boot into the embrasure at our feet while propelling his bulk with both fists atop the merlons. I drove a nine-foot pike so deep into his loins I could feel the point punch through the rear bowl of the pelvis; I set all my weight against the shaft and heaved to drive it clear, while my brother hacked through the brute's right arm till fist and axe toppled in a heap. Still the monster mounted, hurling his bulk with such force against our picket as to bowl off the catwalk first myself, then Elias rising to reinforce, sending the pair of us pinwheeling into the drop gallery to the rear. My brother, on his knees, now swung his axe a second stroke, which chopped the tribesmen at the knee as if felling an oak. The Scyth plunged beard-foremost into the gallery, catching with his bare fist at Elias' throat. My pike was still in his guts. I wrenched it free, tearing out a plate of armor, an ox-hide girdle, and most of the fellow's intestines, which unspooled through the stanchions like a train of sausages. The brute still thundered, clutching with a gushing stump at my privates, before Elias at last succeeded in sawing through the gristle of his neck.

Another score mounted in this titan's train. We fell back before them. Stone rained from our gunners above.

Before the eighth gate, Theseus and half a hundred made a stand. But our king's limbs were so encumbered, his broken left arm bound to his ribs, half-shield welded atop, that he could get but half his weight into his blows. I saw Eleuthera and Stratonike make a run at him in tandem. He fell again. At the gate our fellows hauled him clear beneath a hail of missiles.

My brother and I fled the last hundred steps to the summit. Every man, it seemed, bore another, wounded or maimed. Blood turned the pavement slick. The final gate, that of the summit Fortress, yawned and swallowed us. It closed with a bang; forty men set their shoulders to the crossbar. We were on the summit now. Within the Fortress court, the last Athenian companies milled in disorder. Suddenly from the inner court appeared, to our astonishment, Selene and the girl Stuff! Both were in armor. Their horses were being brought. A watch commander bawled to hold the gate. Selene and the maid were being released!

What had happened?

I tried to push through but the press beat me back. Selene had not seen me. She couldn't hear my cries in the din. I strained toward her; she appeared distraught, as at the commission of some crime or treason. A groom led Daybreak. The horse reared and kicked. At first I thought it was the boy's clumsiness. Then I saw Selene's hand upon the reins; the animal balked and snapped at her in a way no Amazon mount would do, save to a warrior who had lost her *hippeia*.

I saw Selene swat Daybreak across the nose with the flat of her hand, an extremity she would never resort to uncompelled by despair. She sprang to her seat, hauling the bit tight, inflicting pain intentionally, as a ship's master applies the lash to a mutinous crew, then heeled the beast hard and drove him, with Stuff behind, through the portal and out.

The gates boomed shut. The crossbar was heaved into place; the double bolts thrown. The shattered companies of Athens remustered. Into the court advanced Sneak Biscuits. On his back rode Antiope, in armor.

33

THE ARMING OF ANTIOPE

What turn occasioned this I could not then know. I must cobble this recounting at secondhand, from witnesses, each of whom stood present for a portion of events but none for the full sequence.

It had been, as I have said, the lady Antiope's practice in her daily round never to look upon the fighting or permit the babe Hippolytus to do so, but to abide apart in the innermost precincts of the citadel. No other did this. Every breathing soul, it seemed, ringed the battlements night and day, so eager was he for intelligence, well or ill, of the struggle below, and so unable to bear the suspense in its absence. Many bivouaced at these self-appointed posts, refusing to vacate even to eat or sleep. Never—save one appearance on the walls to address her countrywomen and, later, her extraordinary night embassy to the Amazon camp—was Antiope observed outside her cloister. Only with the descent of darkness and cessation of strife, or in the stillness before dawn, would she take the air of the ramparts, and even then made it a point never to look below. Yet surely she heard. It would be impossible not to. With each cry of woe or exulta-tion, so one learned later, the Amazon grew more distraught, uncer-tain if it signaled the end of him she loved or, equally dreadful to her, his vanquishment of one of her own kind. I have been within the citadel under assault, and I can tell you the rock rings with sound from end to end. Worse, the stone plays tricks, magnifying some clamors while diminishing others. You swear the Fortress Gate has been broken in; you arm and hasten out, only to be brought up by comrades' laughter, and see the fight a furlong below.

Apparently the clamor, on this final dawn, had reached such a pitch that Antiope could no longer maintain her truancy. She came out. She mounted to the tower. I know this because men saw her from below and hailed her; others witnessed from within and testified thereafter. They said her face, looking on the slaughter, revealed nothing. Nor did she linger regarding the field, across which men and women were slaying and being slain by hundreds, but turned at once and strode back within.

At this hour, recall, Selene remained in detention at the block-house, with her novice Stuff. My mate Philippus, Dew Lap, chanced then to hold the bell; his post was guard commander; he had charge of Selene.

Suddenly a messenger approached him from the lady Antiope. Selene's horse was to be brought round ready to ride, the dispatch commanded. The maid herself was to be escorted to Antiope at once, by the guard captain in person.

Philippus obeyed in such haste, he testified later, that his corpo-ral and he were packing Selene's breastplate and herald's pennant, she herself cinching her sword and baldric, as all trundled across the court before the Temple of Victory, chockablock now with outdoor kitchens and berths for the wounded. When they entered the palace, they were met by a page at the threshold of Antiope's rooms and redirected to the king's armory.

"You know that kennel, Damon," Philippus told me later, narrat-ing the tale. "It's tight as a duck's ass. Barely room to crook an elbow, as it holds the king's arms and the Companions'. Theseus' armorer was there and had the hole open. Dark as a crypt, one lamp guttering, stinking of bronze and oil and sweat.

"When we entered, the lady Antiope waited at the rear, one foot on the bench before the spear stands. Her hair was dressed and bound, as Amazons do before battle, with her helmet, bossed, on the shelf beside her. Her legs and shoulders were bare. I confess I goggled. Not Theseus himself bore as many scars of battle. At our entry the lady looked up as any commander might, cross and impatient at our tardiness. About both shins she clamped greaves of bronze; her soles were shod in those boots her race call 'fireproofs.' The remainder of her armor inclined against its stand, wanting only the hand to set it about her.

"We had the maid Selene between us, my corporal and I, not sure if the lady wished her held or not. I could feel Selene start at the sight of her queen awaiting armor. Antiope intended to fight, that was clear. But on whose side?

" 'All leave me,' she commanded, 'save Selene.'

"This was impossible.

" 'I must forbid this, lady,' I declared with all the brass I could muster. 'On orders of your lord, our king.'

"The Amazon did not even look at me. Clearly she had called the maid to arm her. It is some superstitious canon of their race that not any lubber may do it. I summoned my globes. 'By command of our lord Theseus, lady, you may not be set at hazard.'

"She met my glance then for the first time. 'If you love your country, Captain, rally every man and hold them for me, in order, in the court of the Fortress Gate.'

"Will you believe me, Damon, when I declare I was compelled to obey her? Her will was so strong. I found myself bowing and withdrawing.

" 'Come, Selene,' I heard the lady commence in their savage tongue. 'I may be wrapped in my death armor only by one who loves me.'

"There is an alcove at the throat of the armory, where the steps turn before ascending. We retreated, my corporal and I. Yet some imperative would not let us depart. We held up there at chamber's gorge. The conformation of the stone carries sound across the apse, so that the speech of the two Amazons worked to our ears as clearly as from one as close as you are now.

"Antiope commanded the maid to arm her.

"Selene refused.

"Here, Damon, I lament my deficiency in the Amazon tongue. Further the women spoke with haste and in a kind of code, as intimates will. I could make out this declaration of the lady: 'I will not stand by and witness another slaughter of innocents,' by which one could only deduce she meant the massacre of Athenian women and children that must ensue when the Scyths and Thracians completed their causeway to the island.

"Selene rejected this, on what terms I could not call clear, but was overridden by her mistress, dictating with emphasis: 'Tal Kyrte must be remembered as warriors, not butchers!' A passionate exchange succeeded, narrated at such a pace that I could comprehend little. The pith seemed to be Antiope's conviction that their nation was doomed, and all that remained was how posterity would remember it.

"The maid Selene dismissed this. 'Listen beyond the walls. Victory is ours!' A dark ejaculation escaped the lady Antiope. 'As the pine pronounced to the axe.'

"Distinctly I heard from Antiope, 'Only one act can make tal Kyrte turn from this folly: the sight of myself in armor contending against them. This will break their hearts, as I read in your aspect, Selene, it now breaks yours.'

"The lady had drawn the maid to her. They spoke in whispers. Both wept. The enormity commanded of the maid had struck both women numb. You could see that Selene sensed, as I, that this act would alter the fate of both our races. Could she summon, as I had not, the spirit to defy her queen?

"Antiope indicated the breastplate before her on its stand. 'Now aid me, my friend, as once you did before.' The lady straightened and aligned herself so that her mate could install the bronze about her. 'I must,' she said, 'be beautiful today.' "

Such was Philippus' report. At the same time Antiope had directed Selene she had, apparently, commanded as well that her own horse be armored and brought round to the court of the Fortress Gate. This site is exceptional in its own right. It is a double gate, with a broad square between. On both flanks ascend galleries from which archers and javelineers may fire upon attackers penned below.

It was into this courtyard now, at the crisis of the siege, that Theseus and the Companions staggered, myself among them, at the extremity of exhaustion. The companies drew up in astonishment to behold Antiope in armor upon her steed of battle. A groom held Sneak Biscuits' reins. This act stood in violation of our monarch's orders on pain of death. The lad went white at his lord's approach. To augment the boy's consternation was the king's aspect in this moment. From the ordeal of battle, the crest of his helmet had been sheared; where the horsehair plume had ascended now hung strips of human hair and flesh. The plate where it fell across his eyes shone, lacquered with blood. His shield, bound to his crippled flank with bands of bronze, was black with that paste of gore and dust which all warriors know from the press of close-ranked combat. The king bore neither spear nor javelin, all long since shivered. His great sword had been sundered at the haft; he clutched the blade butt absent the grip. This too dripped with fluids. With his right hand, whose fingers could no longer be seen, bound as they were in rags and leather to seal their wounds, he reached to the helmet and cocked it back above his eyes. Froth and spittle lathered his lips and chin; he wiped and flung this to the dirt. His teeth he swiped as well, black with blood and grime. His eyes were sockets of exhaustion.

Now he saw his bride upon her armored steed. Clearly he recognized the import of this apparition and the extremity it proclaimed. A terrible groan escaped his breast, as of one who feels the workings of Fate's engine, and knows the mark of his own hand upon the lever. I recall the boy groom's face, reacting with relief that he, the mere agent of this calamity, was too slight a pawn to merit notice. Rather our lord's glance elevated to heaven, to Him who had ordained this overthrow.

The upper galleries of the court stood packed with archers and javelineers, spellbound by the drama playing out in the square below. Outside the gate the massed foe put up a racket ungodly, clamoring for Athens's annihilation.

Antiope reined Sneak Biscuits hard. I did not remark this then, so dislocated were my senses, yet any with eyes could read in her mount's demeanor, smelling the fight and eager for it, that heaven had restored to the Amazon that mastery over horses, *hippeia,* of which she had so long been deprived. My gaze held riveted to her, as did those of every other assembled on the summit at this hour of Athens's extremity.

The lady wore Amazon cavalry greaves, the kind which cover the outboard portion of the shin only, leaving the flesh bare where it pressed against the horse. Her upper legs were scale-armored, her waist cinched in the seven-stranded wale. A breastplate of bronze defended her fore and aft atop a sleeveless jerkin. A black panther skin, the same she had borne from Amazonia, lapped her left side, gorge to hip. From her belt hung a *gorytus* quiver bristling with shafts, a bow of horn and ivory clamped in its case; against her back sat the sheath of a *pelekus* axe; she clutched three horseback javelins. Sneak Biscuits wore a headstall rig of iron over quilted linen, with matching armor plating his neck, breast, and flanks. Every inch of metal on horse and rider had been burnished to a mirror's sheen. The helmet, cocked back on the Amazon's brow, was an eye-slitter of bronze etched with cobalt and timonium. It bore no crest but a solitary band of boar's teeth, lapping the eye slits like a sash. In thirty years of strife on land and sea, I have never beheld a more magnificent-looking warrior.

At this instant two Athenian infantry companies, or such scrambled miscellany as might with charity be called by that name, hobbled into the court from the palace interior, armed and ready to follow Antiope into the fray. At the sight of their lord Theseus in his gore-begrimed armor, the lot drew up in trepidation.

The king crossed to the Amazon, seizing her bridle as if to stay her within the court. Antiope met her husband's eyes. From where I stood, I could see only the nape beneath her helmet. Yet such heartbreak could be read in the aspect of the king, looking up into her face and apprehending the mandate of necessity it told, as to clench my own heart as in the grip of some fell fist. Simultaneously, a thrill coursed along the galleries ringing the court at the sight of this magnificent warrioress, the city's last hope. Nor could a more baneful contrast have been imagined between the gore-mantled lord of Athens and his impeccable warrior bride. Outside, the din of the foe reascended. Would our king hold his queen from action?

From the skirt of the court arose an infant's cry. The babe Hippolytus. He had been brought in by his nurse. At a sign from Antiope the child was borne forward. The sight of his son seemed to unman Theseus' resistance. Again the clamor of the enemy. Did the lady speak? Did the king respond? If they did I could hear nothing, so deafening was the uproar from without.

Antiope motioned for the babe to be passed up to her. Theseus took him from the nurse. Antiope lifted Hippolytus from her husband's hands and set him before her, the infant's back against her horse's mane, his legs straddling the animal's flanks. The Amazon touched belly, heart, and brow in the salute to Ares. Her right hand reached over her shoulder, unsheathing the double axe. She elevated the crescent blades, upright before her. I could see her lips pronounce the anthem of Ares Manslayer,

Blood to iron
Iron to blood

whose import is the warrioress' abdication of hope, her willing release of life and embrace of her end.

With the axe's edge she incised a split upon her own tongue. The child looked on, fascinated. His lips parted in uncoerced emulation. Upon his infant's tongue his mother lanced the matching stroke.

I and the other Companions had crossed to take station at our king's side. I stood close enough beneath the Amazon to see the rawhide ties of her boots and the leather where the quilted pad of Sneak Biscuits' breastplate rode against the whorled hair of his coat. Antiope lifted her son. "Now kiss this face, my love, which you will never see in life again."

The boy obeyed. I turned toward Theseus. His eyes were dead coins. Antiope passed the infant down. At that instant a cry mightier than all ascended from the foe beyond the gate. Antiope resheathed her axe; her right hand rose; she tugged her helmet-facing down.

Theseus could still have stopped her. He was the king; the gatemaster would not open without his leave. Our lord peered into the mask of bronze, which hid forever the face of her he loved.

He stepped back. The gate groaned open.

34

AGONY OF ANTIOPE

⦿⦿⦿⦿⦿⦿

Brothers, I will not bore you with the lore. You have heard the tales. The heroes of that day were your fathers and grandfathers; you know the sites; you have seen the graves and monuments. Some of you fought then in the ranks, while others, lads at the time, owned enough of sense to apprehend the magnitude of events. You youngsters who had not been born, even you have heard the harpers' lays and attended the rites at the House of Oaths and the Amazoneum. No doubt you believe you possess an understanding of the battle and the impact this lone Amazon had upon it. Believe me, brothers, you do not. None has, who was not there to see it.

Antiope advanced from the gate at the base of the Steps. The upper way had been cleared for her by massive bombardment of rock and boulder, the final barrage tonnage held in the west-facing summit magazines, which the gunners released now and which thundered down the zigzag works of the Enneapylon, producing such a storm of stone and dust, colossal and cacophonous, as to drive the Scyths and Getai, Taurians and Thracians and Caucasians massed beneath the Fortress Gate back down the slope in terror. Behind this roiling smokescreen, companies of Athenian infantry propelled the last diehards of the foe from the clefts they clung to above the Nine Gates. The field was cleared. The enemy remustered, massing outside the wall (or what was left of it) of the Enneapylon at the base of the Rock. Down the Three Hundred Steps descended Antiope.

She did not emerge from the gate first, but two Athenian companies, that of Menestheus and Stichios Ox, preceded her. My place was in the former. The foe greeted us with jeers and catcalls but made no move to attack. Then Antiope spurred forth. She did not charge at the gallop, as I have seen carved in reliefs and painted on the bowls of kraters and the walls of hero shrines. She came out at a walk. Nor did she proclaim her identity, citing descent and lineage, as one of her stature had every right; rather, held silent, neither elevating an arm to signal combat's onset nor hoisting the boar's-tooth plate that sheathed her eyes to confirm for all who she was.

Behind her the ranks of Athenians decanted from the gate like winter honey from a jar, sluggishly and tardily. They were terrified. The first line set its backs to the remains of the wall, compelling each succeeding rank to take station before it—the inversion of good order and the very opposite of what their officers had commanded. Still, as each rank accreted, the front advanced. Antiope advanced before it. Clearly no few of the foe took her for a goddess, with such splendor did her armor gleam and by such brilliance did her aspect exceed the common measure of humanity. The hour was still early, the west-facing slope deep in shadow, so that the Amazon, seen from the besiegers' lines, advanced from gloom into flares of blinding dazzle.

Out came Athens's champions, Lykos and Peteos, Bias and Telephos, Tereus, Eugenides, Phaeax, Pylades and Demophoon, the heroes Pirithous (on a splint of iron) with Peleus of Thessaly, Cretan Triptolemus and the Spartan Amompharetus. Last, Theseus.

All yielded place to Antiope. Nor did she acknowledge their existence but, as the paragon in a tiara, shone forth foremost and apart. She elevated the plate of her helmet, revealing her face. Cries rang across all the field.

There is a phenomenon which occurs sometimes among massed armies and even flocks of sheep or birds. Movement at one extremity is communicated, precipitating movement at the other. Fear is the engine. Impelled by dread, a man seeks to withdraw from prominence, to add one pace to the distance between himself and those who seek his slaughter. He backs half a step into the throng, onto the mate at his rear. This fellow, driven by his own fear, yields as well and presses in turn upon the man at his back.

Fear is contagious. Motion multiplies. One man can break an army and one step precipitate a rout.

This is what happened to the foe now. As his upslope ranks stuttered rearward before the apparition of Antiope, the mass compacted upon the ranks beneath on the incline, and so did their fear. The savage, recall, holds his own gods in awe, but even more the gods of his enemies. Looking on peerless Antiope, he perceived an immortal. Who else could she be but a goddess, or a champion with a goddess unseen at her shoulder?

The mass began edging back, gathering moment as a tide in its swing, so that even those at the rear who maintained courage were powerless to stand against their fellows of the fore, but gave way as their comrades retreated upon them.

Antiope advanced.

The mob backed before her.

Another step. Another. Now Antiope elevated her right hand and with a tug seated the armor of her faceplate before her eyes. In the same motion she reached behind her shoulder to draw from its sheath the *pelekus* axe. A cry burst from the companies of Athens. Their ranks swelled forward. The foe's bellied back. . . .

Which champion fell first before Antiope's onslaught? Many cite Harpalus, prince of the Rhipaean Caucasus, whom men called the Bear for the pelt of his chest and whose father, Typhaeus, claimed descent from the North Wind. Harpalus burst at the gallop from the host of the foe, seeking the glory of being first to engage the peerless Amazon. The prince plunged from his horse's back, impaled on Antiope's javelin, which she did not deign even to cast but thrust as a lance, catching Harpalus below the right nipple and driving through the thoracic spine. He crashed to the dust, spitting out his hero's blood.

Next to stand before Antiope's rush was Amorges, lord of all Caria south of the Maeander, who faced her on foot, so brazen was his conceit, seconded by his cousin Arimapachus, prince of Mysian Mariandyne. Their weapons were the whip and the noose, with which they were accustomed to taking down the wild bulls of their country and by which they meant to unhorse the Amazon and dispatch her afoot. Amorges, she shot through the eye slit of his helmet. The shaft penetrated with such force (so the prince's retainers reported later when they came to dress the corpse) as to pierce the skull clean, front to back, and burst forth through the helmet's bronze two hand's-breadths at the rear. Amorges fell as a wall does, and his armor clashed as it toppled. His cousin Arimapachus had snared Sneak Biscuits' neck with the noose and sought now to upend him; Antiope wheeled with such speed as to tangle the prince in his own snare. She jerked him off his feet and dragged him to death across the stone.

The poets tell how Antiope slew next the twins Agenor and Geryontes, princes of the Lykians, who pastured their herds from the Simois to the Scamander. Both stood six feet and fought with the boar-hunter's pike, which they wielded, so men said, with the ease of a fowler his gutting knife. They faced her at the footbridge where the hero shrine of Pandion stands. The first, Agenor, she cut down with the slung axe, the ironhead entering his belly at the navel, tearing through both cuirass and war belt to uncinch the sack of his guts. He bowled rearward, still alive and howling in rage as Antiope vaulted to the earth and, wrenching her *pelekus* from his belly, wielded it to take his head. In an instant she had remounted and spurred to the gallop. The second brother, Geryontes, thrust with his pike as Antiope wheeled to flank him, striking Sneak Biscuits in the hindquarters and tearing off a piece of flesh the size of a cutlet.

The horse wheeled in fury and stove the foe's brains with his hooves.

Next to fall before Antiope's rush was Maimon, son of Saduces of the Trallian Thracians, a youth yet beardless but whose pleas to accompany the expedition had softened his father's heart. Now evil requited the prince's concession to sentiment: his child beaten down beneath the Amazon's axe. She sent to the house of the dead Elpenor and Gigantes, lords of Colchis, and, when they rushed upon her, Ixys, prince of the Macrones, and Otos, war chief of the Copper River Scyths. About her had now rallied four Athenian companies, half a thousand men, led by Stichios Ox and the hero Pirithous, fighting upon one splinted leg, with Telephos of Marathon and Phaeax of Eleusis.

I witnessed only the commencement of this, brothers, for at the instant the first champion, Harpalus, impaled himself upon Antiope's lance, all hell broke loose across the field. Harpalus' fall signaled battle's onset. With a cry the formations swelled and surged and crashed together. My company was swept south toward the Hill of the Muses. Antiope drove hers north, beneath Ares' Hill and into the flat of the marketplace. Here the foe were Scythians, Thracians, and Caucasians. No Amazons. Was this deliberate on Antiope's part? Perhaps she hoped to break her people's will without actually engaging their champions.

Where I had been driven to, in the companies commanded by Menestheus and Peteos, the Tower, our lines engaged Amazons of the Themiscyra, Lycasteia, and Titaneia. The enemy were mounted; we were on foot. I could see Eleuthera at the far left, where Lykos' platoons dueled her, and the other great champions, Hippolyta and Skyleia, Stratonike and Alcippe and Glauke Grey Eyes. Did they too seek to evade Antiope? Perhaps they hoped, as she, for some resolution short of face-to-face. Yet who could hide from her? For such were the cries of jubilation resounding at each blow Antiope struck and each champion she took down, and such the echo upon the compact and enclosed field (for end to end the widest reach was under a thousand yards), that every warrior on every quarter could tell her triumphs.

Antiope was winning. Across two hills we could hear the exulta-
tions of Athenians pressing forward and the dirges of Scythians and
Caucasians giving back.

All who have dueled in massed combat know how swiftly sound
communicates across the field. Groans of overthrow and shouts of acclaim the infantryman interprets untutored and obeys as the wolfpack the howls of its leader. The great tidal surges of battalions may
be accounted not by orders of their captains (for who can hear even
his own name above the din of battle?) but by this measure alone.
Our companies yielded Muses' Hill to Eleuthera; there was nothing
there anyway. In fever we flooded toward Ares' Hill and the marketplace. Antiope! Victory! We smelled it like wolves and stampeded,
baying as we ran.

A boulevard yawed open before us. We were fighting below Market Hill now. The foe were male tribesmen. It seemed the clash had
gone on all day, yet the hour was still early morning. At the southern
entrance of the market stands a colony of cists and crypts. Here my
company, Menestheus', with two of Peteos', locked up with a huddle
of Taurian and Rhipaean clansmen. The enemy had learned enough
of phalanx fighting to know he must seize turf and hold it; this he did
now, with a bitter and brutal stubbornness. His rampart was a line of
chamber tombs; our rushes could not dislodge him. The site spawned
its own species of horror as antagonists overturned the capstones of
the crypts and both fired from behind them and used them to shield
themselves from each other's missiles. As the pitch of the clash in-
tensified, Athenians and tribesmen took cover within the sepulchres
themselves, soles treading upon the baskets containing the bones of
the dead while they themselves dueled and perished. The fighting
was not house to house but crypt to crypt.

In the midst of this I fell wounded. A lintel stone collapsed on
me, shattering the trestle of my right foot. I pitched in agony so acute
it took me blind. A mate whose name I never learned hauled me to
the lee of a tomb, binding my hoof with the jerkin torn from his own
back. He had been hit too, shot through the calf with a Scythian
ironhead. "Do you hear, brother?" he cried, calling my attention to

shouts proclaiming another conquest by Antiope. *"Passa plemmyris peritrepetai,"* my savior cited the proverb: "Every tide turns." He propped me against a boneyard berm and gimped back to the fray.

How long I remained in that posture I cannot say. I saw Selene pass afoot, fighting as an infantrywoman. I blacked out and came to; I thought two soldiers appeared; they seemed to bear me higher up the hill. Someone got wine in me. Lucidity returned.

Now for the first time I saw Antiope. She had reined on the rubble field north of the Cemetery, on that slope where in peacetime the day laborers assemble, seeking work. Prince Saduces, lord of Trallian Thrace, had been searching the field for her, raging to avenge the slaughter of his son. Now he had found her. I saw Selene again, with her novice Stuff. They dashed afoot among Saduces' cohorts, joining the phalanx, which lapped the prince right and left. Directly across massed the lines of Athenians, within which Antiope now wheeled, horseback, to embrace the challenge of the lord of Thrace.

The prince went for Antiope head-on, wielding the two-handed Edonian mace. He meant to decapitate her as the horses passed but at the last moment either lost his nerve or thought he saw a better shot. Instead of bashing with the club, he slung it, sidearm, so that its mace end, which must have weighed twenty pounds, hurtled toward Antiope on the horizontal axis. The great spike would have hewn her in two or taken her horse's head entire had its warhead struck the mark. But Antiope gauged the cudgel's rotation, spurring enough that the killing end pinwheeled past, the shaft only striking her hip. Even so the impact bowled her from her seat. She spilled, weaponless save the axe on her back and the shortsword at her waist. About her collected half a hundred Athenian infantry, the companies that had fought in her train. These scattered like quail as Saduces wheeled his steed, brawny as a draft horse, and, retrieving his mace at full stride, galloped upon the downed Antiope. She met him on foot, slipping his right-handed rush at the last instant, to plunge her blade left-handed into his horse's breast as it passed. So deep did the weapon seat, the burial crews reported later when they purged the field, that shaft and grip were swallowed whole within the animal's flesh and had to be groped for by hand only to be found, let alone drawn forth. The beast tumbled, pitching Saduces. Antiope hacked his head off with her axe.

I could see her as she remounted, several Athenian infantrymen having caught her horse and hauled him back. Her helmet was gone; her hair, gore- and dust-mantled, spread wide in a tangle, wild as a Gorgon's. Both arms shone scarlet to the shoulder. Even her lips ran blood. Her teeth were black with it.

The host of Thracians broke before her. Athenian infantry ravened upon them. Such a shout arose from the field, resounding between the Rock and the Hill of Ares, as to render all interpretation moot. It was the cry of men at the brink of victory.

Now the day hung in the balance.

Now the champions of Amazonia must reply.

Glauke Grey Eyes materialized first, out of the smoke at the shoulder of the fountain house behind the Eleusinion. She was just below me, so that I could see her seat the horseback javelin within the catch of the sleeve extender and call upon the gods to witness her hour of glory. The quarter she had entered from put her behind Antiope, who, pressing forward amid the din of the foot troops, stood unaware of her rival's presence. Grey Eyes could have closed with Antiope and slain her in a hundred ways. Yet she reined in midrush, impelled by honor, and called again, until she saw her countrywoman heed and wheel.

Both Amazons launched at the gallop, but Antiope had the advantage coming from uphill. The flung lances, half again as long as a normal javelin, looked like laundry poles as they crossed in midflight, while each rival, fixing her concentration upon the missile hurtling toward her, heeled her mount to elude its rush. A shaft slung uphill will sometimes "sail," getting too much air under it. Further, the wind had got up, as it will often at that hour. Both mischances combined to deflect Grey Eyes' lance. Antiope slipped its descent, warhead and shaft passing over her shoulder as she pressed her breast to Sneak Biscuits' back. The lance drove on into the stump of a fig tree, splintering as its iron core burst through the foreshaft.

Antiope's javelin, slung downhill and protected from deflection by the shoulder of the slope, plunged from its apogee as its hurler had intended, so that shaft, warhead, and core fused, it seemed, into one balanced entity. It struck Grey Eyes' horse in the meat of the neck, passing through and entering the warrioress midway between navel and pubic bone. The lance drove Grey Eyes through with such force that its warhead shot forth and seated for a second time into her mount, knitting horse and rider. The knight's arms dropped; reins spilled; the weight of her helmet bore her head and neck rearward, lolling grotesquely, as only the dead do. Rider and horse crashed, shearing the shaft that united them as they fell; blood blew from Grey Eyes' helmet as her skull struck the stone.

Alcippe challenged next. Antiope unhorsed her with a blow of her shield and killed her with a javelin snatched from Alcippe's own fist and plunged two-handed into her breast. Bremusa fell then, shot on the run, and, after her, Clonie and Lysippe beneath the *pelekus* axe. Exigency would seem to dictate that a band of champions rally and take Antiope on in a pack. But the code of the plains forbade this. Each warrior must advance alone, sustained by her own valiant heart, to duel her sister woman-to-woman.

Stratonike succeeded in wounding Antiope, a bowshot slung as the antagonists passed which pierced shield, breastplate, and corselet and would have driven through to the vital parts had its warhead connected on the horizontal axis, as the Amazons always shoot at close quarters. Yet somehow the bolt struck on the vertical and hung up between the second and third ribs. The impact nearly bowled Antiope from her horse just the same. She cartwheeled over the hindquarters, spilling to the right side, so that her feet hit the dirt at gallop-speed while she clung with one fist to the mane (the other yet clutching bow and shafts). What man, Heracles included, could absorb such a blow and still haul his weight onto his horse's back? Yet Antiope did it, one-handed, and made it look like nothing. She could not jerk the warhead from her side, so deeply had it embedded, and so broke the shaft off where it stuck, and kept coming. A cry burst from Stratonike to witness this double prodigy, as she read the hopelessness of her cause.

The rivals wheeled and rushed again. This was on the flat, in the saddle between Nymphs' and Ares' Hills, where all houses had been demolished save the wreck of the saddler Euphorion's shop, whose partial walls, waist-high, still stood. The pair hurtled toward this obstacle from opposing quarters, each seeking to use its obstruction to confound the other. Here Stratonike seemed to outplay her rival, abating her rush enough that Antiope must hurdle the first wall while she, Stratonike, still raced on the flat. Their bolts passed in midair, Antiope's overshooting, Stratonike's striking home. The shaft pierced the shield a second time but failed to find the flesh. Now Stratonike hit the wall. Clearance was not high and the horse was fresh. A hundred times of a hundred, mount and rider would have vaulted it with ease. Yet, inexplicably, both forehooves struck. The steed still landed in balance and, had the ground been clear, would have recovered footing even at speed. Yet chance or fate set his landing against the half-demolished second wall, the partition between the saddler's workshop and his family's quarters. The mount spilled, pitching Stratonike. She crashed helmet-first. Her neck snapped and her limbs splayed, unstrung.

What was the number and sequence of those Antiope slew next? Thistle and Xanthe Blonde may be named with certainty, with Electra and Dioxippe, Paraleia and Antibrote. As the champion took each on, she seemed to court her own extinction with enlarging extravagance, so reckless were the tactics she assayed and so ambitious the shots and blows she aimed, not to mention the wounds she received with each clash and the mounting exhaustion to which even the greatest hero must eventually succumb. Clearly Antiope sought to produce the spectacle of her own death, to break tal Kyrte's heart and vitiate the nation of the will to endure. Yet the very recklessness of her attacks worked to preserve her. The other champions overextended, reckoning that only their most singular strike would stand. Their throws miscarried, while Antiope's found the mark again and again. It seemed she would put the army to rout single-handed.

Where was Eleuthera? The sun had mounted to midmorning. The central corps of Amazonia still fought hundreds of yards away, south and east of the Rock, against Ardettos and the Athenian companies which had retaken the Hill of the Muses. Theseus' foot troops worked to pen the Amazons there, to block them from bearing aid to the Scyths and Thracians being cut up by Antiope beneath Ares' Hill. The king's captains were the champions Bias and Demophoon, with the hero Peleus of Thessaly, the Cretan Triptolemus and Spartan Amompharetus. For all the Athenians' valor, however, Eleuthera's squadrons could easily have punched through, or simply circled west behind Market Hill and gotten to Antiope by that route. Yet they didn't.

What held Eleuthera? Perhaps the gallantry of Theseus' defenders. Or Eleuthera and Hippolyta may have hoped another champion of tal Kyrte would overcome their queen. Plain fear may have held them. Yet my gut tells me different. I think they could not, or would not, believe Antiope's revolution. Despite all, the commanders of Amazonia could not imagine their sister taking the field against them. How often this morning had couriers reported Antiope's conquests? Surely Eleuthera and Hippolyta had been informed again and again of the havoc being wreaked by their countrywoman. Yet, all later reports insist, they banished the messengers in fury.

In the end the cries of the field compelled them. You have all heard the famous exchange. The final dispatch bearer, it is said, galloped up to Eleuthera, reporting Antiope's most immediate heroics. "Heaven," the messenger cried, "fights at her side."

"Then I will meet her in Hell," Eleuthera replied.

She sent for Soup Bones, whom her novices had brought out of the fight to catch his wind, and, arming herself with a brace of three horseback javelins, called upon Ares, Hecate, and the Great Mother to witness the rightness of her cause. "Ye gods, if you possess justice as you do might, then guide my lance!"

And she spurred round Market Hill, seeking Antiope.

Where was Theseus at this point? Twenty witnesses render twenty tales. Sense, and facts established in the aftercourse, place him among the infantry holding the saddle between Ares' Hill and the Acropolis. Did he see Eleuthera, ringed by her Companions, gallop north to seek Antiope? If he didn't, surely someone reported it to

him. He seized this moment to break from the fray and mounted to
that knob called the Tailor's Nose. Here, men said, he made signal to
Borges of the Scyths.

This was an intrigue set in motion days prior by Theseus, namely
to buy the clansmen off for gold. Theseus would hand over the treasure of the Acropolis to Borges and the knights of the Iron Mountains, he pledged, if the prince would take this plunder and break off.
Borges had assented. Now was the hour. Theseus raised the signal.

But as often falls out in war, opportunism and the main chance
trump all. Borges was winning. Why back off and settle for part of
the swag, the Scyth reasoned (for surely Theseus held out the plum
portion), when he could carry the day and bag it all?

A volley of shafts greeted Theseus' signal. The tribesmen beat
forward, bellying the Athenians back.

Now onto the field beneath Market Hill, where the Temple of
the Amazons stands today, emerged Eleuthera, crying Antiope's
name. Neither she nor any of her nation owned an inkling of Theseus' botched intrigue. Before Eleuthera's rush (for regiments of
the foe came with her) our troops reeled in disorder, surrendering the
market and the Cemetery, taken this hour at such appalling cost.

The state of the field was this. South and east of the Rock, Amazons and Scyths stood triumphant. Between the Hill of Ares and the
Acropolis, the Athenians under Theseus were falling back, pressed
upon by Hippolyta's Lycasteia Amazons, augmented by Borges and
the Scyths of the Iron Mountains. North, where the Cemetery and
marketplace sprawled beneath Market Hill and the Hill of the
Nymphs, the Amazons, Thracians, and Caucasians fought the Athenians under Lykos and Menestheus, Pirithous and Stichios Ox.

Here was where Antiope was.

To here Eleuthera came.

The pair squared off on the shoulder of Market Hill. Each jock-
eyed to get upslope of her rival. Antiope bore a score of wounds,
gravest being the ironhead wedged between her ribs; she sought to
conceal these incapacities, but the slope betrayed her, compelling
her to favor her right side as she rode. Eleuthera, discerning, seized
the left of the field so that Antiope, if she cast, must do so across her

body. Antiope countered, sheathing her lance and going to the bow. About them on all quarters the fight had broken off, as if heaven itself had commanded. For men are pious in war, and each believed that who won between these champions would seal the fight entire.

Eleuthera launched at once directly across the slope. She had ceded the uphill to her rival, bolting across the face, and as they passed she rose on Soup Bones' belly-band to launch the horseback javelin. Antiope shot. Her arrow crossed Eleuthera's lance in flight, striking the shield of bear-hide, triple-thick and sinew-fused, hard as tortoiseshell, passing through it and the flesh of Eleuthera's forearm to strike upon the iron plate of her cuirass directly below the heart. Here shaft snapped and warhead checked, shy of the fatal mark. Eleuthera's cast flew point-blank, yet sailed, caught by a gust.

The riders came about and rushed again. Eleuthera slung her shield to the dirt. Clearly she had resolved to trade her life for her rival's. She was uphill. She spurred to the gallop, rising upon her belly-band to launch the second missile, heedless of her own safety. Again Antiope's shot rang off her iron breastplate. Again Eleuthera's javelin sailed wide.

With each miss, such groans issued from Amazons and allies as if they themselves had fallen, while jubilation resounded from the Athenian lines, succeeded by lamentations of their own as Eleuthera again did not fall. The Amazon herself rose, coming about, and lifted her voice to the Almighty.

"So, Son of Cronos, you have decided to grant victory to Athens and count as nothing all our nation's valor. Then drive me down foremost to hell, for I will never yield, to them or to you!"

A third time Eleuthera spurred, and a third time Antiope answered. Many observed from closer than I, among them my brother, who was still fighting in the companies under Menestheus that had routed the Thracians. He swears, as do other witnesses numerous and credible, that at the apex of her terminal rush, Antiope veered deliberately, turning Sneak Biscuits' neck so as to expose her own. This much is certain of that pass: Antiope bore no weapon. She galloped empty-handed into Eleuthera's charge.

This was the lady's finish. Eleuthera cast from so close that her javelin's killing point entered Antiope's breast, it seemed, before its butt end had left the sleeve extender in Eleuthera's fist. Antiope bowled over Sneak Biscuits' hindquarters as a doll is swiped from its shelf by a child's angry hand. You could hear the javelin shaft snap as the lady's impaled body struck the stone, not on her back but on her face, her trunk in its armor having cartwheeled through a complete revolution in midair. Her helmet hit first and then her legs. The bindings of her breastplate burst; both greaves sprung from her calves. Eleuthera vaulted to the plain. In an instant the warrioress straddled Antiope's motionless form. The field had gone to stone. Not a sound. Not a cry. So indestructible had Antiope seemed in her hour of glory that not a soul believed she had been brought low. Before all, Eleuthera seemed most acutely stricken. From where I stood, I could see her face clearly. Will you believe me, brothers, when I declare that her eyes pleaded with the lady: *Rise!*

"Ai-eee!" Eleuthera howled, a cry not of triumph but of woe. This dirge resounded from the ranks of Athens, amplified by the foe, until both armies, Athenians at the loss of their champion, Amazons at the perversity of fate, wailed in conterminous despair.

A troop led by Rhodippe and Pantariste swept forward to claim the body of their queen. Two caught the prize by the ankles and made to haul it back to the Amazon lines.

At this instant Theseus burst from the ranks across the way. When he beheld his bride's life-fled form being dragged in the dirt, such a bellow erupted from his gorge as may be made by a bull but not by a man. He even looked like a bull, in his great horned helmet, with the bowl of his shield riveted across his shattered arm, while the jets from his nostrils scalded like steam upon the air. Those close enough to see declared that his eyes showed no white but blood-crimson, and compassed grief of an order beyond feral to primordial.

With a howl Theseus rushed upon the Amazons. They scattered before him. The king did not retrieve Antiope's corpse himself, leaving this to the Companions, who flooded in his train, but only beat the defenders apart from it, then with a roar advanced and called forth their champion.

Eleuthera did not so much emerge as materialize, the ranks of her cohort parting to reveal her. Theseus pressed forward into the breach. He summoned Eleuthera not by her name which means freedom but by Molpadia, Death Song, that citation accorded her by the Iron Mountain Scyths, while he charged the witnessing gods to recall the massacres of the Tanais and the Parched Hills.

One-armed, the king fell upon the Amazon. His first cast took down Soup Bones, piercing the great beast's heart even as Eleuthera spurred him to the clash. No mortal unaided may rush as Theseus did now. Eleuthera perceived heaven's intercession; she wheeled on foot and fled.

The king chased her up the slope of Ares' Hill, within the very ranks of the foe, which parted before the pursuit, then back down to where the Aegeid Gate had stood and now was rubble. Twice Eleuthera stood and cast, but the fury of Theseus' rush had stolen her warlike spirit; her throws spiked short to the dirt.

At last before the ruins of the Temple of Fear appeared Eleuthera's sister Skyleia. "Toward what do you flee, sister?" With these words Skyleia checked the champion's flight and rallied her valor. "Do you seek our mother's womb, to crawl back into it?"

And forming shoulder to shoulder, the pair turned to face the lord of Athens.

Theseus slew Skyleia at one stroke, staving helmet and skull with the club of his mace. Eleuthera, he beat to her knees beneath blows of titanic concussion, breaking first her left hip and leg, then shattering her shoulder. She plunged insensate, shield hammered to pulp. Theseus elevated his club to finish her, and would have, had he not been shot simultaneously through shank and gut. A corps of Amazons swarmed upon him, horseback and afoot. The King's Companions met these and dragged their champion clear.

A melee broke out over Eleuthera's body. At the same time a cry unlike any heard heretofore ascended from the field to the south. This was no shout of war but something other, unprecedented throughout the siege. We did not know it then, those of us on the western quarter, but to the south the foe's order had broken. The Scyths had defected. They had left the Amazons in the lurch.

The mad scrum protracted over Eleuthera's corpse. Toward this epicenter, it seemed, the entire western field had swelled. I had risen, gimping on one leg with my spear as a staff. Mates stampeded past. "On, brother! Claim the body!"

I sank in exhaustion upon a stone. Possession of Eleuthera's corpse changed hands four times. From where I was, dust and smoke obscured the scrimmage. Witnesses later reported that, in the terminal tug-of-war, a corps of two dozen Amazons had formed a front before their commander's corpse and, reinforced by fusillades from their companies massed left, right, and rear, succeeded at last in driving off the Athenians and drawing the body of Eleuthera clear. Preeminent among the warrioresses had been one who had, judging by the blood and dust cloaking her crown to toe, apparently lost her *hippeia*, her mastery over horses, and fought all day on foot.

This was Selene.

BOOK TWELVE

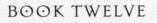

LAST OF THE
AMAZONS

35

THE HOUSE OF OATHS

Mother Bones:

〰〰〰〰〰〰

Here, Uncle broke off, overcome by emotion. For long moments he could not continue. The men of the posse averted their gaze, not wishing to enlarge their comrade's discomposure by their own attendance upon it.

It had been twenty-two days since Damon and other veterans of the original expedition to Amazonia, including Father, had, honoring Prince Atticus' petition, initiated their retelling of our city's history with these warrioresses. The ships of the posse had continued east throughout this interval, entering the Hellespont on the sixteenth day and emerging through the Bosporus into the Amazon Sea by the twenty-first. This night, the twenty-second, the company had beached beneath a promontory called (so local fisher captains told) the Nave of Mercy. It was to this site during their long homeward trek from Athens that a score of Amazons had been driven, separated from the main withdrawing column by that type of blizzard called in these regions "rhipaeans," which strike without warning at that season. Taking shelter beneath the same lee under which our posse now encamped, the maids were surprised by Taphian pirates, whose keep the site apparently was, and overwhelmed. They had been bound and staked to the earth, throats painted for slaughter, when great peals of thunder broke above. Bolts of the Almighty cleft the cavern. The pirates quailed in terror of Zeus Who Protects the Wayfarer; they cut the women free and released them unharmed.

"So too shall I recover," Damon remarked after a few moments. He took wine and, having recomposed himself, picked up his tale where he had left off—with the fall of Eleuthera at Athens, the climax of the battle.

With dark the fighting had broken off, Uncle recounted. Clashes had protracted all day, succeeding the brawl over Eleuthera's body, with neither side able to gain possession of the field. The siege had been broken, however. Our countrymen of the mountain forts, reinforced by the Attic barons and the allies of the Twelve States, had swept in from the north and south and east, driving the Amazons from the Hill of Ares and destroying their camp. This availed little, however, Uncle made clear, as the foe simply fell back, west, to the next line of hills, where she set up fresh bivouacs, still outnumbering our forces two to one, even with the defection of her allies.

Indeed, Damon continued, Borges' Scyths had pulled out at the worst possible moment for their Amazon cohorts. It had gone like this:

Theseus, recall, had contrived an intrigue by which he would deliver to Borges the gold of the Acropolis in return for the tribesmen's defection from the Amazon cause. But the prince of the Scyths had double-crossed him. Finding his troops victorious at that final noon, Borges went all-out after the Rock. Athenian resistance collapsed; clansmen swarmed unchecked up the face. On the summit the sleds and trundles of gold lay plum for the taking, defended by no one but the women, in numbers beneath five hundred, who had been retained by Theseus to toil in the cooking and nursing.

Now one, Dora, widow of the captain Thootes, who had fallen earlier that morning on Market Hill, rallied her sisters to the hour. Yoking the sleds of gold to their own shoulders (for no mules remained), the women dragged these to the brink. There, with great shouts to attract the attention of the Scyths below, they pitched the stuff over. The trolleys plunged, strewing their golden freight.

The world knows the free-for-all that succeeded. Nor must we confine credit to our heroine Dora, for all her brilliance, but honor as well the bronzesmith Timotheus of Oa, whose notion it was to cast the gold not into ingots or bars, which could have been commandeered by the princes while they yet maintained the order of their troops, but to strike it into spits and splashes (and to toss in quantities of lead painted to look like gold). These spilled across the Scythian front like candy at a wedding.

A melee ensued in which no individual of the foe could simply highjack one lump and make his fortune, but each must rake the dirt, seining fistfuls of the elusive pellets, while brawling in his greed not with us, his enemy, but his own fellows. Clansmen stuffed golden berries into skins and quivers, even into their own boots and cheeks, loosing a hullabaloo whose meaning was divined at once by their brothers across the field. These too broke from their order, ravening after the loot.

Now atop the Rock, the women of Athens set up those signals which their captains, routed below, could not. With shields bossed to a mirror's sheen they flashed this message to our countrymen in the forts at Hymettos and Lykabettos, to the upcountry barons and the allies of the Twelve States: "*Boedromesate!* Bring help on the run!" To this day the festival acclaiming this victory is called the Boedromia, and the month of its observation Boedromion.

Frenzy among the clansmen left the southern quarter of the field open to our allies. Their officers wisely reined their rush, channeling the reinforcements' exertions to evacuating our women from the summit. Theseus had returned now from the clash west of the Rock, too wounded to fight but not to command. He let the Scyths sack the city. By nightfall, Damon recounted, the foe had picked the Acropolis clean. Men reported Borges pissing in triumph off the pinnacle. Let him, Theseus reckoned. By this despoiling of the citadel, the prince of the Scyths had resuscitated his standing among his kind, and by his defection from the Amazon cause had revenged himself for his brother Arsaces' death and his own humiliation, which he had bided to this hour to requite.

In two days the Scyths had packed up and gone. The general crowd lost no time following suit. Tribesmen of all nations decamped as well, fearing for their lands and herds back home. Within days the siege remained to be prosecuted by the Amazons alone.

The greater part of Attica was still in their hands. But the fight had gone out of them. They had lost their corps of champions. The marrow of two generations had been decimated. Though in numbers the Amazons still dominated the field, without the Scyths and Thracians their corps could not press this advantage to prevail. Each day our countrymen built back more ramparts; each dawn revealed fresh allies augmenting our fortifications beneath the Rock.

Stalemate had set in. The invaders had no strength to dislodge the defenders from their new positions nor could the champions of Athens oust the foe from their secondary holds. Both sides were too crippled by losses and too depleted in spirit to initiate further assaults.

The land itself lay in ruin. Not a tree remained, it seemed, or a house or gate or so much as a stand of brick against which to rig a tent fly. The sanctuaries of the gods themselves had not been spared, but all, down to the wayside shrine of Pity, had been broken apart, stones conscripted for ammunition. Worst of all was the stench. For days corpses turned up beneath mounds of rubble; rescuers toiled across a landscape of devastation and death.

A perverse malevolence suffused the wrack, Damon reported, by whose mandate, it seemed, no article of site or gear, however humble, might remain unannihilated. So that if you came upon a bench, say, it had been demolished; or a wall, a plate, a child's doll. Down to single roof tiles, every element fashioned by man had been sundered or riven. If by chance the odd object remained intact, someone came along and smashed it. What the Amazons had not reduced to wreckage, our own countrymen beat down themselves, toward no end but alignment with heaven's malice and the pitilessness of war. In the end, Damon testified, you could trek from one end of the city to the other and not find a single usable item, other than weapons and fighting kit. The landscape was a wasteland. When the first wives and children were brought back from Euboea, their despair was so great at the ruin of their country that Theseus had to order such repatriation put off, however fervently the men wished their spouses and infants brought home.

Burials began. For days pyres burned in the camps of both armies. It seemed, Damon said, as if grief were the sole commodity the two sides still owned in abundance. The scale of the calamity, now that casualties could be tallied, overwhelmed both nations' capacity to absorb it. Further, the lines of the foes lay so close across from each other that each could witness the other's rites and attend his or her hymns of woe. From the Muses' Hill, Athenians looked on by the thousands as the Amazons interred Eleuthera. When it came time to raise the mound over Antiope, Theseus dispatched a runner to Hippolyta (who now held sole command of the invading army) to inform her that any would be welcomed who wished to attend.

The entire corps of Amazonia crossed over.

After this, rancor relented between the antagonists. Access to springs and wells, particularly the abundant Klepsydra and the Deep Spring within the Rock, was granted by the Athenians to the Amazons. Our countrymen permitted the foe to water her horses and provided a market for grain and food. The invaders let the defenders return to their farms. It came about that numbers of wounded Amazons were ferried to sites of recuperation on Euboea, while others found themselves tended by their former enemies within that bastion they had striven so mightily to surmount, the summit of the Acropolis.

Twenty-nine days after the final clash, terms of truce were ratified upon that site that would come to be called the Horkomosion, the House of Oaths.

That night the Amazons began to withdraw.

36

THE COMPLICITY OF
THE GODS

⟨⟨⟨⟨⟨⟨⟨⟨⟩

Uncle brought his tale of battle to its close. The hour was late beside the beached ships on the strand at the Nave of Mercy. Damon glanced to Father, as if asking his permission to append an afterword to his yarn. The company remarked this exchange, curious. Father nodded. Damon took a draught of wine and resumed:

"Now, brothers," he addressed his shipmates of the posse, "I will tell you something you do not know. Or rather, confirm that which you may have long suspected."

Damon told of a patrol dispatched to the hill country south of Oinoe, some four or five days after the Amazons' decampment. The troop's captain was Xenophanes, brother of the general Lykos; Damon was sergeant of the first platoon, Father its lieutenant. At that site called the Horns, just below the pass, the company came upon a gang of bounty hunters. The bandits had cornered several wounded Amazons in a herder's hut and were setting up to smoke them out.

"The villains took off when they saw us," Damon recounted. "We kept back, out of range of the Amazon bows, on a rise overlooking the cottage. Suddenly one of the women emerged, on foot, carrying in her arms the body of another. Elias and I drew up in astonishment.

"The maid was Selene.

"She advanced within a hundred feet of our position. She looked dehydrated and emaciated. If she recognized Elias and me, she did not let on. She identified herself to our captain and called out in Greek that the warrior in her arms was her sister, Chryssa, severely wounded but alive. If our commander would guarantee safe conduct out of Attica to the disabled woman, that is, permit her to be borne on a litter to rejoin the Amazon column withdrawing north, then she, Selene, would surrender herself and serve in any capacity we appointed. Such a prize was unheard of, to take an Amazon alive, and excited our captain Xenophanes no end. He ordered my brother and me forward to examine the wounded warrioress.

"We obeyed. We could see even at a distance that the woman's overcloak was the same that Chryssa habitually wore. We both recognized Chryssa's jerkin with its sign of the turtle, and her Phrygian cap trimmed with white marten. But when we got closer we saw that the woman was not Chryssa.

"It was Eleuthera.

"She was alive.

"Elias and I had now drawn up directly before Selene. For our captain's eyes the maid still feigned not to know us, yet it was plain she understood that one word would mean her end and Eleuthera's. I shall never forget the expression on my brother's face. It went without saying that to capture alive the great Eleuthera, whom Athens thought dead and buried, would catapult to fame not only ourselves but our posterity. Down centuries our family would reap the renown of this exploit. My brother met my eyes, then turned back to our captain.

" 'It is the woman's sister, by name Chryssa,' he called. 'I recognize her from the Amazon homeland.'

"At once I confirmed this.

"Selene held her aspect emotionless. She whistled sharply to the tree line. At once two novices materialized (Stuff and another I did not recognize) carrying a reed litter. Elias and I volunteered to escort the outfit north; Xenophanes assented and assigned a detail of eight to accompany us, to protect against the gangs of cutthroats who infested the hills at that time.

"Selene stripped her arms and surrendered herself. Our captain took her into custody."

Here Damon drew up and again glanced to Father, who was seated at his left beside the beached ships. The brothers' eyes met, much as they must have in that hour.

"Why did we do it, comrades?" Damon resumed to the posse. "Perhaps a god commanded, compelling our complicity. Perhaps we could not but acknowledge the greatness of the Amazon nation and reckon the ordeal its corps yet faced seeking to get home, or the need it had of Eleuthera, who was the race's last best hope. Perhaps the selflessness of Selene's gesture touched our hearts.

"In any event we sealed the compact. We told our lie and made it stick.

"Thus Eleuthera was granted passage home. Thus, after certain negotiations and appropriations, Selene came to serve Elias and be governess to our young Bones here and her sister, Europa. And thus did Selene, all these years later, come to break from her indenture, and we, this posse, to toil in her pursuit."

37

A NEW ORDER

❦❦❦❦❦❦

Damon's narration had now brought us to the present.

The ships of the posse continued east. We were now well inside the Amazon Sea and within days, Prince Atticus reckoned, of striking the Mound City. Yet nothing we could see on shore resembled the country that Damon had described as existing as recently as twenty years past.

The plateau beneath which we coasted, which Uncle had portrayed in his chronicle as teeming with horses and game, was scored now in the present with waggon ruts and pocked with rude turf granges. Dirty settlements squatted wherever a rill cut down to the sea. These, we learned, were Borges' property. Vassal villages. They were growing barley and emmer wheat. This was the Scyths' new business. They did not farm the land themselves, such drudgery being beneath their knightly calling, only swept down twice a year to exact tribute. Borges took this tariff not in produce, the villagers told us, but in a potent red stout which the locals stored in huge clay jars with the grains of barley still floating on top. The Scyths ringed these vats like pigs at a trough, sucking the brew up through reeds.

What of the Amazons? We had not seen a single one. Only their graves.

The posse had remarked these in numbers for the prior twenty days. They had appeared on promontories visible from the sea, great barrows heaped up in the shape of crescent shields. When our company landed for fresh water or to give the horses a run, more mounds were found. At the Nestrus and Hebrus rivers our parties trekked inland, led by guides. They were shown fords and passes, sites of battle. More graves were seen at the Danuvius and the Tyras. Clearly Hippolyta's forecast had proved true: those same clansmen who had played servitor to the Amazons at their apex of power had turned predator in their hour of vulnerability.

The posse continued east. With each stop ashore, Atticus inquired of the locals: Had they seen a lone Amazon? Had they seen one traveling with a girl?

The villagers shook their heads.

No Amazons.

No more.

One morning our lookouts spotted wild goats on a headland; Atticus sent in a hunting troop to bag a few for the pot. Beside a stream they discovered a party of women, washing clothes. To our fellows' amazement the maids inquired of our "other ships."

Three vessels had put in on this site two days prior, the women reported. The master of this squadron had asked after us, describing our craft precisely. Atticus sought out the village headman. He returned with a letter addressed to us.

"From Theseus," the prince affirmed to the posse, as astonished as they. He skimmed the roll. "The king has come out from Athens. He has overshot us, so he declares, but will hold for us, east, at the Mound City."

The squadron put back to sea. Within hours two sail were sighted, Athenian, making for us. Our men hauled, cheering. But when the ships came alongside, our countrymen aboard manned the oars and nothing else. They were held at swordpoint by clansmen of the Scyths.

"Your king is in our hands," their skipper bawled across, "and commands you to follow us in."

The Scyths did not board our vessels in mass, only sent pilots over to take us in charge. The dandy posted to Atticus' ship was no seaman but a buck baron of the plains, handsome and shirtless, wearing doeskin trousers and gold jewelry in such quantity it threatened to pitch the ship out of trim from its weight alone. He was in soaring spirits, clapping our lads like long-lost mates. "You hunt the Amazon," he divined. "How much? How much?" He meant for her head, if we got it.

Atticus informed him we did not want her head. The buck laughed as if he would fall down. All Greeks were crazy.

It took minutes to discover that he meant Eleuthera, not Selene.

Who was Selene? He had never heard of Selene! He cared nothing for Selene!

" 'Leuth'ra, 'Leuth'ra," the young blood repeated, shouting, as if we were the numbest skulls he had ever encountered.

Our proudfoot narrated his account. The race of Amazons, who had numbered at their peak above a hundred and fifty thousand, lingered now at their last extremity, down to two or three thousand. The main of this remnant, older women and girls, had long since withdrawn north through the Gate of Storms to the Land of Perpetual Snow in the Rhipaean Caucasus. War parties still ventured south however. One of two hundred had struck the herds of Princes Maues and Panasagoras—Borges' son and nephew—three months ago, driving off two thousand prime stock. A chase had ensued and a battle been fought, north beyond Lake Maeotis, in which half the Amazons had been slain and Eleuthera herself gravely wounded.

Clearly this was the extremity that Theseus had reported to Selene that noon on our farm. It was why Selene had bolted, to offer the Underworld her own life in place of Eleuthera's. It was why the posse pursued her now.

Eleuthera was forty-one years old, our Scythian brave reported, but still preeminent, the last of her race the clansmen still feared. Maues and Panasagoras were scouring every league of the Wild Lands for her now. When they tracked her down and killed her, the last of the free Amazons would be exterminated, and they, the princes, would have won renown everlasting, to eclipse even Borges, and have attained for themselves supremacy of the steppe.

Our buck assumed that we, the posse, were after Eleuthera too. He would not believe our tale of Selene. He had never heard anything so ridiculous.

The shore we coasted was pastureland descending from high plateau. By nightfall the expanse teemed with the hordes of Scythia. Ahead our lookouts reported harbor beacons. Galleys and traders, broad-beamers, could be glimpsed at anchor. Atticus made to put ashore where we were, several miles short of the Mound City, deeming the run-in too risky in the failing light.

"No stop! No stop!" commanded our gallant. He shouted to his mates in the other ships, who at once bared their blades above our comrades' throats. "Fires ahead! Lights! Go on!"

Atticus acceded. The ships made for the channel. Thus, on the ninety-ninth day since their embarkation from Athens, the vessels of the posse rowed in and beached upon that shore whose bastion, the Mound City, had once been the seat of the Northern, or Lycasteia, Amazons, the tribe of Antiope, Eleuthera, and Selene.

38

PRINCES OF THE PLAINS

The first items the Scyths seized were our horses. These would be impounded temporarily, Maues' adjutant assured Atticus and our officers, though it was clear from the glee with which his compatriots took possession of the animals that they would never appear in Athenian livery again.

Our complement was united with Theseus and his crews. The Scyths herded us into one pack, officers alongside men, and drove the lot into a wharfside stock pen whose rails, to keep out wolves, had been topped with rolls of that wicked thorn the Amazons call *agre arra*, "penance maker." From these kennels the captives could view their hosts stripping the ships of all articles of value. Our guards had already performed this service upon our persons. Throughout two nights, which yielded sleep only in snatches, Father and Damon secured me in the pocket between them, backed by the crews as one, offering such glowers to our jailers as to preserve me, a lass at the ripest of ages in these blackguards' eyes, from such uses as they plainly wished to make of me.

The third dawn, Maues and Panasagoras appeared, compassed by their lifeguard of knights. Theseus was hauled forward. It is the nature of the savage not to address but to berate. Our king must endure cataracts of abuse, physical as well as verbal, delivered at such a pitch of outrage, not to say inebriation, as to convince one and all that the sole outcome would be bloody murder. It is all theater to these villains. They champed to torch the ships, which they hated as bearers of evil from afar, and would have, clearly, but for the more attractive prospect of selling craft and crews in one bundle. In the end they detained Theseus, Atticus, and the vessels' captains. The crews were released, or, more accurately, kicked out, with orders to report back by sunset. "The savages reckon we won't stray far," Father observed.

The men were directed by their officers to keep in a body for their own protection. It went without saying that an attempt would be made to retake the ships. Meanwhile, we were free to gawk about the city. Father, Damon, Philippus, and two others—"Beam" and "Mite," who had come out with Theseus—formed themselves into an outfit.

Mite took charge of me. We were all dirty as death, without even shoes. This put us at a level with the locals. I have never seen such a verminous aggregation. In Amazon days, no permanent habitation had been permitted at the Mound City. The place remained grass and earthworks, consecrated for use only at the season of the Gathering and left to God and the elements the other ten months.

Now a year-round city occupied the site. A boomtown. Its denizens were miners and gamblers, merchants, traders in horses and women, slaves, grain, furs, and gold. Father interrogated our new comrades on Theseus' advent. When had the king's ships left Athens, and why? Had Theseus not sworn never to participate in such a posse?

Mite brought the tale up to the mark.

Two days after Atticus' ships had sailed from Athens, Theseus had made to offer sacrifice at the tomb of Antiope, beseeching her favor and protection on behalf of the men of the fleet. The king had made something of a show of this, Mite reported, donating an ox and fifty sheep for a great public feast. Crowds thronged the square, eager for a free feed. But as the priests drew forth the bull for sacrifice, the earth shook. So violent was the quake that the very lintel of the tomb crashed. In the city scores of buildings toppled. Hundreds were killed and injured. That this calamity had befallen, not alone before the tomb of our king's beloved, but on the point of sacrifice of that beast sacred to his reputed father, Poseidon Earthshaker, was an omen whose import it took no seer or mantis to divine.

"The king's luck had turned evil," Mite narrated, "and everybody knew it. I served as wrangler on his spread at Phyle. What broke his heart, I saw, was not just the bane of heaven's enmity, which he had endured all his life, but the treachery and ingratitude of his own countrymen. To behold his political rivals seizing upon his grief to further their own careers—this was the reed that broke the ass's back. Theseus despaired for the democracy, in whose cause he had donated all. The people hated him and called for his blood. What remained for him at Athens?

"In any event, the prospect of a sea voyage, and the chance of roaming again upon the wild plains of the east, no longer seemed such a chore. He packed his kit himself in minutes."

Father questioned Mite further. We had heard that Theseus, en route to the Amazon Sea, had offered sacrifice more than once, seeking to appease the ghost of Antiope.

Mite confirmed this. He himself had trekked in the party twice, at Chalcidician Torone and later at the Nine Ways. "But she never comes. Nothing. Not a whisper."

Damon asked what Mite made of this. What did Theseus want, summoning the shade of his Amazon bride? Did he seek forgiveness for permitting her to fight that final dawn? Did he long to rejoin her beneath the earth? Was communion with her his sole object, voyaging again to the Wild Lands?

"You tell me, sir. He's gone bloody balmy, if you want my part."

That night our captors rounded up both companies, Theseus' and Atticus', and marched us to the earthworks east of the city. Savages in thousands ringed a pit in which men had been bound spread-eagled to scaffolds. They were ours. A score, arrested trying to steal a Tyrian cutter.

The men had been scalped alive and mutilated. Now Theseus, Atticus, and the ships' captains were driven to the fore to witness as the savages applied fire. King and officers were bound to execution posts and beaten with fists and a type of cudgel the Scyths call *oiratera*, "man-breaker." No compulsion of hell or heaven will induce me to recount the tortures these fortune-forsaken souls were compelled to endure, save to note that the spectacle protracted all night, Maues and Panasagoras participating personally and with relish, and our party without exception constrained to look on. Every man anticipated that he too would be dispatched in this fashion, or another equally hideous.

It is the manner of savages, I have said, to thrust themselves into the faces of those they seek to cow, bellowing tirades of abuse, all the while offering kicks and cuffs of stupefying violence. They had learned of Theseus' attempts to summon the ghost of Antiope and scorned this extravagantly.

This is our country now!

No Amazon may enter, dead or alive!

At dawn a courier appeared from Amorges, prince of the Copper River, having ridden, he reported, three days from the north. A war party of six hundred Amazons under the great Eleuthera had been discovered and set upon. The final extermination was at hand.

Ecstatic cries erupted from the multitude. Clansmen bawled for their horses; grooms scattered to rig kit and armor. At once Theseus volunteered our company. We had sailed all this way, he declared, to take vengeance on the Amazons; let us join with our Scythian brothers and finish the job!

The hordes greeted this with derision. Yet such is the perversity of the savage that the princes not only embraced Theseus' plan, reckoning no doubt that they would butcher our party as a final delectation to their banquet of slaughter, but even ordered our men provided with horses and arms.

Theseus entreated one final boon of the princes, that they put out of their misery our comrades under torture or, failing that, permit us to end their agony ourselves.

Maues refused. "The dogs and crows will finish them."

The mob, above ten thousand, mounted and moved out.

39

SPAWN OF
THE DARKNESS

✷✷✷✷✷✷✷

Give the savages this: they can ride. And their horses, plug-ugly beside the steeds of the Amazons, can stand a pounding. Three days and two nights the ruck beat north. Our Athenian troop could have bolted at any moment, but to what end? Bloods in a pack would run us down before ten miles. Damon made me see the necessity of Theseus' ploy, to league with these butchers in their chase.

Somewhere ahead was Europa.

Somewhere ahead was my sister.

So long as she lived, or Father and Damon so believed, they must make for her by all expedients, fair or foul.

The third evening the horde came on the wreck of a battle. You could tell miles off by the ravens and the waggon ruts converging from all quadrants. These carts haul the dames and urchins of the Scyths. We came over a crown and saw them, harvesting the field. The mob must have made three thousand, industrious as ants. The

Scyths scalp and mutilate the corpses of their victims. A war party alone or in enemy territory will take the skulls, which they gild for boozing vessels, but when they range on home turf or know their women are close, they leave the bodies intact for these scavengers to render.

You could tell the Amazon horses even in death by their size and length of bone. Three to five hundred spread across the plain. The Scythian women butchered these for meat, beating back the dogs, domestic and wild, with the same jerking bats they would use to pound the flesh for drying.

As for myself, though I recount this spectacle seemingly void of affect, in that hour my soul was rent with grief and anguish. Was one of those bodies my sister's? Was one Selene's? Maues and Panasagoras scoured the field, seeking Eleuthera's corpse. Whooping broke out when it was determined that the Amazon yet lived. On her trail! The princes could still win the glory of eviscerating her.

I quartered the plain beside Father and Damon. Father's eye scanned each child's remains; consternation convulsed him; his limbs quaked. I examined my own heart. Woe-riven as I was, a cool hardness had settled in my gorge. It was as if heaven had set this challenge before me and I, to my relief, discovered myself equal to it.

I turned to Damon. He was like me, I saw. He knew hate and how to use it. I saw him study me to see if I would crack, and, satisfying himself, proffered a glance so fleeting that an observer would have missed it had he turned but half away, yet which communicated infallibly to me: You are child no longer. I call you woman now.

This look said more. It warned that Father had broken. He cannot endure, Damon's glance pronounced. Therefore you and I, who own strength, must donate ours to sustain him.

All this I assimilated in an instant and shot back to Uncle with a glance.

Now look again, his aspect commanded. I obeyed. Facing to the field of massacre, I felt such emotion rising from the earth as nearly hoisted me from my seat. The blood of these women cried to me. I could hear it, resounding down halls infinite inside me. The call was hate. I recognized it and embraced it with every sinew.

The Reed Sea lay north. To this Eleuthera's remnant had fled. The horde under Maues and Panasagoras abandoned the harvest of slaughter, spurring in this direction. Our Athenian party hauled in the Scyths' train. The ponies our captors had cut out for us were their most balky and least hardy; we fell miles behind, trotting afoot more than riding, and did not overhaul our captors' camp till midnight.

The sprawl of the site was prodigious, extending for furlongs along the Milk River, whose water, glacier-fed, was the color of its name. Maeotians and Copper River Scyths continued to pour in all night. Parties were setting out, seeking Eleuthera's last band. The result was that the camp was unquiet across its expanse, as great companies and herds came and went.

This was when the Amazons struck.

The first thrust hit a mile south of our outfit. Racket and clamor ascended, but with so many herds passing in and out, no one took especial notice. Then the blazes flared. Waggons burst to flame. Riders of the Scyths galloped past, crying the alarm. Now a second assault struck from the west, and a third immediately north.

"Eleuthera," Damon said.

For all the tales I had imbibed over years from Selene, not to say Damon's reports and the trials endured on this voyage, I had never till that moment witnessed a true clash of arms. As the sun's brilliance excels the guttering of a closet lamp, so did actuality eclipse depiction.

Into the lane thundered half a hundred Amazon horse. Their mass appeared so swiftly and with such violence as to snuff the wind within one's breast. No prior citation could have prepared me for such ferocity. The Amazons were hacking through the axles of the waggons, butchering oxen, sowing panic in every quarter. My God, how they shot! I saw a man of the Scyths swing his *sagaris*, cutting an Amazon horse off at the knees. As the whetted iron passed through the gristle and bone, and the beast, not knowing what had hit it, pitched forward onto its face, the warrioress on its back loosed her shaft. The warhead entered the clansman at the plexus of the breast, driving through lungs and spine to exit by three hand's-breadths from his back. He reeled rearward against a waggon; before his groping claw could clutch at purchase, the Amazon had sprung to the turf, taken his scalp, and opened his guts from crotch to apple. He spilled at my feet, alive and gaping horror.

I was in the open. A horse ran me down. I felt its hooves punch the sod a thumb's-breadth from my skull. I plunged clear, toward the steppe and a picket line of Scythian ponies. Two girls my age were freeing the hobbles. They were Amazon novices. One shouted to me, "*Aanikat ehur!*"—"Drive the ponies off!"

They took me for one of them.

A transformation overcame me. "*Ephorit Selene?*" I demanded. "Where is Selene?" Both girls pointed south, where the attack had struck.

I took off for this quarter on the run, crying Selene's name and Europa's. Father tore after me. All about, ghastly carnage was being enacted; conflagrations ascended; men and women dueled and perished. Twice Father caught me and twice I slipped his claw.

I was somewhere in a pocket between two waggons which were overturned and aflame; before me bawled a string of mules, which a line of Amazons were freeing and driving into the night. A score of tribesmen swept onto the site, armed with pike and mace. The Amazons wheeled to repel them. Suddenly a single Scyth caught me from behind and snatched me airborne by the hair. I could not see his face, only smell his breath and hear the swish of his dagger on the air, elevating to slice my throat. At that instant an Amazon axe, slung overhand, pinwheeled over my shoulder from the fore, striking my assailant where teeth and jaw conjoin. The iron drove through the fellow from craw to brow, fixing at the base of his skull between the jawbone and the cervical spine. I crashed to the earth atop the brute, who was still alive and clutching at my throat.

Above me my savior reined. Her hair was jet, greased stiff and flaring. Her face was painted grey and white, the sign of the moon, with circles about her eyes, nose, and mouth. Her mount was sorrel, fifteen hands, and she sat it like a god.

It was Selene.

She signed to me, *Get my axe*.

My heart swelled as if it would burst.

"*Pelekus!*" my tutor barked. The Scyth in the dirt was still writhing, with the axe in his face, while his arms flailed unstrung from command. I seized the haft and heaved. The axe came up with skull and living man affixed.

"Set your heel on his face," Selene commanded.

I obeyed. The axe came clear. Selene held out her hand for me to take and mount behind her.

At that instant Father burst from the darkness. I felt him snatch me by the waist. Damon roared up on horseback.

"Give me the girl!" Selene commanded.

I saw her nock an arrow and draw down.

"Selene!" Damon cried.

I stared down the shaft of my tutor's ironhead. In an instant her bolt would take Father between the eyes.

"Selene, are you mad?"

Damon spurred to cut her off. I saw her bow hand rise. She gave back.

Alarms broke from the south. Scyths rushed in hundreds; the Amazons wheeled and fled. Selene bolted in their train; Damon spurred after her.

I cannot say how I got clear of Father or from what string I tore a horse. I was on the steppe at the gallop. Selene's and Damon's trace ran away beneath the moon. The Wild Lands run in breaks and washes in that region; I tracked the pair over what seemed a dozen ranges. At last their hoof strikes shortened. I came round the shoulder of a rise and saw them, beneath me, half a bow-shot off.

Selene and Damon brawled in the pan of a dry wash. He had got her off her feet. She sprung clear; he caught her again. They had not heard me. Should I rush down? Below, Damon dropped, gasping, onto hands and knees. Selene heaved above him, equally spent. I strained in the starlight. I could see Damon sit up, breathless, onto his heels. Selene stood directly before him. She addressed him not in words but sign.

She sought to send him away. He would not go. He got to his feet and reached for her. She dodged his grasp.

Selene signed that her time was over, the spool of her days had reached its end.

"You have won." I saw her hands frame the speech, but the stroke she made upon "you" carried the meaning beyond Damon as an individual to denote "you Athenians," "you men," "you of the male race."

This sign struck Damon like a blow. "How have I won," he cried in words, "if I lose you?"

He swept across the breach between them. His arms embraced Selene about her hips while he, sinking on both knees, buried his face against her belly. She bent at the waist; her shoulders covered his; her long hair draped his back. I watched, nailed to the site. I could neither command my voice to call nor feet to fly, nor respond to the hoof strikes I heard hastening behind me. Father overhauled me from the rear. Below in the wash I saw Damon and Selene mount. When I found my breath to cry, the lovers galloped away together. Father pinned my limbs with the despair of one who has lost all and cannot lose more. Still I squirted free. On foot I bolted after Selene.

Father did not try to run me down. He mounted and trailed at the trot, letting me exhaust myself, and, two miles on, or five, when I had fallen, he hoisted me in his arms and bore me back.

The Scythian camp, when we returned to it, had rallied from its riot. Clansmen marshaled to aid their wounded and recapture their stock. Father set me down beside Philippus, instructing him to bind my wrists and hold the lead himself, releasing it to no one. I spat when he sought to touch me. Two of our party chanced to pass in that moment and, sighting Father, addressed him as captain, seeking orders. Shall we help tend the wounded? they inquired, meaning the Maeotians and Scyths and Copper Rivers.

Father hesitated, still trembling from his ordeal.

"Let them die," I returned in his stead. "And may their souls wander between the worlds forever."

40

AN AMAZON

꩜꩜꩜꩜꩜

That dawn the Scyths marooned us. They took horses and arms but left our lives. This was no slim fix, however, as the men, many stripped of kit and without even shoes, now possessed neither means of defending themselves nor of obtaining food. The trek to the coast was a hundred and sixty miles.

Atticus called a council to consider what to do. Father did not speak. Theseus likewise held his tongue. Since the Mound City, the king had placed himself under Atticus' command, pledging to earn his keep as a common soldier, and he had done so. At each crisis, however, the men naturally had looked first to him. Yet each time he deferred to Atticus, so that the company, with far less reluctance than one might have imagined, came to accept the king as mate and not monarch. The men were shaken by the horrors of recent days and, no little, by Damon's defection. Numbers besides Father appeared at the point of coming undone. The main voted to strike for the sea. When their count had been tallied, Atticus spoke.

"Brothers, the object of our expedition appears now moot, that is, to apprehend and bring back for trial the Amazon Selene. I daresay we own as much chance of lassoing a griffin. Nonetheless, this remains my charge as commander. Further, speaking as a man, I cannot but believe that Elias' daughter and my betrothed, the maid Europa, remains alive and in peril somewhere north among the foe."

He would not, Atticus said, set the men's lives at further hazard on this commission; he released them to make for the ships and home. He, however, must remain. He would track the Scyths, with Father and others if they wished, or alone if necessary.

You may imagine the murmur that succeeded this. Men on the steppe make seats about a fire (since there is no wood and few stones) by cutting bricks of turf and stacking them into a kind of stand, grassy side up. Theseus, like the others, hunkered on such a perch, to the left of Atticus and some seven or eight men down. He now rose and took up his footstool; without a word the king crossed to Atticus' right hand, where he set this pew down and took station upon it. As one the men burst out laughing. Father and Philippus followed to Prince Atticus' side, Beam and Mite succeeding. In the end, seventeen made to stay, while sixty-some set off south. The mood on parting was so black it was giddy. Eighty-odd men with no horses, no food, and no arms, splitting up to march from nowhere to nowhere.

One may ask how it struck me, a lass of not yet twelve years, to find herself at last upon those Wild Lands on which her fancy had fed from birth. Such ordeals and adventures as I had suckled on, so to say, at my governess' breast, these now had become real. Was I stricken with terror? Did I yearn for home and Mother's bosom?

Not for the time it takes to spit.

I *was* home. This was my country and these, the race of free women, my people. Nor was this fatuity, as it might have been attending Selene's yarns in my childhood bed, but fact I felt in my heart and my guts. What maid could want more than what spread before me? Look left: herds of antelope sprawl to the horizon. Turn right: eland and gazelle carpet the pan. That the nation of free women stood at its extremity only further animated my zeal. These were epochal events; I would be part of them. I felt exalted and lifted out of myself.

The third noon our party sighted smoke. We came upon gear and discarded tackle, next slaughtered animals, then men. The company cadged weapons from the corpses. Philippus caught a horse and used it to round up more. Our outfit had mounts now; Atticus called it together.

Either the Scyths had overhauled Eleuthera's Amazons or the latter had set ambushes to hinder the pursuit. We might come on a battle, Atticus warned the company. He forbade heroics: "Forget Selene. Seek the maid Europa. If we can't secure her to hand, we may be able to treat with the Amazons, if Europa is among them, or with the Scyths if they have captured her."

Atticus ordered me kept back and set Mite to watch. The smoke seemed just over the next hill. But distances play tricks in so vast a country. Night fell and our party still hadn't reached it. We pressed on, fixing bearings by the stars. But the breaks of the plain could not be gotten round in the dark, and when the sun came again, fresh smoke pocked the horizon. It seemed battles raged in every quarter. The ponies we rode were Amazon. "Give them their heads," Theseus suggested. "They will take us in."

All day we kept on, making meals of weevils and prairie hoppers. I ate my shoe. With dawn fresh smoke appeared. We closed on it; this at last was no mirage. Atticus made signal, "Take arms." The company formed into a front. We spurred over the terminal rise.

What we came upon was no battlefield but a graveyard.

The sward before us had been swept scrupulously of refuse and debris. A solitary Amazon held at the crest. Across the slope beneath her, twoscore fresh barrows had been arrayed in a sort of colony, with pyres of bone burned to ash. The mounds were crescent-shaped.

Father reined beside me, studying the field. Amazon dead had been borne to this place to be cremated and interred. Perhaps it was a site of prior significance, he reckoned, or consecrated by this recent fight. Atticus divided the party, one squad to remain in place at alert, while he led the other forward toward the lone rider.

I went with the prince. We could see the solitary Amazon clearly now, above us on the spine, astride her pony. She was painted, with her hair greased stiff, and made no move to make off, rather maintained her post above the leftmost of the mounds, watching the party approach. Was this a trap? Atticus reined, sending a rider ahead. The courier approached the Amazon, communicating with her by sign. He drew rein at the crest, signaling all clear.

Both companies now advanced. The Amazon held motionless. Atticus trotted toward her from the right. I saw her hoist an arm to bid him hold and then sign, to me, that motion which Selene had taught whose meaning is: Come forward, do not delay. I squinted harder.

The warrior was Europa.

The Amazon was my sister.

THE IRON
AND THE MOON

～～～～～～～

In that instant I knew the mound was Selene's. The sensation was of
something cold and keen, like iron, inserted beneath the cage of the
sternum and driven up into the tissue of the heart. I doubled, spitting
phlegm and sputum. Atop the ridge, Damon appeared. He would not
be here, alone, unless Selene was dead.

The pain in my breast exploded, like a great stone dropped from
a height when it strikes the earth and shatters. Shards and slivers
detonated inside my chest. Selene had schooled my sister and me in
the rites of bereavement practiced by the tribes of the steppe, and
Damon's tale had imparted these excesses in detail. Now they
seemed trifles. To scarify flesh or incise the scalp? I would split my
skull and leap naked onto the pyre, such was the grief which compassed and eviscerated me.

Selene.

Selene!

Damon rode down to my side. Did I wail aloud, or did my scream resound only within the cylinder of my skull? I felt his left hand about my wrist, his right hard upon my bridle.

"Not now," he commanded. "Not now."

My flesh felt seared as by coals; I felt my teeth shear through the pulp of my tongue.

Selene!

Rage flushed with such power as I sensed must slay me where I stood. It ascended from my soles in waves, scathing and corrosive. Girlhood's last tatter fell away. I seemed to mount out of myself. Damon. I experienced his agony. It was not like mine. Not grief or rage but despair. For him a void had opened where something precious and unknowable had stood. Here was the marrow. For I reckoned now, for the first time, the coming end of tal Kyrte, the extinction of the free people.

Our party still held at a distance from Europa. I could see her communicating to the fore element, to Atticus, whom she had permitted to approach alone and who now queried her, apparently for intelligence of events, battles and their outcomes, the whereabouts of Maues and Panasagoras, and of Eleuthera and the last of the Amazons.

Clearly the prince was astonished at Europa's apparition, this lass of Athens, his betrothed, whom he had crossed the world in hopes of recovering. I could see him make petition to her—*Depart with me, come home!*—and her rebuff him absolutely and beyond appeal.

Europa's transformation was total. She had become not just another woman but another species. Father had reined-in now on the brow of the slope. That his child was lost to him forever not even the desperate fixity of his purpose could deny. Atticus signed to both troops to follow him; he faced east, the direction in which Eleuthera had fled, and made off.

Damon held beside me. I heeled my pony forward to the mound. At a distance my sister had looked spectacular, wild and brilliant and glamorous. Up close she appeared feral, almost savage. Her eyes had changed. The light in them was different. They were like a wild beast's in their pitilessness and coolness of appraisal. She was not herself, yet more herself than she had ever been.

I must know beyond doubt, Was the barrow Selene's?

Europa confirmed this.

I remarked wounds of my sister's flesh, a score or more. She dismissed my concern. Her glance scanned me sole to crown. Whatever she saw, it seemed to satisfy her.

"Sister," she said, "this is for you."

An antelope-skin sheath lay across her thighs. Within it nested an axe. Europa elevated the case in both hands, as one would proffer an artifact beyond price.

"Selene knew you would come. She commanded me not to depart till I had set this in your hands."

The *pelekus* was Selene's. My sister passed it across. "Mind," she warned, "the edge is keen." I set the sheath atop my thighs and tugged loose the flap.

At once tears scalded. Selene's presence, more vivid even than in life, shone from the whetted iron and coursed up the shaft of ash. I flushed and nearly fainted.

"Are you all right, sister?"

With effort I straightened on my pony.

"Why . . ." I heard my voice ask. "Why did Selene leave this for me and not for you?"

I knew the answer before Europa could speak it.

"Because Selene is not my mother. Because I am not her daughter."

42

ELEUTHERA AND THESEUS

~~~~~~~~~

Moments later Eleuthera appeared. She materialized out of the west with ninety cavalry and fifty in auxiliary, novices and wrights of the *kabar*. Her captains commanded our company to follow.

You may imagine my state. Despair and exaltation commingled with the overthrow of all I had known, of myself, who I was, where I belonged. Yet not an instant could be spared for reflection; heels and quirts must be applied. The Scyths were close. We had to flee.

My sister was made an outrider. I bolted with her before anyone could stop me. Her role was to range to the fore, seeking sign of the foe. From Europa and "Flea," another novice, I learned that Eleuthera's object was the Tanais, two hundred miles east. South first, to get behind the foe, then east to the river. If Eleuthera's cohort could get there undetected, it could track the Tanais north to the Gate of Storms and, through that, to the Land of Perpetual Snows and safety. That the river was the frontier of Scythian country would work in our favor, Eleuthera believed. The foe would search everywhere but in his own wallet.

As for the Athenians under Theseus and Atticus, it would be overstatement to say Eleuthera took them prisoner. She did not deign even to glance in their direction and offered no notice whatever of their king. Yet it was clear she would permit none of Athens's company to make off on their own, lest they give her whereabouts away to the foe.

The combined parties rode and trekked three days and nights, south toward the Mound City, via the breaks to avoid detection. Flea remarked that once her people rode the high plains. "Now we skulk in the coulees." I learned the identities of the remaining champions: Chryssa and Evandre, Althaea and Andromache and Otrete, Prothoe and the Thracian "Stuff." At the fourth dusk foreriders sighted the sea; our companies pulled up to wait for night. The Scyths or others Eleuthera had not counted on, perhaps bounty hunters, had gotten ahead. Our party was cornered but so far unseen. Eleuthera ordered a cold camp.

It was here that she and Theseus finally collided. It came about because of my father.

He had approached Eleuthera, beseeching an audience. When I heard I came on the run. I knew Father would entreat Eleuthera's dispensation, that the Amazons not take me with them. That my sister was gone from him, he had accepted. My loss, however, would be the blow he could not bear.

I raced to the cold fire, around which the main of warrioresses and novices had settled. Apparently Eleuthera had given her answer already, which was that blood calls to blood; she would take no step to debar the child of Selene from following her mother's people. This was communicated to me by Flea and another girl who had been present from the prologue.

Eleuthera continued her address, no longer to Father, but to her companions about the fire, which was of moss and punk in a crescent trench. Here I must digress for a moment to address the aspect of this woman and the impact of her presence.

All that Selene had told of Eleuthera, and all that Damon had appended, was nothing alongside the apparition of this female in the flesh. Eleuthera's years were forty or more, the time of grandmothers among her race; yet her vigor was of one not yet twenty. She was tall, tall as Theseus, and powerful through the shoulders as an oarsman. How she sat her horse! When she galloped down the stream of the camp, her mount's hooves flung spray, which flew, to my eyes, as so many splashes of quicksilver; the axe in its sheath clashed against her back with each stride; I had never beheld anything so lordly or sublime.

Eleuthera's beauty was not mannish, as that of many among the Amazons, but of an order transcending gender. She seemed an entity, not so much of personal or individual being, but the embodiment in flesh of an ideal, and that ideal was freedom. Even her warlike aspect, as spectacularly as this predominated, was but a byproduct of this higher quality. As a flame is pure and may never be made impure, so was Eleuthera. As a lion is without fear and may never be corrupted by fear, so was Eleuthera. Had she ordered me, "March into that fire," not the armies of the earth could have held me back. Had she commanded, "Leap from that cliff," I would have vaulted forth with joy.

She came forward now, before the cold fire. Her comrades fell silent. Eleuthera addressed their chances of survival.

"When the free people's course diverged from *rhyten annae*, 'the way we have always done it'—this was when we went wrong." She was speaking of Athens, I understood, of tal Kyrte's election to abandon its homeland and carry war across the sea. "But what other course did honor leave us? I have thought about this. I believe it is the ordinance of heaven that has called our time to its close. What will become of our nation? We will linger, displaced farther onto the periphery of events. We will hang on, but no longer as a force, only as a curiosity. At last our race will recede into legend. Who will remember us? The wind may be known by the whirl of dust or the drive of flame. But who can see the wind?"

Eleuthera elevated her glance toward where Father, Damon, and

Philippus huddled at the limit of the circle. Theseus had crossed from the Athenian camp and now augmented their party, accompanied by Atticus and several of the captains.

"You will not see us," Eleuthera spoke for their hearing, "but we will be there. Our ghosts will people your nighttime streets, and that part of yourselves that you have driven under in wiping us from the earth will unsettle your slumber. Such violence as we have offered in defense of our freedom will be nothing beside that which you will inflict upon yourselves when we are gone. You have not won, neither your cause nor the gods before whose mandates you genuflect. For we are part of you. In exterminating us, you have slain that which was freest and most noble in yourselves. You have not grown greater by our extinction, but been diminished. Look to it. This is what my heart tells me."

Next morning the plain teemed with Scyths. Thousands had overshot us during the night and trooped now in the direction of the Tanais. Their scouts had not seen us yet. Nonetheless our companies must retreat up the coulee, obscuring our tracks and even erecting a palisade, awaiting the final clash.

That night Theseus approached Eleuthera, offering to use the Athenian ships to ferry the Amazons east. With a rush on the strand of the Mound City, he proposed, our combined parties could overpower whoever held the vessels. The ships' horse stalls would take the Amazon ponies. With a good wind the squadron could beat Maues and Panasagoras to the Tanais and get the women safely on their way.

Such a proposal was epochal. Eleuthera reviled it.

"Shall I survive, Theseus, by the agency of your pity?"

The king responded. "Pity? I have never feared any as I fear you, nor been vanquished by any as you have vanquished me."

Eleuthera regarded him with hate. The company had clustered entire. The moon was dark, the night chill within the coulee. "You have come to our country this time," the Amazon addressed the Athenian, "hoping to summon Antiope from the Underworld to beg forgiveness for the wrong you have done her. She will never come for you. Put this from your mind. You will find her again only in death."

These words scored Theseus to the quick. He seemed to stagger, so that several among the Companions actually started, to brace him up.

"You should have slain her yourself," Eleuthera pronounced, "there at Athens on the morn of the final clash. I would have. But you let her ride forth. You stood aside, permitting her to perform the most infamous act of which she or any soul possessed of honor is capable: to take up arms against her own people. You ruined her, in this life and beyond, because you loved Athens more than you loved her."

This shaft too found the mark. Theseus reeled beneath it.

"I too have betrayed her," Eleuthera continued, "who was far the noblest of our race or yours, for she alone dared yoke sun and moon, man and woman. So I am not unacquainted with the freight of grief you bear."

Eleuthera regarded her old enemy.

"What good has it done you, Theseus, to 'lift' men to 'civilization'? Athens spurns you for it. Those gifts you have set before her, she has spat back in your teeth. Now here you are, come again to us. I should have cut you down the first hour I saw you. I sensed it in my marrow, the *netome* you brought from afar. But Father Zeus is almighty. He has sent Heracles and Jason, and now you, to break the free women. You have not failed His errand."

Such woe stood in Theseus' aspect as seemed poised to fell him to the earth.

"Can you hate me so much, Eleuthera?"

"Hate is a bond, Theseus. And I have hated you a long time."

The king made to speak, as if to pray that such hate be now put away. Eleuthera cut him off.

"The time of the free people is over. And here is the irony, my friend. You who have destroyed us, you of all, Theseus, understood us best and loved us most deeply. You are one of us, and have been always."

At these words the king's self-command broke. Sobs wracked his breast; he dropped upon both knees before Eleuthera. Theseus buried his face against her trousers. The Amazon did not move, or even glance down, only extended her hand after some moments, setting it in clemency upon his curls.

43

PASSENGERS

The Amazon horses must be hoodwinked with cloaks and blankets to get them up the ramps to the ships. They smelled the sea and hated it. Nonetheless they obeyed; all six vessels got away, bearing their complement and an additional hundred and forty—Eleuthera's warrioresses and the wrights of the *kabar*. Every stall was filled save six doubles on Theseus' *Aethra*; these held one mount apiece.

It is no small excursion from the Mound City to the Tanais. Nor could the vessels stop ashore to let the women and horses exercise their legs. The Scyths knew whom the vessels carried; they would stay at nothing to overhaul their prey. Aboard ship the Amazons hunkered, miserable as soaked cats.

Father would not let me from his sight. Or should I call him father? Though he succeeded in keeping me apart from Europa, it was no chore to communicate with her by sign. I would flee with her; I would join my people, the free women of the plains. I bided, confident I could make the jump any time I wished.

On the ships an Amazon with a lurid scar across her cheek and breast took charge of me. She was a captain immediately beneath Eleuthera and, judging by the deference paid her by her country-women, a warrioress of singular celebrity. Her birth name, she told me, was Dosteia. "Though you know me, if Selene spoke true, by another: 'Stuff.' "

How curious is the ordination of the heart. For I, who had held the stopper on my grief so ably and so well (or so I flattered myself), now, at the hearing of this name which had been linked in memory to Selene so vividly and for so long, now I felt the dam of my heart burst. I fell into the Amazon's arms and wept like a child.

Stuff imparted the particulars of my birth, which tale she had had from Selene just this month past. A union of happenstance, such as falls out not infrequently on the land: Mother delivering a stillborn babe, Selene bearing at the same season a healthy girl. Within the private sphere of the farm the switch was made, opposed by none and breathed abroad by none. Even Europa, not yet three years old at the time, was never informed of the truth; she had believed me her sister until only days past.

The question Stuff's tale did not answer was the identity of my sire. It was inconceivable that Father would have betrayed Mother's bed by skulking to Selene's. Who then but Damon? Uncle read it in my eyes the first night we made camp after the burial mounds.

"Do you hate me, daughter?"

Children are cruel, and I was not as grown as I contended. Yes, I hated him. Not for the truth but for keeping it from me. Why must I not know? So I would grow up a proper Athenian girl, to be given to a proper Athenian husband? So none of society would scorn me for my savage dam?

I drove Damon from me and would not speak to him, even on the ships.

Stuff communicated as well the context of Selene's decease. It was not in a fight but a fall, and not from a horse but a riverbank. Selene was gathering willow shoots as treats for her string. "The ground was not stony where she struck, nor was the plunge from a great height. But it broke her neck. She lasted till the mounds were dug for those you saw."

Stuff had a reading of this. She believed that Selene had completed her testament, that is, she had consummated the covenant of the trikona, by which the gods had agreed to accept her life in the stead of Eleuthera's. With this, her task was done. The earth had borne her in its time and now, in its time, took her back.

Eleuthera herself believed this, Stuff asserted, for when Eleuthera offered the tribute over Selene's grave, she did so not in speech, as is customary for one perished apart from battle, but in sign, as the nation reserves for heroes fallen in war.

"Selene believed," Eleuthera had signed, "that she had committed a crime against the people, that is, her failure to take my life and her own when we were wounded and faced capture at Athens. She feared I blamed her these years since, even hated her, for this abdication. I could not hate you, Selene. For this act you performed from love. Not love for me alone, though that was abundant, but for tal Kyrte, for whose weal you offered your liberty, that it might preserve mine. Beyond all others, you have donated your substance to the free people. More, you have made this gift alone, in isolation, cut off from our society and our care. Who has shown such devotion?"

Here, Stuff reported, Eleuthera's composure had broken. Long moments passed before she recovered self-command.

Eleuthera had concluded her eulogy thus:

She made first the sign for "Moon," which was my mother's name, Selene; then the sign for "fallen." Not fallen as in moonset but as a stone or leaf falls. As if, the sign imparted, the moon had fallen out of the sky.

Next Eleuthera made that rotary motion which means the turning of the seasons. *Ektalerin* is the word in the Amazon tongue; its connotation is "that which may be depended upon," as the rising of the sun or the greening of the plains. Only, Eleuthera made the motion in reverse, as if to say, All we have known has become inverted.

Eleuthera had then made the sign for "moonrise." But at the end she turned it by that stroke which makes a statement into a question.

Moon has fallen.
Will moon rise again?

This was my mother's encomium, by which Eleuthera denoted not the woman alone but the nation.

At the fifth noon the armada had entered Lake Maeotis; by the night succeeding it had reached the mouth of the Tanais. The river was even greater than I had imagined. You could feel its current half a mile out.

At fifty yards I made my leap. I dived over the prow and swam for shore. It is a misconception that sailors don't fear the sea. Not one made after me, including Father. They couldn't swim.

Ashore I fled on foot, north along the course of the Tanais, putting miles between myself and the ships before I stopped. Europa would pick me up when the column passed on its trek to the Gate of Storms.

I would be one of them.

I would never look back.

But when horsewomen appeared toward sunset it was to arrest me, by Eleuthera's orders, they said, and truck me like baggage back to the strand. I was delivered into Father's custody. This time he bound my wrists behind me and held the lead as one does on a dog.

The Amazon companies had been assembled, ready to depart. My sister marshaled among them. In moments they would make away. I looked up to discover Eleuthera reining-in above me. She had never addressed a word to me, nor evidenced before this an awareness of my existence, yet it was clear in this instant that she understood all and had commanded all.

"Would you obey me, daughter?"

I saw hope and affirmed this with emphasis. The Amazon indicated Father.

"Then obey him."

And she wheeled and spurred away.

With bitter tears I parted from my sister. We were on a neck of land with a salt marsh at its shoulder. In moments the Amazon column had rounded this, making north. The thicket swallowed them. They were gone.

The ships of the posse had been beached to disembark the Amazon horses. Atticus now gave orders for the men to take their dinner. The site seemed secure, on the far side of this great river, away from the direction from which Maues and Panasagoras would approach. But before the first parties had returned with firewood, horsemen appeared. In minutes the shore was thick with Scyths.

In the scramble to get away, all ships got off but one, Aristides' *Theama*. The enemy sunk grapnels in her and hauled her back to shore. Atticus signaled the other vessels to heave-to beyond bowshot. We could see *Theama* on the strand, swallowed in a sea of savages.

Now for the first time Theseus pulled rank. He commanded Atticus to hold the squadron offshore in safety where it lay. Atticus was to land his men under no circumstances, no matter what he heard or saw.

The king now commanded the tow skiff brought round. He stripped his weapons and, taking only Damon as interpreter, embarked in the gig and rowed ashore.

44

AN ACT
OF STATESMANSHIP

꩜꩜꩜꩜꩜꩜

The Scyths set upon the king and beat him like a beggar. We witnessed from offshore, and I have this also from Damon and the testimony of *Theama*'s crew, who witnessed it on the strand.

Theseus had anticipated such usage; it was why he had ordered the ships to stand off at all events. He offered no resistance to the savages, only endured till his arms, chest, and back were gummed with blood and ash, which the clansmen threw on hot and beat in with whips and quirts.

The princes raged at Theseus for abetting the Amazons' escape. They had chased him in hot blood for days and now took out their frustration upon his flesh. Meanwhile the Scyths had upended *Theama* on the shore, cooping the sailors beneath. The clansmen made a sport of packing blazes at the lip of the inverted gunwale and thrusting burning staves beneath the shell. The smoke quickly reduced the sailors to an extreme state. Theseus and Damon had been bound to stakes and slathered with pitch and turpentine. Up next would be opening their guts and lighting them like tapers.

"Suddenly," as Damon later told, "a great hubbub resounded. Into the camp rode King Borges himself, who is Maues' father and Panasagoras' uncle, and fit to lance both like boils. He was hopping! The bucks, it turns out, had chanced across him, with his own army, on the plain riding in. Why Borges hadn't come straightaway to the shore was he was busy ferrying a pack of his own rustlers across the river and setting them on the trail of Eleuthera and the Amazons, to run them down, if they could, before they got away through the Gate of Storms. Borges meant to take charge of the business personally as soon as he set straight this ruckus on the strand. But when he spied his ancient enemy trussed up and painted for torture, a sea change overcame the old man.

" 'Can this be Theseus of Athens you hold?'

"Borges shoved through the young bloods and commanded them to cut us loose.

"Maues and Panasagoras told him to strike for hell. Borges bawled for his knights. The mob stood one pinch from a bloodbath. The princes were hot. They wanted the ships. They hated the ships. Maues howled in Theseus' face, naming him and all Greeks agents of evil. Borges snatched up a bucket of brine and hurled it over him. The brave howled like a caned dog. The old man cuffed him, hard, beating him back, apart from Theseus.

" 'My apologies, sir,' Borges bayed in that trumpet he calls a voice. 'Youth, it seems, can no longer recognize its betters.'

"How old was Borges then? In his sixties, certainly. He had changed from the seasons of siege at Athens. In those days he wore his tiara even to move his bowels and decked himself with splendid headdresses and tokens of rank. Now he wore a plain cavalryman's cloak and a wolf-skin cap. Even his boots showed no gold. He ordered Theseus and the crew of *Theama* released and made fit to dine as gentlemen.

" 'We shall sup as friends,' he declared for his braves to hear, 'and you shall attend the speech of this great man who by the device alone of some meddling god has fallen into your clutches, for surely absent heaven's intercession you could never have closed within a league of him.'

"One who has not experienced a banquet of these tribesmen cannot know the meaning of extravagance. The Scyths take their liquor neat and mark him of no account who will not duel them horn for horn. By midnight the lot were soused as hogs and as convivial.

" 'Inscrutable are the ways of God,' Borges pronounced for all. 'How else account this usage, that enemies of yore may, by the passage of years alone, become friends? So my heart feels now toward you, Theseus. The rancor I once bore recedes, supplanted by admiration and a sense even of loss at the mates we might have been and the times we might have shared.'

"Theseus applauded his companion's magnanimity. 'Indeed, we own a bond, my friend. That most sublime of all: reminiscence for our vanished youth.' A man of latter years, the king observed, recalls as golden that epoch when his hopes stood high and his strength undiminished. 'What could be more natural for this man than to draw to his bosom all with whom he shared that time, even his foes? Perhaps his foes more than any.'

"Before Borges' seat spread a welter of battle spoils. He lifted an Amazon helmet and turned it over in his hands, admiring the play of firelight upon the bronze. 'Indeed,' the Scyth nodded. 'Each man recalls not the enemy he hated, but the champion who engaged him with such valor.'

"Theseus commended his companion's greatness of heart. Borges, he declared, had grown distinguished with the years. Time has stolen vigor but appended wisdom. Theseus praised the lord of the plains for the lands he had added to his province. 'Nor have you acquired these from insignificant adversaries, but from the most formidable cavalry of the world, the warrioresses of Amazonia.'

" 'Indeed,' remarked Borges, awaiting Theseus' point.

" 'The Amazons too were foes of our youth,' Athens's lord noted. 'Do you not find your heart relenting toward them, Borges, as it has toward me?'

"Maues and Panasagoras broke in, confronting Theseus. He pleads for these women! Beware another Greek trick!

"Theseus put his case to Borges succinctly. Before all, he stressed, the Amazons are beaten. 'Their hour is over; they can harm you no more. Even your young braves must concede this. The Amazons seek only to retire from lands that once were theirs but whose ownership they no longer contest. They fly before you, Borges, to wastes no other nation wants, so inhospitable and remote are they.'

" 'And shall I let them go?' Borges inquired, loudly for all.

"The princes put up a howl. This was seconded by the multitude. Theseus permitted the tumult to subside.

" 'Is not the greatness of a monarch,' he addressed Borges, 'measured by his leniency to defeated foes? Does not the lion turn apart from his vanquished rival, permitting him to retire from the field? The bull elk displays such clemency, and the wolf and the eagle. By such acts do we reckon their greatness.'

"More peals of outrage erupted from the young bloods.

"Borges regarded Theseus. 'Once before, my friend, I took lead from you, believing it gold.'

"All Greeks are cunning, the princes roared. What plot does this one hatch now, he and his countrymen?

"Theseus countered to Borges that he had been deposed at Athens. His enemies now ruled the state. 'My luck has turned evil, Borges. You need have no fear of me.'

"The Scyth smiled. 'What do you care for these Amazons, Theseus, that you should stand before me as their advocate? Is this love, for her whom you once took as your bride, or only soft-headedness in old age?'

"Theseus indicated the princes of the plains. 'Young men see the years stretch before them without limit. But you and I peer down that lane and glimpse its end. Perhaps our freight of winters works upon us, my friend, evoking empathy for others whose time draws to its close.'

"He indicated the Amazon helmet in Borges' hands.

" 'Like ourselves, the race of free women accounts the setting of their moon. But while our nations will live on after us, even prosper, theirs will decline and die.'

"More outcries from the princes. Borges ignored them. His attention held on Theseus.

"He would make a deal, Borges declared. And his sons would abide by it; he would see to that.

" 'I will let the Amazons go,' the lord of the plains promised. 'I will call off the pursuit I have mounted and initiate no other. The great Eleuthera and those who ride with her, I will permit to rejoin the last of their clans beyond the Gate of Storms, and may God preserve them if He will. But if I forswear my vengeance, Theseus, you must renounce something in requital.'

"Our king waited.

"Borges spoke. 'You must never return to Athens.'

"Our lord's crew revolted. 'What is Athens without Theseus? What is Theseus without Athens?'

"Borges let this outcry abate.

" 'I fear you, Theseus, and I fear your city. You are a nest of trouble. Therefore enter exile. Go where you wish. Stay here with me if you like; I will grant you honor and provide all your needs. But never return to your home. If what you have spoken is true, that your countrymen have indeed disowned you, then you will make this pledge. I will forgo my vengeance if you will forgo your repatriation.'

"Maues and Panasagoras protested vehemently. Why listen to this pirate? Why account his word in fixing the fate of these women?

" 'Because,' Borges replied, 'it was by his hand that they were vanquished, not by ours.'

"Borges lifted the Amazon helmet. It was of bronze, rimmed with cobalt and electrum. At its crown rose an emblem in gold of a stag taken down by a griffin. The piece was exquisite; Borges regarded it with appreciation.

" 'Shall we cede them clemency, Theseus, who excelled us in valor, and who fell not by their failings but by ours?' "

45

A RITE OF REMEMBRANCE

Borges kept his word. He permitted Eleuthera and her party, including my sister, to withdraw north through the Gate of Storms.

Theseus likewise honored his pledge. The posse returned to Athens without him. In his absence, stewardship of the state had been conveyed to Prince Lykos, seconded by the barons Peteos, Menestheus, Stichios Ox, and others who had earned preeminence by their valor in defense of the city against the Amazons and by their service to her in the succeeding years. With the ships' return without Theseus, the Assembly formalized this disposition. The democracy retired, such as it had been, replaced by rule of the princes. These governed sternly but well. Within a twelvemonth, report arrived of Theseus' decease, in a fall from a cliff on the island of Skyros, where he had taken refuge. Whether this end came about by an enemy's hand or his own, none could say.

It was Father who recovered most swiftly from events. Restored to the land, he resumed with joy the rounds of the husbandman. He held Mother in more tender regard than ever, and she returned this affection. It was never even discussed that I would be raised apart from them.

Damon tried his best to stand the sire's vocation. But settlement life had never suited him; now with the loss of Selene, he could endure it even less. He shared Father's tutelage of me till I reached the age of marriage. At that time he quit Attica to follow the restless life his soul had always favored. He returned to Athens once a year only, for the festival of the Boedromia.

At fifteen I was betrothed to Prince Atticus. I went uneager and served his house without joy, though he was the best of men and had acted with no slender intrepidity, taking a bride to whom such notoriety attached. In later years I came to love him dearly. Initially, however, in the aftercourse of my rejection from Amazonia, I cared for nothing but this grief. Why had I been cast out? Why had Eleuthera banished a child of her race, who wished only to live and die in her service? Why had she let my sister stay, yet sent me home?

At seventeen I was delivered of my first babe. With what bitterness did I endure my term! For I reckoned that with the birth of this child I would be bound beyond disseverment to my husband and to the race of men.

Then you came, Alcippe, my eldest, whom I named, inspired by heaven, after that great champion, "Powerful Mare," of Amazonia. Succeeding you came your sisters—Enyo and Adrasteia, Xanthe and Glauke, Skyleia and Stratonike. Watching you grow and thrive, at last I understood.

You were why Eleuthera had sent me back. You, my daughters, seven without a son, for such has been heaven's will. And you seven have likewise borne only daughters, that the city marvels and looks on you with fear and awe.

Now daughter, Alcippe, eldest of our line, rise and take up the antelope-skin sheath before you on its stand. Bear it to me. Unbind its bands.

There. The *pelekus*. Selene's own, the double axe of Amazonia.

Withdraw the weapon. Display it before your sisters and daughters. I have honed it to a razor's keenness.

Now come you forward, daughters. Kneel, each in order. Receive the iron.

We make this cut by our own hand, that no enemy may say he drew first blood. Take this on your tongue, whetted edge of your mothers, which is Selene's, which is Eleuthera's, which is Antiope's and Hippolyta's and all of tal Kyrte's.

Blood to iron
Iron to blood

Here was Eleuthera's object, mandated of me as she and her last clans withdrew beyond the Gate of Storms. That by the blood of my mother, Selene, borne forward by me and all I would bear, would the nation of Amazonia not perish but endure, here, in the belly of the beast.

Blood to iron
Iron to blood

Attend now and never forget! The blood of champions courses within you. Be worthy of them! Draw strength from them! They are your flesh and sinew, indisseverable, ineradicable down all the tracks of time.

46

AMAZONEUM

꧁◎◎◎◎◎◎◎◎◎◎꧂

Now crows the cock. The moon is down.
  Night withdraws.
  Day approaches.
  Now must we rise and take our stations.
  Bathe and garland yourselves, my daughters. Dress in your finest.
Form in procession as I have instructed you. March with me and all
Athens to the Temple of the Amazons, the Amazoneum. There the
priests of the state will initiate the festival of the Boedromia, honor-
ing their fathers' conquest of the army of women. We too shall ob-
serve this. But not as they.

  Hear me, daughters. Stand in your places today. Let the nation
see you. They will part before you, in awe and trepidation, and draw
you to them at the same time. Take no satisfaction of their honors;
rather, pity them. God has bent them to His will no less than ourselves.

When I was twenty and had borne my third child, a message came to me from the East. Its author, through his courier, bade me commit it to memory. I obeyed. Each year on this day I recite for myself and for you its text, which has come to comprise our order and our benediction.

Damon to his daughter, greetings.

It was my wish to return to Athens, as I have each year in this season of the Boedromia. A wound, which I fear shall prove fatal, detains me however. You will be the last of our line, my child, you and those you bear. Instruct them as I tell you. Serve with them as my surrogate in this day's ceremony and all to come. Hear, please, with my ears, see with my eyes.

When you come to the Amazoneum today, stand not with our tribe of Athens but take station at the crown of the Hill of Ares. Mount to that eminence from which you can see the mound of Antiope before the Temple of Mother Earth and the crescent-shaped barrow of Molpadia, our Eleuthera, with the line of Amazon graves receding toward the Itonic Gate.

Attend the speeches of the politicians. Bear with patience their trivialization of events and their citations offered of men and women whose worth they can never know.

Look you now to the footbridge at the northern limit of the marketplace. Don't see the manicured grounds and cane-swept square. Turn instead with the inner eye. See with me. See what I would see, were I standing at your shoulder. Perceive this site not as she stands now, rebuilt and reconfigured, but as she appeared on that eve succeeding the terminal truce, when the race of free women withdrew forever into history.

There where the road now leads to the Ceramic Gate spread a field of rubble. This was our Athenian camp. A tent hospital occupied the west-facing slope. Before this sprawled staked ditches, hide-and-timber palisades, and the anticavalry trenches called leg-breakers. Behind extended the kitchen kennels and a picket line for

the horses (twelve) and mules (fifteen), which comprised the total-
ity of Athens's mounted brigade. A breastwork of stone ran from
the Eleusinion, itself rubble, to the facility that had housed the
Custodians of the Market. Tent flies and laundry lines bedecked
this position; some four thousand manned it, none of whom had
bathed other than in their own spit for months. The footbridge of
Cranaus was a pile of rocks with boards spiked atop. The spring-
house was a hole in the ground. Where the plain abutted Market
Hill, more lines of our troops extended.

The oaths of peace had been ratified the morning before. Still
the war was not over. Still all held to arms. Watch discipline was
maintained. The company of which Elias and I were a part held
the post at the western shoulder of the Hill of Ares, where the
Amazon camp had stood. Directly above us was the temple the
warrioresses had erected to their progenitor, the god of battles,
roofless as all their cathedrals. Our troops had preserved it intact,
fearing heaven's wrath.

On the next hill west extended the lines to which the Amazons
had withdrawn.

The hour approached evening. I was dead asleep, anticipating
my watch, which was to commence at sunset.

Someone shook me awake. Such was the state of anxiety
within which all dwelt at that time that I sprang to my feet in
alarm, groping for spear and shield. No one else moved. I drew
up. Every face had turned west toward the enemy camps.

The Amazons were pulling out.

Along the length of our lines, two miles from end to end,
every jack of Athens rose and stood in silence.

The Amazons passed out on horseback in column of twos.
The Corps of Mounted Archers comprised the center, with their
male auxiliaries, the kabar, on foot at either flank. The day was
dry and dusty; the parched plain gave up clouds beneath the
horses' tread. The descending sun struck these, rendering the column in profile, silhouetted against the sky.

Warrioresses and novices advanced by nation, Themiscyra

first, then the Lycasteia, Chadisia, and Titaneia. Those of us who knew them, which by this point meant the defending force entire, could reckon each by the standards they bore and the way they sat their ponies. The column ascended into view on the east-facing collar of the Hill of the Pnyx, tracked across this, then down the saddle at the border stone of Melite, from which it mounted to and traversed the Hill of the Nymphs. The corps skirted Market Hill, inclining east to the Ceramic Road, by which it continued north in the direction of Acharnae. Into view ascended a seemingly endless procession of horses and warrioresses. These bore their totems at battle height, eagle and bear, lion and wolf, aurochs and griffin and ibex. Each rider advanced in armor, burnished to a mirror's sheen, with her helmet likewise dazzling, bow and quiver at her knees and her axe in its sheath between her shoulders. I have never witnessed a spectacle of such splendor or such despair.

Down our lines someone loosed a cheer. The men picked it up. Three great hurrahs arose in honor of the column.

A hymn commenced, from our countrymen manning the ramparts beneath the Rock. I turned to Elias. The anthem swelled. "Fall of the Titans," the same we had heard the Amazons themselves encant upon the pursuit to the Tanais.

Now the hour of their passing
Younger wait to take their place
Even they weep, who have them vanquished,
Never more to see their face

All evening the column remained in view. Elias and I took horses and followed along the Acharnae Road. At Holm Oak Hill we drew up. Flanking the march, remnants could be seen of other wild tribes, males, razing what little remained intact after their months of depredation. The Amazons with great solemnity passed on, leaving the province unmolested, until at last they vanished over the Leuconoe grade.

All that remained visible, from where Elias and I reined, was *the churned impress of the column's track in the clay. Upon this now descended shore birds in their multitudes, seeking the grubs and beetles harrowed up by the horses' tread. In moments, it seemed, these had picked the trace clean. Then wheeling in the failing light, they too receded, leaving darkness to close upon the wake of the free women, effacing in its fall the furrow of their passage.*

AUTHOR'S
NOTES

ON THE HISTORICAL REALITY
OF THE AMAZONS

When we think of ancient Athens, the city we customarily call to mind is that of Plato, Pericles, Socrates; the Classical Athens of the fifth century B.C. *Last of the Amazons* takes place in a far earlier Athens, eight hundred years earlier, to be exact.

That Athens might be likened to Chaucerian or Elizabethan London—modest in comparison with the imperial colossus she would become, yet already a burgeoning metropolis stamped with her own uniquely Athenian character. Her king was Theseus, a true historical figure, though his exploits come down to us as lore and legend. Theseus, the poets declare, slew the Minotaur and, later, abducted the Amazon queen Antiope (some call her Hippolyta) from her homeland on the Black Sea and brought her to Athens as his bride.

The year was 1250 B.C. or thereabout. The Trojan War lay a generation in the future. It was an era when history butted up against mythology, when legends like the Amazons may truly have existed.

Plutarch says they did. (I'll pass over other interesting but, to me, less convincing evidence, such as recently unearthed warrior-women's graves in the Amazon homeland of southern Russia, and the battle murals of the Painted Stoa and the Parthenon metopes.)

Plutarch states that an army of Amazons and Scythians attacked Athens during the reign of Theseus. That this force overran the country to such an extent as to make their war camp within the city itself, directly beneath the Acropolis, "is certain," Plutarch declares, "and may be confirmed by the names that the places thereabout yet retain, and the graves and monuments of those that fell in the battle."

Plutarch lived in the first century A.D. If the Athens he knew truly had sites whose names derived from that ancient battle, common sense bids us ask: Did the Athenians simply make up such names, inventing the siege of the Amazons out of whole cloth? Consider the analogy to our own forefathers. Would white Americans have fabricated names like Dakota and Seattle and Massachusetts if Native Americans had never existed?

Can we take Plutarch's testimony seriously? If we can't embrace outright the historical reality of warrior-women, then certainly we can suspend disbelief.

It may add perspective to recall that scholars of the nineteenth century scoffed at the reality of the Trojan War. Homer's *Iliad* was honored only as inspired myth. Then Schliemann excavated Troy and academics ate their words.

Perhaps in the future a bulldozer gouging a new subway route in Athens will scrape against an undiscovered tomb and into daylight will emerge the bones of Antiope. Perhaps archaeologists, skeptical today of the reality of warrior women, will hold in their hands the war queen's very weapon, the double axe of Amazonia.

A NOTE ON SPELLING

To transliterate or not to transliterate; that is the bane of any writer who tries to transpose into English words and terms that are perfectly happy in ancient Greek.

My solution is a cockamamie mishmash, part pig-Latin and part porky-Greek.

I've simply selected, on a case-by-case basis, whatever word looks and sounds best to me. Thus the reader will find in a single sentence "Cephisus" (Latinized) and "Eridanos" (Greek); "Lykos" on one page and "Lyceum" on another. Even buildings have not escaped this deranged approach. I like the Latinized look of "Amazoneum," but also used the Greek "Eleusinion."

For such inconsistencies, I beg the reader's indulgence.

SPECIAL THANKS

To my outstanding editors, Shawn Coyne and Bill Thomas (in alpha-
betical order), not only for shaping and elevating the material but for
championing it in the real world. Few readers (and not too many
writers) appreciate, or even know, all the contributions that a great
editor makes. Thanks, you guys. Without your friendship and support, I would be floundering and so would this book.

Huge thanks too to my fellow inkslinger Printer Bowler of Mis-
soula, Montana, for an exceptionally astute unofficial read. It was a
pleasure, P.B., to steal your most excellent ideas.

And again to my comrade in arms, Dr. Hip Kantzios of the Uni-
versity of South Florida, who has been a friend and invaluable mentor since the first hour of my embarkation upon the wine-dark seas of
ancient Hellas.

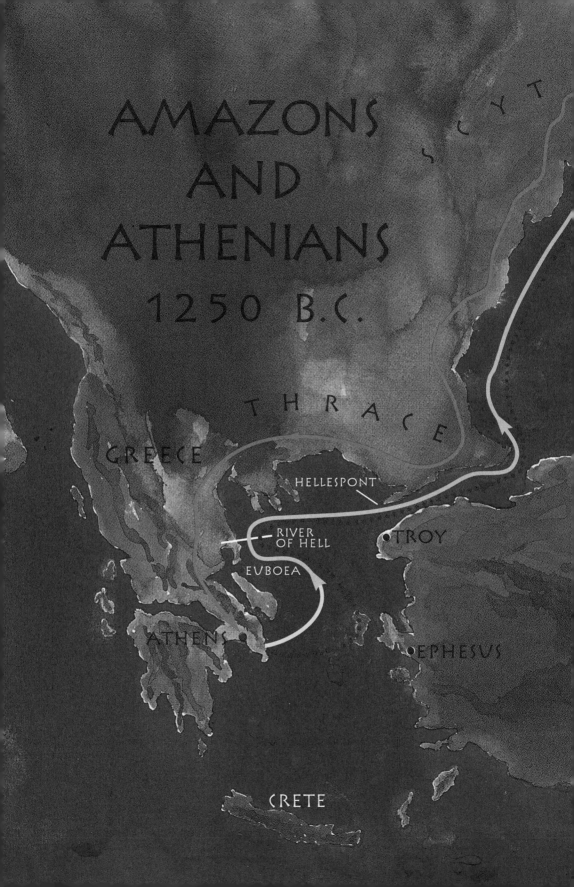

AMAZONS
AND
ATHENIANS
1250 B.C.

SCYT

THRACE

GREECE

HELLESPONT

RIVER
OF HELL

TROY

EUBOEA

ATHENS

EPHESUS

CRETE